Another Love

Amanda Prowse has always loved crafting short stories and scribbling notes for potential books. Her first novel, *Poppy Day*, was self-published in October 2011. Her novels *What Have I Done?* and *Perfect Daughter* have been number one bestsellers.

Amanda lives in Bristol with her husband and two sons. She is the author of several acclaimed novels and short stories.

www.amandaprowse.org

Also by
Amanda Prowse

Novels
Poppy Day
What Have I Done?
Clover's Child
A Little Love
Will You Remember Me?
Christmas For One
A Mother's Story
Perfect Daughter
The Christmas Cafe
My Husband's Wife

Short Stories
Something Quite Beautiful
The Game
A Christmas Wish
Ten Pound Ticket
Imogen's Baby
Mrs Potterton's Birthday Tea

Amanda Prowse

Another Love

HEAD
&ZEUS

First published in the UK in 2016 by Head of Zeus Ltd.

This paperback edition first published in the UK in 2016
by Head of Zeus Ltd.

9 7 5 3 1 2 4 6 8

A catalogue record for this book is available from
the British Library.

Paperback ISBN 9781784972196
Ebook ISBN 9781784972165

Typeset by e-type, Aintree

Printed in the UK by Clays Ltd, St Ives Plc

Head of Zeus Ltd
Clerkenwell House
45–47 Clerkenwell Green
London EC1R 0HT

WWW.HEADOFZEUS.COM

This book is for anyone who has lived in a house that lurks beneath the shadow of alcoholism. It's for anyone who has waited with a nervous swirl in their gut, to see what comes next. Anyone who has stood next to a drunk and questioned everything they know. Anyone who has ever wondered, *how long can I live like this?*

It's not until you are stone cold sober in the company of a drunk that you realise, despite how long you have known or loved them, that you don't really know them at all...

Prologue

My darling Celeste,

This letter might come too late for us both, but either way, I feel compelled to put pen to paper. I read a quote the other day that said, 'Imagine when you die and arrive at your final destination, God says, "So how was heaven?"' It floored me. I lay on the carpet and shook with fear. My ideas about God and indeed heaven are sketchy, but this made sense to me because my life was wonderful. I had it all. People often say that, don't they? But I really did, and I guess that's the hardest thing for me to fathom, how I unpicked my existence strand by strand until everything I held dear lay in a pile like a fine knitted garment reduced to knotty wool.

It's as if there are two of me. The shy me, the nice me. Smiling and enjoying the good fortune of others, wanting to do good, wanting to love and be loved, wanting nothing more than to laugh and laugh some more; the woman who puts her family at the centre of everything. That woman is smart, interested and interesting. She wakes with a spring in her step and a lift to her heart, happy to have a place in the world, a woman who looks forward to the future.

And then there is the other me, the one who has another love, a love that can't be broken. A destructive, all-consuming love that casts a long, dark shadow over all that is good. This other love is so strong that she will do anything, anything if it means they can slope off together and snatch some illicit moments of pure, pure joy. This woman is mean, angry and easily led. She is reckless, cruel and self-centred. She scares those around her, and she scares herself a bit too. And it doesn't matter how forcefully I tell myself to keep her at bay, how firm my resolve to leave her buried, she is made of stronger stuff than I can defeat. She is hardened metal against my softened will, she is omnipotent and magnificent and in her presence I can do nothing but cower.

When she is around, I can feel the tension in the air like a storm brewing on the horizon. I can almost see the bruised purple clouds rolling in. I can feel my face change from pretty to ugly. So very ugly. I feel my muscles tense and my eyes bulge. My mouth spews vile, aggressive slurs and I don't care whose ears are on the receiving end. Even yours my darling girl. I become angry for angry's sake. It's as if I *want* to wreak havoc. And while the nice me, the other me, claws away inside, mortified at her behaviour, there is nothing I can do. I can't find a way out.

There is no salve for the guilt I feel, no cure for the nagging remorse at how I treated you, no remedy for the deep sadness at what I have lost.

I carry a picture in my mind of a time long ago. A snapshot of the life that used to be mine. I am standing at the sink, filling the kettle to make tea for those I love and you are little, maybe four, and you are sitting on the floor in your pyjamas, singing 'You Are My Sunshine' out of tune. Your voice is loud, and you are happy! Happy just to be at home with me, safe and warm. I wish I could go back to that day and start over. I wish I could have one last chance to do things differently. But deep down I know that I could be given an infinite number of chances and I would not change a thing. I would still end up here alone with this pen in my hand, shaking, with my heart fit to burst and my nose and throat thick with tears. I would not change a thing because I can't.

It may sound strange, but I wish I'd been diagnosed with a different sickness, a more visible one. Something that twisted my body, broke my bones or blistered my skin. Something that would make people look away and shield their children. Even that would be preferable. Anything other than to have people think that being like this is my choice.

It is not my choice. It is not my choice!

Who would choose this?

Celeste

It's been quite a week. On Wednesday I got back in touch with the therapist, Erica, who I haven't seen since I was a teenager, and today I start, on her recommendation, writing things down.

'Why should I write it all down?' I asked as she handed me this spiral-bound notepad and pen, like I was still a child and had no way of securing either. I chose not to point out that I've just graduated from Southampton Uni with a 2:1 in Human Geography. I wasn't being flippant with my question; I genuinely wanted to know how it would benefit me.

She gave a small sigh, as though the answer were obvious, pulling off her glasses and waving them as she spoke, a neat trick. It not only gave her a prop for distraction, reminding me of the photographer who clicked his fingers over my dad's head to make me look in that direction while he snapped away, but also because without the sharp focus of my pained expression, my querying smile, she was able to speak freely, regurgitating facts and ideas without my sentiment as a diversion.

'Because if you are able, with honesty, uncensored, to capture the key events that have shaped you, it will help you make sense of your upbringing, help you reach an understanding. You said you were worried about your childhood in some way *tarnishing*

4

the life you and Alistair might have; this exercise will provide clarity, help you move forward, enable you to have a good look at how your thought processes and behaviour have evolved.'

'You make me sound like a Pokémon.'

'A what?' she asked, with a little crease at the top of her nose and a curl to her top lip, as though I was speaking a different language. I wanted to ask how she could have got to fifty-eight and not know what Pokémon are.

Erica was keen to talk about my mum's letter. I was keen not to. It's too distressing; I literally can't look at it. I've placed it in a drawer, mentally parked it and will dig it out when I'm feeling... stronger, I guess.

Okay, so here goes. Purple ink? What was Erica thinking? It's such a frivolous colour for such a serious undertaking; maybe that's the point.

My name is Celeste. I am from Bristol and I am twenty-one. I am the daughter of Romilly and David Wells. I'm teetotal, like to swim, love to walk. I own too many pairs of trainers and not enough pairs of heels. I'm allergic to nearly all mascara and crave smoked mackerel. I can only cook one passable thing, chicken and ham pie, and I am engaged to Alistair Hastings, who I met on a field trip in Dorset. The day I met him I was wearing wellington boots and my hair was plastered to my head with rain. I looked at him and I knew, knew that he was the one I wanted to spend my life with. I can't say his name or think about him without smiling. I'm absolutely crazy about him. He is smart, kind and funny and he would definitely have laughed at my Pokémon reference. He's a farmer and thankfully a dab hand in the kitchen, as long as what needs dabbing is meat, potatoes and veg.

Erica said to go back to the beginning. For me that starts with toddlerhood. I remember being three very clearly. Well, actually, that's not strictly true. I remember aspects of being that age. Certain facts and images float to the top, bright and distinct like the scarlet waxy globs inside a lava lamp. I suspect these memories are not that interesting to anyone but me, like the time I hid in the cupboard in the hallway, sitting on a roll of carpet, listening to my mum's voice as she made out she didn't know I was there. 'I wonder where she could be?' she said, extra loudly, making sure the words filtered through the door that was pulled to, letting in a crack of light and a glimpse of the hall floor. I banged my feet on the floor in excitement, knowing that any second she would fling open the door and discover me and I would leap into her arms and she would hold me close and spin round in a circle with my head buried in her shoulder and the scent of her perfume rising up.

These were the years before, when I only ever pictured my mum with a stomach full of love and the desire to be near her, always. This was the time when I thought she could make everything better, when I trusted her to provide a haven for me, a home that smelt of sugar cookies and encircling arms. Before…

One

'Does it really matter?' Romilly whispered, looking up with a pained expression, holding a side plate in each hand. Both were white but had different patterns around the edge. On one, a delicate double silver line; on the other, a tiny bird and leaf pattern in relief.

'How do you mean?' David shook his head, confused.

'Well...' She put the plates on the table and pushed her glasses up her nose, then patted the scarlet creep of embarrassment that bloomed on her chest. 'I mean, you only eat off them and when you're not putting food on them, toast and whatnot, they'll be shut away in a cupboard.' She sighed. 'I'm tempted just to go for the plainest, the cheapest, and not worry about it too much. I don't think it really matters.'

She felt her cheeks colour in case this was the wrong answer, knowing David's mother, Sylvia, would not understand her indifference to things she felt were vital. Sylvia did this, stressed the things Romilly must do in order for her wedding, and by implication her marriage, to be successful. *'A good wife should want to cook for her man. You have to overlook his occasional grumpiness – that's men for you, troubled and tired with all that responsibility!'* This had

7

made Romilly smile, as if being male carried with it a certain weight that, being a mere female, she could never fully comprehend. And on hearing about a male friend of theirs who intended to accompany his girlfriend into the birthing pool: *'Good God! I expect the poor chap will need counselling after that! It's just not natural!'* There was so much that Romilly wanted to say to her future mother-in-law, not least that it was in fact the most natural thing in the world and did she realise it wasn't 1953. And also, with all her pearls of wisdom and sage advice, how come her own husband had done a runner before they'd hit their tenth anniversary? But of course she never would, because for all her faults, Romilly was not mean. And she had to concede that the wiry, opinionated American had managed to grow the gorgeous man she was going to marry.

'You really don't care, do you?' David smiled, walked over to the table behind which she hovered, and picked up a dinner plate.

Romilly shook her head, sending her thick red hair shivering down her back. 'Plates is plates.'

'I don't think I have ever loved you more.' He carefully touched a finger to the delicate china on the table before reaching for her hand. 'Just so you know, we have about twenty minutes to get you home or I swear I am going to shag you here and now on this very table.' He nodded, darting a look at the carefully displayed chinaware.

'But we're in the middle of John Lewis!' she whispered, staring at the shoppers in close proximity. Even the thought that they might have overheard was enough to send her pulse racing.

'Nineteen,' he countered coolly, folding his arms across his chest.

'David!' Someone might be listening. She gathered her cardigan around her slender form and tucked the long strap of her bag over her hunched shoulders as she stood.

'How are we getting on here?' The lady smiled as she approached. She had been wonderfully helpful and seemed excited about their impending nuptials, even though Romilly was sure working in the wedding list department must have left her a little jaded about the whole palaver; there were only so many times you could show genuine enthusiasm for the description of pale ivory taffeta and a horseshoe seating plan.

'Oh! Goodness!' Romilly had hoped they might be able to slip out of the store unnoticed. 'I... I am so sorry, but we are not going to make a final choice today. But thank you for all your help. We'll be back, very soon,' she added nervously.

'We're going to sleep on it,' David said authoritatively.

'Righto. Well, you are absolutely right. You mustn't rush your decision. They do need to be exactly what you want; after all, you have to live with them for quite a while. Tell you what, I'll make a note of the samples you like and pop them in your file with your wedding list. The name is...?'

'David Wells. And my wife-to-be is Romilly. Miss Romilly Shepherd.'

Romilly felt her stomach bunch and her face break into a smile at his words 'wife-to-be'.

'And the date of the wedding?' the woman asked as she jotted down notes in a maroon leather hardback book, held up to her chest.

'In six weeks.' Romilly blushed. 'Six weeks from today. Saturday the eighteenth.'

'Sorry to interrupt, but that's seventeen minutes, Rom.' David tapped his watch and gripped her by the arm. The woman stared at him quizzically.

'I'm so sorry to rush off. We have to erm…' Romilly whispered over her shoulder as David pulled her from the store with some urgency. They ran across the road towards the car, laughing.

Romilly lay on her tummy, kicking her legs up behind her. The tangled white sheet covered her modesty as she stared at the beautiful man sitting against the headboard who was to become her husband.

'You are very handsome, you know. I still get shocked by it. I look up and it hits me in the chest, the realisation that I am marrying a very good-looking man. I like it.'

David smiled at her. 'We are going to have fine-looking babies.'

'Sooner rather than later, if we carry on like this.' She laughed and lay back on the mattress, reaching over to the bedside table for her glasses.

'Ooh, yes, please! I can turn you into a proper housewife. You can stay at home and grow babies and cook supper, forget all this getting your PhD nonsense!'

'I thought you loved me for my brain?' she simpered.

David shook his head. 'That's just what I told you to get you into bed. But now I have and you are trapped, I can come clean and say that it was purely your sexy little bod and that red hair that did it for me.'

Romilly smiled. 'I really don't want to be flattered by that. I want to be offended, outraged…'

'But you are, admit it.' He nudged her arm with his toes.

She laughed out loud and leant forward to kiss his ankle. She was beyond flattered, *thrilled*, in fact, to be viewed in this way! She heard her mum's voice, a constant refrain through her childhood, correcting anyone who referred to her as ginger, insisting she was strawberry blonde and then, as the shade darkened over the years, either Titian or auburn. It made her feel like her very red hair was something of a negative.

Romilly had been five when her sisters were born. As far as she was aware, this was when her dad had begun retreating to his shed, where he still liked to lurk all these years later, 'sorting out his bits and bobs' or 'fixing and pottering', as if living with four women was more than any man could cope with. Maybe it was.

Carrie and Holly arrived like marshmallow meteors: soft and sweet and wreaking devastation on her little world. It was as if her parents had ordered them straight from the Disney Store. *'We'll take two identical, blonde, pretty, cute, well-behaved, characterful babies, please! Oh, and make them gigglers and good sleepers, that would be great!'* From the moment the twins were born, every journey her mum made took double the time it should. Everyone in their Wiltshire postcode, from milkmen to old ladies, would stop her, hand on arm, to stare and beam. 'Will you look at them little poppets! They are beautiful! So pretty!' And her mum would beam back, because they were and she had made them. After a second or two, her mum would place her hand on

Romilly's back and push her forward an inch, saying, 'This is Romilly, their big sister. *She's* very clever!' Trying to include her, consoling her with the sticking-plaster of being bright. 'She really is very clever.' This her mum said more times than Romilly could count, sometimes followed by 'Aren't you?' And Romilly would nod and smile, because she knew this was what was expected, despite the sinking feeling in her stomach that meant smiling was the last thing she felt like.

Even though she noticed that the twins were much admired – it was hard not to – it didn't occur to her to feel jealous. Not a bit. She loved her little sisters, loved their cuteness, the constant burble of conversation, their excitability that made even the most mundane day feel like a party. She didn't need the constant reassurance from her mum that she had her own gifts, no matter how hidden. In fact, the relentless bolstering led Romilly to conclude that she must be not quite good enough; otherwise, why would her mum feel the need?

She had, over time, developed a shell into which she could retreat, just like the much maligned common garden snail. She liked all invertebrates, but insects were her special thing. She hid her face inside books and chose bigger and heavier glasses, prompting her classmates to make jokes about *Coronation Street*'s Deirdre Barlow. She took to offering her views in a whisper so as not to offend or dominate, happy to hide in the shadow of her sunnier, prettier sisters.

Romilly grew up, left school, won a place at Bristol University and was happy. Content. Not that life was always perfect, far from it, but she had never seen the point of craving what she didn't or couldn't have – longer legs, better skin or a flashier car. She was one of life's satisfied. Unlike her sisters, she had never sat with her nose inches from the table while holding out a finger to measure the precise amount of orange juice their mum had poured into each of the three glasses. She had never whined, 'She's got more than me!' She was just happy to get the drink.

At least that was the case until she met David. David Wells. David Arthur Wells, to give him his full but rarely used name. She couldn't say the words without smiling. Because as she said them she pictured his face, his beautiful face, and then she let her mind's eye travel down to his hard chest, and then she pictured his muscled arms closing around her, tightly, and she remembered the feeling of utter, utter bliss as she submitted, losing herself against him. And that made her smile all over again.

The first time he'd sat next to her in the library, Romilly had tried not to show her surprise, tried not to notice him. She hoped he hadn't seen her neck bulge with a huge swallow of anticipation as she surreptitiously ran a finger around her nose and mouth, searching for any untoward secretions.

He flashed her a smile and she blushed and went back to her books, leaning forward so that a curtain of hair fell over her face. She squinted at the text and continued to read. *Onychophorans are soft-bodied, full-lipped, beautiful boy sitting next to me... For God's sake, Rom, concentrate.* She gave a small cough and tried again. *Onychophorans are soft-bodied, muscly arms, gorgeous face, and smells wonderful...* It was pointless.

Engrossed in her prop, she didn't see him lean forward to write on the side of her notepad, so close she could feel his warm breath against her skin. It sent a shiver down her spine, making her skin taut beneath her goosebumps. With his hand at an awkward angle, he scrawled, *Can I borrow a pen?*

She pulled her hair across her face and hooked it behind her ear, raising her eyes to his. 'You've got one,' she whispered, pointing a finger towards the biro with which he had written the request.

Wide-eyed, he tapped his forehead lightly in mock admonishment. Leaning forward again, he wrote, *I'm a klutz!*

She got it. He was taking the piss. She shifted in her seat and twisted her body away from him, trying to ignore him. She wondered what had prompted the strange interaction. Maybe he was just trying to amuse himself. Nerd-baiting had been popular when she was at school, but she'd hoped that university would be different. She heard the scrape of a chair on the next table and felt him turn towards the sound; an accomplice maybe? Ah, yes, that would be it, a dare. *Well done, Mr Good-Looking. Job done.*

The next day, however, he sat next to her again. This time he took his biro and drew a smiley face on her folder. She felt confused, welcoming the interaction but so unsure of his intentions that she feared making a fool of herself. She reciprocated in the only way she knew how, by drawing a ladybird on his folder. He encased it in a bubble and added an arrow pointing in her direction, above which he wrote, *You.*

Her scrawled reply was swift. *A ladybird? Really?*

To which he replied, *It's the eyes...*

She had the last word. *And the spots!*

On the third day, he greeted her with a whispered, 'Hey, Bug Girl!'

She smiled, very much liking the idea of being his Bug Girl, happy to have this connection. Even if it was only because he admired her bookishness, it was still a thrill.

They quickly established a ritual whereby whoever arrived first would place their rucksack on the seat next to them and ward off anyone else with a steely stare. Their contact was confined to the library. This was unsurprising as Romilly rarely ventured to the Student Union bar and was not a frequenter of the bars and clubs favoured by David and his cronies. And David had never even heard of the volunteer programme at Bristol Zoo, where she spent many hours in the butterfly forest explaining lifecycles and other fascinating facts to the general public.

Three weeks after their first encounter, they met in the stairwell. Heading in opposite directions and both with large folders held tightly against their chests, they hovered, she above and he below. It felt coincidental but also opportune; it was what she had been longing for, a chance meeting. Both were rooted to the spot, unmoved by the tuts and yells and the trundling feet forced to navigate around them. It was as if they were each in a force field of their own, singled out from the crowd and marked as being of special interest.

For the first time, he spoke to her in a voice louder than a whisper. 'Hey, Bug Girl.' And all of a sudden she felt a spike of envy. It was an unfamiliar sensation, a bit like hunger and fear and anger all swirled into one. She could taste the sour note of jealousy that blossomed on her tongue as she stuttered her response. For she knew beyond a shadow of a doubt that boys like David Wells didn't fall in love with bookish, ginger-haired, spectacle-wearing girls like her. They went for leggy, long-haired gigglers like Carrie and Holly, girls who knew sexy stuff and weren't afraid to be manhandled, unfazed at the prospect of their T-shirt riding up or inadvertently flashing their pants.

Romilly had never been that sort of girl. Being clever was her thing, her nose always firmly inside a book as she crept from the library to lectures and back again. The boys that courted her were the ones who also studied science and who also wore specs and who knew every word to the entire series of *Star Trek: Deep Space Nine* and weren't afraid to spend an entire coach journey to Dartmoor and back again proving this. David was in another league entirely and it was a league in which she wasn't even a minor player.

'It's Romilly.' She nodded.

'David Wells.' He smiled.

They continued to sit close to each other in the library, getting to know each other little by little via whispered exchanges, some gentle teasing and the scrawling of information and ideas in gel pen across each other's notes and files. They would then stroll back to halls together, down the steep pavements of Park Street or up towards Whiteladies Road, meandering and chatting, whatever the weather.

'How can you spend all day, every day, studying one tiny creature?' he asked one afternoon as they ambled nonchalantly along. 'Don't you ever get bored?' He prodded the textbook in her arms, whose cover displayed various pictures of the mayfly, her insect of special interest, about which she would write her dissertation.

She wrinkled her nose beneath her glasses and took her time in forming a response. 'Quite the opposite. The more I learn, the more I want to learn. I don't think there can be anything as fascinating in the whole wide world, absolutely nothing, as a creature that is born knowing it will catch only one sighting of the moon. Just one! A creature that seeks the sun, knowing it has to live an entire life in a day! That's incredible, don't you think? The very opposite of boring. And that question is actually comical, coming from you, Mr Numbers. I mean, accounting and finance? Now that's proper boring! I mean, God, if I had to look at numbers all day, I'd just say, shoot me now.'

She glanced up at him uncertainly. Had she gone too far? *Shut up, Romilly! Just shut up! You're rambling because you're nervous. He'll think you're a loser.*

His suggestion of a date came a whole month later, as they stood on the steps of the Wills Memorial Building. It left her speechless, quite literally staring at the space above his head, wondering if it was a joke or whether it was even worth it. The disappointment of him rejecting her after one date was possibly more than she could bear. She figured that if there had been any romantic intentions on his part, he would have made his move a while ago.

His expression was searching. 'So, is that a silent "Yes, I'd love to come for a light supper on the docks," or a silent "Sod off"? I can't tell.' He laughed, that easy laugh that showed his beautiful teeth.

'I'd love to,' she squeaked.

'Yes!' He punched the air, and for the first time in her life, Romilly felt like a prize.

Tessa, a girl in her halls, had insisted that she have a drink before she went off to meet him. Dutch courage, she called it, although there was nothing Dutch about the Russian vodka shot that she hurled down her neck. Romilly wasn't fond of booze, didn't like the taste much, apart from sickly sweet cocktails, fizzy wine and Pimm's and lemonade in the summer. But this was not the time to be picky; booze flowed in every room on campus and she needed something to give her confidence, anything that might loosen her tongue and enable her to shine a little in front of this beautiful boy.

It was just the one measure, but as the alcohol glazed the back of her throat with its heat, she felt her eyes widen and her cheeks flush. She smiled at the warm glow, which, she had to admit, took the edge off, just a little. She had ditched her glasses and positively shimmied out of her halls.

From that night on, she and David fell effortlessly into coupledom. They were always invited out as a pair and referred to as a unit. It felt great.

The day she took David to her parents' house in Pewsey, Wiltshire was one she wouldn't forget. Nerves had rendered her silent. Trying to control the quake in her gut, she wondered what he would make of her ordinary family in their ordinary house. Her dad, who grew enough tomatoes to keep Heinz in production; her mum, who scoured the hob until the shiny surface lifted; and her sisters, who lounged on the sofa in their tiny shorts and vests, sending pheromones out into the atmosphere with their utter, utter gorgeousness.

Carrie and Holly did a double-take at the sight of their sister's catch. He was far, far from the dorky, scrawny bibliophile that they'd been expecting. Her mum went into fussy overdrive, telling him just how clever her oldest daughter had always been, while force-feeding him Victoria sponge, homemade of course. She had whispered to Romilly through a sideways mouth as they ferried plates and cups to the kitchen, 'You should have told me!' Romilly was perplexed. Should have told her what? That David was good-looking? Well mannered? Smart? What would that have meant, two Victoria sponges? Her dad had packed him off with an old Raspberry Ripple container piled high with ripe, earthy-smelling 'tommyatoes', as he called them.

Romilly waited for David to end their relationship, convinced that it would only be a matter of time before she, like her mum's hob, lost her shiny veneer and he got distracted by something newer, glossier and less timid. She woke each day with nervous anticipation that today might be the day he came to his senses and binned her. A couple of glasses of wine before they saw each other became the salve that ensured she could cope with whatever occurred. She soon discovered that if she topped herself up with a couple more glasses when they arrived at their destination, and downed the odd tequila slammer chaser, she became someone else entirely. And that someone else was the kind of girl no man could resist, particularly the fabulous David Wells.

With the syrupy booze flowing through her veins, she felt taller and sexier and was not averse to hitching up her skirt and dancing where and when the mood took her. David would sit back in slack-jawed admiration, a little the worse for wear himself but delighted and enthralled by the smart, sexy girl who garnered appreciative looks from other Bierkeller drinkers.

Cocktails flowed and became the backdrop to their social life. Sometimes the evening would end with Romilly doing the honours, propping David up like a sack of spuds, his arms dangling forward, his speech slurred. She would manoeuvre him in and then out of a cab, then dump him onto the single bed in her room. As he lay there, pissed and snoring, she would stare at his profile and touch her finger to his cheek, feeling wave after wave of love for him, before pulling the duvet up to his chin and tucking him in.

One night, when it was her turn to be ferried home in an inebriated state, she lay with her arms crossed above her head on the pillow and told him for the first time that she loved him. 'I really, really, really, really do. Like proper love, not just sexing love, not just one-day-Mayfly love, but proper love.' She grinned as he sank to his knees and stroked her hair away from her face.

'I love you too, even when you're pissed. I just hope you remember this in the morning.' He laughed.

'Write it down for me!' She reached towards the bedside cabinet, knocking a half-filled glass of water onto the carpet. 'David, David, write it down!' she insisted, waving her hand in the general direction of her desk, cluttered with books, pens and biscuit crumbs.

'Okay! Okay!' He stood with palms upturned and found a pen and stack of Post-its. On the top one he wrote, *I love you, Bug Girl, and you love me. We are joined forever. Proper love. Do not forget this!* Then he stuck it on the shade of her lamp and budged her into the corner to make room for him to sleep.

When she woke up, shivering and smiling at the duvet thief who had hogged not only the majority of the inadequate bed, but also the bed cover, her eyes fell upon the yellow square fluttering on her lamp. She felt a jolt of joy that left her breathless. These were happy, happy times.

Romilly worked hard at her studies, arriving at the lab full of enthusiasm, throwing herself into every experiment and reading her textbooks late into the night, determined to get the First she knew she was capable of. Whenever she was on top of her workload, she would down her syrupy dancing juice and vamp it up for her man.

On occasion, her nagging insecurity still reared its ugly head. Any message that went unanswered or any apparent distraction on his part would send her reeling to a dark place. Fearing the worst, with muscles coiled in tension, she would wait for the inevitable 'It's not you, it's me....' conversation.

One evening they'd strolled across the Downs and along Ladies Mile, hand in hand under the full-canopied trees whose leaves had begun their transformation into shining golds and russets. The air was Bonfire Night bright and the blue-grey sky seemed to accommodate more stars than usual. The two walked along the footpath that skirted the Avon Gorge, breathing in the cool night air and chatting as they went.

Eschewing the lure of the bustling pubs, they made their way along the Gloucester Row. Romilly hesitated, taking tentative steps out onto the suspension bridge, trying to quell the leap of fear in her gut. She looked up at the magnificent structure as night closed around it, the cliffs of the gorge blurring into shadow behind the bright light of the bulbs illuminating it. It mattered little that this incredible feat of engineering had held fast for the last one hundred and fifty years; she still pictured the taut stays snapping and the tons of Meccano-like metal collapsing into a twisted pile two hundred and fifty feet below, with her buried somewhere beneath.

Halfway across the bridge, David stopped suddenly and stood in front of her. He took her hands inside his and drew a deep breath.

Romilly held his gaze. This was it. *Don't cry. Don't give him the satisfaction. It's okay, I knew it was never going to last.* As her thoughts whirred, she watched him struggle to start, the wind licking his face, lifting his dark fringe. His lips were dry and he swallowed, as if he had a lump in his throat. *I always knew that someone better than me would come along and steal you away, so just say it, get it over with and don't patronise me, just give it to me straight.* She remained silent, not wanting to make it easy for him.

'Rom...' He exhaled from bloated cheeks and shook his head, looking into the distance.

This was clearly harder than he'd thought and that gladdened her, made her feel a little less disposable.

'It's okay. I know. I know what you're going to say.' She blinked, trying to keep the catch from her voice, looking down at the river far below and imagining flinging herself into it. Was it true that you died or lost consciousness before you hit the water, she wondered? Or was that just a white lie, trotted out to ease the pain of the bereaved?

'You do?' He stared at her.

She nodded.

'Okay then.' He released her hand, ran his fingers through his hair and waited, breathing out slowly.

After an interminable pause, he raised his voice. 'So, come on! Tell me, Bug Girl! Is it yes or no? Don't leave a guy hanging.' He peered over the edge at the twist of the River Avon beneath them.

Romilly glanced across at the cars scurrying along the Portway like rows of common ants, purposefully following the same meandering path in two opposing, evenly spaced lines.

'Come on, Rom! I don't like this pause. It was bad enough when I first asked you out. Is this also a silent "Yes, I'd love to," or is this one meant to be a silent "Sod off"?'

'What do you mean?' she asked.

'I mean, are you going to marry me or not?'

'Am I going to... what?' She needed it repeating as she gripped the side of the bridge for support.

Despite the other pedestrians, mostly tourists coming from the Leigh Woods side of the bridge, who giggled at them, their cameras poised, David dropped down onto one knee and took her hand inside both of his.

'Romilly Jane Shepherd, you are amazing. I've never met another girl like you. You make me laugh, you look after me when I'm sloshed and you are the smartest, most interesting person I have ever met. I love you and you love me, proper love that lasts forever, so will you marry me?'

Romilly stared at him and felt her mouth fall open as her knees bobbed with weakness. He wanted to marry her. David Arthur Wells, who could pick anyone in the whole wide world, had chosen her. She leapt into his arms as he held her fast and kissed him passionately on his beautiful mouth.

Celeste

When I was little, I used to pore over their wedding photos. I think it gave me reassurance that there had been this wonderful, romantic time and that it wasn't all bad. I find them hard to look at now, for obvious reasons. They're lovely actually. Mum and Dad seem so young! My mum looked ecstatic, wide-eyed and slightly shocked, as though the whole affair had taken her by surprise, like those brides you see on the telly whose other halves have arranged the whole thing and they just have to turn up on the day and say 'I do'.

She wore a huge meringue-type dress that dwarfed her frame. And she held a stunning bouquet of lilies and trailing ivy that did the same. She has the stance of a little girl who's playing dress-up and has slipped into her mum's frock. Her shoulders are slightly hunched in every shot and she's always peeking upwards, as though she's an imposter who's afraid she might get turfed out of the cream taffeta creation at any moment.

The thing that stands out to me is the brooch on her bodice. My dad gave it to her on the morning of the wedding and it's the most stunning thing – a mayfly. The body is made up of tiny little jewels and the large wings are slivers of turquoise shell, almost transparent and edged in silver. When the light catches them, you can see all the blues and greens of the rainbow. It was her most special possession.

God, suddenly I really miss her. The number of times I used to sit on her lap and she'd show me the brooch and tell me about how Dad had given it to her. I asked her once why she loved it so much and she told me that these beautiful creatures weren't on the earth for very long which made them all the more precious. I got upset, asking, *who looks after their children?* She told me that the mummies might not be on the earth any more, but that it didn't matter, they were always able to watch over their babies, however far away they went.

I would love to go back to that time.

There's one wedding picture that's my favourite; it's beautiful. My dad is standing below my mum on a step and is looking up at her. Aunty Holly and Aunty Carrie, who were bridesmaids, are mid throw, letting handfuls of pale petals fall all around them. The image is so sharp, I can almost smell the blossom. People are crowded around them, lots of uni mates and other relatives, their arms in the air and all smiling, but it's as if Mum and Dad can see only each other; their eyes are locked and they really do look deeply, deeply in love.

I know Mum got pregnant quite quickly after they graduated and married, which, now I'm the same age, seems really young. And I guess that's part of the reason for re-visiting Erica, I have so many doubts, not about Alistair and I, none at all, but plenty about my ability to be a mum. I look at my friends who have had strong, positive role models, who have learned how to bake or fix a car, all because the women in their life showed them how and I worry that I didn't have that. I worry that the defective gene that meant my mum was off the rails might have been passed on to me and I don't want to give my kids a life like that. I really don't.

Not that we are planning on anything soon. We are going to wait, at least that's the plan. Well, he says that's the plan but then romanticises about showing his son the ropes on the farm. I've told him we might not have a boy and even if we do, he might not want to run the farm, he might want to be a ballet dancer or an astronaut. I've also suggested we might have a girl who is dead keen to take on the role. He laughed and said the Hastings don't have ballet dancing or astronauting in their blood, just farming, and that our daughter will be far too smart to lug hay bales in the rain. So I guess that's me told!

Two

Romilly ran her fingers over her cookery book collection in the alcove by the hob and adjusted the weighty volumes until they looked just right. They had mostly been wedding presents and while she had cracked the spine of one or two and admired the glossy pictures of stylised food that made her mouth water, she had yet to actually try making any of the recipes. They were more like props to help her and David play house, on a par with the pasta maker, electric shredder and ioniser, all of which had been gratefully received and exciting to unwrap on their return from honeymoon, but now gathered dust on various surfaces throughout the flat. She found it instantly off-putting to flip open a page and read 'go grab the rosewater and fresh nutmeg from your larder' when her 'larder' contained nothing more fancy than gravy granules and a sausage casserole mix. She knew her cooking skills were a little basic, she was more a 'jar of sauce over pasta for a quick supper' and 'shop-bought apple pie' kinda gal. Not that David seemed to mind, and that was all that mattered to her.

She covered her face with her hands and took a deep breath. 'Please don't get stressed, it's only my mum!'

She jumped as David snuck up behind her and kissed the back of her neck. 'That's easy for you to say, but I'm so nervous, I feel sick.' She swallowed, her voice small, her palms a little clammy.

'That's mad! I don't know why you get into such a state – she loves you.' David twisted her around until she was looking at him and placed his finger under her chin, pushing her face up so she had no choice but to stare him in the eye. 'And especially now that you're going to give her her first grandchild, she'll love you even more! Not as much as me, of course, but close. Remember the plan? We'll tell her after pud!' He hunched his shoulders and grinned, childlike in his anticipation.

Romilly nodded, not wanting to quash his obvious excitement. 'I just know how your mum likes everything to be just so.' She glanced around the disordered kitchen of their Redland flat and recalled Sylvia's tone the previous Christmas. '*A jar of cranberry sauce? Goodness me, I've never seen such a thing!*' Anyone listening to her expression of disdain might have safely assumed that Romilly had let the neighbours' cat crap on the table. '*It almost seems like more effort to drive to a store and buy one, when it's so quick and easy to whip up a fresh batch, nothing much more than a few cups of fresh cranberries and some dark sugar. David Arthur has always loved my homemade sauce, haven't you, darling?*'

It wasn't that Sylvia was intentionally nasty; far from it. She had been overly generous to the newlyweds and always said the right thing, but it was the *way* she said it. '*So glad David has found someone sensible and homey*' or '*Ah, is this where you grew up? Very sweet!*' Maybe the South Carolina drawl distorted her meaning, but no matter how Romilly tried to ignore her misgivings, she thought the flash in Sylvia's eyes and the brevity of her smile spoke volumes. She knew that mother and son shared a close bond, but for her part she hoped that when her own child was married and trotting towards their thirties, she at least would know to loosen the reins and let them fly.

David didn't like to talk much about his parents' divorce, but Romilly knew that the family had come to the UK for his dad's job, a senior role with an energy company, and that Sylvia had been the dutiful wife, keeping a beautiful home, hosting dinner parties and sitting on the PTA of the local primary school, doing all she could to adapt to life as an expat. David's father was also putting in the hours, setting up a flat near his City office with his young PA, Gigi, and flitting between the two very different women. This was until an unexpected pregnancy forced his hand. He chose his shiny, young, pregnant girlfriend, taking her back to Charleston, South Carolina, where the baby turned out to be a false alarm and Gigi left him for a riverboat captain who spent his days fishing for catfish up and down the Cooper River. Sylvia had hated fish ever since.

Perhaps David was right, perhaps she needed to be less sensitive. And she was in complete agreement with him that the delivery of Sylvia's first grandchild was going to make a huge difference.

'So, tell me about your pretty sisters. What adventures are they having?' Sylvia asked as she leant against the countertop and watched as Romilly set the lamb to rest and then finished cooking the veg and spuds.

I get it – prettier than me and not as boring either; off having adventures. 'Well, Holly is still working in a bar in Ibiza and showing no signs of coming home. She's loving it. And Carrie has just started her nurse's training and already has her eye on a handsome junior doctor called Miguel, who is equally smitten, apparently, and she's convinced he'll propose once he gets to know her. Poor chap doesn't stand a chance!'

'Oh, Pat must be delighted!'

'Yes, Mum's proud of her, of course. Nursing is tough and the pay is so poor for what they have to do. It's admirable.'

'No!' Sylvia laughed and batted the air. 'I meant planning to land a doctor! That's a real coup, huh?'

Romilly stuck out the tip of her tongue, licking away the words that gathered in defence of Carrie and indeed her mum. *My sister is self-sufficient, not a gold digger. Dr Miguel would be lucky to have her.*

'Tell you what, Sylvia...' She opened the drawer and pulled the cutlery into a bunch, shoving the metal bouquet with its spiky tines into her mother-in-law's hand. 'Would you mind putting these on the table? Lunch is half done, I'm just waiting on these veg. Oh, and while you're there, could you find some napkins as well?'

'Su-ure!' Sylvia replied, making her way to the table in the large square entrance hall that doubled as a dining room.

Romilly watched her leave the kitchen, then hurried over to the fridge. She grabbed the Chablis from the door, withdrew her arm and smiled at the cool, half-full bottle that sat in her palm. Working quickly, she unscrewed the lid and closed her eyes as she placed the hard bottle edge to her mouth, liking the feel of the glass against her soft mouth. Tilting it, she savoured the earthy, fruity scent that danced up her nose.

As soon as the wine slipped down her throat, tasting sweet but leaving a mineral-like zing on the back of her tongue, she felt better. In the last few months she had discovered that her dancing juice was also really good at making her feel calm. She continued glugging until she was sure she'd had a glass-ful, took a deep breath, fastened the screw top and replaced the bottle in the fridge door. Half filling a glass with water, she took a large mouthful and swilled it around before swal-lowing. She then popped a little rectangle of minty gum and continued to tend to the food.

She and David had agreed to cut back on their drinking. It was not only the foundation to all their socialising but had also become part of their daily routine, a little ritual that she very much looked forward to. At stressful points in the day, just the prospect of cracking open a bottle of wine that evening, or flipping the lid on a couple of cold beers had the ability to lighten her mood and revive her interest in the task at hand.

Now she was pregnant, abstinence was the general rule. Some of their friends insisted she stay away from the grog, while others advocated that one glass to keep mummy relaxed and happy was not going to do any harm. She decided to go with the one-glass theory, but only if she really felt the need. Surprisingly, this required major changes. It was amazing how much a part of their lives alcohol had become and if she was being completely honest, the idea of socialis-ing without having a drink felt a little pointless. Nonetheless, the image of their baby taking shape inside her tum was usually enough to steer her towards sparkling mineral water. Today, however, having to cope with Sylvia without the aid of a little tipple was too much to ask.

'Ta-dah!' She held the stainless-steel salver above her head as she sashayed up to the table, then placed the leg of lamb, veg and roast potatoes in the centre.

'That looks fab!' David smiled at his wife. 'Clever girl.'

'So you *like* lamb now?' his mother asked.

'I love it. Well, I love the way Rom cooks it.' He nodded at the platter.

Romilly smirked as she picked up the serving fork and spoon and settled back in her chair. 'I might not know every-thing, but I know how to keep my husband happy!' And she gave her mother-in-law a subtle wink.

Sylvia opened her mouth but was uncharacteristically lost for words.

It was, as agreed, after pudding that David disappeared into the kitchen and returned with a bottle of champagne and three gold-rimmed flutes, glad of the chance to use the rather frivolous wedding gifts.

'Ooh, champagne!' Sylvia clapped her hands, her long, glossy red nails shining like talons. 'What are we celebrating? Your new love of lamb?'

David chuckled. 'No, Mum, much better than that. We have some news—'

'Ah, finally you are getting a house! Thank the Lord!' Sylvia placed her palms together as if in prayer and flicked her eyes skyward before addressing Romilly. 'I remember your mum saying she quite liked cosy, but I find the lack of space suffocating! Quaint is good an' all, but Lord give me space!' She fanned her face as if to demonstrate her discomfort. Romilly pictured her doing something similar at her parents' cosy cottage.

'Actually, we *are* going to buy a house, as soon as I'm fully chartered in two years, but this is rather bigger than that.' He reached across the table and took his wife's hand into his own. 'We are having a baby!'

Sylvia leapt up with tears in her eyes. 'Oh my God! My baby is having a baby! How did that happen?' She squealed, took her boy into her arms, then walked around the table to stare at her daughter-in-law.

'This is wonderful. Really wonderful! I shall knit! I shall crochet things and I can buy little iddy-biddy socks and beautiful clothes! Oh my, this is really something, you clever, clever kids!' Sylvia kissed Romilly on the cheek and held her close. It was the sweetest, most sincere kiss she had ever given her.

The three laughed and wiped away tears as David poured three flutes of champagne.

'Not for Romilly, dear. No alcohol now she's in the family way.' Sylvia lowered her head and patted the table, as if to give the statement gravitas.

'Oh, one'll be okay!' Romilly reached out, taking the stem between her thumb and forefinger.

David raised his glass. 'To Wells Junior! The best linebacker this country has ever produced!' He grinned at the nod to his mother's heritage.

'Now, wouldn't that be something,' Sylvia said, smiling.

'Might be twins!' Romilly added, reminding everyone that this ran in her family. 'Might be twin *girls* and that means I'll have to find *two* successful men to palm them off on!' She laughed loudly and sipped at her champagne.

With the dishes washed, Sylvia dispatched and night drawing its blind on the day, David climbed into bed beside his wife. 'I think you could say she was pleased.'

'She really was. I can't picture her crocheting at all!' Romilly laughed as she slid down under the duvet, her red hair spread across the pillow like a fiery curtain. She removed her glasses and placed them on the bedside cabinet. 'I'm in the lab tomorrow, so I don't have to be up too early.'

'Lucky you.' David chuckled. It felt strange that he was now immersed in the world of work, putting on a suit and looking very grown up, while his wife was still a student, working towards her PhD. He turned onto his side and propped his head on his raised palm. 'Can I ask you something, Rom?'

'Of course!' She sighed and closed her eyes.

'I just wanted to say...' He paused.

'What?' She opened her eyes, noting his hesitancy.

'I... I think Mum's right. I think you shouldn't drink while you're pregnant.' He avoided her gaze.

'Yes, I know. We've already agreed that. But it was only a little sip of champagne and it did us all the world of good!'

'Are you sure that was all you had?' he asked sheepishly.

Romilly sat up. Her tears hovered near the surface as her cheeks flamed in humiliation. 'God, David, you make me sound like some old lush! I'm not stupid, I'm a scientist!' She hated the echo of her mum's affirmations. *This is Romilly and she's clever...*

'I know! Darling, I know you're not stupid.' He ran his

thumb up the outside of her arm. 'But I don't think it's a good idea to drink. It might be bad for the baby.'

Romilly stared at him. 'You think I would do anything, anything at all that might be bad for this baby?' Her voice was distorted, her vocal chords pulled taut with shame and anxiety.

'Not intentionally, of course not!' He sat up.

'Christ, David! I checked it out and the guidelines say no more than two units twice a week. And so the odd glass of champagne is absolutely fine!'

Leaning across the bed, David lifted her thick hair from her shoulder and kissed the pale bare skin of her décolletage, where her nightie fell away. 'I love you, Rom, and you are going to be the best mum in the whole wide world, I know it.'

She felt her shoulders relax and she gave him a small smile as she watched his lips moving once more. He wasn't done.

'But...'

'But what?' she whispered, feeling like the girl in the stairwell who couldn't believe that he was talking to her.

'I know you drank most of that bottle of Chablis that was in the fridge.'

'What? Are you checking up on me now? Did you put a marker on the bottle?' she snapped, feeling the throb of embarrassment at his confrontation, mortified that he had unmasked her dishonesty, her greed.

'I'm not checking up on you, no. Of course not. I just know it was nearly full and then it wasn't. I only mention it because I want what's best for our baby and what's best for you.' He kissed her again.

'Oh, David!' Her tears sprang from her as her breath stuttered. 'I'm sorry. I'm so sorry! I just got so flustered about your mum coming over and I was nervous and I just thought I'd have a sip and then I swigged it, without really thinking. It's more out of habit than anything else. A bottle is just a couple of our big glasses each and I'm so used to that. I haven't had any for days, so I figured a couple in one day was the same difference.'

'It's okay, Rom. It's okay. Please don't cry!' He held her against his chest.

'I love you, David, and you love me, don't you?' She sniffed.

'I do. Proper love, Bug Girl. You know that.'

'Yes.' She nodded against his skin. 'Proper love. I'm sorry.'

'Don't be sorry, it's all fine. We just need to make sure you don't get stressed and that I support you as much as I can. It's going to be great.'

'I love you, please don't leave me.' She gripped his arms and pushed against him as he stroked her hair.

'I'll never leave you.' He kissed her gently on the head. 'You silly thing.'

'I'm sorry,' she repeated. 'I am, David. I'm sorry. I love our baby and I'm sorry.' Romilly lay against him until her tears abated and sleep overcame her.

'You warm enough, darling?' Pat shut the window in the conservatory, where the family sat together on the creaking three-piece wicker suite.

'Yes, I'm fine, Mum!' Romilly nodded and smiled. It felt lovely to be so looked after by everyone.

'I cannot believe you are up the duff.' Carrie shook her

head. 'I'm going to be an aunty! That's just awesome. And way better than being a mum.'

'How do you figure that?' Romilly asked.

'Trust me, since I've started nursing I've see plenty of saggy boobs and jelly bellies. Not that babies aren't cute, they are, but is it worth that? I don't think so.' She twirled her blonde hair between her fingers. 'This way, I get to keep my figure, go mad at Baby Gap, take the little weenie out for trips and then give it back. It couldn't be any more perfect!'

Their mum joined in. 'Goodness, Carrie, you don't know the half of it! Imagine what my boobs and tum were like after having you twins.'

'I'd rather not, thanks.' Carrie mimed retching.

'My stomach was never the same again. For years I needed a good corset to take up the slack. Your poor dad was in shock the first time I got undressed, and boing!, everything went south.'

'Mum! I think we get the picture!' Romilly raised her eyebrows at David, who looked decidedly pale.

'And don't get me started on my pelvic floor!'

'La la la la!' David sang with his fingers in his ears.

They were all howling with laughter as Romilly's dad, Lionel, came in from the garage with a bottle of Prosecco. 'Here we go!'

'Ooh, just in time, Dad! Mum was telling us about her post-pregnancy pelvic floor.' Romilly grimaced.

'Lovely.' Lionel smiled, as though he didn't have the foggiest idea what she was talking about. He popped the cork and poured the fizz into the waiting glasses. 'Are you having one, Rom?' he asked.

David shot her a look.

'It's okay, David. There's no need to look at me like that! I know I'm not allowed any!'

'Oh, I don't know about that,' Pat offered amiably. 'I think a little bit of what you fancy does you good. People go nuts with the whole pregnancy thing nowadays. Blimey, I used to give you lot a dab of whisky on your dummies to settle you.'

'Yes, Mum, that's a great idea!' Carrie rolled her eyes. 'And what if you fancy a little bit of crack cocaine or a little bit of cyanide, is that good too?'

'I don't think it's quite in the same league as a sip of Prosecco.' Romilly sighed.

Lionel coughed. 'Here's to the wonderful news that soon we will be welcoming the next generation. A grandad! What a marvellous title that is!'

'And I'll be a very proud grandma,' Pat added.

Romilly felt a flush of joy at how happy her parents were at their news.

'Wish Holly was here.' Her dad sighed.

'I shall Skype her later, fill her in.' Romilly smiled.

'So do you think it might be twins?' Carrie asked eagerly.

'No, 'fraid not. It's just one baby! I've had that confirmed.' She patted her tum with its minuscule baby bump.

'It usually skips a generation,' their mum pointed out.

'That's such a shame. Just the one, how boring,' Carrie said.

Romilly stared at the remains of the chilled Prosecco and found herself wishing that she could have a glass.

Celeste

I have lots of good memories of my mum; good days, lots. It wasn't as if every day of my childhood was blighted, not at all. There were some days with Mum that were my best ever days, literally the best ever. That's the thing, when she was on it, she was the greatest mum in the world! It was almost as if she was making up for the other times. She was funny, interesting, patient and carefree.

One day in the summer holidays, I was about four or five, she took me to Canford Park, not far from where we lived, where there was this big rectangular pond surrounded by a beautiful rose garden. I was wearing my little blue sandals and we practically skipped there, hand in hand. She put a tartan blanket on the paving by the pond and as we sat staring at the water, she told me even more about the mayfly. She told me they were precious because they were only on earth for such a short space of time and she told me she thought they were the most beautiful creatures ever created. 'Apart from you,' she said, and she touched my nose. Then she bent close to me and whispered, 'Imagine if they were aliens, taking on the form of mayflies, not wanting to hang around too long in case they are discovered. They arrive on this beautiful planet, learn as much as they can and then shake off their bodies to go back and report what they have seen!'

She made it sound so real, so possible, and I was fascinated.

We ate cheese sandwiches that had got a little hot and melty in their plastic box and then we lay flat on our tummies and stared at the murky green water, dipping sticks into the gloopy weeds and flicking water droplets at each other. Mum threw her head back and laughed and then, as if on cue, there they were: four mayflies, as if she had magicked them just for me! They hovered right in front of us, like toffee-coloured jewels above the water. Their little wings caught the light, beautifully iridescent and beating so fast just to stay in one place that it looked exhausting.

Mum was transfixed. 'Look they're watching us!' Her face lit up and she said, 'It doesn't matter that I've seen them a thousand times before; every time is like the first time. I find them so beautiful. I wish I didn't know the fate that awaits them, but I do, and I can't un-know it.' If only, standing there then, I had known the fate that awaited my Mum. Maybe I could have done something to stop it.

Three

David walked up the driveway with a confident stride, his shoulders square, one arm behind his back and a grin splitting his face. Romilly leapt up from her perch on the front step and ran to meet him. Clamping one arm around his waist, she tried to reach behind his back with the other, stretching and twisting to find his hand, which he then raised above his head, beyond her grasp. The little steel bundle glinted in the sunshine as it jangled. She jumped up with her arm extended, trying to grab his clenched fist.

'Give them to me!' she screeched, her fat plait thumping against her shoulder with each bound.

'You want them?' he teased. 'Come and get them!' And, keys in hand, he twirled off the driveway and onto the patch of grass in front of the house that had officially been theirs for the last hour or so.

Romilly's new, well-paid job and David's promotion meant they could just about afford this beautiful, modern, mock-Tudor detached house in Stoke Bishop. One of Bristol's grander suburbs, it was within easy reach of green space as well as the motorway. Romilly knew it must be a desirable postcode from the way everyone boasted about it, regardless of whether they lived in one of its cul-de-sacs or on a grotty rat run.

When the details had landed on the doormat of their Redland flat, she had oohed and aahed, wondering if it really was within their price range. Realisation that it was, just, had sent her pulse racing. Their first visit, with the toddling Celeste in tow, had more than lived up to expectations. Despite the pressure of David's grip on her forearm reminding her to keep cool, not to appear overly keen and not to get her hopes up, she had rushed from room to room, taking in the large, well-lit spaces, the abundance of storage, the neat double garage and the flourishing back garden with its patio and outdoor table and chairs nestling under a huge green umbrella. It was perfect.

Ignoring her husband's advice, she'd beamed at the charming Mr Brooks, telling him of her plans for the garden and that she could definitely live with the kitchen until they had more money to remodel. There and then she bought the dream as well as the bricks and mortar. She imagined hosting her family for Christmas, envisaged her dad nodding at the lavishly appointed table as her mum beamed with pride. She wanted to see Sylvia's face as she ushered her for the first time into the twenty-six-foot kitchen where they would eat brunch and American pancakes. And as they turned to leave, she pictured Celeste descending the wide stairs, pausing on the half-landing in her wedding dress while she and David stood in the hallway below, blotting tears and gasping at her beauty.

She chose not to share this last image, thinking it might appear a tad over-zealous to be planning that far ahead for their little girl, who had only just mastered the art of going nappy-free. Learning to live without a padded back-up had proved quite a trial for Celeste. After numerous accidents, she seemed to have come to the conclusion that, when she felt the need, she should whip off all her clothes – shoes and socks included – and run to the potty, as though she could only perform this ritual when in the altogether, or 'nudey-dudey', as they called it. Romilly and David hoped Celeste would get the hang of it before too long, unable to imagine her receiving the call of nature as an adult and shedding her kit in the middle of Sainsbury's.

The purchase of their new home had been smooth and problem-free and the charming Richard Brooks from Savills had called only an hour ago to say the keys were ready for collection. Sylvia had agreed to pick up Celeste from nursery and to then take her for a stroll and lunch, giving them time to get the move underway without their inquisitive little girl under their feet.

Laughing, David lowered his weary arm and gave in to his excited wife, who grabbed the keys in both hands and leapt around the grass with her prize clutched tightly to her chest. She ran up the path, then reached back with her hand outstretched.

'Come on. Together.'

Walking forward, David took her hand and both of them smiled as she placed the new key in the unfamiliar lock and turned. It really was some house, and it was theirs!

The front door eased open and the two found themselves in the bare, echoing hallway, a vast space compared to the rather cramped flat they had lived in ever since they'd graduated.

Romilly placed her hand over her mouth. 'I can't believe it's ours!' She let the tears of joy brim.

David pulled her towards him and kissed her, gently at first but with a force that built into a passionate, hard snog. 'Let's christen it,' he whispered into her ear.

'We can't! We've got the removal van arriving any minute and we've...' She struggled to remain composed as his hands roved under her jumper and lingered on her curves. 'We've got no curtains...' she managed, between kisses. 'People will see!'

'I've got a solution.' Gripping her hand, David opened the cupboard under the stairs and stood back, sweeping his arm forward, like a doorman at a flash hotel.

'You want me to get in the cupboard?' She giggled.

'It's perfect!' He smiled. 'Cosy and hidden, and there are some carpet off-cuts on the floor so it's comfy too. Come on!' he urged, pulling his jumper and T-shirt over his head and letting them fall in a heap by the door before unbuttoning the fly of his jeans and letting them drop too.

Laughing, Romilly dragged her jersey over her head and reached behind her back to unhitch her bra, which pinged off and landed on her husband's discarded garments. She smiled at her man, giddy at the daring of the deed and in the half-light of the hallway, managed to lose some of the self-consciousness that had dogged her since she'd given birth.

She had given up drinking. By the time she'd finished breast-feeding, she was so used to not drinking that it was a lot easier than she thought. Her head was clearer, her sleep sounder and her energy levels higher now she wasn't battling the inevitable hangover. There was, however, a downside, in that the odd glass of wine and a couple of lime-laden gins had made her feel sexy, had chased away the last of her inhibitions and encouraged her to relax, especially between the sheets. Sober sex meant she was acutely aware of her lumps and bumps, her slightly saggy tum and her nervous touch.

This outburst of passion was good for them: spontaneous, rushed and wonderfully physical. It was rare that they were both home, without Celeste and not too tired to take advantage of the frisson. Kicking off her jeans and trainers, Romilly climbed into the dark, slightly fusty space and lay down. Laughing, David joined her after closing the door. She wrapped her arms around his neck and kissed him.

'Did you ever think when you sat next to me in the library that it would lead to this? This grown-up life in this grown-up house?'

He held her face in the dark. 'I didn't, Bug Girl, but you know the best thing?'

'What?' she whispered as he met her skin to skin.

'We get to do grown-up things in our grown-up cupboard!'

Suddenly, Romilly froze and gripped his arms. 'What was that?'

'What was what?' He sighed, slightly irritated by the diversion.

'I heard something!' Her tone was urgent.

'No you didn't.' He bent his head and kissed the side of her neck.

Romilly closed her eyes and tried to let the moment take her, before shoving at his chest and sitting upright. 'David! I did hear something! I think someone's at the door!' She pushed her husband.

'All right! Stop pushing me!' He laughed.

'It's not funny!' She giggled, hiding her fear. 'I heard someone knocking! It might be the removal men! Oh shit!'

'Okay, okay, just calm down.' The sound of rapping was now clear and crisp in their ears.

'Calm down? David, we are stark bollock naked in the cupboard and the only way out is into the bloody hallway where the window has no curtain and there is glass in the front door and whoever is knocking will see us!'

'Sssssssssh!' David wheezed his laughter.

'I don't see what's funny!' She felt around on the cupboard floor to see if the previous owner had miraculously left a blanket or a large dressing gown in the vicinity. They hadn't. 'Supposing it's our new neighbour?' she squawked. 'Or the vicar!'

'Why would the vicar call?' David giggled.

'I don't know!' She shrank back against the wall. 'What are we going to do?'

'Okay...' His voice was calm. 'This is what's going to happen. I'm going to crawl out and put my jeans on and open the door as though nothing is amiss. I'll either get rid of whoever it is and come back and join you, or if I can't, if it is the removal men, I'll usher them upstairs and come and knock on the door and you'll know it's safe to come out. You can then grab your clothes, scurry to the loo, pop them on and reappear. Okay?'

She felt her pulse quicken. 'Couldn't we just make out we aren't in?' She grabbed his leg.

'No! They've only got this afternoon to unload the lorry or we'll have to pay for an overnighter and another day tomorrow. It'll be fine. Trust me.' He kissed her on the forehead as the knocking grew louder and more impatient.

She grabbed his leg. 'So, when do I come out again?' Her mind had gone blank.

'When I knock! It means they are upstairs and the coast is clear.'

With that, he left her alone in the darkness. She could hear his voice but couldn't quite make out the words; he was being loud and friendly. *Hurry up, David! Don't bloody chat, get them upstairs. This is my worst nightmare!*

Suddenly, the knock came. Romilly sprang into action. Crouching forward onto all fours, her foot caught the edge of the spare piece of carpet. As she fell, the door flew open and she landed flat on the hall floor. With her head down and eyes low, she spied her clothes with her underwear sitting neatly on top. She lunged for the pile. As her hand touched the cold denim of her jeans, Romilly looked up for the first time. And there, standing in the hallway, was her mother-in-law, looking shocked, and her little girl, who pointed at her naked form.

'Nudey-dudey Mummy!'

'Yes, darling, nudey-dudey.' Romilly scrabbled herself into a sitting position and picked up her pants before sliding her foot into the leg hole, as if it was the most natural thing to be doing on this sunny afternoon.

'Did you do a wee-wee?' Celeste asked, toddling forward and helping by passing her mum her bra, assisting in the way Romilly had assisted her on numerous occasions.

'No, darling. I... err...' She was trying to think of what possible explanation she might give when there was a distinct whistle from the open front door. Romilly, now in her pants and trying desperately to re-hook her bra, smiled at the three removal men who were crowded on the front step and giving each other wide-eyed looks. Slowly, she gathered her jeans and top and made her way to the downstairs loo.

'Hi there!' She waved. 'Just give me a mo and I'll pop the kettle on.' She smiled as she disappeared into the tiny cloakroom.

It wasn't until early evening, when Sylvia had left, the removal men had off-loaded the last of the boxes, and Celeste was sitting on the floor engrossed in her dollies, that Romilly and David had the chance to collapse in a helpless heap on their sofa.

'Why did you knock?' She beat at his chest through her tears of laughter.

'I didn't! It was Celeste; she was like a little homing pigeon. She literally marched straight in and banged on the cupboard door.' He wiped away his tears at the memory.

'You could have shouted out, warned me, said something!'

'Like what? I was standing there with my mother!'

The two laughed until they cried, gripping each other tightly. Celeste, alerted by the fun, toddled over to the sofa and climbed up to sit on them.

'Do you like your new house?' Romilly asked as she brushed her little girl's hair from her forehead.

Celeste gave an exaggerated nod.

'Do you like your new big-girl's bedroom?' David asked.

'Yes.' She nodded again, before giving an involuntary yawn.

'Are you sleepy, baby?' Romilly wrapped her daughter in a hug, kissing her scalp.

'Why don't you go get her off to sleep. I'll find a cold bottle to celebrate our new home and we can make a night of it.' David grinned.

'Don't know. I'm a bit out of practice at drinking.' She kissed his hand, which rested on her shoulder.

'It's like falling off a bike, Rom. You'll be fine.' He winked, trying to remember in which box he had packed the wine glasses.

'Or like falling out of a cupboard?' she quipped, still giggling as she carried her little girl up the wide staircase of their beautiful new home.

Celeste

We moved into our family home when I was two. The plan was for me to have a raised bed with storage beneath. The storage never materialised; instead there was a gap of just over a foot in height, where a broken doll used to lurk, living on a dusty mat with a discarded sock and sticky wrappers, evidence of chocolate bars that I had eaten illicitly. This gap was my hiding place whenever going downstairs felt scary. It was dark and cosy and I imagined it was the place that alien mayflies went to die. I talked to them sometimes, asked them what it was like to live in a different world and whether they were sad to leave their children behind. That imaginary world under my bed was like my safety blanket, a small space that was all mine. Mum found me there once or twice and one time, she lay on the floor and put her hand under the bed until it found mine and we lay there in the dark, me under the bed and her on the rug with my hand safe inside hers as she sang to me. It was the song she always sang, 'You Are My Sunshine...'.

And the house, for which I will always have a key, pulls me back. I know it so intimately that I can picture it and smell it with my eyes closed, even when I'm on the other side of the world. Dad mentioned moving once, after Mum... but I'm glad we didn't.

Glad he didn't pursue it. I think the look on my face must have spoken volumes. I just can't imagine leaving the house where our story sits between the bricks and lurks in every scuff on the wall, behind the plants and trees in the garden. No matter what was happening in my life, that house, my room, was the one constant. Even though there were times when I would retreat to the gap under the bed where the alien mayflies lived, squeezing my eyes shut to try and block out what was going on all around me, it was still home.

Four

Three years after they moved in, on a remarkably similar day, a removal truck blocked the Wells' cul-de-sac from morning until late afternoon. All the residents noticed it, but no one complained. Instead, they peered at it from behind the net curtains or had a good gawp while they tended to their bins or watered their tubs. Everyone tried to glean clues as to who the new occupants might be. Was there a kid's bike to be seen? A teenager's drum kit? Fancy sofas?

Romilly and David hadn't regretted stretching themselves financially while they were so young, knowing that things would continue to get easier as they headed for middle age. But with both of them still under thirty, that still felt like a long way off. Romilly was highly regarded at work and her pay reflected this; apart from a sometimes irritating commute, her job was everything she'd hoped it would be. David's career continued to go from strength to strength and he was on track to become one of the youngest partners in the firm. His mantra hadn't changed: 'Have you noticed, Rom, that the harder I work, the luckier I get?'

Such was the nature of the neighbourhood that everyone found a way to accommodate the inconvenience of the large truck that didn't look to be going anywhere any time soon. They drove up onto pavements, waving good-naturedly at the new arrival and shouting out offers of tea and biscuits as they exchanged names.

Sara Weaver, they soon discovered, was a divorcee. She had bought the house from the Hensons, who had traded in their 'highly sought-after four-bed, three-bathroom home with landscaped back and front gardens' for a cool four hundred grand, with which they then purchased a snazzy apartment in a gated community in Naples, Florida, issuing invitations to all the neighbours to visit them whenever they wished. This struck Romilly and David as particularly funny, given that the Hensons only ever socialised at Christmas, when they threw their annual cocktail party, roping in the older kids in the area to serve canapés and stack the dishwasher for a tenner each. They were quite certain that if they did turn up in Naples with a suitcase in tow, the Hensons would duck behind the breakfast bar and hide out like a Victorian widow being chased for overdue rent. Still, it was nice to be asked and just for a minute or two picture themselves in that Florida sunshine while Mrs Henson whipped up a batch of her much admired eggnog.

Sara Weaver was a different kettle of fish entirely; she was about as social as they came. Even the removal men seemed to be having a great time, whisking tables, metal bedsteads and a washing machine up the path as though they were feather light, encouraged by Ms Weaver's raucous laughter, gentle ribbing and generous helpings of tea and Mr Kiplings. It felt more like a street party than a hectic removal day.

She appeared at their front door the day after she moved in. Romilly had been polite, neighbourly, as 'Call me Sara!' leant against the kitchen worktop, telling her how her dentist husband had done a runner with his dental assistant, leaving her high and dry after six years of marriage. She had of course taken him for as much money as she could, threatening to make him wait the statutory five years for his divorce, which would have proved most upsetting for his very pushy new beau. She had given him his divorce, eventually, but it had cost him. Sara had been wronged and, as she explained, felt no qualms at the fact that the new Mrs Weaver and her ex were shacked up in a flat on the wrong side of Whiteladies Road; she was certain that his earning capacity would see him back on track in no time.

Romilly found everything about her fascinating: her tight jeans, heels and vest, which were more appropriate for a nightclub than a neighbourly pop-in, her tendency to overshare, her loud voice, and her laugh, which was only ever a sentence away from erupting. Romilly placed her hand on her daughter's shoulder and pushed her forward. 'This is Celeste. Our daughter.'

Celeste stood in front of her mum, her thick, mousey-brown hair hanging against her pale face, from which large eyes shone.

'Say hello, darling!' Romilly prompted.

'Oh, wow! She's gorgeous!' Sara gasped.

Romilly grinned. Yes, she was.

The little girl walked forward and gave a shy wave.

'Oh goodness, you're so pretty! Do you go to school?'

Celeste took a step backwards as Sara bent down and looked her in the eye.

'I go to Merrydown Juniors. I'm five,' Celeste whispered, wary of the woman who acted as familiar as Aunty Carrie and Aunty Holly but was actually a stranger.

'Oh, I can tell you are a Merrydown girl! But I would have thought you were at least seven.' Sara's eyes twinkled.

Celeste beamed, delighted by the compliment, and ran off to watch the telly.

Sara straightened. 'Do you work, Rom?'

Romilly was a little taken aback at the woman's presumption, abbreviating her name when it was usually only family and close friends that called her 'Rom'.

'Err, yes. I'm a scientist. An entomologist.' She still got a kick out of announcing her non-standard profession.

'Good God!' Sara raised a carefully shaped eyebrow. 'A what?'

Romilly laughed. 'I work for a biopharmaceutical company. I'm an expert on insects, so I help them look at how best to protect crops, keep bugs away and things like that.'

'Oh shit, it's not that GHD stuff, is it? The one that if you feed it to chickens they get born with three heads and if it gets into my cornflakes my tits will fall off?'

Romilly giggled out loud; Sara was quite unlike anyone she knew. 'I think you mean GMO not GHD and no, it's nothing to do with that. Your tits are quite safe.' She giggled again.

'Good. I would hate to think of all that money of Neil's going to waste!' She placed her hands under the inflated cups and pushed her breasts upwards. 'You have great tits too, if you don't mind me saying.'

Romilly stared at her. 'Err, no! I just don't think anyone has ever said that to me before – my husband possibly, but certainly not on our first meeting!'

'Well, he should have. You have a fab set and great hair; you've got that whole Jessica Rabbit thing going on.'

Romilly laughed, loudly. 'I think Jessica Rabbit was slightly more hourglass than me and definitely didn't wear glasses, or cardigans.'

'Rom…' Sara placed her hand on her arm. 'I always say there are a dozen people waiting to put you down and knock the confidence out of you, so don't do it to yourself. You are a very sexy lady and you should celebrate it!'

'You think?'

'I know!' Sara winked.

'Would you like a drink?' Romilly liked their new neighbour. She liked her very much.

Sara looked at her watch. 'It's nearly five o'clock and in my house it's practically illegal not to have a glass of plonk at this time.' She banged the countertop. 'You and me are going to be great mates, I can tell.'

Romilly smiled and went to the fridge. She didn't need an excuse for a glass of wine, but having someone to drink it with made a welcome change. David rarely shared a bottle with her any more. He'd embarked on a health kick a couple of years earlier and had become very conscious of what he ate and drank. He seemed to be always training for some marathon or other and watching his calorie intake was now second nature. These days he only drank occasionally and could be quite disapproving of Romilly's daily plonk. It was the one thing they regularly clashed over.

It didn't matter how many times she explained to him how everyone drank wine, literally everyone! The lady in the post office, the girl in the chippy, practically every parent at school and even her parents, he still made her feel guilty, casting tense glances at her when she reached for the bottle before, during and after dinner. And if she was being honest, she found his reaction unfairly censorial, irritating. It took the edge off her pleasure and encouraged her to act furtively.

It wasn't as if she got rolling drunk or was too inebriated to function, it was just how she relaxed, how she shrugged off the stresses of the day. A harmless habit. If she didn't drink half a bottle of wine in an evening, she couldn't sleep. If she didn't drink half a bottle of wine before a social event, she couldn't go, because her nerves would get the better of her; and if she didn't drink half a bottle of wine before Sylvia arrived, she simply couldn't cope.

She hadn't confided in her husband how the thought of a cold bottle of wine waiting in the fridge could get her through the most challenging of days. If she got caught in traffic, lost her keys, mislaid her handbag or struggled over some particularly troublesome data in the lab, all of these things could be eased by simply picturing the honey-coloured reward that awaited her at the end of the day. It was her only vice. She didn't eat vast quantities of chocolate or take-aways and she had never smoked or taken drugs, all of which would surely take a far greater toll on her health than the odd glass of plonk.

The two women took up seats at the pine kitchen table and chatted and laughed as they polished off not one but two bottles of Sauvignon Blanc. Romilly found her new friend hilarious, enjoying the raucous tales of single life and how Sara was making up for lost time after years of being stuck in a dull, lifeless marriage.

'My husband was like the fun police! I can see that, now I'm out of it.' Sara laughed. 'He was like this big atmosphere hoover who came in and sucked the joy from whatever I was trying to do. I wasn't allowed to have any fun! None at all. I feel sorry for his poor bloody dental assistant, who will have to put up with him, the miserable bastard!'

They were halfway through the third bottle when the sound of a key in the front door caused Romilly to sit up straight and narrow her eyes at the kitchen clock. It was 7.30; she had completely lost track of time.

David strolled into the kitchen, clutching his car keys and laptop. He was surprised to find the two sitting at the table in semi-darkness, leaning heavily on crooked arms and snorting laughter at each other's comments. He flicked on the central light and eyed the stranger.

'David! Hello!' Romilly called out, shielding her eyes from the harsh bulb. 'This is my new friend, our new neighbour, Swara...' Her laughter rippled from her as she hiccupped. 'No, no, it's Swara!' She beat the tabletop with her palm. 'Swara!' Again she tried and failed to get the name right.

Sara stood up and wobbled on her heels as she held out her hand. 'Hello, Mr Accountant, I am Swara!' She giggled, tilting her head in a coquettish manner.

David nodded, ignoring her outstretched hand. 'Where's Celeste?'

As if on cue, she ran into the kitchen. 'Daddy!' She flung her arms around his leg and looked up at him. 'What's for tea?' she asked, her voice small.

'You haven't had your tea?' He bent down.

She shook her head.

'Tell you what, why don't we go up the Stoke Bishop chippy and you can have chicken nuggets? How about that?'

'Yes!' The little girl jumped up and down on the spot; this was a real treat. She ran towards the front door.

David hovered in the kitchen and glared at his wife. 'It's 7.30, her bedtime, and she hasn't even eaten! I suggest you get yourself together while I get the food. We can talk later.'

He barely registered their new neighbour. As he ushered his little girl from the hallway and closed the front door behind him, a ripple of laughter followed him up the driveway.

Romilly waved Sara off, feeling a mixture of happiness that her new friend was only a couple of doors away and dread at the showdown she felt would inevitably come when David got back with Celeste. She decided to set the table for them, as a way of making amends. Wandering back into the kitchen, she gathered two white dinner plates from the cupboard. As she carried them across the room one of them slipped from her hand and shattered into tiny pieces on the ceramic floor tiles. Her grip loosened and the other quickly followed with a loud smash.

Romilly knelt down to retrieve the bigger shards and winced at the sharp bite of pain in her knees. It threw her forward, causing her to place her palms on the floor, and she instantly felt a similar sting in them too. Sitting back against the cupboard door, she stared at her palms; they were bloody, with fragments of white crockery embedded in her skin. Her knees were the same.

Without thinking, she ran her hand over her face and felt the slivers stuck in her hand scrape her cheek. She started to cry. Her hands and knees hurt, her face throbbed and her palms pulsed. She could feel the warm trickle of blood over her arm and wrist.

With her head hung forward, she sat on the floor and waited for David to come home. David, who could make everything better. A small part of her figured that if he found her tearful and bleeding, then he wouldn't be quite so cross about her and Sara getting tipsy and forgetting to feed Celeste and put her to bed. At least that was what she hoped. She didn't have to wait long; it was less than ten minutes before she heard the car pull into the driveway.

'Mummy! We've got chips!' Celeste yelled excitedly from the hallway.

'David!' Romilly called out weakly.

Her daughter appeared in the doorway and seemed to freeze. Her little chest heaved and she looked scared.

'It's okay, Celeste.' Romilly smiled through her tears. 'Can you get Daddy?'

Celeste didn't move. Rooted to the spot, her eyes scanned the mess on the floor, darting between the broken china and her mum, who had blood streaked across her face and running from her knees where her tights were ripped.

'What the f—' David yelled over his daughter's shoulder, remembering she was present before he swore. 'Hey, Celeste,

I tell you what, sweetheart, you go and eat your nuggets and chips in front of the telly, while I help Mummy, who has had a little fall. But she's okay, aren't you, Mum?' He did his best to sound jovial, like it was all some sort of a game.

Romilly nodded her head. 'I'm fine.'

'Come on.' David guided their daughter from the room.

'I... I need tomato sauce, Daddy,' Celeste murmured as she made her way to the sitting room, clutching her paper-wrapped supper and glancing back towards the open kitchen door at her mum, who sat slumped with her head on her chest.

David darted back into the kitchen. 'For God's sake, Romilly!' he whispered through gritted teeth as he opened the cupboard by the kettle and pulled out the ketchup. 'What on earth happened?'

'I fell over,' she managed.

'Don't move, love. I'll be back in two secs.' He rushed from the room, ignoring the crunch of their best china beneath the sole of his brogues.

Romilly began crying again. Sad that he had sounded mad but happy and guilty that he had called her 'love'.

David switched on the other main light and bent down next to her. 'What on earth have you done?' He touched the point on her cheek where a scratch was bleeding.

'I dropped the plates and they smashed and then I knelt on them and I've cut myself.' Her tears came afresh.

'Okay. Don't cry, darling. It's okay. Let's try and get you cleaned up.' His tone was level, kind.

He grabbed the dustpan and brush from the cupboard under the stairs and cleared the space around her. Then he filled the mixing bowl with hot water and a dash of Dettol. Setting it on the floor, he took off his suit jacket, looped it over the back of a dining chair and knelt down beside his wife. With a wad of kitchen roll dipped in the water, he dabbed at her cuts, beginning with the one on her face, which thankfully looked a lot worse than it was. Next he tended to her palms, removing the fine splinters of china as she winced, then mopping the wounds clean. He did the same with her knees. Finally, he cut strips from the sticky roll of fabric plaster and covered the cuts.

Supporting her gently under her armpits, he helped her stand, then guided her up the stairs and towards their bedroom.

'Come on, one more step,' he coaxed. 'Nearly there.'

Romilly flopped onto the bed, turned her face towards him and began to sob. 'I'm sorry, David. I broke two of our wedding plates. I'm sorry.'

'It wasn't the first time and it won't be the last. It doesn't matter.'

'Matters to me...' She sniffed.

'What matters a lot more is not getting Celeste off to bed on time and forgetting to give her her supper.' He sighed and his jaw tightened. 'I thought you'd learnt your lesson on that front, after... after that day at your parents', with Russian Viktor and the Pimm's.'

'Oh, David, I'm so sorry. I promised it wouldn't happen again, and I never meant it to. I promise I didn't.'

'Daddy!' Celeste's voice came chirruping up the stairs. 'The telly's gone all fizzy. I want to watch my programme?'

'Just a tick!' he shouted. 'I'll bring you a glass of water when I come back up, Rom,' he said as he made for the door.

As Romilly lay there listening to the distant chatter of the two people she loved most in the world, images from that horrible episode with the Pimm's kept galloping into her head. It was summer and the whole family had spent the day in the garden at her parents' house. Everyone was in high spirits. Carrie was running around the garden in her shorts and T-shirt, her arms outstretched like a child impersonating an aeroplane. 'My Holly's home!' she yelled. She ran up behind her sister and lifted her off the ground, spinning her round with her legs in the air. It mattered little that they were in their twenties; when they got together after any time apart, they reverted to their thirteen-year-old selves.

'Put me down, Car!' Holly screamed, thumping her sister's locked wrists. 'Help me! Rom, for God's sake, help me!'

Romilly had chuckled and remained anchored to her seat. She winked at David and smiled at Dr Miguel, who laughed nervously. It was the first time the doctor had seen the twins together; he was trying desperately to impress Carrie's family while also working out what his role was. He shouldn't have worried, however. Spending an hour showing an interest in their dad's greenhouse, and downing two helpings of their mum's trifle was enough to guarantee just about anyone Carrie's hand in marriage.

Holly's latest beau, Viktor from Russia, had made a fierce bucket of Pimm's. As soon as Romilly sat down, he'd ladled a generous measure of fruit and booze into her glass. She had sipped away throughout the afternoon, accepting Viktor's frequent refills, which he offered in lieu of making conversation in his limited English.

'Darling, I don't think you want any more of that.' David pointed at her glass.

'What? It's only like fruit and lemonade, there's nothinginit, spoilsport!' She rolled her eyes in his direction.

David glared at the meaty Viktor, waiting for an opportunity to have a word with him out of Romilly's earshot. It might have seemed funny to get her plastered, but she had a little girl to look after and it was him that would have to pick up the pieces later on. The chance never arose, however, as Romilly stuck close to Viktor and his generous ladle all afternoon.

It was only as evening loomed, when she stood up to join her sisters and her mum in an impromptu dance on the lawn, that Romilly realised just how much she'd drunk.

'Oh, now she gets up to help, when I'm no longer in danger! Come on, Rom! She's had her jiggle juice, David, and she's ready to party!'

Holly screamed her laughter at the exact moment that Romilly's legs gave way. She had tripped on a divot that would not have troubled sober legs. Stumbling forward, Romilly ploughed into her mum, who had a rather sleepy Celeste in her arms. Romilly sent Pat tumbling to the left, and as she fell, she dropped Celeste with a hard thump on the ground.

The little girl screamed, as much in shock as any real pain, the soft grass and mud having cushioned what could have been a very nasty impact. David leapt from his deckchair, casting his beer to one side as he scooped up his daughter, kissing her face and shushing her quiet while he stroked her hair. 'It's okay, darling, you're fine,' he repeated, over and over. 'You're okay.' Dr Miguel checked her over. Seemingly nothing was broken, but a giant egg-shaped bump was growing on her forehead, topped with a purple bruise.

Romilly lay on her back with her arms cruciform, looking up at the twilight clouds, watching them float overhead as mayhem reigned around her. She could feel the weight of David's angry stare, her mum's acute embarrassment and the twins' hysteria as they flapped and squawked in panic. Viktor's loud, inappropriate laugh cracked the air like thunder.

'Why are you laughing, you prick?' Holly shouted at him, and despite his lack of English, he was left in no doubt that he would soon be Viktor the ex-boyfriend from Russia.

David blocked the sky as he reached down and took Romilly's hand, pulling her upright. She stood on the spot where she had fallen and wobbled as if on springs.

'Think we'd better get her home,' David murmured, embarrassed, as he awkwardly kissed his mother-in-law and nodded to Dr Miguel and Viktor.

After strapping Celeste into her car seat in the back, David went to retrieve his mandatory tub of tommyatoes from Lionel. While he was gone, Romilly turned from the front seat to look at her daughter. The bloody, blue bruise on her little forehead looked angry.

'What the fuck?' Romilly slurred. 'What the fuck's going on?'

Celeste wailed in response.

'Why is she crying?' David asked as he climbed into the car, his jaw jutting with anger.

'Fuck knows!' Romilly laughed, loudly.

'Charming.' David was beyond furious, but he knew that having a row right then would be pointless and would only increase Celeste's distress.

They were only a few miles from home when Romilly woke in the front seat. The car was too hot and the air was thick. The motion of the car swaying from lane to lane on the M4 was all it took; it was almost simultaneous: as she opened her eyes, she vomited. A sticky pink foam splattered across the dashboard and windscreen.

'Jesus Christ, Romilly!' David yelled as he punched the hazard-lights button and coasted over to the hard shoulder.

Celeste, woken by his shouts, immediately started screaming and then she too started vomiting, the smell of her mother's sick having this effect on her.

David wound down his window as they sat on the hard shoulder. His daughter was crying and shouting from the back seat, with sick dripping from her chin and outstretched arms. His wife was crying and vomiting into the footwell, puking all over her shoes, her handbag and her dad's punnet of tommyatoes. He literally did not know which way to turn and so he sat, paralysed with fear, anger and a good measure of disgust, trying to remain calm. A police siren whined behind him. He loosened his seatbelt and climbed out of the car to greet the officers, wiping sick and a few chunks of strawberry and cucumber from his thigh as he did so.

Romilly narrowed her gaze and watched in the side mirror as the officer put on his hat and approached David, who stood by the verge with his hands in his hair. He looked like he might be crying as he explained the unfortunate situation in which he found himself. She saw the policeman take a step forward and pat his arm, which made her smile. Everyone loved David Arthur Wells.

The memory of this last image made Romilly turn towards the bedroom door just as David came in with the glass of water. She smiled weakly at him. He didn't smile back.

'I don't much like the new neighbour,' he said curtly as he set the glass down on the bedside cabinet.

'You don't know her!' Romilly forgot her contrition and leapt to Sara's defence.

'Neither do you,' he countered. 'Obviously I'm not saying be rude or ignore her, but don't encourage her to be friends. There's something about her I didn't like.'

Fun police… Romilly felt a small giggle leave her mouth at the thought, as David switched off the lights and left her to sleep.

Celeste

Sara Weaver. Now there's a name I haven't considered for a while. I used to love her. I really did. My mum told me often enough that she was her only friend and so I was grateful to her for that. I wanted someone to look after Mum and for her to have fun with, just like I did with my friends. And Sara was fun to be around. She was different. She knew the words to songs on the radio, not old people's songs but songs that my friends and I liked, and she could make me laugh. She wasn't like any other adult I knew. She didn't follow the rules and she liked to make a mess. She used to come into our house like a wind, shaking up the quiet and changing the way things felt, and when she arrived I'd see Mum's expression lift and so I wanted her to be there as much as she could. My mum would call her, giggling, when my dad left for the day or had nipped out, like giving her the nod that the coast was clear, and that made it seem illicit, naughty. And it felt like I was in on the secret, like one of the grown-ups, even though I didn't know what the secret was. It was exciting.

One day we pulled every cushion from every sofa and chair in the house and built a fort and then, when I was in it, Sara jumped on it, trapping me inside and squashing me. It was funny at first, I was giggling fit to burst. But then she put more weight on the top, might even have fallen asleep, I don't know, but it felt like an age that I was inside, in the dark, unable to move my arms and legs and feeling the weight of her pressing down on my chest. My giggles had meant I'd lost my regular breathing pattern and no matter how hard I tried to fill my lungs, I couldn't. I felt a tightness in my chest and I was very close to sheer panic, when she suddenly moved and flung the cushions high and wide until I was free and we both lay on the floor. I was laughing so hard from relief, but then my mum picked up this bean-filled cushion and stood there whacking me with it, and the three of us laughed and laughed until we cried. I cried really hard then, and I didn't want to laugh any more.

When my mum put me to bed that night, I told her that I had been scared and that I couldn't breathe and she said it was best that I didn't tell Daddy, she placed her finger under my chin and lifted my face to hers, 'we don't want to worry him, do we?' I shook my head. She then held me tight and kissed me, whispering into my ear, 'you can throw all the bottles away with me tomorrow, we shall go on a secret mission!' She knew I liked the sound of the glass smashing after you dropped it into a little hole in the top of the bottle bank.

Then, of course, as I got older and heard my dad speaking frankly about Sara's influence on my mum, begging Mum not to even go out with her, I stopped loving her and started to mistrust her. I felt guilty about all those times I'd laughed with her and began to see that it was in some way disloyal to my dad. I could see she was the wedge between my parents, the thing keeping them apart, or so I thought. And I began to hate her for that.

As I say, I haven't thought about her for a very long time, but now I suppose I feel sorry for her. I'm pretty indifferent. I can see that she was an enabler. She encouraged my mum to drink, so they could both have a good time. But Mum wasn't forced; she was a consenting grown-up who wanted to go along for the ride. In fact, I see Sara a bit like an instructor, a boozing tutor, picking my mum up, taking her out and helping her to get better and better at drinking. They relied on each other. So I don't blame her, not any more. If it hadn't been her, there would have been another Sara. Mum would have found someone else to show her the ropes, help her become an expert at her chosen sport. Of that I'm absolutely certain.

Five

'Can you see the difference?' Romilly held the two fragile glass slides up towards the light and stared at them, holding them slightly to the right so that Warwick the intern could see them too.

'Not really.' He swallowed, looking nervous.

'That's okay.' Romilly smiled, polite and patient, trying to put the young graduate at ease. 'Let me show you in a different way.'

Warwick followed her to the end of the lab bench, where the microscope was set up.

She pushed her specs up onto her nose and squinted over the lens, silently twisting and adjusting the settings until she was happy. 'Right, take a look now.' She moved to the side and nodded for him to take over.

The young man sighed and placed his eye close to the eyepiece. 'Oh!' he exclaimed.

'Go on,' she coaxed.

'Erm... I think the seed on the left has tiny new radicles on the base and the one on the right doesn't.' He lifted his head and stared at his mentor.

'Exactly! Well done, you!' She beamed. 'And that means,

Warwick, that there is something about the seed on the left that the grey field slug didn't like! This is marvellous. Really marvellous.' She clapped.

'It's exciting, isn't it?' he said, flushing.

'It really is.'

Romilly logged the data and tidied her workspace, as was her habit. She knew her colleagues laughed at her OCD-like meticulousness, but it was a trait she couldn't alter. It was just one of her quirks that they affectionately ribbed her about, another being her need to work alone. 'There's no "I" in team!' her colleague Tim regularly shouted at her from the other side of the lab. To which she always replied, 'And there's no "Do I look like I give a shit?" there either!'

'You're a lone wolf, Rom!' Tim yelled at her now, impressed by her latest finding.

She gave a high-pitched howl in response, as she always did when he said that.

Romilly eventually hung up her lab coat an hour after her official workday should have ended. 'Bye all, see you tomorrow! Good job today, Warwick.' She noted the lad's beam of pride as she waved to her colleagues, then began fishing one-handedly in her bag for her keys as she made her way to the car park.

'Rom!'

She turned to see who had called her. 'Sara?' She was surprised to see her neighbour waving from a car window by the gate. 'What are you doing here?' Romilly was taken aback, wondering if all was okay with the house. Questions and scenarios flashed through her head. *Burglary? Fire? Where is Celeste?*

'Yeah, I'm good. How are you?'

'Fine.' She felt a little confused by the exchange, as though it was normal for her friend of six months to turn up at her place of work and hang out in the car park.

'Hope you don't mind me pitching up, but there's a new cocktail menu being launched tonight in town and I have a VIP invite that's a plus one. So, as I don't have any other friends, I thought you might like to jog along with me. Please don't make me go on my own!' she begged, hands pressed together as if in prayer.

'I can't just go out, Sara! I have to go home.' She looked at her watch. It was about now that the afterschool sitter would be packing up to leave, and David would be heading home too. 'They won't have supper without me. I need to get back.'

'Can't they eat without you just once? We are talking VIP!' Sara raised an eyebrow suggestively. 'When's the last time you went out and had a giggle, like you didn't have a care in the world? A good old bloody giggle!'

Romilly bit her lip, pulling her oversized handbag into her waist like a shield. 'I'm not sure. David thinks you're a bad influence on me and I think he might be right!' She laughed.

'Yes, because David is a fellow member of the fun police, the atmosphere hoover club. I can tell. And what's more, he can tell that I can tell, if you follow!' She roared with laughter. 'Come on, Rom! You're not having enough fun! What's one evening?'

Romilly laughed too and with a heady jolt of carefree abandonment shooting through her veins, she jumped in the passenger seat and swiped her phone to send David a text, explaining that she was working late and to go ahead and eat without her. She shoved the phone in her bag, too nervous to study his response.

Sara punched the air and shouted 'Yes!' as though her team had just won the cup. 'You can lose that ponytail for a start!' She reached across and pulled at her friend's hair. 'Let the mane loose!' she shrieked.

Romilly laughed and did as she was told, teasing off the elasticated band and letting her hair fall in lustrous waves over her shoulders. She shook her head and raked her fingers through the shining red mass.

'Oh my God, your hair is amazing! All you need is a bit of this...' Sara dipped low and plunged her hand into her handbag that sat in the well by Romilly's feet. The car swerved a little to the right. They both gave a nervous giggle as the driver of the Volvo coming in the opposite direction beeped his horn.

'Fuck off!' Sara waved back. 'I'm trying to get to my lipstick!' she shouted, as though this was explanation enough for her meander across the lane. 'Here.' She handed Romilly a berry-red tube of sparkling lip stain. 'Go on, pop it on. It is so your colour. It'll accentuate your hair and as you have next to no eye make-up on behind those shades, we need to make your lips pop. That's the rule: dramatic eyes or lips but never both. Did you not learn that at beauty school?' she lisped in a fake American accent.

Romilly shook her head. 'No, I must have skipped that lesson. Too busy learning the periodic table.' Pulling down the sun visor, she tentatively drew the wand across her mouth, staring at the instant, glistening pout that was bright and did indeed make her mouth pop. It didn't look like her. 'I've never been very good with make-up. I think because I wear glasses and I can't see too well without them, I'm nervous of eye shadow and stuff. I only wear a bit of mascara. I guess because David and I met at uni, he knows what I've always looked like and it would feel odd to suddenly walk around with a face full of colour. I'm just not that type.'

'You are a stunning woman, who seems to hide her looks away, and that's a shame. One day you'll look in the mirror and you'll be eighty-six, everything will have gone to rat shit and it will be too late to explore just how gorgeous you are! You don't want that, do you?'

Romilly shrugged and thought of her mum. 'I've never really thought about it. My sisters were always the pretty ones and they are really good-looking – you know, blonde, long legs, smiley, they've just got that cute thing going on and they always have. I was different, really...'

'Says who? God, blonde and cute is ten a penny. You are *so* gorgeous! You just don't know it. You're like one of those sexy secretary types who suddenly shows up at the end-of-year party and whips off her goggles and everyone realises they've been dictating notes to Jayne bloody Mansfield all year without realising it!'

Romilly smiled at her friend's theatricality. 'Hardly! And I don't want to be a secretary type or a starlet, I want to be taken seriously. I'm a scientist.'

'Yes, so you've mentioned. But every woman wants to be sexy, scientist or not! Now, let's get this party started!' Sara leaned across again and opened the glove box, from where she produced two mini bottles of Möet et Chandon. They were pretty little things, with pale pink labels and pale pink foil.

'Ooh, fancy!' Romilly chuckled.

'Get them open!' Sara banged the steering wheel dramatically.

Romilly did as she was bid and popped the corks. Sara didn't seem to mind that the spray from the bottles shot out over the pale grey leather interior of her Mercedes. Romilly placed the foaming lip of the bottle to her mouth and savoured the sweet bubbles that burst on her tongue. As with any first sip, it was as if a beautiful note played in her head, a note that she knew would become a full symphony the more she drank. It was the music of distraction, playing a tune that took her to a different place, where she could be anyone and anything she wanted to be.

They parked the car at a meter just up from the Bristol Royal Infirmary and made their way to Zero Degrees. They linked arms like they were old, old friends.

'Hey, Sara! How lovely to see you!' A pretty waitress with a white pinny tied high under her bust greeted her friend. Romilly had to admit to a frisson of excitement that her companion was known. It was a little bit of celebrity that seemed to elevate her by association. 'Come on, let's get you a good spot near the bar.' The waitress took Sara's hand and led her through the tables, past groups and couples enjoying after-work beers and intimate suppers.

'Cocktail?' The waitress smiled, her hands on her hips.

'Ooh, go on then. Surprise us!' Sara flashed her best smile.

The waitress clicked her fingers. 'Leave it to me!' she said, and skipped off.

Sara opened another button of her shirt and adjusted her hair around her collar before folding her manicured hands together on the tabletop. 'And by the way, who exactly was it that told you that?'

'Who told me what?'

'That you weren't *that* type? That you had to be a bit mousey, hide your fabulousness!'

Her voice was loud and Romilly wished she were a little quieter.

'I'm not sure. I don't think I do—'

'You do!' Sara interrupted her. 'You hide away behind your specs. God, you have this inner sparkle, this glow about you...' She waved her hand in an arc and Romilly could almost see the fairy dust falling down in a glittery shimmer. 'But when David walks into the room, or when you were leaving work just now, it's like you're stooped, apologising for something, God knows what. And it's sad to see, because you are amazing!'

'I don't always feel amazing. I often feel a bit...' She hesitated, not sure how much she should share, if at all.

'A bit what?' This, Sara whispered.

Romilly looked up at her new friend, who she had to admit was very easy to talk to. 'A bit invisible. And a bit nervous that everything I have might be taken away from me.'

'Why do you feel like that?' Sara tilted her head, earnestly.

'I don't know. But I always have, like nothing is permanent and so I have to tread carefully, to make it last, eek it out before it all disappears. A bit like a mayfly.'

'A what? Is this your three-headed chicken-feed stuff again?' Sara gripped her boobs in mock horror and was back to screeching.

Romilly shook her head in faux disapproval just as the waitress reappeared carrying a round tray bearing two tall cocktail glasses. The drinks were a vivid shade of orange that faded to amber at the base and each had a wedge of pineapple stuck on the side and a neon-pink straw with a parasol poking out of the top.

'Good grief!' Romilly giggled, glad of the change of atmosphere. 'What on earth…?'

The waitress bobbed and placed one in front of each of them. 'Ladies, I give you our finest, strongest Mai Tai. Double shots for good measure!' She winked and squeezed Sara's shoulder as she passed.

Sara raised her glass. 'Here's to our new friendship, many moments of laughter and releasing your inner siren! Cheers!'

Romilly picked up the cool glass and clinked it against her friend's. 'Cheers!' she echoed, drawing on the straw and letting the cold, ice-filled booze slip down her throat. Before she'd even swallowed that first sip, she was already looking over Sara's head to see about ordering a couple more.

Two hours later and the party for two was in full swing.

'This is your one! This is your one!' Sara banged the table and laughed.

'Issit?' Romilly had lost track.

'Yesyes yes! You have to mime it, come on!' she shouted.

The intro finished and the lilting tones of Coldplay's 'Every Teardrop is a Waterfall' filtered through the sound system. Romilly stood. In her mind, she was centre stage, confident that the group of suited blokes on the next table were nodding in time to the music as she held the floor. She sang along with gusto, swinging her red hair and winking at the handsome bartender. Sara gazed at her, wide-eyed and clearly proud of her performance. Romilly could feel the spotlight on her as she let the adoration pour over in waves. She felt like a star, someone who knew more about pop culture than germ culture, someone who was more comfortable in a fur coat and sunglasses than a white coat and lab goggles. And it felt good!

The reality was a little different. The men on the next table snickered behind their hands and winced as they listened to her drunken warble. One leant over to his mate and whispered, 'Some poor sod's at home waiting for that!' His mate shook his head in commiseration as they both shielded their eyes.

Romilly didn't know the words but compensated by making a low-level humming noise, with her mouth open, and repeating the odd word that became clear after it had been sung. 'Fall… waterfall… everyone… dance!' she shouted, loudly and off-key. Her eyes were half closed, her head tilted back so she could see her audience. Her hair hung forward, partially obscuring her face. Her feet were firmly planted on the spot while she twisted and swayed the top half of her body, half in time to the music. Her blouse gaped open to reveal her flesh-coloured bra. She stopped singing at one point to strum an invisible guitar. This sent many of the diners and drinkers into hysterics, laughing hard at her. Laughing at the woman who prided herself on being a professional, on her cleverness. Sara's contribution was to take out her phone and snap her buddy, mid performance, while occasionally singing along, her fingers tapping the sticky tabletop in a space between the mass of empty cocktail glasses and beer bottles.

Romilly had no memory of leaving the bar or climbing into the taxi that took them across the Downs and out towards Stoke Bishop. She let her head loll on Sara's shoulder as they rolled closer to home. She swayed on the doorstep and waved to her friend, who was carrying her heels in her hand as she tiptoed into her empty house. Romilly watched her disappear and remembered for the first time that David would be waiting for her and that he wouldn't be best pleased.

Leaning on the front door, she pulled back her shoulders and smiled, removed her phone and widened her eyes, trying to see the exact number of missed calls and unread texts. She couldn't make out the digits, but knew it was a lot.

'Shiiiiiiit!' She giggled.

Pressing the little phone icon, she slid down the door until her bottom rested on the front step.

'Where are you?' This was how he answered the phone. He sounded angry, his breath coming in short bursts.

She couldn't help the laughter that escaped her mouth, because despite his tone and the fact that she knew she was in trouble, he was asking where she was and she was in fact on the other side of the door, and that was funny! She lifted her loosely bunched fist and tapped on the door.

David, with the phone still in his hand, opened the door rather quickly, causing her to fall backwards. She lay with her back on the doormat, staring at her upside-down husband.

'AreyouinAustralia?' she garbled.

'For God's sake, get up!' he growled, looking out into the cul-de-sac before reaching down to pull her by the shoulders all the way into the hall.

'I've been worried sick! Your text said you were working late, I called the office, they said you'd left at the normal time. I've been imagining all sorts. I've phoned everyone I could think off. I even put Celeste in the back of the car in her pyjamas, trying to make it an adventure, and we drove around looking for you.' He pushed his fingers through his hair. 'I've had the worst night you can imagine and look at you! Look at the bloody state of you! Who were you with?' He clenched his jaw.

'My friend!' she slurred.

'Which friend? Who?'

'Swara.' She giggled from the floor.

David nodded as if this only confirmed his suspicions. 'Stand up. Get yourself upstairs, clean up and go to bed. I swear to God, I can't stand to look at you!'

Romilly clung to the wall as she manoeuvred herself into a standing position. 'S'proper love, David. It is. Properlove.' She reached a hand out to him.

He opened his mouth as if to speak, but then her knees buckled and she leant on the wall for support. Without warning, her head span and the sickly sweet contents of her stomach rose up in her throat.

Celeste

I remember waking up in what seemed like the middle of the night. It was dark outside and I heard a strange sound, as if someone was throwing buckets of water at the window or cracking the vacuum-cleaner flex on the tiled hall floor, the way Dad did sometimes to make me laugh. He used to make a kind of lasso and snap it down against the floor, shouting 'Yeeeeehaaaa!' in an exaggerated American accent. I was going through my *Toy Story* phase and was quite in love with Jessie the cowgirl and it used to make me laugh, partly because this wasn't like my dad at all! He was normally serious and busy, preoccupied with his computer screen or his newspaper, so the few occasions when he went all silly were precious. Very special indeed.

I was curious and a little bit afraid, as if I could sense that all was not quite right. I pulled back the sheets and crept from my bed, across the landing and quietly down the top few stairs until I had a view of the hallway below. I sat on the top step, nestled against the bannister, hidden, watching.

Mum was bent over with one hand on the wall, her hair hanging forward over her face; I thought that was odd as it was usually tied up. Her silky blouse gaped open and I could see the lace of her bra. She groaned and mumbled something, and then a blast of watery vomit shot out of her mouth and landed on the tiled floor with a really loud splat. The smell was absolutely disgusting. It made *my* mouth fill with water, as though *I* was going to be sick. I cupped my hand and put it over my nose and mouth. Then I noticed that the floor was wet, covered in watery puke and little pieces of carrot and shredded chicken. My mum had no shoes on and her bare feet were covered in sick. Her toenails were painted red and they glowed like embers through the vomit. It was horrible.

She stood upright as Dad came from the kitchen. He was angry, I could tell by his straightened back. His arms were locked around a bowl full of soapy bubbles and there was a sponge floating on top.

'I'm sorry...' Mum slurred. Everything about her looked blurry, like she was smudged. Her red lipstick was messy, her eyes were pink and there was black mascara running down her face. She was like a sad, scary clown.

'Stand still!' Dad was whispering, but it was like he was shouting. It made me nervous and my tummy shrank.

Mum was crying again, saying 'I'm sorry' a lot. Then she stepped forward and slipped in the goop, only just managing to stay upright by grabbing onto Dad's shirt. The water in the bowl sloshed over them both and a large puff of foamy suds landed on the side of her hair.

This time Dad shouted. 'For fuck's sake, stand still!' And then it was as if he remembered why he mustn't shout because he jerked his head towards the top of the stairs. Our eyes locked. And he had this expression I'd never seen before. I've never forgotten it. He looked sad, but it was more than that. He looked ashamed. Really ashamed.

Six

Romilly placed the dishwasher tablet in the little trap and shut the door. The machine gave off its satisfying beep, meaning that the dishes were being taken care of.

'Celeste, come on, your porridge is ready!' she called up the stairs.

Her little girl skipped down the stairs in her school uniform and took her place at the kitchen table. 'Can I have honey on it?'

'Of course! A super swirl for my super girl!' She winked as she flipped the lid and let the golden goo twist in a perfect loop, lying like a thick river on top of the creamy oats.

Celeste smiled. The neater her honey, the more she liked it, having inherited her mother's desire for things to be exact, ordered.

'Morning, morning!' David sang as he flicked the kettle.

'You sit down, I'll get toast.' She hummed.

'Goodness me! It's not my birthday, is it?' He smiled, taking a chair opposite his daughter, giving her a quick wink before opening *The Telegraph* to catch up on the headlines.

'No, thank goodness, because if you're a year older, it means that I'm not far behind! And ageing is not something

I want to rush. But I'm not working today, so I've got time to spoil you both.'

Romilly pushed her glasses up onto the bridge of her nose, feeling a twinge of guilt that she had phoned in sick that morning. She noted the twist in her gut as her thoughts turned to the last few weeks. The pressure had been building for a while now and she was certain that her job was in jeopardy. It felt easier not to go in, to blot out the fear, just for one glorious day.

She smiled at David. 'You will start with breakfast and fresh coffee, and I should think the day will end with a nice homemade supper, maybe even a pie.'

'Wow! You won't hear any complaints from me.' He beamed.

'I like your cooking, Mummy,' Celeste said.

'Oh, Rom, did you hear that? She likes your cooking!' David pulled a wide-mouthed face to make them both laugh.

'And why not? I'm a good cook when I try!' She laughed as she poured the hot, dark brew from the cafetière and placed it in front of her husband.

'Do you know, Celeste, when I met Mummy, she could just about manage beans on toast. We lived off biscuits and crisps that she kept in a cupboard in her room. We were like a couple of little mice, nibbling away. It was horrible!' He added milk from the jug to his coffee.

'It wasn't horrible, it was wonderful! I liked being a little mouse. I was totally preoccupied with studying. Cooking for you, me or anyone didn't enter my head. In fact I sometimes think if I didn't have to shop and cook for you two, I'd still live off biscuits and crisps and the odd bit

of toast. I'd go back to being like a little nibbling mouse.'
She smiled.

'Heaven forbid!' David grinned at his wife, holding her
gaze.

The last few days had been lovely. Back-to-normal lovely,
with both of them making an effort to erase the horrible
memory of that night when she had let them both down,
being so sloshed she had lost her dignity and so drunk she
had forgotten him. Neither wanted to go through that again.
It had shocked them both for very different reasons.

He had banned all wine and spirits from the house and
she had willingly agreed, wanting to do anything that would
put them back on track. What wasn't so easy to control was
the desire for booze that had been ignited inside her. It was
on a different level now. She found herself thinking about it
more, wanting it more and taking the opportunity during her
working hours to indulge, which meant she could keep it
from her husband.

Romilly placed a glass of orange juice in front of her
daughter. 'I think we'll walk to school. What do you think,
Celeste?'

'Yep, good!' She nodded.

Romilly locked the front door behind them and clutched her
daughter's hand as they made their way down the drive. Sara
drove past in the Merc with the top down. 'Well, hey! It's my
partner in crime!' It was the first time they'd bumped into
each other since their night out.

Romilly nodded, embarrassed at the memory and mortified to be reminded of it in front of Celeste. She looked at

Mrs Rashid opposite, who was sorting her recycling in her dressing gown, and felt a shiver of revulsion that they had brought their unsavoury behaviour to this quiet cul-de-sac in Stoke Bishop. A place where families lived, where people trimmed back their hedges and mowed their lawns, stopping only for a cup of tea and a natter, and where Mrs Rashid felt comfortable to be pottering outside in her PJs.

'Where are you two girls off to? Need a lift?' Sara ran her tongue over her front teeth, checking for lipstick.

'Can we, Mum? Sara's car's got no roof on it!' Celeste jumped up and down.

Romilly pulled her daughter close alongside her. 'No. Thanks, Sara, but it's rare that I have time for the walk and we can have a proper chat. Plus the fresh air will do us the world of good.'

'Oh, a proper chat, my favourite thing. Well, enjoy your walk and have a great day, Celeste. Rom, if you can get a late pass, you know where I am!' And without waiting for a reply, she pulled her large-framed sunglasses from her hair and placed them on her face before roaring off up the street and onto the main road.

'What's a late pass?' Celeste asked as she skipped along-side her mum on the pavement.

'What would you like for tea? If you could have anything, anything at all?' Romilly was keen to change the subject.

It seemed to do the trick. Celeste immediately placed her finger over her lips, as she did when she was thinking, and hummed. 'I like pizza or I like roast chicken and red jelly.'

'Roast chicken and red jelly, eeuuw, on the same plate?'

'No, Mummy!' She laughed. 'Or one of your pies.'

Romilly arrived home with the heavy carrier bags of supper supplies making her fingers cramp. Walking into the kitchen, she dumped them on the floor and noticed that the little red light of the answer phone was winking. With a trembling finger, she pressed play and stood back.

'Romilly, hi, it's Mike Gregson here. I think we need to talk, so do call me back. You have my direct line and my mobile number, or if it's easier, call Marta and let her know when's a good time and I shall endeavour to call you back when it's convenient. Thanks, Romilly. Talk to you soon, I hope.'

She rushed forward and deleted the message, pressing the button again and again and only feeling content when she heard twice over that there were 'no new messages'. She didn't want David asking any questions.

Her heart thudded and she felt the beginnings of a headache. Her hand shook as she unloaded the ready-to-roll pastry, chicken fillets, leeks and tub of cream onto the work surface. She put the shopping away and emptied the dishwasher. Glancing at the digital clock display on the cooker, she noted that it was 10.15.

Romilly ran the vacuum cleaner over the bedroom floors and folded the linen from the tumble dryer. She was considering what should be her next chore, undecided between watering the tubs in the garden or cleaning the bathroom, when the phone rang. Without too much thought, she sat on their bed and answered it.

'Romilly, hello, it's Mike Gregson here.'

'*Shit!*' she mouthed. Dr Gregson was her boss. She felt her stomach drop, making her feel sick. She hadn't expected him to call again so soon.

'Hi, Mike, how are you?' She concentrated on keeping the quiver from her voice, tried to sound normal.

'I'm good. Very good, thanks for asking, but the reason for my call is that I am more concerned with how you are.' He was a kind man and his tone was one of genuine concern. She pictured his eyes crinkling at the sides as he spoke.

'I'm great, apart from this bug that I emailed Marta about. Still not over it, I'm afraid, and I didn't want to give it to anyone else.' The lie caused her cheeks to flame. She removed her spectacles and wiped the sweat that had gathered at the corner of her eyes.

'Yes, I was sorry to hear that.'

There was a pause while both considered where to go next, each wondering whose line it was. Both knew that she lying, which made it all the worse. It was Mike that finally drew breath.

'The thing is, Romilly, I'm a little worried about you.'

'Oh, there's no need, really. I'm sure I shall be right as rain in a few days or so.' She swallowed, trying to strike the right note between jovial and poorly, willing him to end the call with a cheery goodbye.

There was another awkward pause.

'I am fond of you, Romilly. We all are. You are an absolute asset to the team.'

'Thank you.' Her voice cracked.

She thought about the day last week, early afternoon, when Tim had cornered her in the lab. 'This is really awkward, Rom, and you know we're mates, right?' She'd nodded. Yes. Yes, she knew that. 'But have you been drinking? I'm embarrassed to have to ask you...' Her denial had been swift and emphatic; she had switched to aggression, the first form of defence. 'I'm sorry, Rom,' he'd said with a look of utter mortification, 'this isn't easy for me, it's just that...' *What?* She'd snapped, daring him to disclose more. 'You've made a few mistakes recently and that's okay, we all get tired and stuff happens – do you remember how I mucked up that batch of samples shortly after Phoebe was born and I was just too tired and you helped me? That's what it means to be part of a team, isn't it. We all cover for each other. But...' *What?* Again she'd barked at him, her eyes narrowed. 'Warwick has asked if he can switch to a new mentor and I think that's probably a good idea. He's noticed, in fact I've noticed too, that you smell of booze sometimes and you don't really seem that with it.' She pictured Warwick's open face, keen to learn, and she closed her eyes, humiliated. She hadn't been sure Tim would raise his concerns with the powers that be, but clearly he had. *Thanks a bunch, Tim, you bastard.*

Mike drew her back to the present. 'You truly are an absolute asset, but I need you to be safe, Rom.' He spoke slowly. 'I need to know that things are okay with you, especially as you're working in a hazardous environment. You understand that, don't you?'

She closed her eyes and spoke to the darkness; it was somehow easier than with their wedding photo staring back at her. Images from that incredible day flashed into her head – the beautiful brooch he'd given her, the girl she had been, the feeling of absolute wonder that David Arthur Wells wanted to marry *her*. 'I do.'

'Good. That's good. I am here as and when you want to

talk to me. You have some close friends here, you know, friends who care very deeply about you.'

She knew this was his way of saying don't be mad at Tim.

'But first and foremost I have to think about safety, everyone's safety, not just yours. Do you understand where I'm coming from?' His voice was firm but warm.

'I do.' She nodded. From now on she would need to be a lot more careful.

She made her way down to the hall and headed straight for the cupboard under the stairs. Opening it, she stared at the shoe rack, crammed with trainers in various stages of decay, boots, rollerblades, sandals and flip-flops. It was their little family, represented in so many bits of footwear. Stepping forward, she took her right wellington boot from its slot and tipped it upside down. The bottle of Chardonnay slid from its dark hiding place.

After carefully replacing the boot, she nipped into the kitchen and took a knife to the seal, carefully unwrapping the strip of plastic and twisting off the cap. There was no point in pretending: she didn't reach for a glass or even a mug but simply put the bottle to her mouth and tipped her head back as she lifted it. The familiar thrill of placing the hard glass against her lip hadn't dulled. The wine slipped down her throat, giving her an immediate, sharp jolt of euphoria and relief that tingled along her spine and fired out along her limbs. She smiled and closed her eyes, feeling instantly better. It was like the very best medicine.

Pausing, she thought about Tim's interrogation and Mike's slightly condescending tone. What was it to do with them how she lived, what she drank? It was up to her. Taking up the Chardonnay again, she polished off the plonk as she stood in the middle of the kitchen. Then she inhaled deeply, letting the feeling of bliss wash over her, before rinsing out the bottle and replacing the cap.

Pulling on David's gardening shoes that were at least three sizes too big, she carefully carried the bottle out into the street. The Rashids' car wasn't in their driveway; they'd probably gone to the supermarket or over to their son's to babysit. After a quick glance up and down the road, Romilly hurried across the block-paved driveway of the house opposite, lifted two empty jars of pasta sauce, a bottle of olive oil and an old jam pot, before stowing the empty wine bottle at the bottom of the box and replacing the items so no one would notice. Back inside the house, she ditched David's shoes, cleaned her teeth, gargled with mouthwash and turned up the radio as she danced round the kitchen to Absolute 80s, feeling a huge sense of relief that all was now right with the world.

David walked through the door at half past six.

'Wow! Something smells good.' He smiled at the sight of his wife busying in the kitchen and Celeste setting the table for supper. 'I rather like you not working, if this is what I get to come home to every night!' He winked at his beautiful, academic wife, knowing that a week of staying home and playing the domestic goddess would have her climbing the walls. He grabbed her around the waist and kissed her cheek and then her mouth.

'Yuck!' Celeste yelled from the table.

'You wait till you get a boyfriend and then marry him, you won't think kissing is yuck then.' Romilly laughed.

'Mum's right,' David said as he slipped off his jacket and removed his tie.

'I'm never going to have a boyfriend and I'm never going to get married!' she shouted.

'You don't know that!' Romilly snickered as she cut the pie and drained the tender-stem broccoli.

'I do, because boys are horrible, they won't let you play football even though you are better than Billy and Hamal and they call you Celery even though your name is Celeste, which is nothing like celery, which I don't even like.'

Romilly and David stared at each other, torn between wanting to laugh and wanting to reassure their little girl that boys could be a bit daft at times and that when she found her voice and her confidence, she wouldn't mind being called Celery so much. They settled on a conciliatory, 'Oh, darling!' and a hug.

David and Celeste picked up their cutlery and exchanged comments on how lovely their supper looked, while Romilly popped into the garage and returned with two chilled bottles of Spanish lager. David watched as she popped the lids and set one by his plate and another by her own.

'Beer on a school night?' He laughed, wary of spoiling the atmosphere. 'Not sure if I want one actually.' He concentrated on forking a tender chicken chunk into his mouth.

'Don't be boring, David, it's only one beer! I thought it would go nicely with the pie. If you don't want it, leave it.' She sighed. The truth was that if he didn't have one, she felt that she couldn't either and this made her anger flare.

David picked up the cool, slippery bottle and held it up towards his wife. 'You're right, it's only one. My training can wait. After all, I'm eating pastry and cream, how much harm is a beer going to do?' He clinked the neck of the bottle against hers and they both sipped.

Dinner was a success. David and Celeste had cleared the table and stacked the dishwasher while Romilly soaked in the bath. With their daughter now sound asleep, the two turned off the main light and switched on one bedside lamp before slipping beneath the duvet. David opened his arms as Romilly removed her glasses, placed them on the bedside table and wriggled up to him before laying her head on his chest. He held her tight, running his fingers through her beautiful Titian locks. 'Your hair will always fascinate me. It was the first thing I noticed about you.'

'Was it?' She smiled against him.

He nodded. 'I saw you walking out of the Student Union one day and your hair was so bright, it was like everyone around you was two-dimensional, flat, beige, but you were solid, 3D, standing proud and in focus with this shining head of hair that caught my eye. I only saw the back of you and I told Rob that you were probably ugly, as any girl that was that fit from the back had to have something bad going on at the front.'

'How mean are you!'

'Not really. It was a case of self-preservation. I wouldn't have been able to sleep if I'd known what was waiting for me at the front.' He sighed. 'I kept looking for you and then one day, in the library, there you were, my Bug Girl, with your nose in a textbook. And I just stood by the door, staring at you. Your face... those enormous eyes hiding behind your glasses. I had never seen anyone that was such a combination of sexy and vulnerable. I didn't know whether to wrap you in cotton wool or shag you!'

'David!' She batted his chest, laughing.

'It's true! I fell for you hook, line and sinker. And that was that. I knew you were the one.'

'Proper love,' she whispered.

'Yes, proper love.' He kissed her scalp, then slid down the bed until they were nose to nose and kissed her again, hungrily, on the mouth. The two held each other fast as they celebrated their deep love in the way they had been doing since university, the main difference being that now they weren't squashed into a single bed whose fitted sheet kept escaping from one corner, and they kept the noise down not so he wouldn't be found out, illicitly staying over in the girls' hall, but so as not to wake their little girl.

Skin to skin they lay, arms and legs entwined. 'That was lovely.' She kissed the base of his throat, enjoying the flames of satisfaction and contentment that flickered inside her.

'It was,' he breathed. It felt good to lie there, still in each other's arms, without an alarm or a chore, just enjoying the now. 'I knew from the first time I stayed in your room that I would do anything you ever asked me.' He smiled.

'Well, if I'd known that, I'd have made you get up and get me tea!' she quipped.

'I would gladly have made you tea, even though I don't think you owned any mugs other than the one with your toothbrush in.'

'That's probably right.' She chuckled, picturing the chipped mug on the side of the sink with dried toothpaste and a paperclip in the bottom. It was always lovely to share the details of those days, a reminder that they were bound by their history. It made her feel secure.

She sensed his sudden hesitation and waited for him to speak.

'And I still would, you know, Rom. I'd do anything you asked me, including make you tea, anything, if I thought it would make you happy. I'd move, have another baby, change my job, anything, anything to make us work, and to ensure that we keep working in the future.'

Romilly shrugged her arms free and scooted across the mattress to her pillows. 'I get the feeling you're saying that because you want to ask *me* to do something,' she whispered. 'You know, like, "Ooh, Celeste, Daddy really wants to try some eye drops, but he can't because they're yours! Do *you* want to try them now?"' She smiled at the memory.

David propped his head on his crooked arm and gazed at his wife. He looked close to tears. 'I love you.'

His expression removed any trace of her smile. 'I love you too. But that sounds very much like question avoidance.' *Don't leave me. Please, don't leave me, David.*

'You're right, I do want to ask you something.' He licked his dry lips.

Romilly reached for her glasses and popped them on as though what might come next required her full focus.

'I... I want you to stop drinking. I want you to give up booze completely for a month. That's all. Just a month.' He patted the mattress.

'Why a month?'

'To see how you feel, to make you think about how much you do actually drink and...'

'And what?'

'I guess to see if you can.' He snatched at a loose thread on their bed sheet.

Romilly pulled her knees up and placed her head on them. Her tears were swift to find release; her breath came in shallow pants. 'David… David…' It sounded like she was begging.

'Come on. Come on now, don't cry!' He coaxed her from the bed. 'Let's go get that cup of tea.' He kissed her face and they shoved their arms into dressing gowns and stumbled downstairs.

They ended up on the sofa. The only light came from the moon that flooded through the sitting room window. Romilly sat crying, facing David side on, her feet under his dressing gown, resting against his thigh. Half an hour passed in which she sniffed and he sat in silence, waiting for her to speak. Eventually she dried her tears, blew her nose and began.

'Can I have that cup of tea?' she whimpered.

'Course. You stay here.' He sprang from the sofa, placed the grey faux-fur throw over her toes and left her alone for five minutes.

She cast her eyes over their sitting room. Interior design had never been her thing, but what they had achieved was comfortable, if a little predictable. She had selected items from catalogues and room sets and simply copied the way the sofas, mirrors and lamps had been arranged. It was only when she went inside houses like Sara's, where there was a vivid splash of colour, a feature piece of art or a clever idea to use space, that she realised just how safe their decor was.

David sat back down, handing her a large mug with a

bumblebee on it, her favourite, which she held gratefully between her palms.

'Shall I put a lamp on?' he asked, his voice soft.

'No.' Romilly knew that it would be easier to be honest without being able to fully see his expression.

'Are you warm enough?'

'Yes, thanks.' She stroked the throw. His desire to make her as comfortable as possible still surprised and reassured her. They sipped their tea until Romilly found her voice in the half-light.

'I remember when the twins were born. I was only little, but I felt this huge shift in my world, and I couldn't explain why, I didn't really have the words. But I felt... I felt spare, like my parents had finally got the babies they desired and I was just... spare. I know that if the twins had come first, they would never have had me. I heard my mum say that to Aunty Di once.'

'Oh, people say all sorts, especially when they're run ragged and their kids are babies. And you know what your mum's like, she lets her mouth run away while her brain is still catching up. Your parents love you, they always have. They're so proud of you!' He squinted at her, trying to find the relevance.

'I know they are, but I also know how I felt. Maybe I'm not describing it properly, but I didn't feel like anyone really, truly wanted me, not until I found you. And you wanted me and yet you were perfect. You are perfect, and I felt like, at any moment, you'd see that I was just very average and dump me for someone less ordinary.'

'I love you, I always have and you are completely extraordinary.'

She flexed her toes against his skin.

'Do you still feel like that, Rom, that I might dump you?' he asked softly.

'A bit,' she whispered. 'Yes. Sometimes.'

David shook his head. It was a wee while until he spoke. 'I try every day to make you feel valued. I always have.'

'I know, I know, and you do.' She briefly laid her hand on his arm. 'I just can't help it.'

'It makes me feel like shit that I can't show you how I feel, that you don't have faith in us.'

'I do. I do have faith in us… It's just…'

'Just what?'

'It's not you, it's me—'

'Did you really just say that?' David felt the beginnings of a smile on his lips. He reached over and pulled her towards him. 'Oh, my beautiful Rom. My Bug Girl.'

She laid her head on his shoulder.

'You are a complex puzzle to me, Rom, you always have been and it's one of the reasons I love you so much. I love that I have always had to try and figure you out.'

She wasn't sure she wanted to be a complex puzzle but nuzzled against him anyway.

'But I'm a bit worried about you, a bit worried about us,' he continued as her heart skipped a beat. 'You've always come alive, become more confident after a glass of plonk and we've had some crazy, crazy nights, haven't we?' He laughed and kissed her scalp.

Romilly thought back to the evening at Zazu's Kitchen on the Gloucester Road that had felt like a party. Dinner and drinks had ended with tables being pushed against the wall and the whole room chatting and singing like they were all friends, spurred on by the liberal measures of wine and her uninhibited desire for everyone to raise their glasses in communal toasts. And then there'd been that time at the Harbour Festival when she'd become separated from the group and they'd found her trying to skateboard in front of the Lloyds Amphitheatre with a bemused gang of teenagers, who clearly hadn't known what to make of the drunk woman in the floral frock with skinned knees.

'But it seems to have become more than just a way to loosen up on a night out, hasn't it? Is that a fair comment?'

She nodded.

'And the thing is, Rom, I know it's a problem or at least becoming a problem, because I don't mention it, I feel I can't mention it. I'm scared to. You know, like when someone's fat and you can't use the word fat in front of them, which means you know they've become fat.'

'Like Jay...' She smiled.

They laughed, thinking of their friend who had swapped his evening run for pizza eating and PlayStationing and had ballooned.

'Yep, like Jay. I can no longer make fatty jokes at his expense because it's too near the mark, too real.'

She looked at her husband, all too conscious that he didn't really want to talk about Jay or his weight. 'So what word can't you say in front of me?' She bit her lip.

He shrugged, which told her all she needed to know.

She pulled free from his hold and sat on the sofa with her legs crossed on the cushion, watching him. 'I drink more than I tell you.'

He nodded, his eyes downcast, as if this wasn't news.

'I... I drink when I find a situation stressful, or if I feel nervous or anxious.'

'Do you often feel nervous or anxious?'

'Yes.' She nodded.

'Do you feel like a drink now?' he asked, holding her gaze.

'Yes.'

He massaged her left foot with his thumb. 'Has it got stronger over time, your desire to have one?'

'Yes.' She nodded again.

'I mean, at uni you always came out of your shell when you drank, and it was a laugh. You seemed to bloom when you were a bit pissed. And I suppose if I'm being completely honest—'

'I need you to be,' she interrupted.

'If I'm being completely honest,' he continued, 'I've enjoyed seeing you like that. Fun and more confident, adventurous in every sense.' He smiled at her and squeezed her toes. 'But since we've had Celeste... I don't know, something's changed and I find myself wishing you wouldn't drink. It's not funny any more.'

His words were like tiny swords that further hacked at her self-esteem. She felt small and useless. *I don't want you to think less of me. I want to be a good mum to Celeste.*

'Do you...' he swallowed, 'do you drink every day?' he whispered.

'Yes.' Her response was barely audible.

'How much have you drunk today?' He hardly dared ask. She heard the waver in his voice.

There was a pause. She considered how much to tell him, wanting to exorcise the secrets that hovered in her mouth but feeling a deep shame at her weakness, her greed.

'I've had a bottle of wine and three bottles of beer,' she managed through a fresh bout of tears. She could tell by the way he shrank back against the cushions that he was shocked.

'You've drunk that today? While you were here on your own?'

She guessed he wanted Sara to be implicated so he could blame her, offload some of the responsibility onto her.

She nodded.

'I see.' It was all he could think of. 'Do you *want* to stop drinking every day?'

'I do, I do, but I love it. I really like drinking and it makes everything feel better.'

'But that's the trick, isn't it. It only feels like it's making things better, whereas actually it's making things worse, creating a whole other set of problems. I know you know this, Rom. You're smart.'

'That's me, smart.' She gave a wry smile.

'Let's do what I suggested, let's try for a month and see how we go. Do you think we should get some help? Go to the doctor or find a therapist? I don't really know how this works or what's best.' He looked at her with a lost expression that she could hardly bear to see.

'No. No.' She was emphatic. 'I don't want to get anyone else involved. I really don't. I can do this. I know I can. I just need to be strong and stay in and not be in charge of the shopping and little things like that.'

'Okay, if you think that's best. Why don't we get Holly to

come and stay? She's back from Ibiza for six weeks and I bet she'd love to spend time with you and Celeste.'

'You mean so she can babysit me, keep the gin under lock and key and report on progress?' Romilly gave a weak smile.

'Yes. That's exactly it. I'm worried that if you're here alone or I'm not back from work or if anyone should come over who's a bad influence on you...' They exchanged a look. 'You wouldn't be able to resist.'

'Okay.' She nodded.

'We can do this if we're completely honest with each other. It's all about communication. You need to tell me how you're feeling, and if there's anything I can do at any point to take the edge off or help you, then I will. We're a team, me and you, okay? A team. A team without secrets.'

David sat forward and cradled her to him as she cried.

'A team without secrets,' she repeated, closing her eyes and feeling swamped with guilt at what she wasn't telling him. Firstly, that she had actually drunk two bottles of wine and three bottles of beer that day. And secondly, that from simply talking about it, she was now desperate, desperate for a drink and could think about little else other than the bottle of wine that was nestled inside a wellington boot in the cupboard under the stairs. It was as if it was calling to her.

Celeste

Around the same time as the vomiting incident, when I was about six, she came off the booze for a few weeks. I can't remember how long for exactly, but I do remember that for a while she was like the perfect mum. Really attentive and great. Aunty Holly was staying with us and she was brilliant. She was so funny – still is. I love her. It was a happy time.

One day she picked me up from school and she was excited. She got like that sometimes, a bit childlike, I suppose, like she had a secret or a surprise, and on this occasion she did! I jumped in the car where Holly was waiting and instead of going home for our tea, we went up to the zoo in Clifton. She'd packed a picnic and the first thing we did when we arrived was set out our blanket and eat our sandwiches and crisps and we were all so happy that we laughed at everything. Everything! A fat lady who walked past, the way my orange squash splurged out of the bottle when I squeezed it, every animal shriek and noise. We just sat on that blanket doubled over, laughing, giggling and rolling around. We were having the best time ever and that was before we'd even seen an animal.

I remember seeing a girl about my age, she was walking along the path and her mum was marching ahead of her, and I could tell she was angry and the girl looked really sad and I remember thinking what a waste it was to be sad and angry at the zoo. It's funny, I can't remember too much about the creatures we saw or what happened, but I can vividly recall that picnic on the grass and the deep, deep love I felt for my mum. It was late afternoon and still sunny. Her hair was loose, sitting about her shoulders, and when the light caught it, it looked like fire. It was really quite beautiful.

Then a week or so later she took me into town and I was allowed to get my ears pierced. I couldn't believe it! I'd been nagging her for a while as a few of the girls in my class had earrings. I never thought she'd agree, not in a million years, but just like that, with Aunty Holly in tow, I found myself sitting on this high stall while a woman who smelled of cigarettes held the little gun thing at my lobe. I was petrified and at that point would gladly have backed out had I been given the choice!

I remember sitting in the middle of this jewellery shop and she was holding up huge garish chandelier type earrings saying, 'ooh these are nice Celeste!' and I sat there giggling, with a mixture of joy at the situation and absolute fear that she might actually make me wear them!

We went to Claire's Accessories after and Holly bought me this huge diamante tiara and mum got me a pair of little silver studs that I still have. I wore my tiara to McDonald's and all the way home. When I walked through the door, Dad was on the phone. He did a double-take and frowned like he was really cross, but then he looked at Mum who was smiling and looked so calm and pretty, and I saw his face relax into a kind of half smile that was happy, but bemused, like he wasn't quite in on the joke. I looked in the mirror in the hall, twisting my head so the light caught the diamonds on my tiara and made it sparkle. I twiddled my newly placed earrings and couldn't wait to get on with the business of growing up. I guess that's because I didn't know what the next few years would bring.

It was a lovely time, though. The house felt different. Dad was much more relaxed, laughing and making jokes like he used to. I guess it was because he didn't have to worry about what was waiting for him when he came home from work. What sort of mood Mum would be in. It was the same for me, coming home from school. For those few weeks while Aunty Holly was there, we were like a proper family. Mum would read me a story every night and I didn't have to get my dirty socks out of the washing machine for school or pretend I didn't mind not having any snacks for my lunchbox like my friends did. And I didn't have a tense tummy any more and I didn't once crawl under my bed. Until this time, I'd thought it was normal to always have a bunching feeling inside; it was only when the tension disappeared that I even realised it wasn't normal.

Mum understood all that, I think. One night, when we'd driven home from school, we stopped on the driveway and instead of jumping out of the car like we usually did, she sat staring at the windscreen. I sat still, not sure what was happening, and then I realised she was crying. She told she me was sorry and I asked her what for, like I didn't know what she was apologising for, but I did. It was for all the crappy days when she couldn't be bothered or was out with Sara or she had drunk at home and I'd seen her pissed. I think that was what she cried for, as if when she was off the booze, she could see things clearly – the bad as well as the good. I wanted to comfort her, but I didn't really know how, so I started to sing 'You Are My Sunshine', as that was what she sang to me sometimes and I knew it always made me feel a lot better.

Seven

'What am I going to talk to her about?' Holly whispered across the bathroom as she sat on the loo, holding a small mirror up to her face while she applied her make-up, gurning in different angles, trying to reach her lashes and all of her eyelid.

Romilly continued cleaning her teeth. Growing up in a small house with one bathroom, this had always been normal to them.

She spat the minty foam into the sink and patted her mouth with a towel. 'What do you mean? Same things you talk to anyone about! She's American, her English is perfect. And besides, you've met her lots of times.'

'I know I have, that's the problem. I find her a bit... I don't know... preachy, a bit annoying and a bit like I want to hit her around the head with a wet kipper.' Holly grinned at her sister.

'Shhhh!' Romilly held her finger up over her mouth and her face flushed scarlet. She tried to contain her giggles but at the same time was embarrassed at the thought that Holly's voice might have carried. 'Please don't hit her around the head with a wet kipper and don't let David hear you say that, she is his mum after all.'

'Come on, Rom, you can't tell me you actually *like* her!' Holly said loudly.

'I don't not like her.' Romilly made a neutral face, tactful as ever. 'And she has always been very generous to us, helped us with the deposit for the house, bought things for Celeste, you know… She tries in her own way, and I want her to feel welcome, always. It can't have been easy for her bringing up David on her own. I can't imagine what it must have been like, but her husband sounds like a right sort. Left her for his secretary, just dumped her and David when something shinier came along.'

'Maybe that's why he's so solid, dependable?'

'Mmm, could be. He never really talks about his dad.' Romilly checked her teeth in the mirror.

'What was his name?'

'Why?' Romilly was wary of giving Holly too much information.

'Just curious.'

'Cole. Not that she ever mentions him.' She fixed her sister with a stare.

'I can't imagine Sylvia married, and I certainly can't imagine her having sex.'

'Good God, Holly! Why would you want to?'

'I don't!' She giggled. 'She's just not that type is she? I bet she thinks you and David don't do it either. She just seems unaware, detached.'

Romilly laughed. 'Oh, don't worry, Holly, she knows we do it! Firstly, we have a child—'

'Good point.' Holly winked at her sister and fired an imaginary pistol at her, made from her thumb and forefinger.

'And secondly, she once discovered us almost mid act.' She placed her hand over her eyes. 'Oh my God, I can't believe I'm telling you! It was the most horrific moment of my life! She saw me naked on the hall floor and David only half dressed!'

Holly laughed loudly. 'Why were you on the hall floor?'

'It's a very long story, but basically we had been having sex in the cupboard under the stairs.' Romilly blushed.

'Oh my God, you bloody weirdos! That is classic!'

'I knew I shouldn't have told you. You are not to mention it, ever. Ever! Not even to Carrie! Swear!'

'Scout's honour.' Holly giggled.

'And I mean it, Holl. Be nice to Sylvia.'

'Message received.' Holly stuck out her tongue and rolled her eyes as she applied a fourth coat of mascara.

'I'm being serious. You have to be nice to her, do what I do and just let anything she says that's a bit off centre roll off you like water off a duck's back.'

'I wi-ill!' Holly laboured the point, sounding like a petulant child. 'Does she know you're under house arrest?'

Romilly laughed. 'I am not under house arrest and no, she doesn't. We'll just lie and say that you're here because I like you and not because you're my jailer.'

Holly put her mascara wand back in her make-up bag and pressed powder under her lower lashes. When she'd finished, she looked up at her big sister. 'Are you an alcoholic?'

Romilly turned from the mirror and stared at her beautiful sibling, who had used the word that everyone had been very careful to avoid saying in front of her. The word David couldn't summon, the word she dodged in her own head. She felt slightly sick at the accusation. Of course she wasn't an alcoholic. Was she? How would she know if she was? In her mind, alcoholics were people who drank before breakfast, who swigged from brown paper bags in the park, toothless people with matted hair who shared cans on the pavement and shouted at random strangers from their bits of cardboard in the car park. Not people like her who simply liked a drink or two to boost their confidence and help them relax. But the wine bottle had been calling to her more and more often lately. What did that mean?

'I don't think so.' She held her sister's gaze.

'Well, that doesn't really answer the question. I mean, I don't think I need to lose weight, but the waistband on my jeans tells me differently. And Mum doesn't think she needs a hearing aid, she just believes that everyone in the world, including everyone on TV and the radio, is now whispering just to annoy her. She actually thinks it's a worldwide conspiracy designed to irritate Pat Shepherd, and chief conspirator is Anne Robinson, as she can no longer hear the questions she asks on *The Weakest Link*.' She mouthed the punchline: 'Did you not get the memo?'

Romilly gave a short laugh. 'I hear you. Loud and clear. And I know what you're saying.' She sighed. 'I guess the answer is that I think I have the potential to be an alcoholic and that's why it's important that I just kick it. And that I do it now before I slip any further.' It felt simultaneously scary and empowering to say the words out loud.

'I'm very proud of you, Rom. You're doing great.' Holly was sincere.

Romilly smiled at her. Physically, she felt a lot better. Her skin had a healthy glow, her hair was glossy and she had put on a little weight in all the right places. She decided not to confess that today, two weeks in, it was just as hard as it had been on day one and that if she had the chance, she'd be off to stick her hand in that wellington boot quicker than you could say 'Mine's a pint'.

Not an hour went by without her thinking about having a drink, picturing herself holding a large glass, imagining the tang of a cold, earthy white against her lips. She even dreamt about the stuff. It was enough to send her nuts. To quash the cravings, she took long baths, snacked, cleaned the house, watched television, tried to master the art of painting her beloved mayfly (with varying success), chatted to Holly, walked around the garden or shopped; anything rather than submit to the longing for the taste of booze.

She didn't even have work to take her mind off things. Some time after her first official warning from Dr Gregson, she'd been caught downing a half-bottle of wine in the Ladies at the lab. Instead of having another go at her, Dr Gregson had phoned David. She'd heard them both offering earnest sentiments, swapping theories and ideas about what might be best for her, as though she were a child or a thing. It was enough to turn anyone to drink. And the upshot was, she was on indefinite leave, 'for health reasons'.

'Thanks, Holly. I don't know if I would have managed without you here.'

Holly ignored the compliment. 'I was talking to Carrie about it.' Romilly smirked at her sister's endearing lack of guile. 'We're worried about you, Roms. I mean, we both said that it's strange how we drink a lot, and I mean a lot – we arrive somewhere with a party-head on, we get pissed, we dance, we laugh, we make fools of ourselves – but then that's it. We don't think about doing it again until a week or two later, or we might go for months without going on a bender. But with you it's always seemed a bit different.'

'In what way?' Romilly was giving Holly her full attention now.

'You're so quiet and sensible normally, and it's like you can't get your party-head on *until* you're pissed. Then when you do… whoa! You go way crazier than we ever would, like you don't have the same limits.'

Romilly grimaced. 'That's probably true.'

'Oh God, do you remember that barbecue at Mum and Dad's? The one with that prick, Russian Viktor?' Holly rolled her eyes.

Romilly nodded and gave a tight-lipped smile as her cheeks flamed.

'I wonder why that is?' her sister mused.

'I don't know.' *But I wish I did.*

'Are you scared, Rom?' Holly whispered.

'I am a bit, Holl. Yes.'

'That's understandable. But don't be. It's all going to be fine.'

'What do Mum and Dad think about it all?' She knew her sister would have discussed it with them.

'As you'd expect, Mum thinks it's a lot of fuss over nothing and that you should just pull yourself together. After all, you've got this posh house and a lovely husband, what have you got to drink about?'

Romilly smiled, knowing this was exactly how their mum functioned.

'Dad left the table as soon as we started discussing it and went to the shed or the greenhouse to check on his tommya-toes or build some piece of crap that Mum can bin when he's not looking. The usual.'

'As a family, we're not very good at talking about stuff, are we? Unless it's good stuff. I mean, we can talk about good stuff till the cows come home, but anything that might make us uncomfortable, we just all stay zipped!'

Holly laughed. 'It's true! The guy I work for in Ibiza tells me about the family discussions they have around the table. They talk about everything – you know, money worries, the kids – it's so healthy. They have this open, supportive little network, which means there's always someone to pick them up if they fall, someone watching out for them, because everyone knows everything.'

'You really love it out there, don't you?' Romilly smiled. 'You get this happy glow when you talk about it.'

'I do love it. I mean, I miss everyone, particularly Carrie—'

'None taken!' Romilly interrupted.

'But it's quite nice when people want to know me for me and not because I come as part of a pair.'

'I can understand that. God, Holly, I feel a bit edgy.'

Holly jumped up off the loo seat and held her sister tightly. 'It'll all be okay, you know. David and you can do anything, we've always said that. With your brains and all that love, you can do anything you set your mind to.'

Romilly hugged her sister close. It was just what she needed to hear. 'Thanks, darling. I'm so lucky to have you and Carrie. Very lucky.' And she meant it.

'Granny's here!' Celeste shouted excitedly from the hallway.

'Yay!' Holly gave Romilly a loud kiss on the cheek, then grabbed an imaginary kipper in her hands and made out to swipe her sister about the head. As the two made their way downstairs to greet Sylvia, Romilly shot Holly a hard stare as a reminder to be nice. They did their best to control their giggles.

'Well, you didn't tell me my granddaughter had turned into a supermodel!' Sylvia yelled at them as they hovered on the stairs.

Celeste smiled at her mum over her shoulder, showing her two large front teeth that didn't quite fit her six-year-old mouth yet; they sat at an unusual angle, making her less supermodel, more scrum half. Romilly and David had quietly commented on her goofy gorgeousness, loving this stage in her development.

'Look what I found, Granny!' Celeste opened her palm to reveal three fat woodlice curled into her hand.

'Oh my!' Sylvia jumped back.

'Don't be scared, they're dead,' Celeste said matter-of-factly. 'They look like tiny little armadillos! They're so cute!'

'Remind you of anyone?' Holly whispered in her sister's ear.

'Cuter when they were alive, I'm sure!' Sylvia said, wrinkling her nose in distaste.

'Kettle's on!' Romilly smiled as she kissed her mother-in-law and made her way into the kitchen. 'How was your trip?'

'Fine, but I was very glad to see David at Temple Meads.

The train was jam packed; thank God I'd booked a seat. I was in the quiet carriage, but still people were chatting and talking loudly into their phones.' She tutted. 'I had to stand up twice and point to the sticker on the window, in case they hadn't realised. I even had to tell the ticket guy to keep it down, he was talking very loudly to a man about connection times at Didcot Parkway!' She sighed as she took a seat at the kitchen table.

Romilly caught Holly's eye; they were both imagining the relief those poor passengers must have felt when Sylvia disembarked. They probably had a little natter or a group singsong in celebration.

'And what about you, Holly? Are you still working in that bar or have you found a career?'

Holly ignored the scorch of her sister's warning stare. 'Oh, I left the bar a while ago. Yes, I've found a career and I'm really good at it!'

'Well, good for you! I told Pat she wasn't to worry, that you'd find your feet eventually.'

Holly gave a sideways smile, unwilling to divulge that she now ran a chain of three high-end cocktail bars and lived in a beautiful apartment in Santa Eulalia, overlooking the sea.

'What is it you are doing now?'

'I'm a stripper!' Holly announced with her arms held high over her head and her left knee raised.

Romilly gasped and Sylvia's eyebrows shot up.

David came into the kitchen with a large holdall. 'I'll pop this straight upstairs for you, Mum.'

She nodded at him.

'All okay?' He looked from face to face, trying to interpret the awkward atmosphere.

'Yep!' Celeste beamed. 'Aunty Holly is a stripper,' she announced.

'Well...' David struggled for words. 'There we go. I'm sure she's a very good stripper. Like I've always said, Celeste, whatever you do, give it a hundred per cent and err... you'll be really good at it.'

Romilly sprayed her laughter over the work surface, Holly giggled loudly and even Sylvia couldn't help but see the funny side. 'David, really!' She shook her head, laughing.

Their evening was fun. Romilly watched, delighted, as Sylvia and Holly found common ground. The foundation for their exchanges was a seam of sarcasm, as each tried to outdo the other. Celeste had been allowed to stay up late and was thoroughly enjoying the grown up banter. Romilly refused Sylvia's offer of a beer with their Indian takeaway, noting David's sideways glance as she opted for water instead. Celeste read from her reading book and later proudly recited her three lines for the end-of-term play. The four adults applauded enthusiastically, all agreeing that she was going to be the best Peasant Number 8 that had ever graced the set of *Robin Hood and his Merry Band of Thieves*.

The laughter was slowing, yawns were interspersing the conversation, and thoughts were turning to the plump pillows and clean white sheets upstairs, when the front door-bell rang.

'I'll go.' David jumped up.

It was unusual to have visitors at this late hour. Romilly stood and, aided by her sister, gathered up the silver-lined white paper bag, in which sat a thick crust of naan bread, and started to stack the empty foil containers that were sticky with thick sloshes of spicy red sauce. Everyone heard the wail that came from the hallway. Romilly abandoned her task and rushed from the room, to find Sara leaning against the wall, tears streaking her face as she struggled to find her breath. David looked on helplessly.

'I'm sorry, Rom, I didn't know who else to go to. I just need someone to talk to!' she sobbed. Her voice carried the recognisable slur of a drunk.

'It's okay, nothing's that bad,' Romilly cooed as she put her arm around her friend.

'What's the problem here?' Sylvia, with typical candour, asked from the doorway.

'She's pregnant!' Sara screeched, beating her fists against her thighs. 'All I ever wanted was a baby, that was all I have ever wanted, and he wouldn't let me, and he's been with this tart for no time at all and she's fucking pregnant!' She bent forward, hanging onto Romilly's arm.

'Come on, Sara, let's get you home,' Romilly said quietly, keen to shield Celeste from further upset.

'I don't... I don't want to be on my own. I'm so lonely!' She looked up imploringly.

'It's okay. I'll take you home and I'll sit with you for a bit. Is that all right, love?' Romilly turned to her husband.

David nodded, unsure how else to respond. An awkward silence descended on the hallway. Romilly could just imagine the whispered conversation that would ensue once she'd left the house.

The two women made their way along the pavement to the house at the top of the cul-de-sac, where Sara had left the front door wide open. Romilly eased her over the step and kicked the door shut before guiding Sara into the sitting room, where she slumped down on the sofa and cried loudly.

Romilly let her eyes linger on the beautiful hand-embroidered cushions, designer rug and vast pieces of modern art that turned the rather bland, rectangular sitting room into a fashionable pad. The two pale lilac chandeliers that hung at either end of the room were dimmed, casting diamond-like shards of light into the room. There was a half-eaten pizza in a box on the floor, which gave off a strong smell of onions, and an empty tumbler lay on its side next to it.

'Don't cry, Sara. He's just not worth it,' Romilly offered, hoping that might help.

Sara lifted her head and pulled herself into a sitting position. She looked ugly. Her eyes were swollen and her lashes were glued shut with the goo of old make-up; her nose ran and her mouth drooped.

'But he *is* worth it!' She cried fresh tears. 'He *is* worth it and I fucked it up! I fucked it up, Rom! I loved him and he left me and it was all my fault. I had a fling, a stupid, bloody, pointless fling, and he left me and she was ready to jump into my shoes. I always knew what she was about. He told me I was being stupid and there was nothing in it, but I knew. I could tell by the way she looked at him and looked at me and I didn't like it. She was biding her time.'

Romilly was a little shocked by the revelation. It threw a very different complexion on her original understanding that Sara had been wronged by a man with too much money who had simply had a change of heart.

'And now she's pregnant! She's having his baby...' Sara bent forward as though felled. 'It was the one thing I wanted, Rom. The one thing I wanted was a baby, his baby!'

'I don't know what to say to make it better, Sara, but I know it will all look a lot different in the morning.' She looked around and realised that, despite the glitzy decor, the house felt cold; it had a distinct lack of heart, with nothing that spoke of happy memories, family or shared laughter. 'Can I get you a cup of tea or something?' she whispered, using the voice that calmed Celeste when she'd had a bad dream or was in a tizz over something.

Sara nodded, but her eyes were half closed. She listed sideways onto a pile of cushions. It looked as if she might have fallen asleep.

Romilly made her way into the kitchen, filled the kettle and set it to boil. It was strange being in a house that had the identical layout to hers but was entirely different. Opening the cupboard where in her own kitchen she kept her mugs and cups, she was faced with cereal boxes, a tin of crackers and a packet of pasta; it made her feel uncomfortable and like she was snooping. Eventually she located the cups and placed one on the side, with a tea bag resting in the bottom.

She scanned the fridge in search of milk. Her eyes roamed the shelves, which were sparsely stocked, bar the odd piece of Clingfilm-wrapped veg and an old pot of greying coleslaw. She stopped searching when her gaze fell upon a bottle of Prosecco, slick with beads of condensation and standing proudly in the door. The sight of it caused a strange reaction that was partly physical, as if she wasn't in control but on autopilot. Her mind screamed instructions at her. *Don't touch it, Romilly! You've done so well, two whole weeks! Don't do it! Don't!*

Instinct told her to act quickly, before she had a chance to listen to any counter-arguments. If she didn't seize the moment, she could quite possibly talk herself out of what she was about to do. Gripping the bottle, she quickly pulled it from the tray, listening to the delightful clink as its weighty base touched against a jar of pickle. Yanking, she peeled the foil and twisted the wire cage that housed the cork, working quickly before turning the cork inside her palm and easing it free with her finger and thumb. Her heart raced and she breathed deeply in eager anticipation. The excitement made her smile and her pupils dilate, just the prospect, the thought of knowing she was going to be able to have a drink, filled her with a heady combination of relief and joy.

Maybe I could just have one little taste... She liked the shape of the lie in her thoughts; it eased her guilt as she brought the cold green glass to her soft lower lip. Slowly, she tipped the bottle, letting the cool fizz froth over her tongue.

It was instant. As she took the first slug, a whoop of euphoria travelled from her mouth to her brain and exploded like fireworks inside her head and in the pit of her stomach. She closed her eyes and continued to glug from the bottle, pausing only to catch her breath when the bubbles clogged her nose and throat and forced her to slow, to take a second before continuing, as quickly as she was able.

It tasted fantastic! Better than she had remembered. It was heaven, and the calm that spread through her left her in a state of near ecstasy. With every gulp, thoughts of her family slipped from her mind. The promises she'd made to David and Holly were quickly erased.

As usual, before she'd emptied the Prosecco, her thoughts were already turning to what she might be able to drink next. She finished the bottle and belched twice, even enjoying the sour tang of the regurgitated bubbles that travelled up her throat and hit the back of her tongue. She reopened the fridge and scanned harder this time, but she couldn't see any more bottles or cans, nothing of interest. She looked under the sink and was about to wake Sara and ask her what else she had, when she turned to the bookshelves at the back of the kitchen and struck gold! The bottom two shelves were lined with a shining cornucopia of bottles in an array of shapes and sizes. The labels alone were enough to send a shiver through her: Bacardi, Bombay Sapphire, Courvoisier, Smirnoff. She chose the Courvoisier simply on the basis that she didn't mind it neat and rather liked the short, fat bottle with the long slender neck.

Not wanting to disturb Sara from her slumber, Romilly sat at the breakfast bar and listened to the sound of the tight, stubby cork easing from the top. Inhaling the pungent fumes, she sipped gingerly at first, until she found her flow. Then she began pouring the golden brandy into her mouth, letting it slip down her throat.

An hour passed. Things had started to get a little hazy and Romilly had removed her glasses and had her hand over her eyes. There was a knock at the front door and she heard an indiscriminate burble coming from the sitting room in response.

'It's okay, Sara. Stay where you are, honey. I'll get it.' Romilly took a deep breath and opened the door wide, a smile fixed on her face. It was Holly.

'How's she doing?' Holly peered over her sister's shoulder.

'She's sleeping a bit. Best thing,' Romilly said quietly.

Holly stood up straight and folded her arms across her chest. 'Have you been drinking?' Her tone was accusatory and reminded Romilly of their mum.

'No!' she replied, rather more loudly than she'd intended.

'Romilly, I can smell it on you and you look—'

'I look what?' She held the doorframe for support.

'You look a bit sozzled.'

Romilly snorted her laughter. 'Sozzled? Now that's not a word you hear every day! Sozzled!' she repeated as she giggled.

'I thought you were supposed to be taking care of Sara?'

'I am! I am!' She pointed at the sitting room. 'She's sleeping.' She placed her finger over her pursed lips.

'I think you should come home now.'

'I think you should mind your own business.'

'I mean it, Rom. You should come back, try and get to bed before David sees you.'

'Oh, really? Well, I'm not afraid of David! He's not my boss! He's not like the boss of Romilly! Even if he thinks so, he'snot!'

'Are you coming or not?'

'Not.' She swayed.

'For fuck's sake!' Holly swore some more, then strode off down the path.

Romilly shut the front door and walked back to the kitchen. She was surprised to find Sara sitting on the other side of the breakfast bar, sipping brandy from a tumbler.

'Was that your sister?'

'Yes, my bossy sister. I told her to go away, cos I'm busy drinking your wine and your brandy.'

'You can have what you want. I love you Romilly. You're my only friend,' Sara whined.

'I'm not. You have lotsofriends.'

'I don't.' Sara started crying again, wiping her tears and snot up into her hair. 'I love him so much! I don't want to live here by myself. I want to go home and I want us to have a baby.' She sobbed. Romilly patted her back and poured herself a tumbler of brandy.

Neither knew how much time had passed when the doorbell rang again. 'Avon calling!' Sara shouted, sending them both into a spiral of chuckling and wheezing. Sara slipped from the high stool and returned a minute later, sucking in her cheeks and with a furious-looking David in tow.

'I've come to bring you home, Rom. Holly is packing her bags and I thought you might want to say goodbye to her.'

'She's my friend...' Sara purred.

David flicked his head in her direction. His eyes flashed, his pupils like pinpricks. 'Don't talk to me.' He held up a palm.

'No, no! David, you don't understand...' Sara walked forward.

'I said don't talk to me, and I meant it,' he hissed through gritted teeth. He looked close to tears.

Striding forward, he took his wife by the arm and pulled her from the stool she was perched on. For some reason Romilly found this funny and she giggled as she reached back to grab her glasses from the countertop. Her laughter only made him even more angry. On the way out, he held her up when she tripped over the front step, then marched her stumbling along the pavement. 'Hello, Mr Rashid!' Romilly waved at their kindly neighbour, who had been outside to check that his garage door was locked, as he did every night before retiring. He returned her wave and ambled inside. David sighed in relief that he hadn't seemed to notice that anything was amiss.

'What on earth is going on here?' Sylvia asked from the kitchen.

'Nothing is going on.' Romilly made a fair attempt at Sylvia's American twang. 'I am being forced home by your son, who is behaving likeaprick. Do you remember when you caught us fucking in the cupboard?' She bent double, laughing hysterically.

'Romilly!' Holly yelled from the sitting room.

'Oh yes, thas right, Holly, you can have a go at me too! Miss Perfect is in the house!' she shouted, raising a fist in the air.

Woken by the shouting, Celeste pattered out of her bedroom and crouched, wide-eyed and frightened, behind the bannisters at the top of the stairs.

'Hey, Holly, thasright, isn't it? Miss Fucking Perfect, coming here like you're betterthanme, telling me what I can and can't do. You only got GCCC's, or whatever they're called, you didn't get a degree. You're thick as mince, and that otherone, both too stupid...' She swayed on the spot, keen to make her point.

'Mummy?' No one had seen Celeste creep down the stairs and into the hallway, where she now stood with her little chest heaving and tears streaming down her face.

Sylvia rushed forward. 'It's okay, darling. Mummy isn't feeling too well…'

Romilly snorted her laughter and gave her daughter a double thumbs-up as she wobbled.

'Why don't you and I go back upstairs and have a story, darling? To help you get back to sleep. I'd love that.' Sylvia took her granddaughter by the hand. 'You can choose.'

David pulled his wife into the kitchen. 'You sit there and don't move,' he snapped, 'while I make you a coffee.' His hands shook as he reached for the coffee jar and spoon.

Holly poked her head round the door and dabbed at her eyes with her sleeve. 'I'm off, David,' she managed through her tears.

David kept one eye on Romilly as he went over to his sister-in-law. 'Don't cry, Holl.' He shook his head, mortified and at a loss as to how to make things better.

'I'm okay.' She jutted her chin and threw back her shoulders. 'Say goodbye to Celeste for me. I don't want her to see me blubbing like this.' Her words only seemed to make her cry harder.

Romilly lifted her head from the cradle her arms had made on the countertop. 'Don't go! Don't go anywhere, Hollywood. That's what we used to call you, isnnit, Hollywood and Carriewood!' She laughed loudly. 'Stay here, come on, we can chat, jusstayhere…' Her head flopped forward again.

David followed Holly to the front door.

'I'm so sorry, David.'

'Why are you sorry? It's her that's behaving badly. I'm… I'm…' He struggled to find the words. 'I don't know what to say.'

'I thought I could keep her on the straight and narrow, but apparently I can't.' Holly gave a small smile and wiped her eyes. 'It's hard to talk about, but I think she might need professional help, David.' She kissed him on the cheek and made her way to her car at the bottom of the drive.

'I think you might be right,' he muttered as he closed the door behind her.

Celeste

It was the first time I felt unsafe. I don't mean in imminent danger or that anyone was going to harm me physically, but I did feel a shift in my world, as if all the things I thought I could take for granted, I couldn't. It was as if everyone was pretending and I'd seen through it. Mum was swearing and shouting. Aunty Holly was crying, and Dad looked so angry, I thought he was going to hit Mum. I'd never seen him so angry. It was even worse than the sick night.

Granny Sylvia was not her usual self, either. She took me upstairs to read me a story, but her eyes kept darting towards the landing every time someone shouted or a door slammed, so she kept losing her place and having to start at the top of the page again. I couldn't concentrate either. Both of us were waiting for the next yell or slam. She kept patting me and saying, 'It'll all be all right,' but it didn't feel all right, far from it. It was one of the only times I'd seen my Gran tearful. I asked her if it was all my fault. 'Why would you think that?' she closed the book and I told her. 'Because I went on and on about having my ears pierced and I knew that Mummy didn't really want me to get them done, but then she did and I think I made her and then Holly got my tiara and I know Dad didn't really like it, and I wish

I could go back and say that I was joking and not get my stupid ears pierced in the first place!' She held me close and rocked me back and forth and she said, 'whatever is going on with Mummy and Daddy is nothing to do with you. You are the very best thing that they have!' but I didn't believe her, like when she used to tell me I was like a super model, I knew I wasn't. I wasn't even the third prettiest in my class.

Looking back, I can see that her words were as much about reassuring herself as me. I remember in the months following, lots of people asking me, 'Are you okay?' which only added to the feeling that things were not okay. I didn't want to have to tell my friends about what life was like in our house and so I stopped talking to them, afraid I might let something slip. I became quite withdrawn and quiet. And once I'd started to be quiet, it was really hard not to be, as though that was how I was now and I couldn't remember what it was like to be perky and noisy.

It was ages before I could go back to sleep.

Eight

The place was luxurious: a large Georgian house that sat in its own manicured grounds in rural Somerset. Its guts had been scooped out and replaced with a modern, open-plan interior and minimalist decor. It reminded Romilly of the time she was presented with a pineapple in a restaurant, when she was about twelve; when she'd lifted the lid, it was full of lemon sorbet and glacé cherries and not the lush, sweet fruit she'd been expecting. It had been a bitter disappointment and a salutary lesson that things weren't always what they seemed. *I shall call this place The Pineapple*, she decided and couldn't help wondering what had happened to all the original fireplaces, flooring, old bricks, light switches and doors. She felt a nostalgic ache for the building, wondering what tales it could tell.

The grey-haired woman behind the glossy white desk leant forward, her elbows resting on the dust-free surface and her elegant hands twisting together beneath her elfin chin. 'We have a different approach here. We are not a hospital, although many of us are medics. We like to think of ourselves as a health-and-wellbeing-restoration retreat. And our pro-gramme will be adapted to suit you, Romilly. Typically, clients are given diazepam or similar to help combat the cravings and side-effects of withdrawal, but you've decided against that route, I understand?'

David coughed. 'We've discussed it at length and we're concerned that Rom might be swapping one dependency for another, so we feel that the organic approach might suit her best.'

The doctor nodded. 'Here at Orsus, we look at the individual and find ways to reprogram the need, the desire, but there is also a physical aspect to detoxification, which of course you will be well aware of, Romilly.'

'What... what will I actually do here?' Romilly asked, her nerves evident.

'We offer one-to-one counselling and we also encourage residents to participate in group counselling and other joint sessions, such as yoga and art.'

Romilly looked at David. Group participation was one of her least favourite things. *'There's no "I" in team!'* She gave a faint smile.

'You'll be prescribed specially tailored vitamin infusions twice daily, as well as a complex range of supplements to help your liver get back in shape. Each afternoon you'll be given our signature hay-bed detoxification treatment, which most clients find very restorative.'

David nodded at the woman. Her firm but kindly tone inspired confidence and gave him hope that this might be just what Romilly needed. He turned to his wife, who looked hunched, as if trying to fold into herself and disappear. 'It all sounds great, Rom,' he said coaxingly.

Romilly stared at him. It was easy for him to say, but it

wasn't him who was being made to participate in group therapy and bloody hay beds.

'We serve nutritional, organic juices four times a day and a light, healthy meal in the evening, designed to reawaken your appetite. Although sometimes your body is so busy adjusting to the alcohol withdrawal that it just doesn't really want to eat, so we leave that up to you to judge. As I say, you are in control and you are always given choices.'

Romilly was only half listening now. She was distracted by the large oak tree whose branches were tapping against the Georgian window frame to their right. She'd spent a lot of time looking at oaks in the past, researching acute oak decline and the oak jewelled beetle that was a possible culprit. It was a beautiful thing with metallic blue wings, she remembered.

'We are very aware that this isn't a one-size-fits-all treatment, so we will constantly monitor how you're feeling and what's working. How does that sound, Romilly?'

Romilly stared back at the woman. 'Oh, err, sorry...' She pushed her spectacles up along her nose and squirmed in the leather chair. 'I was just thinking about, err, my work actually.'

The doctor sat forward. 'Is your work important to you, Romilly?'

'Yes, yes it is. Was... But...' Romilly swallowed the lump in her throat as the tears started to prickle. She turned to David. 'Don't leave me here, David. Let me come home with you. Back to you and Celeste. I feel like I should give it another go. I'll go back to work and everything will be how it used to be—'

David bit back his own tears, reached over and took her hand inside his. 'It's okay, love. I'll be phoning Dr Harrison—'

'Lorna, please,' the woman interjected.

He smiled briefly. 'I'll be phoning Lorna every day and when she gives me the nod, I'll jump in the car and come and sit with you and it won't be long before you'll be coming home.'

The doctor nodded, as if he'd given the right answer. Romilly hated the condescension that was coming off the two of them. She began to feel resentful towards the co-conspirators, like she was being forced into being there. She bit her lip to stop herself reminding them that she wasn't stupid. *How smart do you have to be, to end up here, then, Rom?*

'This isn't a prison,' Lorna said. 'You're free to leave whenever you want, but we would strongly encourage you to stay and really immerse yourself in the programme. The first seven days are critical. We give you the choice to stay or go, because we've found that the more flexibility, the more personal choice there is, the more we are empowering you to choose recovery from your dependency. Does that make sense?'

Romilly gave an awkward nod. 'It does, yes. But I would question that first assumption that I actually do have a dependency. I mean, I absolutely know that I drink too much and that I can get a little... out of hand...' An image flashed into her head of her being sick in the hallway and Celeste watching from the stairs. She closed her eyes briefly. 'But the word "dependency" makes me think of full-blown alcoholics and I don't think that's me. I really don't.' She looked at her hands, trying to still them in her lap. 'In fact, what I want to say is, I *know* that's not me.'

An awkward hush came over the room before Lorna spoke.

'Can I ask you to look at this?' Lorna tapped the keyboard on the desk in front of her and pointed to a PowerPoint slide that had appeared on the blank wall behind her.

Romilly squinted at the bullet points on display.

'I want to ask you these questions out loud and I want you to answer me honestly, okay? And don't worry, it's not a test; you can't fail. It's just to give me an insight and maybe to give you an insight too. So, the first one...' Lorna cleared her throat. 'Do you ever feel guilty or ashamed about your drinking?'

Every day, every single day. I hate how much I drink. I'm so, so ashamed... 'Sometimes.' She blushed.

'Okay, good. And the next one is, do you ever lie to others or hide your drinking habits?'

I lie every day, to everyone, and I go to great lengths to hide what I drink... She pictured the wellington boot full of wine and the stash of miniatures in her toiletry bag that she swigged from while she was on the loo. She nodded. 'Sometimes.'

Lorna smiled. 'Okay. And do you have friends or family members who you know are worried about your drinking?'

She saw herself in the bathroom with Holly. *I was talking to Carrie about it. We're worried about you, Roms.'* David squeezed her hand. Romilly nodded her response.

Lorna pointed to the next question. 'Do you need to drink in order to relax or feel better?'

I can only relax when I've had a drink. It's always been that way, but now it's worse, I need a drink to feel better; I need a drink to get through the day. 'I guess,' she whispered.

'Have you ever blacked out or forgotten what you did while you were drinking?' Lorna's voice was soft; probing but kind.

Romilly didn't realise she was crying until she went to speak and the answer came out in a croak. 'Yes.' She immediately thought about that horrible morning when she'd woken to find that Holly had left. She'd wondered where her sister was and why Sylvia was a little frosty over the breakfast table and Celeste so withdrawn.

'And finally, do you often drink more than you intended to?'

I always, always drink more than I intended to. I only ever plan on one sip, a little taste, but I can't do that. I can't. Not any more.

Romilly nodded and looked at David, ashamed that he had to hear all this. *Don't leave me, David. I love you...*

After unpacking her clothes into the sleek, touch-door wardrobe and lining up her shampoo, conditioner and toothpaste on a glass shelf above the pale grey marble sink, she sat on the bed and felt her legs sink into the thick white duvet. She swiped at the tears that coursed down her face, replaying the moment David had turned his back to leave her, his mouth contorted with crying. 'David!' she'd called along the corridor as they faced in opposite directions. 'Proper love, Bug Girl,' he'd managed, before Lorna had placed her hand on his back and walked him to his car.

'You can do this, Rom. You can,' she whispered as she placed the photograph of her, David and Celeste on the bedside table and ignored the tremor to her hand.

There was a knock on the door.

'Come in.' She sat up straight, alert, feeling her pulse quicken and her cheeks flush at the prospect of interaction. A fresh wave of nausea swept her body, leaving her hot and sweating. Her joints ached and there was a twist to her stomach that made her muscles tense. Dry mouthed, she smiled at Lorna, who entered with another, younger, woman dressed in a pale blue tunic that buttoned up on her shoulder; the Orcus logo was embroidered below the buttons and her hair was tied up in a long, dark ponytail swinging high on the back of her head.

'How are you doing, Romilly?'

She was relieved that Lorna was still being as kind as she had been when David was there. She'd feared that might have been an act, put on to convince him that this really was the right way to spend a large chunk of his monthly salary.

'I'm okay. You know...' She bit her lip.

'I wanted to ask you, now we're alone, did you have a drink before you arrived here today?' Lorna held her eye. 'Again, there's no wrong answer. We just want honesty. It's important because the timing will help us monitor your reaction to alcohol withdrawal and decide how best to treat you. I'm not trying to catch you out, I promise.'

Romilly considered her options and concluded that honesty was probably the best policy. She nodded. 'Yes, I did.'

'Well, thank you for telling me that.' Lorna smiled. 'This is Gemma and she will be your programme mentor.'

Gemma stepped forward and raised her hand in a wave. 'Hi, Romilly.'

She waved back, which felt a bit ludicrous, like they were playing one of the games that had kept Celeste entertained at nursery.

'Romilly, is it okay if I just go through your toiletries and bits and bobs?'

'What for?'

'It's a check we carry out on all new arrivals,' Gemma explained. 'Just to make sure you don't have any substances that might cause harm to you or any other clients if they were to get hold of them.'

Clearly this was quite routine for her, but Romilly could only reflect on Lorna's earlier assurance that this was not a prison.

'Sure.' Being in this environment was exposing enough; it mattered little if they went through her things.

Gemma commenced unzipping her suitcase and felt around beneath the lining. Then she nipped into the bathroom and peered inside her toiletry bag, before unscrewing the lids of her shampoo and conditioner and having a sniff of both. 'Could I ask you to hop off the bed?' She smiled.

Romilly did as she was asked, standing against the wall while Gemma dropped to her knees and lifted the mattress with one arm, running her other arm up under it until she touched the wall. She then patted the duvet and pillowcases and turned her attention to the wardrobe, looking inside the pair of trainers on the floor and tipping the slippers up and giving them a shake. Similar treatment was given to the drawer, which contained her underwear.

Eventually Gemma placed her hands on her hips and sighed. 'Great. Thanks for that, Romilly. We can't be too careful and it really is in your best interests. Do you think you might have brought anything in here that maybe you shouldn't? If you have, this is a good opportunity for you to tell us about it.'

'Where would I have put it?' Romilly answered, with a tad more irritation than she'd intended. The waves of sickness and sweatiness were making her feel quite unwell.

'Oh, you'd be surprised.' Lorna laughed. 'We've had items lodged in the cistern behind the loo, behind ceiling panels and in just about every orifice you can think of!'

Gemma shook her head. 'I can tell you this for nothing, when I was trying to kick the booze, I'd have popped anything anywhere, if it meant I could get a drink when no one was looking.'

That's how I feel, right now. I'd give anything for a drink, just a sip. Some wine, anything. I know you mean well, but you don't understand. Just one little taste would help me, make me feel better and then I could think straight and make a proper plan for how to fix things...

'How are you feeling right now?' Lorna narrowed her gaze.

'Okay. Not great. A bit sick,' she confessed.

'We can give you something for that. Gemma will give you a tour and then drop you at the treatment rooms and we can start you on the path to wellness. How does that sound?' Lorna smiled encouragingly.

Sounds like something I want to run away from...

After half an hour spent hooked up to a drip in a white-walled, white-floored, windowless room, Romilly actually felt a bit better. Not only because of all the good stuff going into her veins, stuff that would apparently help flush out the toxins, but because being sat there with a needle in her arm felt quite medical. And that made her feel like she was ill. Not nuts, or weak, or demanding or selfish, but ill. For the first time, she felt some of the guilt that had bound her so tightly for so long start to fray at the edges.

Gemma showed her to a communal area that was bright and airy. Light flooded through the floor-to-ceiling bi-fold doors. One wall was covered in luscious silvery flock wallpaper; the other walls were white and contained a huge TV screen and a series of boxy bookshelves filled with interesting-looking coffee-table tomes. Large, luxurious silver sofas were arranged opposite each other like equals signs, with low, reclaimed-wood coffee tables between them and over-sized potted plants on console tables at the back. Vast chrome lamps with white coolie shades were peppered around the space. It reminded her of a fancy hotel lobby; she half expected to see a couple of business types holding a meeting and a clutch of impatient guests glancing at their watches as they waited to check in.

The people on these sofas, however, were clearly not businesspeople or hotel guests. They were people who, like her, were trying to get better.

Gemma pointed to the sofas. 'Go make yourself comfortable, Romilly. We'll be bringing round juices in a minute or two. Don't look so scared. They're a friendly bunch.' She smiled, inclining her head towards the residents. Most of them were in pyjamas or tracksuits. Some were listening to music, others were browsing magazines or just sitting there in silence. 'The only rule we have here is that you can't mention alcohol or brand names or names of specific drinks. You can talk about drink issues, but we find it doesn't help if we are more specific.'

It was strange, but even Gemma's innocuous comment caused the image of a bottle of gin to spring to the front of her mind. She swallowed, wanting so badly to drink from it. 'I think I might go back to my room, if that's okay?' Her voice was small and her face trembled as her whole body shook.

'Yes, of course.' Gemma placed her hand on her arm. 'I'll be up in a minute. I'll wait for your juice and bring it with me.'

Romilly nodded as she made her way along the central atrium wall towards her room. An uncomfortable heat washed over her in waves and left her flushed, sweating and with a strange feeling of emptiness that was horrible and nothing to do with hunger. Her stomach churned with sickness and her fingers were constantly clenching and unclenching as she bit down hard, enjoying the sensation of grinding her teeth.

She was removing the rather unwieldy key-ring, a neon-yellow ball, from her pocket when a voice made her jump.

'Hey, neighbour!' he offered, with an enthusiasm and energy that bordered on sarcastic.

'Hi,' she whispered. She was in no mood for making new friends, especially not with a plummy-voiced, floppy-haired boy who, ridiculously, had turned up the collar of his navy

Jack Wills polo shirt and tied a cricket jersey around his waist. Who was he going to impress in here?

'I'm next door.' He pointed. 'This your first day?'

She nodded.

'I thought so. I know the room's been empty since I arrived. How are you finding it? Have you tried the steak? The beach isn't far and there's a lovely stroll down to the town if you fancy a wander after dark.'

'Sorry?' She eyed him with irritation.

He laughed. 'Nothing! It's just my "welcome to Torquay" sense of humour.'

'Are you from Torquay?' she asked quietly.

'No.' He shrugged. 'Bristol. You're not in the mood for a chat, are you, Red?'

She shook her head and pushed open her door.

'Well, when you are, come say hi. I'm Jasper, by the way.'

Romilly looked at him. The cocky kid was in his early twenties, she guessed, and seemed to find the whole situation quite amusing. He was right about one thing, though: she was in no mood for a chat.

Celeste

Dad told me Mum had gone away, but he was non-specific about where or when she was coming home. A couple of years previously, she'd gone to the States to speak about insects at a conference. It felt like ages that she was away. When she got back, she brought me loads of goodies: comics, a teddy, some slippers with pom-poms on and some actual NASA space food, ice cream and mashed potato that you had to add water to. I added the water, but the food tasted disgusting. It made me think that maybe I didn't want to be an astronaut after all.

I instinctively knew that this was a different kind of trip because this time she didn't call me and Dad didn't tick the days off on the calendar and we didn't plan her welcome-home banner. In fact Dad hardly mentioned her at all, as if I might not realise she was gone. Still, I convinced myself that she was at another conference and I tried really hard to stop myself worrying that she might have only got a one-way ticket.

Granny Sylvia came to stay a lot and she and Dad had this timetable on the fridge with little slots that they filled in – *Bake biscuits for lunchbox*; *Celeste to Brownies*; that sort of thing – so they knew who was doing what. It was pretty much exactly the opposite of what happened when Mum was there. There were no spontaneous outings to the park any more, but it was reassuring to know I would always be collected from school on time and that there would always be something proper for tea. And they never forgot to kiss me goodnight.

Granny Sylvia wasn't Mum, though, and I didn't want Mum to think I'd swapped her. One afternoon, our teacher, Mrs Hopkins, handed out slips of paper about some meeting at school. We were supposed to give them to our parents and return them to her as soon as possible. She told us very firmly that our parents were to sign the slips and circle the time they would like to attend. My heart hammered in my chest. I placed mine between the pages of my reading book and popped it in my bag. I kept picturing it there. I couldn't sleep, worrying about it. I cried in the bath whenever I remembered it, and I lay in bed for hours, trying to think of a solution. I didn't want to bother Dad with it and Mum had disappeared, so she couldn't even sign it, let alone turn up for the meeting. I just didn't know what to do. Then the answer came to me, really late one night after I'd tossed and twisted for ages under my duvet.

The next morning I woke early, sat at my little desk and carefully removed the note from my reading book. I tore the slip off, not worrying that it wasn't straight. I took a felt-tipped pen and wrote *Romilly Wells* on it in my best writing. And then I drew a big red, yellow and green flower on it, with a smiley face. I drew flowers on most things; I was trying to perfect them. I decided this wasn't enough of an embellishment, so I put two stickers on it too, one of a rabbit holding a dandelion and the other saying 'Great Teeth!' that I'd been given when I went to the dentist. I arrived at school and handed it in to Mrs Hopkins. I was certain she'd think it was from Mum.

Nine

She had to admit that, apart from feeling a little out of sorts, physically uncomfortable and missing home so badly she almost couldn't think about it, the first day and night at Orcus weren't too bad. She had declined the thick, gloopy, carrot-based juice that Gemma had brought her and had similarly dismissed the thinner green one that smelt like soil and had appeared some hours later. The surroundings were luxurious and everyone was friendly. So far, so good. Whether it would help her kick the booze, she wasn't sure. It all felt a bit tame, if she was being honest. At some level, she'd been hoping for a sterner intervention, a shock to her system that would leave her swearing off alcohol for life. She needn't have worried. On day two, the shock came.

Romilly woke with an empty, gnawing pain in her gut that made her double over into a foetal position. She wanted to spend the day curled up and hiding, but Gemma and her colleague Neil had other ideas. 'We'll get you hooked up and the infusion will make you feel better, I promise.' Gemma was as usual, stern but kind.

Romilly shook her head; her hair was stuck to her face and scalp with sweat. 'I just... I just want to stay in my room.'

'I know, sweetheart, but you can't. We need to get you hooked up to the IV and get the good stuff into your system. Come on, up you jump.' Gemma pulled back the duvet.

'Why don't you fuck off and leave me alone! I'm not a child!' Romilly roared. Her outburst shocked her more than it did her carers, who had heard it all a thousand times before.

'You don't mean it, Romilly, and we're not going anywhere, so come on, up you get!'

She hauled herself into a sitting position and tried to stop her jaw locking tight and her muscles spasming with tension. It was the most uncomfortable state she'd ever found herself in. 'Please can I j... just stay here?' she whispered, shivering and contrite now, ashamed of her tantrum.

'Fraid not. Do you want to shower now or later?' Neil asked as he tidied the towel from the chair and folded her dressing gown, which she'd flung from her bed in the night.

'Later.'

She reluctantly left the confines of her room, accompanied by Neil and Gemma. *Not like prison, my arse*, she thought as they escorted her to the treatment room.

Romilly sat in the chair and closed her eyes as they inserted the needle into her arm. Her teeth ground together, her body ached and wave after wave of sickness washed over her, starting in her gut and rolling out like a tangible, tumbling thing, not content until it had curled along her limbs and up to the top of her head, filling her completely with the horrible sensation of emptiness, starvation and a stomach-churning need for a drink. Her face and palms were sweating and she smelt. Not just a regular, wake-up-and-need-a-shower smell, or end-of-a-busy-day, need-a-bath smell, this was something else. She stank and she knew that if she could smell it, then so could others. And then the diarrhoea started.

Her tears, when they came, were of frustration and embarrassment. She kept thinking about Celeste and wondering what she was doing at that very moment. She pictured her on her way to school, chatting to her dad as he dropped her off en route to the office; in the playground, doing skipping with her friends; back home, watching *Blue Peter* all on her own; snuggling up with Teddy under her little ladybird duvet. She cried even harder. *I'm sorry, my darling girl. I miss you so, so much…*

On day four, Romilly was called into Lorna's office.

'David has phoned every day and sends his love.'

Romilly had to stop herself glaring at the woman. *That's my husband you are talking about! Don't you dare send me his love. You don't know him, you don't know us! I just want to talk to him.* Instead, she simply nodded.

'I understand it's hard not talking to your family.' Lorna had correctly read her expression. 'But it really is for the best. It can be a huge distraction from the task in hand and it's far better to give the programme your whole concentration.'

Romilly shrugged.

'How are you sleeping?' Lorna's tone was level.

'I'm not really.' She removed her glasses and rubbed at her eyes, which felt full of grit, before replacing them. 'I find it hard to drop off, my mind is churning so much, and then when I do, it's almost getting-up time. I've had some terrible dreams.'

'What about?'

Romilly took a deep breath. 'I dream I'm drinking and I'm

in a kind of holiday resort and my whole family are sitting back, having dinner, shocked and horrified by my behaviour and it's like I'm watching myself from above. I stagger in the street and I can hardly stand. I take my clothes off and I'm yelling and swearing. It makes me cringe and makes me feel guilty, but then when I wake up, I long for the drink that I had in my dream and that makes the dream guilt feel real, and makes me feel like crap.' She picked at her cuticles.

'Do you want to break that dream down further?'

Oh, for God's sake! It's obvious, isn't it? 'No, I think I can read it quite well.'

'Are you managing to take any of the juices? They are so good for you, bursting with lovely organic veg, and they will really help.'

'I'll try and have one today.'

'As you'll understand, being a scientist, when your body is used to getting its calories from alcohol, your bowel and intestines can take a while to adjust to processing regular food again. Juices are a great way to ease you back in. Are you drinking plenty of water?'

An image of a metallic-green *Cicindela splendida* she'd seen while she was at a conference in Florida flashed into her mind. She'd spent ages watching as the tiger beetle lapped up the morning dew on a leaf, getting the water it instinctively knew it needed. God, that seemed like a lifetime ago now.

'Yes. I'm drinking plenty of water.'

'And you have a group counselling session now?'

'Yes, I do,' Romilly whispered, trying to sit up straight and at least look engaged.

'How are you finding them?'

Pretty pointless. I can't see how listening to a bunch of strangers talk about how well or badly they're doing will help me stop wanting a drink. 'Okay. Yes. Fine.'

Lorna shifted in her seat and closed her laptop. There was a second or two of silence before she spoke and Romilly felt her face flush, as though she might be in trouble.

'The thing is, Romilly, there are two strands to being here. One is physical; trying to almost recalibrate your body so that it no longer expects alcohol and can cope without it. And the other is psychological; trying to understand why you choose to drink and how you might break your dependency. And that is only really possible if you *want* to break the dependency.' Lorna gave Romilly a searching look. 'When you're fully committed to stopping drinking. Do you understand?'

'Yes. Thanks.' Romilly nodded her understanding and left to go and join her group therapy class.

'Red! I saved you a seat,' Jasper called out, pointing at the comfy leather recliner next to his.

She kicked off her shoes and sat down, curling her feet under her.

'I wonder what the main feature is. Hope it's a *Die Hard*, they're my faves. I went to get you popcorn and a Coke, but I didn't like the look of the queue and didn't want to miss the trailer.' He grinned.

She gave him a sideways smile. 'Thanks.' She found him irritating but had to admit that she'd miss him if he weren't there to lighten the mood.

'I wonder what revelations lie in store for us today?' he whispered. 'My money is on Brendan finally breaking down and confessing to his cross-dressing ways.' He nodded at the quiet older man with the large bushy moustache and mass of grey hair that was so naturally bouffant it resembled a wig.

Romilly bit her lip as he continued undeterred. 'Or Mary the speedy blinker revealing her "Love" and "Hate" tattoos, which she has on each tit. What do you reckon?'

Romilly looked at the neat fifty-year-old woman who picked holes in her cardigan and had already shared, in a voice little louder than a whisper that she'd worked in local government for the last twenty years.

'I think you're going to get me into trouble.' She widened her eyes at Jasper and sat back, waiting for the session to begin.

Mario the therapist was confident, nice-looking and consciously sympathetic. He cocked his head and knitted his eyebrows in concentration at whoever was responding to his question, as though the words they spewed contained insight and wisdom and weren't just the ramblings of a would-be-drunk. As usual, he began the session by leading a five-minute relaxation exercise, getting everyone to breathe in slowly through the nose and out of the mouth, designed to get them all to a calm place. Then Helen, a fortysomething fashion designer from west London, was given the floor.

'This is my fifth attempt at coming off booze,' she began.

Weak... The word leapt into Romilly's head uninvited as she appraised the slightly grimy, slightly lost-looking middle-aged woman in front of them. Her self-pitying tone didn't help, either.

'And I know this time it's different because I am free to go and yet I'm choosing to stay. I think that's a really good sign. It means I'm here because I want to get clean and if I want to get clean then that's over half the battle.'

There was a little ripple around the circle of smiles, a few nods and one or two claps.

I'm not like you. I'm not anything like you. I live in a nice house in Stoke Bishop, I have a wonderful husband and a beautiful daughter at Merrydown School. I'm not like you. I'm not like anyone here. I just want to go home.

'The holistic programme, the juicing, everything has really helped me. I never thought I'd want to swap alcohol for health, but I do! I want to be healthy.' This earned another ripple of encouragement. 'At my lowest point...' Helen paused and spoke more slowly, staring at the floor. 'At my lowest point, I was on the game and the men I went with paid me in vodka.' She looked up, catching the eye of several in the circle.

What the fuck? Romilly tried to hide her disgust and suspend judgement, but it was difficult.

'I could never have imagined falling so far, but I did and in a way I needed to hit rock bottom before I could start to climb back up. That's it, really. I am feeling confident about my future and I want to keep feeling like this and so I'm going to do everything I can to get better, every day.'

Helen shrugged her shoulders and tucked her long blonde hair behind her ears. Mario looked overwhelmed as he walked forward to embrace her, rewarding her openness with a hug and a gentle, sincere squeeze on the arm.

Romilly sat with Jasper for their evening juice, sipping the beetroot, ginger and celery concoction through a fat straw.

'This is way better than steak and chips!' He clinked his glass against hers and she tried hard to suppress the image of cold glasses of wine that popped into her head.

'Do you find *everything* funny?' she asked.

He considered this as he swallowed the purple iced puree. It was sharp and he sucked in his cheeks then stuck out his tongue. 'No, I don't. But I'm very good at hiding behind my funnies.'

'How old are you, Jasper?'

'Twenty-two. And you?'

She smiled. 'Twenty-nine.'

'Is this your first time in therapy?'

'Yes.' She nodded. 'And you?'

He tipped his head back and laughed. 'Oh God, no! I've lost count. I've been everywhere, including to three clinics in America, one of them in the desert, where I was supposed to chant away my demons while sitting in a pit and holding a special stick. Another was in Spain, where we were encouraged to hike up the Sierra Nevada and eat only what we could catch—'

'That sounds harsh!' she interjected.

'Not really. I found a pretty boutique hotel and managed to catch a platter of tapas and a fine bottle of local red.' He winked at her. 'I've had stints in several clinics all over the British Isles and now here, again.'

'You've been here before?' She was surprised. It hadn't occurred to her that you might return again and again.

'Yep. My parents will send me anywhere and do anything rather than sit and talk to me about what's going on in my crazy, messed-up head.' He tapped his leg nervously. 'It seems it's just too much to ask for them to figure out how to live a life where they don't have to lock their booze in their gun cabinet.'

'So what *is* going on inside your crazy, messed-up head?'

'My brother died, in a car accident.' He stared at the floor.

'Oh God, I'm sorry.'

Jasper nodded his acceptance of her condolences. 'Unfortunately, it was me that was driving the car, illegally, aged sixteen. And it's fucked my head and I will take any drug or drink, practically anything I can get hold of, just to blot out all feeling. And my mum and dad can barely look at me, let alone help me. He was brilliant and handsome and funny and now he's nothing and it's my fault. It's pretty fucked up.' His smile had faded and he now looked like the young man he was, a very young man who was scared.

'Does it help you, being here?' she whispered, feeling a wave of affection for this damaged boy.

'I think the distraction is good, but does it cure me of my addiction? No.' He held her stare, pale and unsmiling.

'Then why do you do it?' she asked, softly.

Jasper placed his juice on the table and folded his hands in his lap. 'It's the only thing my parents understand, sending me away. It makes them feel better to be doing something and then when it doesn't work, they feel less guilty because at least they tried something. And they get even angrier with me because of how much they're spending, but it's just a clever ruse, they say that's what they're angry about, the cost, the futility, but really they're angry because I killed their son. So it serves a purpose. And I understand. I do. They don't really keep track of where I've been and for how long, but you get my point.'

He thumbed his nose and reached for his juice with a

shaking hand. 'I guess it's a routine that's familiar for me too. When I was eight I was sent away to boarding school and then after the accident I was sent to live with my gran up in Scotland, then when I failed to get any A-levels, despite a very expensive education, they sent me to work in an orphanage in Africa and then when I came back and started serious boozing, they started sending me to rehab. My mum likes to read about places on the internet that offer fabulous cures, the more innovative the better, and she sends my dad the link and he books them there and then.'

'Do you work?'

Jasper shook his head. 'No, I'm too busy marching up and down the Sierra Nevada looking for a decent bloody hotel!' And just like that, they were back to joking.

'Do you work, Red?'

'Yes. I'm an entomologist.'

'What's that? Is it something to do with mummies and the Sphinx?'

'No, that's an Egyptologist! Quite different.'

He flashed her a smile that told her he knew very well what the difference was. His expensive education clearly hadn't been entirely wasted.

'I work for a biopharmaceutical company, but I'm on leave at the moment.' She nodded. 'I don't know when I'll be going back. Everything is a little hazy in terms of dates and milestones and I think that's the thing I find hardest. If I knew I had to go through this for x number of days but would feel better by y, then I could hack it; it's the uncertainty, the vagueness that I struggle with.'

'Because you're a scientist. You deal in facts, data.'

'Exactly!'

He laughed. 'Well, I'm sorry to be the one to break it to you, but that's pretty much the only certainty you have as an alcoholic: the uncertainty. That horrible feeling that you never quite know what tomorrow is going to look like, no matter how determined you are when you fall asleep.'

'I'm not an alcoholic.' She realised she had said it out loud. Pausing, she looked at Jasper, who smiled and once again gathered his juice into his hand.

'I tell you what, Red. I've seen a few in my time and you do a fucking good impression of one.' He shook his head as he sipped at the mashed beetroot.

Celeste

The morning Dad told me we were going to visit Mum was the first time it even occurred to me that she might be ill. I'd lived for weeks with my stomach bunched into a tiny ball, imagining all sorts. At first I genuinely believed she was working away. But then I'd hear Dad whispering into the phone, too quietly for me to get what he was saying but loud enough to know it was secret. I knew there was something terrible going on. I'd crawl into the gap under my bed, staring into the dark, too scared to even move, trying to guess what was happening and watching the tiny alien mayflies crawl up and down the mattress over my head.

My main thought was that they were giving me away and didn't know how to tell me. Mum had gone to get the people they were giving me to, while Dad was quietly making the plans. Whenever Dad was extra nice to me, I thought it was because my departure was imminent. I used to lie ramrod straight in the gap, close my eyes and promise to keep my room tidy and to try and eat broccoli and not to be so noisy; anything just as long as I could stay.

So it was quite a relief when Dad told me where we were heading. I'd been waiting for him to say 'Get in the car' and I held my breath, expecting to hear where my new family was and where he was taking me. When he told me we were going to visit Mum and that she was in a kind of hospital, I laughed out loud. But then I started to run through a list of reasons why she might be sick. Did she still have all her limbs? Would she recognise me? I bit my nails right down and tried to stop the squirm in my tummy that made me feel sick.

'She's really looking forward to seeing you.' Dad smiled.

'Has she still got all her arms and legs?' I asked.

A little confused crease appeared at the top of his nose and then he smiled again and stroked my hair. 'Her illness isn't anything to do with her arms and legs. It's a bit more complicated than that, but I promise she'll be feeling a lot better, a lot calmer and kinder.'

I held onto his every word like it was a promise. It was the first time I'd been introduced to the concept that Mum might be ill and wasn't just being mean to me. I thought about the time I crept up behind her in the kitchen, she was standing by the sink and I planned on giving her a hug, but as I reached up to touch her, she turned around and yelled. The dark green bottle in her hand smashed down in the sink and I heard the glugging sound as something that smelled like perfume trickled down the sink. She screamed, her eyes flashing and she shouted at me, 'for fuck's sake! All I want is five minutes peace alone, that's all just five fucking minutes!' I think that was when I started to think that maybe her life would be better if I wasn't in the house at all. I hadn't meant to make her jump or make her spill her drink. So dad's insight was helpful. It made it easier, in some ways, like she hadn't chosen to be horrible or to leave me.

I don't remember much about the place she was in, except

for the way it smelt, like synthetic lemon. It reminded me of air freshener. Everywhere was clinical, shiny and white. I know she was pleased to see me. I remember her hugging me too tightly and I wanted her to let go. It felt like the time when Aunty Sara trapped me in the fort made of cushions. It felt like suffocating.

Ten

'Are you warm enough?' His tone was overly formal as he turned the dial from blue to red on the dashboard.

'I'm fine.' She hated the stilted awkwardness that sat between them like a sheet of glass, making them strangers.

'Celeste has made you a gift. It's a jewellery box, I think.' He smiled at the road ahead. 'But be warned, when I left, she and my mum were trying to figure out how to disguise the big hole in the middle. I suggested she fill it with jewels, but she wanted to put a candle in the middle, so God only knows what you're going to walk into. You might want to practise your delighted face.'

'I don't have to practise it,' she said, affronted. 'I'll be delighted just to see her, hold her. I've missed her so much.'

'Of course.' He coloured in apology.

'I know it's only been four weeks, but it feels like a lot longer. It's so isolated there, it makes you feel removed from the real world.'

'I suppose that's the idea.'

'Yes. Probably.' She nodded, unwilling to admit that just travelling in a car, being on the motorway and having the freedom of a phone in her hand made her feel a little out of sorts, almost as if she had too much freedom.

'How are you...? I mean, are you...?' He tapped the steering wheel with his thumbs and bit his lip, worried about saying the wrong thing.

Seeing the man she loved so nervous around her sent a crimson blush of awkwardness over her face and chest. She adjusted her glasses.

'I am doing great, David. I haven't had a drink since the morning I got there and I feel healthier than I have in a long time.' She thought it best to cut to the chase, deal with the elephant in the room, or in their case, the car.

'So, I don't know how to ask, really...' He swallowed.

She twisted her body to face him. 'David, you have to be able to talk to me. We're a team without secrets, remember?'

Her heart raced at the prospect of having to mention her disgusting secret, the greedy need for booze that had taken hold of her for a while. She was, however, confident that she was not like the people she had just spent weeks sitting with and speaking to and observing pouring out their hearts in therapy. She liked a drink, yes, that she couldn't deny, but these people were addicts and the two things were very different, despite what Jasper had said.

Dear little Jasper... The half a brown envelope with his phone number on it lay folded inside her handbag; the other half had disappeared into his pocket with hers hurriedly scrawled on it. He had been sincere in his offer to be there if ever she needed anything, although she couldn't imagine how that might come about. It was very sweet of him nonetheless.

He coughed. 'Okay. And you're right, Rom. So I guess what I want to ask is, are you fixed, do you think?'

Romilly couldn't help the spurt of laughter that fired from her mouth. He glanced sideways at the passenger seat and laughed too. Her tears quickly followed. She was like a rainbow, formed by both rain and sun, with tears streaming as she laughed hard.

He placed his hand on her thigh. 'It's okay, Rom. It'll all be okay.'

More tears came at the realisation that if he wondered if she was fixed, he must have considered her broken. And who wanted anything broken? *Don't leave me, David. I need you.*

As they pulled up onto the driveway, Romilly scraped her hair up into a knot and pinched her cheeks. A banner made of A4 sheets sellotaped together had been strung across the front door rather haphazardly, with *Welcome Home Mummy* printed across it in a riot of felt-tipped colour. The letters to the left were large, the W taking up a whole page; the ones to the right got smaller and smaller, where an impatient hand had run out of space. The effect was wonky but wonderful.

At the sound of the car, Celeste came running down the driveway. She buried her face in her mum's chest, gripping her in a tight hug around her midriff before carefully patting both of her mum's arms and legs. Romilly clasped her shoulders. They stood fast, neither wanting to let go, both of them thankful that they were on home territory again, not in the clinic with everyone watching.

'I missed you, baby. I missed you so much – you have no idea!' Romilly kissed her little girl's face, inhaling the scent of her and enjoying the feel of her little body in such close proximity.

Sylvia hovered on the doorstep, holding a tea towel and smiling. Romilly nodded in her direction, both grateful for all she had done for David and Celeste in her absence and envious that this woman had stayed in her home and played house while she was out of sight. She stood tall and gripped her daughter's hand, trying not to feel like a visitor to her own home.

'I made you a present, Mum!'

'How lovely! A present is just what the doctor ordered.' She spoke without giving the phrase too much thought.

'Did he make you better?' Celeste looked up at her mum, hope written all over her face.

'It was a she doctor actually, and yes she did.' She beamed, quite convincingly. *I can do this, baby. I can do it for you and I can do it for your dad. I won't let you down.*

Celeste's smile of relief split her face. 'It's a jewellery box, but it's not only a jewellery box,' she babbled as she skipped up the path, 'it's a candle holder as well.'

Romilly glanced back at her husband, who was lifting her bag from the boot. 'Well, that sounds like a marvellous invention! Jewellery box candle holders, it's genius!'

'Welcome home.' Sylvia planted a kiss on her daughter-in-law's cheek. 'There's a chicken in the oven and a peach cobbler in the fridge. You look well, Romilly.' She was sincere and Romilly felt guilty for the negative envy that had flared only seconds earlier.

'Thank you, Sylvia. And thank you for... everything.' She peeked over her shoulder and into her clean, tidy home.

'I have a cab on the way, so I'll leave you guys to it.'

'Oh no! Stay and eat with us?' Romilly levelled.

Sylvia shook her head. 'Uh-uh. You need time with David and Celeste and I shall get out of your hair. But I'm on the end of the phone, so at any time, if you need anything, just call. London's not that far away.' She picked up her bag and kissed her granddaughter goodbye.

Romilly watched as David accompanied her down the driveway. As Sylvia stood holding her son and whispering into his ear, Romilly felt her aggression flare. 'What are you two whispering about?' she muttered under her breath.

'Come on, Mum! Come on!' Celeste pulled her by the arm.

She tried not to look at the cupboard door as she passed, tried not to picture the bottle that lay hidden and seemed to call to her as loudly as a jungle drum. She shook her head, pulled her shoulders back and headed into the kitchen to admire the rather lovely, if gaudy gift her daughter had made. The man-sized tissues had been discarded and the outside covered in pink tissue and large, plastic diamonds and rubies. In the middle sat a fat church candle; this too had a couple of precious jewels glued to the top. She had never loved anything more.

The four months following her return were happy times. Romilly felt, for want of a better word, clearer. She found new joy in her freedom and shrugged off her shyness. Celeste was a little more clingy than normal, but that was to be expected. Romilly did all she could to reassure her little girl that she wasn't going anywhere. They enjoyed a newfound closeness, and had fun, even doing the most mundane things.

The first time they went shopping together, she smiled to herself as her little girl dithered over her cereal choice in the supermarket. 'Come on, Celeste, get a wiggle on. They're all the same anyway! Just blobs of cereal covered in enough sugar to topple a walrus.'

'But I like them.' She smiled her gap-toothed smile at her mum.

'Yes, you like them *because* they're coated in enough sugar to topple a walrus.'

'And I like walrussusses.'

'You like walrussusses?' She laughed.

Celeste nodded.

Romilly rushed forward and swooped her little girl into her arms, holding her around her rib cage. She let her slender legs dangle as she waltzed with her this way and that in the aisle, singing 'I am the walrussusses'.

Celeste threw her head back and chortled, hoping none of her classmates were in Tesco Golden Hill that Saturday morning. She gripped her mum's shoulder as Romilly swirled her up and over the line of approaching trolleys, ignoring the tuts of other shoppers trying to reach round them for their porridge oats and Frosties.

'All okay, madam?' A blue-suited manager with a name badge rocked on his heels with his hands behind his back.

'Yes, thank you.' Romilly smiled. 'Could you point me to where I might find your walrussusses?'

'Mum! Stop!' Celeste reached up and placed her small hands over her mum's mouth, her wide-eyed delight suggesting she wanted the exact opposite.

Everyone, David included, did their best not to mention

her 'little holiday', as her mum had apparently referred to it. They simply shared in the joy of her being back home and returned to health. And Dr Gregson's call, when it came, had been frank and sweet.

'We need you back. Things don't run quite so smoothly without your obsession for accuracy and tidiness.'

'Is that right? I prefer to think of it as a good eye for detail and efficiency that saves us all a lot of bother in the long run!' She laughed, pushing her specs up onto her nose.

'How are you doing, Romilly?' He had lowered his voice.

How was she doing? 'I'm good. Better and sharper, I guess. And really enjoying this time as a stay-at-home mum, if I'm being honest. Spending time with Celeste is just bliss.' She smiled, picturing their cycle ride in the grounds of Blaise Castle the day before, racing around the winding track that took them up to Henbury Golf Course, then stopping for ice creams on the way home.

'Well, don't you go getting any ideas. We need you back here, as soon you're ready.'

She wasn't sure if he was being honest or simply trying to encourage her by making her feel valued. Either way, it worked. She put the phone down and felt a warm glow of confidence spreading through her. Everything was going to be okay.

With Celeste tucked up in bed, David stacked the dishwasher while she studied the *New Scientist*. 'What's that you're reading?' he asked, pulling out the chair next to her and turning to face her.

She looked up as if noticing his presence for the first time. 'It's a fascinating article about how ants protect caterpillars in exchange for a sugary secretion – a reward, if you like. Isn't that just incredible?'

'Eeuuw!' David pulled a funny face.

She smiled at him. 'You stick to accountancy, Numbers Boy.'

He reached out and twisted her towards him. Removing her glasses, he placed them on her magazine before kissing her tenderly on the mouth. 'I was just transported back to the library, when we used to whisper to each other and you scribbled on my folder and I kept looking at it, chuffed because it meant you'd noticed me.' He kissed her again.

'*Me* noticed *you*? God, I couldn't believe my luck. Still can't.' She leant forward and placed her hands around his neck.

'I love you, Miss Romilly Shepherd. My Bug Girl,' he whispered.

'And I love you. Proper love.'

'Yes.' He nuzzled her neck with his lips. 'Proper love.'

David stood and pulled her from the table. He led her by the hand up the stairs of their lovely home and into one of the poshest bedrooms they had ever slept in, and it was theirs.

The next morning, Romilly stood at the sink and yawned. 'Not too much milk, Celeste, you'll just spill it everywhere.' She rolled her eyes as her daughter drowned her Cheerios, the current cereal of choice, while she pushed the plunger on the cafetière and poured the strong coffee for her and David.

'Ooh lovely, thank you.' He winked at her as he bit into his toast and honey and scanned his paper.

Celeste shovelled Cheerios into her mouth at an alarming speed. Her cheeks bulged.

'Whoa! Slow down, missy!' Romilly tutted.

Celeste tipped her head back, trying to contain her mouthful. 'I have to eat them quickly sho they don't go shoggy,' she explained, showering her school jumper and the tabletop with little milk-sodden, sugary Os.

Romilly laughed.

'Oh, I meant to say, I got an email from Lorna at The Pineapple, that restaurant you went to,' David stated matter-of-factly, stealing the minute of relaxed laughter to drop the news. He had adopted his wife's fruit analogy to keep the true nature of the place from Celeste.

'Oh yes?' Romilly felt her pulse flutter at the mention and the usual creep of embarrassment along her neck, a reminder of her shame and guilt at what she had put them through, along with an uninvited flash of desire for a drink. It was ironic that the very mention of the place that had provided her with a cure of sorts had the opposite effect.

'She was just checking in, asking how things were, you know...' He kept his eyes on the broadsheet.

'Interesting she was checking in with you and not me.' Romilly raised her eyebrows.

'I guess she thought it would be good to get my perspective.' David smiled weakly, still uncomfortable with the topic and acutely aware of all the times when it would have been impossible to have got an honest answer out of her.

'You should tell her about our evening, ask her what she thinks of *that* for progress?' She smirked over the top of her spectacles, her mouth twitching mischievously.

David coughed and sipped his coffee. Romilly recalled the feel of his skin against hers, the way she had lain there afterwards, wrapped in a sheet and chatting to her man as he sat propped up against their luxurious buttoned and velvet-covered headboard. They had laughed, remembering their uni antics, in particular the time she had snuck into his room and had to hide under his bed with several unsavoury items of sports attire until the warden had finished his chat and left. She had emerged with an old Haribo packet stuck to her bare bottom. The memory had made them guffaw into their palms and pillows, trying not to wake their daughter, who was asleep down the hallway.

'I'd rather she didn't get in touch, and if I'm being honest, I'd rather not talk about The Pineapple. I'm just happy to be getting back to normal.' She ran the hot tap and washed her hands.

David watched her busying herself in the kitchen. 'I can't argue with that.' He smiled and took another bite of toast.

It was inevitable. She knew at some point that she would bump into Sara. Bristol was like a large village and the postcodes within it even more so. Their lives were separated by nothing more than four driveways and a couple of rows of wheelie bins. Romilly was walking back from school, having waved her daughter off at the gates, and was searching through her handbag for her keys. The sound of a front door closing caused her to look up. She saw Sara jogging down the path and knew that interaction was unavoidable. She briefly considered running up the drive and quickly disappearing into the house, but by the double flick of Sara's head, Romilly knew she'd been spotted and to try and hide felt silly.

'Hey, Sara.' She waved as her friend drew close.

Sara nodded and glanced uneasily at Romilly's sitting-room windows. 'God, I haven't seen you for an age. How are you?' Again her eyes flicked towards the house.

'I'm...' She lifted her arms and let them fall by her sides. 'I'm getting there, I guess. I suppose the answer is, I'm better than I was the last time I saw you.'

Sara inhaled and looked skyward. 'Oh God, yes. I shouldn't have come crashing into your family time like that. I feel guilty that I gave you the opportunity.' She shook her head.

'The opportunity? Don't be ridiculous! It wasn't your fault, I think I was probably looking for an excuse to get out of the house, if I'm being honest.' She recalled the heady feel of the cold Prosecco against her mouth and felt her palms flash heat. A punch of desire hit her stomach. 'How are things with you?'

Sara bit the inside of her cheek as her tears gathered. 'I'm finding it hard, actually, to come to terms with their baby news.'

'Yes, of course.' Romilly had quite forgotten about that.

'And I miss you! I'm finding it hard that I don't have you to talk to.'

'Things have been...' She struggled to find an acceptable excuse.

'It's okay. David made it quite clear.' Sara fished in her bag for a tissue.

'David made what quite clear?'

'He came up to the house a few weeks ago and told me I had to stay away from you and Celeste. He was really mad. I was a little scared, to tell you the truth. He told me if I came near you or had any contact with you, then he'd take action.' Her tears fell. 'I don't think he realises that I don't actually have anyone else.'

Romilly was stunned. 'I don't... I don't know what to say.'

'There's nothing to say.' Sara hitched her bag up onto her shoulder and turned to leave.

'I think it just needs a little bit of time, Sara, to let the dust settle. It will all be okay.' She smiled.

Sara nodded. 'I hope so. I really do miss you.'

Romilly watched Sara walk down the street before letting herself into the house and grabbing her phone.

'When will he be back at his desk?' Romilly was curt. Her husband wasn't answering his mobile and now she couldn't get him at work. She was furious.

'I'm not sure. Would you like me to leave him a message?' The woman sounded apologetic on his behalf.

'No, thanks.' Romilly pressed the button and threw her phone onto the kitchen table, watching it slide, saloon-like, a good half a metre. She thought about the bars in the Wild West, depicted in so many movies, pictured the moonshine liquor being sloshed into dirty shot glasses. Her stomach growled with a feeling that was close to hunger but had nothing to do with food.

Walk it off, Rom. Do something.

She climbed the stairs and stripped the beds, balling the bed sheets, duvet covers and pillowslips into a mini mountain that she hurled down the stairs with gusto.

Angry thoughts whirred through her head. *I can't believe he spoke to Sara like that, warned her off having contact with me. What am I, a child? It makes me look so dependent, like I have no judgement. I wouldn't dream of doing that to him.*

She felt her face break into a sweat and her tongue salivate in anticipation. She cleaned her teeth for the second time that day, liking the sensation of minty freshness and not wanting to dilute it with food or anything else. She jogged down the stairs and as she stooped in the hallway to gather the laundry from where it had fallen, her eyes were drawn to the handle of the cupboard under the stairs.

Romilly stood still, as if caught in a moment in time. *I just want to see it. I won't drink it. It will just help me, knowing that it's still there.*

Abandoning the sheets, she turned the handle and ran her hand over her collection of shoes and the shiny silver rack on which they sat in pairs. She looked at the floor of the cramped space and remembered that day when they had moved in... Her fingers touched the toes of her wellington boots. She pulled her hand back and placed it on her chest. With her eyes closed, she made herself remember how she'd felt walking back from Celeste's school only half an hour ago: healthy, elated, clear. *Don't do it, Rom. Don't do it. Just walk away. Walk away now.*

A surge of longing started deep in her stomach, swirled through her body and rushed up into her head. She opened her eyes wide and almost lunged for the boot. Grabbing it from the rack, she was instantly, painfully, aware of its lightness. A whimper escaped her mouth. Quickly replacing it, she reached for its twin and felt a huge jolt of anger that it too was empty.

'No!' she screamed. Flinging shoes and boots from the rack out into the hallway, where they fell in dull thuds on the pile of laundry, she yelled her frustration at the walls. 'What have you done? Where is it? This is nothing to do with anyone but me! How dare you cleanse the house, like I'm fucking incapable? Why haven't you hidden all the sharp knives and locked away the car keys?'

She tore around the house in search of a bottle, any bottle. The miniatures in the bathroom had been removed from under the cotton-wool balls in her drawer. The half-bottle of brandy that she made creamy peppercorn sauces with, which David liked slathered over well-done steak, had been rooted out from behind its shield of herbs and spices. The beer fridge in the garage was empty and the floor-to-ceiling wine rack held nothing but two bottles of slimline tonic water and a two-litre bottle of Coke.

'For fuck's sake!' Romilly stood still and tried to calm the fury that fired inside her. Though she knew it was a disproportionate response, she couldn't control it. Now all she could focus on was getting a drink.

Her breathing came fast, leaving her a little lightheaded. She stormed into the kitchen to find her car keys. As she gathered them into her palm and located her purse, her mobile phone rang from the kitchen table.

'Yup?'

'Rom, it's me!' He sounded chipper, which only served to irritate her even more.

She sighed in frustration. Her husband did this, announced it was him calling, as though his number, picture and ID didn't pop up on her phone screen every time she accepted a call from him.

'I know.'

'I missed your call earlier. I was in a budget meeting with the team. All okay?' If he was nervous or concerned, he certainly wasn't showing it.

'I saw Sara earlier.'

'Oh, right. Did she come round?' he asked quickly.

'No, don't worry, she hasn't broken any ban that you might have imposed. She didn't even set foot on the grass. I bumped into her on the pavement, which I think is still a public footpath, but you might want to check.'

'Why are you sounding like that?' He'd dropped his voice now.

'Why?' she laughed. 'Because you can't go around telling people to stay away from me, David. You can't threaten people and choose who I can and can't talk to! I'm a grown-up, in case you hadn't noticed!' She heard a door close in the background and figured that he had either found a quieter place to talk or had shut his office door.

'Listen to me, Rom. You need to calm down and listen to me.'

She felt her jaw tense. In her current state of agitation, being told to calm down had the opposite effect.

'I told her to stay away because she's trouble, she's not good for you.'

'Why?' she fired back. 'Because I'm so weak she leads me astray?'

'Something like that, yes!' He paused and she could picture him pinching the top of his nose in regret. 'I don't trust her and I don't like the person you are when you're with her and have been drinking. That's the nub of it. And you've worked so hard to get this far and you're doing great.'

His encouraging tone was the last straw. 'I'm not a kid! This is not the playground, where you get to keep the nasty girls away from me! I can do what I want, with whoever I want!' she yelled. Her muscles were flexed in angst and her throat was sticking, dry.

David was quiet for a second or two before he spoke. His words were slow and considered. 'But don't you get it? I would do that. I would keep the nasty girls away from you in the playground. I would do anything to protect you from anyone that might hurt you. I would do that for you and I would do that for Celeste, because you are the only two things I care about. I couldn't give a shit about Sara or anyone else. I only care about my family, about you.'

'I know that, but did you stop to think about how that might make me feel? Imagine if I came into your office and started telling the people you work with not to sit with you or instructing you on how you should do your job?'

'That would be completely different and if someone at my work was trying to hurt me, I'd be glad of your intervention!'

'I can't talk to you because you are far too clever. You obviously have an answer for everything and I can't respond because I'm too thick and I need you to intervene in just about every aspect of my bloody life!'

'That's not true and I need you to calm down, Rom. I need you to just take five, sit down, have a glass of water and call Holly or Carrie for a chat. Or do you want me to come home? I can shuffle a meeting and be home within the hour. Would you like me to do that?'

'No. What I would like is for you to give me a bit of space and a bit of bloody credit!' She ended the call and swept through the hallway, jumping over the laundry mountain and its crown of random shoes, boots and the odd stray flip-flop.

Romilly parked the car on the forecourt outside the Co-op on Stoke Lane and roamed the aisles. She didn't want to make it too obvious, so she lingered in the bread section, carefully choosing a brown loaf for its health properties, before making her way to a stack of kitchen roll that was on special offer. She popped two packets in her basket before walking briskly to where the booze was kept and almost nonchalantly throwing in some bottles as though they were an afterthought. She didn't study labels or peruse special offers, she just grabbed what was to hand and tried to look indifferent.

A woman wheeled her trolley in the opposite direction. Romilly stared at her, watched as she wandered the aisles with a spring in her step, casting items into her trolley with an almost choreographed grace, stopping once to consult a list before smiling, folding it and putting it in her handbag. Romilly nosed at the contents of her trolley: bread, milk, jam, oranges, olive oil, courgettes, loo roll, liquid soap. Regular items for a regular life.

She wanted to tap the woman on the shoulder and ask her a few questions. How do you get to be like that? How did you get to be a regular mum and wife? One that doesn't wake up with the image of wine behind her eyes, one who doesn't plan her every action, trip, nap and job around her quest for alcohol? One who doesn't feel her palms sweat and her limbs shake at the thought of not being able to drink?

How did you get to be like that? She wanted to know, she wanted more than anything to learn how to be a mum like that, because this wasn't living a life, it was more like fighting a battle.

It had been four months, two weeks, four days and five hours since her last drink, but she knew she was about to break her fast and the prospect was as exhilarating as it was distressing. Alcohol had its hooks into her and it was pulling her over the line from right to wrong.

'Hello!' the woman chirped, engaging with Romilly, who had been staring at her for a while.

Romilly felt her neck turn scarlet and her chest burn with the embarrassment that was never very far away. 'Hi,' she whispered.

'Are you okay?' The woman cocked her head to one side, making her ponytail swing across to her right shoulder.

Romilly looked down at her own basket, at the bottle of vodka that nestled between the two bottles of red wine and the packets of kitchen roll that she had placed on top, as a decoy. The sight of them made her laugh. Who was she trying to kid?

'I'm fine. Thank you. Just picking up...' She paused and looked at the woman. 'Just picking up my booze. I need to drink it, it's like my medicine, except it's not because it doesn't make me better. It makes me worse. I haven't drunk for a while, but I want to and I'm going to.'

The woman stared at her, her eyes darting from the bottles that clinked in the basket to the spots of colour on Romilly's cheeks and nose. 'Do you need me to call someone for you?'

'No I don't.' Romilly felt her tears bloom at the woman's kindness.

'Are you driving?' She looked concerned.

'Yes, but as I say, I haven't had a drink in a long time.' She nodded assertively.

'Well, I hope your day's good,' the woman offered gently as she made her way to the checkout.

Romilly drove home with the bag of groceries on the passenger seat. As she turned into the cul-de-sac she was dismayed to see David's car in the driveway. Pulling up behind it, she applied the handbrake, killed the engine and unclipped her seatbelt, but she didn't move, preferring the quiet of the car, which cocooned her, kept her from the outside world. It was some minutes before David spotted her from the sitting room and rushed outside. He bent low, peering through the windscreen, clearly trying to judge her state. He tried the passenger door handle and was frustrated to find it locked.

'Can you open up, Rom, please?' His eyes darted over the road to the Rashids house, which was quiet.

She pressed the little key icon above the door handle and all the locks jumped.

David opened the door and lifted the plastic Co-op bag from the front seat. The unmistakeable clink of glass bottles knocking against each other rang out like shots. He peered into the confines and then looked at his wife, who stared ahead.

'I haven't had any.' She spoke without facing him. 'I wanted to drink it, more than I can tell you, and I probably would have downed the lot if you hadn't been home, but you are and so here we are.' She bit her lip.

He placed the bag in the footwell and climbed into the passenger seat. 'I am really, really proud of you. I am. Proud of you for not just opening it and drinking it and proud of you for being honest with me.'

'You cleared the house out, removed all the drink.' She looked up at him. 'You found my secret stashes.'

'Yes. Lorna told me that you would probably have hidden alcohol around the house and I laughed at her. I thought it was highly unlikely. But then there it was.' He shrugged.

'I'm sorry, David. Sorry about the way I spoke to you earlier. I know you meant well. I just wanted to shout at someone. I wanted a proper excuse for how angry and wound-up I was feeling.'

'I understand. I do.' He took her hand and held it in his lap. 'More worrying to me is how close you came to drinking. So, the question is, what do we do now? I can't be rushing home from work every day to check on you. We need to figure out what we can put in place to help you.'

Romilly sobbed noisily. 'Do you ever... do you ever wish you were married to Ponytail Mum with the shopping list? I mean, you must regret being married to someone like me who's such a pain in the arse.'

He raised her fingers to his mouth and kissed their joined knuckles. 'I don't know who Ponytail Mum is, but I know that I love you, Rom. Proper, proper love. I don't want anyone else, I never have. It'll all be okay, we can do this, you and me, the team without secrets.'

She nodded and wiped her nose on her sleeve.

Celeste

I could feel that things were on the slide, sense it. Dad picked me up from school one day, which was unusual. His tie was loose and he smelled a bit sweaty, like he had been rushing. I clipped in my seatbelt I asked him, 'what's a p'zedd?'

He twisted the key and looked in the rear view mirror, trying to navigate the school entrance.

'No idea. Come on! Come on!' he shouted at the sudden burst of traffic that held us up. I wasn't done and tried again. 'Billy and Hamal said that Mummy is a p'zedd and I don't know what it is, I was going to ask my teacher but I remembered when they told me that swear word, that word for poo that starts with sh...'

'Yes! Thank you Celeste!' he raised his hand to stop me 'I remember.'

I told him I didn't want to get into trouble and had saved my question up all day. He seemed to calm and turned to me, sighing, resigned 'what's the word again?'

'P'zedd' I repeated it best I could, I even tried to imitate their Bristolian accent, which was a bit stronger than mine. He stared at me and took his hands off the steering wheel. He looked floppy like the strength had left his core. He turned his head to look out of the driver's window, facing away from me then and he whispered, 'It's piss-head and it's a horrible word and it means someone that drinks too much wine.'

I nodded, instinctively knowing it was something not to be repeated and that my mentioning it had somehow wounded him. 'I think Aunty Sara is one too.'

'She's not your Aunty.' He looked at me again, his eyes blazing.

The rest of the car ride passed in silence. I wished I hadn't asked him and decided that next time anyone called my mum a horrible word I would keep it secret from my dad.

Eleven

She noticed a certain edginess in her husband as time went on. It felt like he was waiting for her to mess up and that made her jittery. Every night when she climbed beneath the sheets and the day had passed without incident it felt like a small victory, as though she had passed a test. Only for her it was a test that never ended, more of a continuous assessment, and with the dawning of each new day she could only hope that she would make it through to the next round.

Romilly trod the stairs with a tray full of glasses, mugs and toast plates that she'd found by the sides of beds and on the desk in the study. She cautiously navigated the stairs in her socks and headed for the dishwasher, which she was surprised to find was already whirring away.

'Oh!' She set the tray on the countertop and looked at the machine with her hands on her hips, as though this might bring her closer to understanding why it had been activated.

'You should have brought those down earlier.' Sylvia marched in from the garden and nodded at the tray and then the machine. She had been staying with them for a fortnight and was driving Romilly nuts.

Romilly bit her lip and felt her pulse quicken and her cheeks flame, as they always did when she was being criticised. 'I didn't know I had to.' She gave a short laugh. 'It was more or less empty a minute ago. Thought I'd shove these in.'

'I prefer to get it going.' Sylvia flicked the switch on the kettle and reached into the cupboard for a mug.

'It's rubbish for the environment and expensive to run it with just a few things in. I always fill it right up and try and use it just once a day.' She hoped she sounded both firm and friendly.

'Oh gosh, that would drive me crazy!' Sylvia flipped her hand in front of her face as if swatting an invisible fly. 'I don't like the thought of all those germy dishes lurking in the corner, I'd rather put it on as and when, keep things fresh.'

Romilly couldn't think of a single retort other than, *'This is my kitchen, not yours! Why don't you piss off and go waste water, time and electricity in your own house!'* So she stayed quiet.

But Sylvia wasn't done. 'And since when did you care about the environment? You have the heating on and the window open in the bedroom. I mean, that *is* crazy! Where are you trying to warm, Mars?'

I want a drink. I can feel the need swirling in my tummy. So I shall have a coffee... Romilly reached over her mother-in-law's head to find her mug. She pulled a couple of cups from the front of the shelf and looked behind them, then flicked her head to the draining board and the table.

'I can't find my mug,' she said, trying to think of where she might have left it, knowing it wasn't in the almost empty dishwasher.

'Which one?' Sylvia looked up.

'The one I always use. It's a half pint, huge, with blue and green stripes around the bottom and a bumblebee on the side. David bought it for me a couple of years ago and it's my favourite morning mug—'

'Oh, darling, I threw it out. It had a huge crack in it and I thought it might go at any time, so I threw it.'

'You threw it?' She tried to keep the edge from her voice.

'Yes! It was broken!' Sylvia tutted, as though Romilly was being petulant.

Racing out to the wheelie bin, she threw back the lid and lifted out the leaky bin bag and a Sainsbury's bag full of trash. And there, nestling in the bottom, sitting in a grimy, oily soup of dripping waste, sat her mug or at least what was left of it. It was in pieces: the eye of the bumblebee looked up at her. Romilly felt her tears gather. She knew it had had a crack in it, a teeny hairline crack that had fractured the glaze and had been present for some while, if not always. She'd had plans for her china companion; it was to be promoted to pen holder once it lost its handle or became chipped. But that was before Sylvia had decided to stick her oar in and take the decision to end its life there and then.

'Okay, Romilly?' Mr Rashid called. His lilting Indian accent turned her flat 'R' into something to be rolled, enjoyed. She loved the way he said her name.

'Not crying over spilled milk, are you?' He chuckled at his own joke.

She stood in her pyjamas staring into the wheelie bin and gave a brief smile in return. *No, Mr Rashid, I'm crying for much, much more than that.*

When Carrie and Holly turned up later that morning, Romilly joked that she'd always thought she and David lived in a big house until her mother-in-law arrived and suddenly it became the smallest house in the world. It was as if everyone was on top of each other and there wasn't an inch where you could find privacy or even talk without being overheard. Holly had opened the cupboard in the hallway. 'What about in here, Rom? This looks like quite a private space!' Carrie joined her laughter, clearly up to speed on her naked-shame story. Romilly beamed. It felt great to be giggling again. Her own mum was lined up for a stint of Romilly sitting once Sylvia had returned to London. She felt quite trapped. She knew that this informal rota was probably necessary, but that didn't make her like it any the better.

Literature had arrived that very morning from The Pineapple asking if she wanted to go for a week of retreat, a kind of top-up to her earlier treatment. Without showing it to David, she'd ripped it in two and then did the same again, putting the quarters in the bin. For the first time in a long while she thought of Jasper, who knew how to play the system. She remembered his funny words in group therapy about Brendan and Mary and it made her smile. She really hoped he was doing okay. He was a good man.

It had been five months, two weeks, three days and nine hours since she had drunk alcohol and while the hot flashes, muscle spasms and insomnia had abated, her desire to drink had barely faded. She knew she was in a danger zone, vulnerable, and so did David.

*

It was the day after Sylvia had gone and her mum was arriving at the weekend, leaving a forty-eight-hour period when she would be unsupervised.

'If you want, I can try and come home at lunchtime and in the afternoon?' His leg jumped up and down under the kitchen table, dancing with nerves.

'I've told you, I'll be fine. Please, David.' She pushed her glasses up to adjust them.

'Is that "Please, David, leave me alone", "Please, David, stop nagging" or "Please, David, eat your breakfast and shut up"?' He tried to make light of the situation.

'Actually it's all three.' She grazed the top of his head with a kiss.

She was aware of him watching her like hawk, gauging the steadiness to her hand as she poured Celeste's Cheerios into the bowl, saw the way he glanced at the coffee she gulped, wondering if she'd slipped something into it while he was showering.

'Are you sure you'll be okay today?' he asked as he closed his laptop and stowed it into his workbag.

She took a deep breath. 'For God's sake! I love you, but you make it hard for me to act naturally. When *you* can't relax, it makes *me* jumpy and then you misinterpret it. I can feel you watching me and I know you can't help it, but it's like living in front of a two-way mirror. You're making me a nervous wreck and that makes me want to drink. I'm sorry to be so blunt, but there it is.'

David inhaled and closed his eyes. He was trying to picture it from her perspective.

She took a step towards him. 'I spoke to Mike Gregson and I'm preparing to go back to work. I can't wait! I'm going a bit stir-crazy here. But your expression, the way you look at me...' She shook her head. 'It makes me wonder if I'm capable of anything, especially going back to work.' She heard her boss's words and cringed as she thought of that day. *I have to think about safety, everyone's safety, not just yours...*'

'I remember when I was young, badgering my mum to let me cut the bread for toast and she kept saying that if she gave me the knife, I'd cut myself. I asked every morning, but she wouldn't let me. She just didn't trust me. And then one day I kept on and on so much that eventually she let me have the knife, but as I gripped it, she kept screaming instructions at me, out of the blue – "Not like that!" and "Mind your thumb!" And I was such a wreck I put the knife down and let her do it. I didn't want to try any more, because she had unnerved me so much. I couldn't do it.'

David stood up from the table. 'I will let you cut the bread, Rom, I promise. I'll try. And you're right, I can't help it. I want to watch you and be with you all the time. I guess I'm just waiting to catch you if you fall.' He stared at her.

'Yes, I know, love. But I feel like I might fall *because* I'm so busy watching you watching me that I'm not looking where I'm going.'

He pulled her towards him and hugged her close.

'Urgh!' Celeste shouted her disapproval as she raced into the kitchen and skidded across the floor tiles in her socks. She came to a standstill at the table, where she sat down and started shovelling her breakfast cereal into her mouth. Romilly laughed at her and kissed her husband again.

'Go to work and don't worry about me,' she whispered. 'Call any time and if I need you, I will shout, okay?'

'Okay. I love you, Bug Girl.' He nodded, kissed her nose and left.

Romilly spent the day cleaning the house and changing the linen in the spare bedroom in readiness for her mum's arrival. She still had an hour before Celeste needed collecting from school, so she picked up her phone and pressed the contact she hadn't used for a while.

'Rom!' Sara was evidently pleased to hear from her.

'Hey, you, I was just wondering how you're doing?'

'It's good to hear from you. Is this allowed?' Sara half laughed.

'Well, I won't tell if you don't.' Romilly giggled.

'I'm okay. You know... Same really. I'm actually in Torquay, coming home tonight.'

Romilly smiled and for the second time that day thought of Jasper. 'Have you been on holiday?'

'Not exactly, more a little dalliance, a diversion, by the name of Greg. A barrister, who is promising to keep me warm on a cold winter's night. He's rather lovely.'

'A barrister? Wow! From dentist to barrister – you can't half pick 'em!'

'No! No!' Sara roared her characteristic laugh. 'A barista – he makes coffee!'

Romilly also laughed long and loud and felt some of the knots slip from her muscles. It felt good to chat to her friend for so many reasons, the main one being that she didn't treat her like a fragile thing, like something that might fall or someone that might break.

*

Pat arrived, hauling her suitcase up the driveway with tight-lipped determination, as though she had come to make good, clean up and generally fix everything. She was like a cross between Mrs Doubtfire and Inspector Gadget, but with less electronic wizardry and more knitting.

'Right.' She stood in the middle of the kitchen and Romilly could see it was with a flicker of disappointment that she cast her eyes over the pristine surfaces, organised fridge and fruit bowl that shone with succulent, organic fare. She correctly suspected that her mum had hoped to find a much less orderly set-up that was crying out for her steady hand and the swish of a bleached mop.

Pat clapped loudly. 'Cup of tea!' she announced, as if this at least was something she could do.

'It was really lovely to see the twins last week. We had a good old laugh.' Romilly smiled as she thought about her sisters and how they had commandeered the sitting room, drinking coffee, chatting and generally teasing each other, as they always had. It had felt good, like old times.

'Yes, well, everyone is worried about you, Romilly.' The way her mum's voice went up at the end told her this was a somewhat inconvenient state of affairs.

'I know, Mum, and I'm sorry I've upset everyone.' She swallowed.

Her mum wrinkled her nose as she studied the box containing the green-tea bags that Sylvia favoured. 'I don't know what it's all about really, love. I am trying to understand, but it's like Aunty Karen, isn't it?'

Romilly shook her head. 'In what way?'

'Well, she was always bloated, felt a bit poorly, had problems with her back passage and so on. Eventually her doctor sent her for tests, which all sounded a bit hippyish, if you ask me – she had to hold a piece of metal and chant, or something. Anyhow, turns out she's a coeliac!'

'Are you saying I might be a coeliac?' She was really confused now.

'No!' Her mum tutted. 'I'm saying that Aunty Karen loved bread! She did. She was the first with her hands in the sandwich tray at any family event. Loved her bread, but she can't have it, so she doesn't and that's that. And surprise, surprise, she feels a lot better for it.'

Romilly stared at her. Her mother had only been over her threshold for approximately fourteen minutes and Romilly was already looking forward to the day when she would be heading home again. She shook the thought from her head, knowing her mum was only trying to help. An image of her dad, coming in from the shed at that very moment, abandoning his greenhouse and sprawling uninterrupted on the sofa, smiling and taking full control of the remote, made her realise that he too probably needed this break.

'I see what you're saying, Mum, and you're right in a way. I just need to not drink and everything will be okay.'

'That's right!' Pat turned to her with her palms raised, as though this was a breakthrough moment. 'I mean, you've never known your limits, have you? And before you get huffy, I'm not going to mention that horrible day with Viktor the Russian—'

'Even though you just did.'

'But only to tell you that I'm not going to. Anyway, my point is, you have never been good with drink. I can't count the times I've had to remind you that a drunk girl is not a pretty girl.'

Romilly stifled the giggle that wanted to burst from her throat. She knew this was far from funny.

Her mum wasn't done. 'So, what I'm saying is, you need to pull yourself together, love. You need to think about what your little episodes are like for Celeste, and what you're putting poor David through. And your work can't be too happy that you're loafing around at home...'

Romilly was aware that her mum was still speaking, but she'd tuned her voice out. Her tears bloomed and slipped down her face. Her mum, making the tea, didn't notice.

I can barely stop thinking about what I'm doing to Celeste and David. And I'm desperate to go back to work. I've got research to see through, projects to monitor. And I wish... I wish I had something wrong with me that people could see, because then they wouldn't feel like you do, that I just need to try and pull myself together. I could not be trying any harder. It takes all my strength not to give in, every second of every minute of every day.

Celeste

Both my grandmas are completely bonkers, but in different ways. My mum's mum is comical. She never stops talking, not for a second. She's always busy and if there isn't a chore to be done then she'll find one, like organising the peg bag. And I'm not even joking. She came to stay with us for a while and I remember her taking all of the clothes pegs out of their bag on the washing line and putting them all back inside, in neat little stacks!

She says she likes to feel useful, but I think she just doesn't like to sit still, doesn't want too much thinking time, maybe. She always loved my mum, but I don't think she ever understood her or her illness. She'd often say things like 'A month in a bloody luxury retreat, I should be so lucky!' Now I'm older, I can see that's quite a horrid thing to say, as if Mum had been living it up. She just couldn't get her head around how Mum could have a loving family, a beautiful home and a good job and yet choose to throw it all away. But that's the thing, she didn't have any choice. No choice at all. She was sick.

Granny Sylvia always treated me as an equal, even when I was seven or eight. That was great in some ways, she got how I was feeling. We talked about how scared I was and she said that was fine, as everyone was probably a bit scared but that adults were better at hiding it. I asked her if she'd ever been scared and she spoke in a voice that I hadn't heard before, softer, 'I was once so scared I thought my heart might stop. My husband, Cole, your Grandpa, he was the finest man ever to stroll down Main Street. The day he married me I thought all my ships had come in and I was happy, so happy. We moved over here and had lived a wonderful life. Then one day he told me he was leaving me, and the life I lived was going to come to an end. And even though he was talking, I couldn't hear his words, like on the TV when the sound and picture don't quite match and I remember thinking, how do I carry on? How do I do this? I was mighty scared then, more afraid than I had ever been.'

'What did you do?'

She sat up straight as if remembering that it was me she was talking to.

'I got my house in order, toughened up, swallowed my fear and dusted myself off!'

And just like that her stern voice was back. She kissed me and said 'Keep at 'em!' and I wished then that she were more like Nanny Pat, who would tuck me in and plump my pillow and linger in the doorway until I'd nodded off.

Twelve

Ten months, three weeks, six days and three hours. This was how long it had been since Romilly had last had a drink. She'd been back at work for two months and she felt good. Returning had been strangely nerve-wracking: being handed her car keys, wallet and bag and waved off as though it was just any other day at the office. She'd been as nervous as if it was the first day of school.

David had put on his 'everything is fine' face. She hadn't confessed to him that there had actually been something rather comforting about being supervised, even though it had driven her crazy at times. It was a similar feeling to falling asleep knowing someone was down the hall keeping an eye on you. Her fear of having the freedom to go out and source a drink was acute. She hoped beyond hope that she wouldn't act on it, as though the choice wasn't hers to make.

There was also a strong sense of embarrassment about walking back into the lab where Tim had cornered her on that horrible, horrible day. His words still made her cringe. *This is really awkward, Rom, but have you been drinking?* She needn't have worried. As soon as her hand touched the handle, he shouted, loudly, 'Oh, finally! Here she is. Just as we've nearly finished all the hard work, she turns up to tell us what we did wrong and grab all the glory and probably have a quick tidy-up as well!' He downed his pen and strode over to the door.

'You know me too well.' She smiled, welcoming his loose, brotherly embrace.

'I do. I have also been keeping track of all the days when it was your turn to make the tea.' He sprinted to his desk and pulled a piece of paper from under a stack of books. 'And, according to this, you owe us six hundred and forty cups of tea or coffee and three hundred and forty-six bourbon or custard-cream biscuits. You will, however, be relieved to hear that you don't have to make them all today; any time over the next month will be fine.' He smiled.

'I've missed you, Tim.' She pushed her glasses up onto her nose and tucked her hair behind her ears, ready for business.

'Oh, don't think you can get out of tea duty by going all mushy on us!' He winked. And just like that, she was back in the fold.

Months had passed and her period of absence wasn't even remembered any more. This made her feel happy and confident in her role. As Romilly hung up her lab coat and said her goodbyes for the night, she did a double-take, surprised to see the familiar Mercedes in the car park. Sara was leaning on the bonnet. Her legs were crossed at the ankle and she was on her phone. Romilly looked to the left and right as if to check that it wasn't a set-up and David wasn't about to leap from the bushes and shout, 'Aha, caught you!' She wandered over, feeling embarrassed that they'd had so little contact in recent months and unnerved at Sara's sudden appearance.

She walked slowly, hoping her friend's call might end soon. It didn't. Romilly found herself hovering in front of her awkwardly, trying not to listen to the detail as she chatted to Greg, her beau, and practically ignored Romilly, as though she was not standing in close proximity, in the car park of the lab at which she worked. Finally, Sara cooed her loving goodbye and slid her phone off.

'Right, that's that,' she said, folding her phone into her palm as though this were a pre-arranged meeting and not their first encounter since they'd stood awkwardly on the pavement trying to find common ground while Sara confessed to having been banned from her friend's life. 'You look gorgeous!' she exclaimed.

Romilly plucked at the mustard-coloured tunic with the embroidered front panel, ridiculously flattered by Sara's comments. She'd forgotten that Sara had the ability to do that.

'Fancy a curry?'

'A what, sorry?' The invitation was so random, it threw Romilly a little.

'A curry! I've been gagging for one for weeks but didn't fancy dining alone. Why don't we take my car, go get some food. Doesn't have to be a late one.' She raised her palms as if in submission. 'We can have a good old catch-up over a ruby and be back in time for bedtime stories and cocoa. How does that grab you?' She smiled.

Romilly thought of David and Celeste, who were expecting her home, and recalled the last time Sara had met her from work, so casually and without warning, and how that had ended up.

'I would like a curry—'

'Great!' Sara interjected. 'Let's try the new one in Clifton village, it's supposed to be fab.'

'But I'm not sure I can tonight.'

'Oh, come on, Rom! It's just a curry, us two sharing a naan and putting the world to rights. To be honest I could do with a chat.'

It had been months, literally months since she'd done anything other than work or pace the rooms at home. A curry in Clifton sounded wonderful. 'Okay. But I'll have to pop home first, let David know where I'm off to. I don't want him worrying.' She kicked the tarmac with the toe of her shoe.

'Sure. Shall I meet you there then? I'll go ahead and get the poppadums on order and see you there in, what...?' She looked at her phone screen, presumably to gauge the time. 'In about an hour?'

'Okay, lovely.' Romilly smiled, feeling a frisson of excitement at the prospect of going out socially and happy to be with Sara, who had the knack of making her feel good.

Pulling on the handbrake, she practised yet again what she was going to say. It reminded her of when she was a teen and used to lie to her parents about staying overnight at a friend's so she could go to a party. It was the same sensation: the metallic taste of deceit overlaid by the sweet promise of doing something fun.

'Look!' Celeste ran towards her mum the moment she walked in the door. 'I've got new teeth!' She bared her gums to show the stump of a little ivory-coloured button poking through the back of her gums.

'Hey, that's so great! Congratulations on your new teeth!' She kissed her face, following as her daughter skipped into the kitchen.

'Okay, so we have a choice.' David was preoccupied with the shallow plastic ready-meal trays in his hands. 'Can I tempt you with lasagne or carbonara?' He shuffled them in his hands. 'I don't mind which, so you get to choose.'

'Actually, I don't want either. I'm going out!' She tried to sound casual, but her eyes flickered nonetheless.

'Oh.' His eyebrows knitted together as he placed the cartons on the work surface. 'Where are you going?'

'Don't you mean who are you going with?' She asked the question that she was dreading hearing, as if bringing it to a head herself might spare them both the dance of getting to the point.

He stared at her but said nothing.

'Don't look so worried. I'm just going out with Tim and the guys from work for a curry. Kind of team building, I suppose. I didn't think you'd mind.'

'I don't.' He glanced at Celeste, who was busy colouring in a picture of a gingerbread cottage. 'Are you sure you feel up to it?' he whispered.

'Yes! It's a curry and a catch-up, it'll be fine.' She nodded.

'Do you want me to drop you off?' he offered, sweetly.

'No, that's fine, I'll jump in a cab and one of the guys can drop me back. Parking in Clifton at this time of night is a nightmare.'

'Okay.' David sighed, as if steeling himself. 'If you want to leave early, or want picking up, or anything's bothering you, or you feel uncomfortable in any way...' He let this trail. 'Then text me and I'll be there before you can say "chicken tikka masala".' He kissed her nose. His lips were hot.

She could tell he was nervous, but she was determined to show him that she was capable of leaving the house without getting drunk. 'I love you, Mr Wells.' She smiled as she wandered over to hug her daughter goodbye and give her instructions for bed.

'Proper love,' he reminded her as she shut the front door behind her.

Celeste

It's weird, isn't it, that the older you get, the better you're able to look at the map of your life to date and spot the markers, the pivotal moments of change, after which nothing was ever quite the same again. It works for good things and bad. Like the time I first saw Alistair. It was pouring down with rain. He practically marched towards me, stomped through the haze, as though his message was urgent. I turned and watched him striding across the field, waiting to hear what vital information he had to impart. He even jogged the last few steps, as though in a desperate hurry. But when he reached me, he didn't say anything for a few moments, just put his hands in the pockets of his Barbour and looked out towards the horizon. I followed his eye line and gazed across the sloping landscape towards the big sky. It was dark, menacing.

'You should see the sunrise from here. On a clear morning, it's the most beautiful thing you'll ever see.'

'I'd like that,' I said, as though it was an invitation.

He stared at me then and I him, and instead of feeling embarrassed or awkward about looking at this stranger whose name I didn't even know, it felt wonderful, natural, as if it was expected, the right thing. As if I knew he was going to be important to me and so I had to catch up, learn him.

And, looking back, I can see that the night Mum went out for a curry was the same. It changed things for all of us. And for her, it was the beginning of the end.

Thirteen

Opening just one eye hurt.

She closed it again quickly, battening down her fluttering lids, trying to shut out the shaft of light that had shot through her pupil and pierced her brain. She opened and closed her mouth, licking her dry lips and swallowing. Her tongue was thick, her spit rancid and strands of her hair were in her mouth, a couple down her throat. She gagged. She placed her hand under the covers and felt her thighs wet with the slippery aftermath of sex. A film of sour sweat sat slickly on her skin and her gut churned with the desire to shit or vomit or possibly both. She shivered, as if poorly.

And yet, unbelievably, these were the joyous seconds. These were the happy few moments of oblivion before realisation dawned and her whole world came crashing down. She wondered if there had been a noise or whether the thunderclap that rang out inside her skull had been heard by her alone. Its ricochet as devastating as any bullet.

Holding her breath, she slowly peeled her eyes open. The first thing she saw were unfamiliar wardrobe doors of cheap pine and then dusty floral curtains that fell a couple of inches short of the window sill and sagged from the pole that tried to support them. They let the daylight in. Morning light, to be precise. The room had that particular spicy smell of boys, an acrid combination of feet, sweat, trainers, sex and dirty sheets. She swallowed the bile that rose in her throat.

She was naked. Clinging to the edge of a brown nylon duvet cover, she slowly turned her head to the left and suppressed the scream that built in her throat. A naked back was turned away from her. Pustules and angry spots peppered the greasy skin between the shoulder blades that were muted under a comfortable layer of fat. The man had dark hair and was sleeping, mercifully.

Raking through her jumbled thoughts, she tried to remember something, anything that might give her a clue as to who he was and how she had ended up in this place. Wherever this place was. But there was nothing, not even a hint.

Romilly slipped from the bed with trembling limbs, desperately hoping that he wouldn't wake. Her head pounded as she reached for her scattered clothes and handbag that lay on the bedroom floor, resting on top of greasy pizza boxes, which were stuffed with dough crusts and used, branded napkins, next to discarded boxer shorts and a wet, stinking towel.

She crept onto the landing, narrowly avoiding a muddy-wheeled mountain bike resting against the banisters and a clotheshorse crowded with items dried stiff as card by central heating. She pulled her mustard-coloured tunic over her head, concentrating on not vomiting and not waking anyone else that might or might not be asleep behind the closed doors of this rather ordinary house.

Glancing at her wrist, she noticed her watch was missing. She swiped her tears with the back of her trembling hand.

With a sudden, urgent need to pee, she trod the landing and pushed open the door that was ajar. It was a regular bathroom, the kind you might find in any three-bedroom semi. The bath was avocado green and filthy, with a collection of hair nestling around the plughole. The shelf above the sink was loose, tilting forward and threatening to disgorge its listing cargo of toothpaste tubes, hair wax and loose Q-tips. She hovered over the loo, trying not to look at the slicks of piss and the dark brown streaks in the bowl, cursing the noisy stream that threatened to wake her host. Straightening, she caught a glimpse of herself in the mirror. Her breath snagged in her throat as fresh tears fell.

Her cheek was creased with the fold of an unfamiliar pillow and her skin was grey. Mascara sat around her eyes in a blackened smear, with darker, heather-coloured bruises beneath. Her fingers shook as she raked her fringe forward.

Tiptoeing down the stairs, she slipped out of the front door and tripped along the street until she found a road sign. She slid the screen of her mobile and noted the time, 7.15.

'Taxi.'

'Yes, hello, can you pick me up please?' she whispered.

'Where from?' The man's voice was hurried.

'Erm... Seddon Road.'

'Is that Seddon Road, St Werburghs?'

She nodded. 'Yes.'

'Where to, love?'

She sat back on the low wall and sobbed hard, swallowing the tight ball of distress and shame that sat in her throat. Noticing for the first time how filthy her feet were, stuffed into her high heels.

'Stoke Bishop.' *Home. Please take me home.*

She focused on not being sick as the taxi pulled into the cul-de-sac. Fishing in her bag, she found her glasses, which were loose, out of their case and a little out of shape. They sat crookedly on her nose and she could feel they were off centre. She felt out of place, bedraggled and grubby among the manicured lawns, weed-free shingle and netted, organised recycling bins. The rusty cab shuddered to a halt on her quiet instruction. She was certain the knocking engine and wheezing brakes would set all the John Lewis custom-made blinds twitching. Her stomach lurched once more, as she reached into her handbag for her purse, unsure if she had any cash. She briefly imagined the humiliation of having to walk up the drive and ask for money. Thankfully, her fingers found a twenty-pound note, scrunched into a section along with two others and a couple of receipts.

She handed the man the twenty without making eye contact, aware of the disapproval and amusement that dripped from him. They hadn't chatted, but she knew he'd been stealing glimpses of her bowed head as she'd sat exposed and vulnerable in the back of his car.

'A good night then?' He smirked.

It wasn't his words that distressed her so much as the judgemental manner in which he delivered them. She felt diminished, ashamed that this pot-bellied stranger knew a secret about her.

Doing her best to ignore him, she clambered across the grubby velour upholstery. Trying to look purposeful and confident, she held her house keys in her shaking palm and smiled, flicking her hair over her shoulder, hoping this would fool whoever might be watching into thinking that all was well. Her fingers gripped the key as she tried to steady her nerves. It slid to the left and right, missing the little slot each time. Taking a deep breath, she narrowed her gaze and concentrated. Miraculously, the key found its target and with one push the door swung open.

'Mum!' The sweet, angelic voice rang out from the kitchen, where breakfast was in full swing, the *Today* programme burbled in the background and the smell of freshly brewed coffee filled the air.

Romilly stood rooted to the spot, running her hand through her hair and smiling, powerfully aware of the pungent scent of sex, sweat and booze that lingered around her. Her lip trembled as she rallied her thoughts. *No time for tears. Keep it together.*

Celeste was in her school uniform. She raced out of the kitchen and skidded to a stop on the Italian floor tiles, placing her small hand on the wall. 'Is Aunty Sara still in the hospital?'

'The hospital?' Romilly coughed. Her voice was creaky, unused.

'Yes.' David's voice boomed from the doorway. He blotted his mouth with a white cotton napkin. His eyes were blazing, gleaming chips of flint in their centres. His face was grey with fatigue and there were two high spots of colour on his cheeks. 'Where you have been all night,' he spat. 'Sitting with her after her fall.' His stare never left her face, angry but imploring.

'Oh, yes.' She nodded.

'What happened to your neck, Mummy?' Celeste touched her own as if to add clarity to the question.

Turning, Romilly lifted her fingers to her neck and faced the oversized gilt mirror. Her legs threatened to fold beneath her and a sob left her throat as she stared at her reflection. The right side of her neck was a mass of ugly, raised, purple and red love bites.

'I don't know,' she whispered. This was the horrible truth.

'Did *you* fall over when Aunty Sara did?' Celeste whispered too.

She couldn't stop the hot tears that ran from her eyes, snaking rivers that left clear tracks as they cut across her grimy skin. Her daughter pushed forward and buried her face in her mother's jeans. Romilly placed her hand over her little girl's mousey-brown hair, unable to meet her husband's gaze. There was only one thought that reverberated inside her head, the fact that only millimetres of cotton separated her darling girl's face from the stain of sex left by a nameless stranger.

Celeste

I came down the stairs one day just before lunch and the front door was open. I popped my head out to see if Mum had gone to the car or was putting the bin out; she didn't know I was there. I gripped the side of the door and peeked with one eye. She was still in her pyjamas and her head was hanging forward, she looked a little floppy and still half asleep. I saw her crouch down by the recycling bins and lift out the empty bottles. She picked up a red wine bottle and held it up to her mouth, tipping it higher and higher until maybe a drop or two found their way into her mouth. She threw it onto the grass and kept rummaging, sorting and didn't seem to care that the bottles were wet with rain and the odd twig. I was fascinated and frightened at the same time. I watched her dive forward as if she'd struck gold and I guess she had, an old gin bottle. She couldn't get the lid off quick enough and clutched at the green glass, like it was the most precious thing. This too she tipped until it was vertical, her mouth hanging open, hoping for a trickle, a drip, anything, I watched her shake it up and down, not willing to admit that it was empty. She then stared at the lid and brought that to her mouth. I saw her tongue dart out and work around the inside. It was horrible. I have never seen anyone so desperate, so unaware of what else was going on around them than my mum at that moment when all she wanted, actually no, all she needed, was a whiff of booze because even that was better than no booze at all. And then she caught my eye and I heard her mutter *'fucking nuisance'* under her breath. I'll never forget the look in her eyes. Guilt, shame, and something like anger. It was the first time I remember her swearing at me.

Fourteen

With her hair still damp from her bath and a foul hangover dulling her senses, she pulled her jersey sleeves down over her shaking hands and rested them on the kitchen table to try and steady them a little. A strategically knotted pale pink pashmina covered her neck. The house was very quiet.

'Where's Celeste?' she whispered.

'She's staying at Amelia's house. Amelia's mum took her home with her straight from school, she seems very nice.'

Romilly nodded. Even that small movement hurt her head. She had spent over an hour in a hot bath, trying to scrub away the dirty feeling that clung to her like a new skin, scratching at her scalp until it hurt and lathering herself until a layer of grey scum floated on the water. She lay there long after the bath had turned tepid and could have stayed there all day, locked away with her shame and her distress, trying to make sense of what had happened and how. The hardest part was that she had no one to blame but herself. It had been a relapse of the worst possible kind. She had no memory, none after leaving the house to go and meet Sara and then waking up that morning... *Oh God! Oh no!* Every time she pictured the second she'd opened her eyes she wanted to vomit and her body shuddered involuntarily.

'I don't know if you're hungry?' she asked, softly.

He shook his head, his tongue resting on his top lip as though he was deep in thought.

'I think there might be some cheese and crackers if you—'

David spun round and yanked open the kitchen cupboard with such force that it slammed back shut. The second time he pulled at the handle, he elbowed it open to make sure as his hands plunged inside. Romilly shrank back in her seat as he started grabbing at the plates, flinging them with gusto onto the ceramic floor tiles. They shattered, instantly and loudly. Fragments and shards flew up around him.

Romilly was shocked; she pulled her bare feet up onto the chair and knotted her arms around her shins, watching wide eyed and with sagging shoulders as he went back for more. His face bore an expression that was new to her. His mouth was set in a snarl. When all the plates were smashed, he started on the cups and saucers. When the cupboard was empty, he collected the two glass tumblers that languished on the drainer with remnants of orange juice lurking at the bottom and hurled these too onto the floor. He then leant on the sink and took deep breaths through his nose, exhausted by his efforts. His fingers were coiled into fists and his arm muscles corded with tension.

'Have you looked in the mirror?' His voice had an edge to it that she hadn't ever heard before.

She didn't know whether to answer, so instead she just shook her head slightly.

Without saying anything else, he sidestepped the broken mass on the floor and grabbed the top of her arm, pulling her from the seat. She managed to find her footing just in time, as he half lifted, half dragged her to the large mirror in the hallway. He pulled the pashmina from her neck and let it fall to the floor. Holding her shoulders, he thrust her close to the glass.

'Look,' he hissed. 'Look at yourself!'

Romilly squinted and took in her hair, limp and plastered to her head where she hadn't washed out the shampoo and conditioner properly. Her skin had a pale, almost bluish tinge and the side of her neck bulged with numerous blood-ied, plumped crescents the colour of blackberries, the sight of which made her feel sick all over again.

'D... David, I—'

'No!' he shouted. 'You don't get to speak. You only get to listen.'

He dragged her by the arm back into the kitchen and pushed her towards the table. The broken china cracked under his brogues, making a sickening crunch that sounded like bones.

'It's only ever been you, Romilly, despite what you think and despite what you've worried about. Only ever you. My friends thought I was nuts, did I ever tell you that?'

She stared at him, again unsure if he wanted an answer, afraid of doing the wrong thing.

He continued, facing her with his chest heaving and his arms folded across his torso, as though he was holding himself together. 'Do you remember the first time I took you to meet them?' His bottom lip shook, as he and Romilly both pictured that evening when they'd been first-year university students and the world was their oyster.

'So, Rom, let me introduce you to everyone.' David had grabbed her by the hand and pulled her over to the table in the pub garden. Channings was a popular haunt; they usually had at least one drink there, either on the way out or on the way home.

Romilly had stood and stared at the benches crammed with unfamiliar faces: four boys and two girls who all seemed to know each other. The girls were sitting together and wore matching floral headbands, indicating that they were mates, in a special club whose members coordinated if not their outfits then at least their accessories. She'd felt her cheeks flame and knew it wouldn't take much to make her cry; her nervous tears fluttered in her chest like an anxious bird, one she wished would take flight.

The evening passed in a bit of a blur. She was conscious of David's friends asking politely about her course and her plans for the coming year, but with every round of drinks that arrived at their table, her concentration strayed further and her posture became more slumped. If the anxious bird in her chest hadn't flown from its cage, it was certainly asleep. It was Romilly who suggested they start the drinking games, banging her glass on the table and shouting over the others, 'Fuzzy Duck! Come on! Don't be so boring. Fuzzy Duck! Fuzzy Duck!'

As David had taken her by the hand to lead her from the table at closing time, she had duly waved and blown kisses to everyone, apart from the two girls, whom she christened, loudly, 'the groovy headband twins!' before laughing raucously. David had turned to his mates and mouthed 'Sorry!' as he tipped an imaginary glass up to his mouth to show she'd had one over the eight, not that any of them needed to be told.

He took another step and the crockery made a sickening crack.

'I'm sorry,' she whispered.

'What?' He cocked his head to one side.

'I... I said I'm sorry,' she whispered again.

'I'm not sure if you're apologising for that night, or for every fucking night since when you've made a fool out of me and embarrassed yourself! Or maybe you're sorry about last night, when you effectively put the final nail in the coffin of our marriage? Because that's what you did. How do we come back from that? How do we? You tell me, cos I don't fucking know. I don't...'

He turned and kicked at the smashed crockery. Swivelling back to face her with eyes bright, he drew breath. He wasn't finished. 'I know, let me throw a few names at you and let's see if you can tell me what they all have in common. Okay?'

She gave a small nod, too nervous not to play his game.

'Right, here we go.' He coughed to clear his throat and poked out his thumb. 'Marnie and Jack.' And then his index finger. 'Mikey and Anna.' Then his middle finger. 'Jo and Liam.' And then his next. 'Adam and Fi.' And the next. 'Charlotte and Jay, Simon and Bridey, Jerry, Fiona M... Are these names ringing any bells for you, Rom?' He leant forward. 'Tyler and Rowena. Mags. I nearly forgot about Mags!' He held up his outstretched fingers as if they had puppets on them and walked forward with tears glinting in his eyes. 'I could go on, but I've run out of fingers!' He gave an unnatural chuckle. 'Go on, have a guess.'

'They... they're our friends.' Her voice quivered.

'Wrong!' he shouted loudly, then slapped the table, hard. It made her jump. 'They *used* to be our friends. Big difference. And do you know why they aren't our friends any more? Do you?'

She shook her head.

'Come on, Rom, have a guess.' His fake smiley tone was just as unnerving as when he shouted.

She shook her head again.

'No? Well then, let me help you. It's because of you. Because of you and your drinking. Still don't know what I'm talking about? I know, here's a new game, it's called match the event with the couple. Are you ready?'

She stared at him, as nerves rendered her silent.

'So, whose wedding did you wet yourself at and tell the groom's mother to fuck off? Want another? Whose birthday did you ruin by getting so hammered that you screamed and shouted songs in the restaurant so loudly and out of control that they asked the whole party to leave? Whose child did you fall on during their summer picnic? Whose wife did you inform that you'd seen him shagging her friend at university, four years before they met? At whose toddler's birthday party did you use the C-word, making the boy's ninety-four-year-old grandma cry, actually cry? Shall I go on?' His voice broke away in sobs as he folded forward, the strength finally leaving him.

'All these people...' He swallowed. 'All these people that made up our life. Our friends! One by one, you've driven them all away because you drink too much. You drink too much!' he shouted, wiping his nose and his tears. 'And I should have said it a long time ago, but I've covered for you, made excuses for you, lied for you! Because I loved you.' He shook his head and leant forward on the table. 'But I can't do it any more. I can't. I won't.'

David stood up straight, took a deep breath and looked at his wife. 'It ends now. It ends. I haven't wanted to see the truth; I've chosen you over everyone, over every person who has told me that you are toxic, that you have a problem. I've dropped them and stuck by your side, for your sake and for the sake of our little girl. But enough is enough. This morning it was as if the filter fell from my eyes and I saw what everyone else sees. And I am done.' He raised his palms and let them fall by his sides.

'Please! David! I—'

'Stop, just stop.' He shook his head, disgusted. 'It's too late for that. There is nothing that you can say and there is nothing I want to hear. It's done.'

Turning on his heel, he scrunched his way over the broken china, walked out into the hallway and closed the front door behind him.

Romilly shivered as she stared at the pile on the floor. She remembered sitting in John Lewis holding a side plate in each hand, trying to choose between two patterns, one edged with a delicate double silver line and the other with a tiny bird and leaf pattern in relief. 'You really don't care, do you?' he'd observed and she'd shaken her head. 'Plates is plates.'

'I don't think I have ever loved you more,' he'd said. And he'd meant it. Romilly let her eyes fall to the china now lying smashed on the tiles and her tears finally came. It was done and it was her that had done it.

With an aching heart and words of regret spilling from her mouth, she crept from the kitchen, carefully avoiding the mess on the floor, wary of cutting her feet. She sobbed as she stepped into the hallway, opened the cupboard door and reached for her wellington boot. She turned it upside down, letting the bottle of vodka fall into her palm with a satisfying thud.

Celeste

I wouldn't say that I was fully aware of what was going on, but I knew that something was odd in my house. I started staying overnight with my friend Amelia and her family, and it's like with anyone, you don't realise how weird your own family is until you go and stay with another, and then you realise that everyone does things differently.

Amelia's mum didn't make her clean her teeth before bed, which I thought was the best thing in the world! At home I used to hate having to leave the warm duvet, where I'd been having a story or just playing with my toys, to go and stand on the cold bathroom floor and clean my teeth. But my dad was a stickler for it. Being at Amelia's was like a holiday, an adventure. Her mum used to kiss me goodnight and tuck me in when she did Amelia and she smelt of talcum powder and cooking, unlike my own mum, who smelt of chewing gum and something sour.

I can remember telling Nanny Pat years later that I never cleaned my teeth before bedtime when I stayed with my friend and she said something to the effect that they were bad parents. This makes me laugh now. They might not have made Amelia clean her teeth, but her mum never got so pissed she lay unconscious on the floor and her dad wasn't going to give himself a bloody hernia through trying to fake happiness and paint on a smile every day, even when his whole world was tumbling down around him.

In fact one of the things I love most about Alistair is his family. His parents are lovely, very warm and welcoming, and they don't ask me too many questions about Mum; they clearly aren't obsessed or fascinated with my situation. They make it easy for me to be with them and they love me and I love them. Dad sometimes calls Alistair's dad and they go for a pub lunch together. I like the idea of them being friends, it just makes everything straightforward. I'm very lucky really.

Fifteen

She stared at the mini whiteboard with her name on it, or an attempt at her name. It read *Ronald Wells*, which was close enough. 'I think that might be me.' She pointed at the sign and bobbed her head at the man with the green padded gilet and the inscrutable expression.

He gave a stiff nod and lifted her suitcase. 'Willkommen.' He was polite but cool as he grabbed the handle and led her out into the early morning air and to a waiting minibus, for which she was the only passenger. She chose a seat midway back, against the window, and wrapped her coat around her form as the vehicle pulled out onto the road.

The drive to the lakeside clinic took them along mountain ridges and down country roads. The bright blue Austrian sky was pierced by rows and rows of closely planted, snow-topped evergreens that reminded her of arrows pointing upwards. Romilly wound down the window and breathed deeply. The air was so pure, it was how she imagined the air in heaven might taste: sweet, clear and beautiful. It was like imbibing goodness. She blew into her cupped hand and sniffed at her breath; it smelt predominantly of mint, with only the faintest trace of vodka discernible to a knowing nose.

She hadn't tried to form a picture of where she was heading and anyway her imagination could not have prepared her for the magnificent sight that greeted her. The vast lake was so broad that on this cold morning, with a haze of fog hovering on its surface, she couldn't clearly see the other side. What she could see, however, were the large wooden houses along its shoreline, with their high apex roofs and prettily carved balconies and window boxes. The houses were set in generous plots containing outbuildings, wood stores, boat sheds and vegetable beds. Romilly noticed that the plots didn't seem to be fenced off; it wasn't obvious where one property ended and the next began, which made the place feel friendly, communal, as if there were literally no barriers to being neighbours. An image of Sara flashed into her brain.

Long wooden jetties protruded from each piece of land into the lake. Some had fibreglass tenders tied to them, sitting high in the water; others had canoes upturned and drying out in the morning air. One or two had a pair of chairs at the end, facing outwards, which immediately conjured thoughts of long, lazy summer days. Romilly pictured herself watching the sun rise and set over the hypnotic water and in that fanciful imagining; David was by her side, where he had always been. It was breathtakingly beautiful; like a scene from a calendar, she thought.

Barely a ripple disturbed the surface of the lake. Its reflection was immaculate, as if someone was holding up a pane of glass to the reeds and spiky grasses that grew in clumps along the banks and around the jetty piles. Even at this early hour, couples were out briskly walking the path that encircled the water, kitted out in close-fitting Lycra and thermal gloves and hats, with long ski poles looped around their wrists. To Romilly, they looked impossibly happy and healthy, lifting their poles high by way of greeting and smiling widely as they called 'Morgen!' or 'Gruß Gött!' at each other. She glanced briefly at the lakeside Bäckerei but could summon no enthusiasm for the breads and pastries advertised on their handwritten signs; she was in no mood for organic rye bread with plum compote, poppy seed and hazelnut strudel or even a Viennese coffee. She wasn't in the mood for much.

Would a few weeks at the Rechtsmittel Klinik restore her appetite, her health, her marriage? It was a potential lifeline at least, Romilly reminded herself. And she had Sylvia to thank for it, which had come as a big surprise. When David had thrown in the towel, it was Sylvia who'd talked him round. Instead of the 'I told you so' reaction Romilly had expected, her mother-in-law had insisted that David give their relationship another go. She'd berated her son for giving up after just one attempt at treatment. Would he have walked away so fast if Romilly had been suffering from a different illness, she'd asked; if she'd developed a physical condition that rendered her useless and needy? Of course he wouldn't! Romilly had only been able to stare at the woman who was shouting her corner when she had no voice of her own. She knew that she would always, always be grateful.

The clinic that Sylvia had found and paid for was an ugly concrete splat on the otherwise picture-perfect Carinthian landscape of southern Austria. It reminded Romilly of a 1950s low-rise office block, the sort that in Britain usually housed a local government department. She stared at the abundance of concrete and the large sliding metal-framed windows that she instinctively knew would be screwed shut. Its anomalousness brought to mind what one of her uni professors had said of a similarly ugly building in Bristol. 'Ah, but just think, Miss Shepherd,' he'd intoned as he gestured out of the window at the fine Bath stone architecture of Clifton, 'you are inside looking out and surely it would be far worse to be outside looking in? Fortunately for you, this building is not part of your landscape, it is theirs!' It gave her comfort to think of that now. *Miss Shepherd. Whatever happened to her?*

She placed her hands against her thighs to try and stem their shake, thanked her silent driver and went inside. The interior was a little better than the outside; it was still bland, gloomy and dated, but at least it was spotless. The straight lines and fuss-free minimalism of its original seventies decor made it look strangely up-to-date, which made her suddenly think of her dad; she gulped down a tear as she pictured him in his shed, hoarding once-fashionable walnut-veneer wardrobes and doors, adamant in his certainty that, like everything else, their distinctive grain would come back into fashion one day.

A young girl with piercing blue eyes and a blonde plait roped on top of her head showed Romilly to her quarters. 'Your room.' She stretched out her arm as she stated the obvious. 'You unpack and then you have induction.' Her tone was cold, officious. And with that she was gone.

Romilly looked at the dark green linoleum floor, which she was sure would stick to her bare feet on cold mornings. A low, single bed was pushed into a corner, its garish orange bedspread the only splash of colour against the depressing magnolia walls. A narrow Formica-topped table with two slatted shelves beneath it sat against the wall opposite and in a nook between the wall and the window stood an open-fronted wardrobe with four plastic hangers.

Sitting on the bed, still wearing her coat and with her back against the wall, Romilly thought of David. She heard his angry tone during their row, recalled the cold, forced hug he'd given her when he'd left her at the gate earlier that day. Again she saw the expression of disgust on his face as he'd made her look in the mirror. She thought of Celeste, her darling girl, and her face crumpled in tears. She pictured the two of them lying on their tummies, dipping sticks into the pondweed at Canford Park, smiling at the mayflies that hovered over the water as the sun glinted off their wings. 'I miss you. I miss you, baby, and I'm sorry. I want to come home. I want to come home,' she whispered, hoping that her words might drift across land and sea and fall into the ears of her little girl, who right about that time would be having her morning break at school and making up a dance routine with her friends or simply running around. Her heart lurched at the prospect of not seeing her for weeks. It felt like a sentence.

'Hello!' a woman boomed from the hallway. She knocked briefly on the door as she entered. She was solid. Her arms, revealed where her sleeves were rolled to the elbows, were like hams. Her complexion shone with a rosy glow and her eyes were bright. She was tall too, six foot at least, and she wore white clogs, white trousers, a pale denim shirt and a white cloth apron. Her dark hair was twisted into a bun. A man stood behind her, partially obscured, a doctor or nurse, judging by his upside-down watch and similar medical attire.

'I'm Ulli and this is Ralph. We are your coordinators, and so, welcome!' The woman smiled. 'How was your journey?' Her accent turned the 'j' into a 'ch'.

'Fine, thanks.' Romilly sniffed up her tears.

'It's a big step for you, being here, being away from home.' Ulli closed her eyes briefly in a gesture of understanding.

Romilly nodded. Yes it was.

'But it's good that you are here, and when you go home you will feel like a million dollars!' She gave another smile.

I don't want to feel like a million dollars, I just want to feel like Ponytail Mum. I want to feel normal. I want to not feel so crap. I want David to love me again. I want to be there for my daughter.

'So!' Ulli shouted. 'First we need to get you settled and we need to check your things, is that okay?'

'I can unpack.' Romilly glanced up at Ralph, who had stepped forward.

'We are happy to do it,' he offered, unsmiling.

'It's just a precaution,' Ulli said.

The Pineapple had been swankier, but the check-in procedure at both clinics was the same. Romilly watched as Ralph methodically felt his way through her clothing and opened the bottles in her toiletries bag, sniffing at the synthetic apple and peachy scents of her shampoo and conditioner.

'Okay.' Ulli smiled, satisfied. 'We'll give you half an hour to settle and then we'll come back to take you to the Med Centre, where we will start your medication and talk you through what to expect during your stay.' She nodded briefly and left the room, with Ralph following in her wake.

Romilly hopped from the bed, closed the door and turned the key in the lock. She reached down into her pocket where the lining had been cut away and pulled the hem up, enabling her to feel around inside it. Her eyes blinked in blissful relief as her searching fingers closed around the three miniature bottles of vodka she had snaffled from the plane. The thin silver metal lid gave a satisfying snap as she twisted it off. Placing the little round neck against her bottom lip, she felt the familiar euphoric lift in her stomach, welcoming the medicine that made everything feel better, gave her clarity. She popped the other two bottles into her snap-lock plastic bag and, with a silent vote of thanks to Gemma at The Pineapple, stashed them in the cistern behind the loo.

At the Med Centre, Ulli indicated for Romilly to sit on a plastic chair, one of seven lined up in the corridor along a glass wall. 'Dr Nagel will be with you soon.' Ulli nodded and left her to ponder the neat alpine rockery in the centre of the adjacent courtyard.

A door opened and a man in his early fifties took a seat along from her. 'It's like waiting outside the headmaster's office, isn't it?' he joked. He had a British accent, but some of his vowels had a distinctly American twang.

'I don't know, I never had to wait outside the headmaster's office.' *I was good at school, I was clever. My problems started after I'd left.*

'I bet you were a prefect. I can tell.'

Romilly turned to look at the emaciated man, who had rather laughably spiked up his thinning hair with wet-look gel and carefully crafted his pencil-thin beard to run along his jawline, up his tanned cheeks and above his top lip. He wore a large silver skull ring on his index finger, battered cowboy boots, leather jeans and a tight black blazer with a white T-shirt underneath. His posture – one leg stretched out in front of him, not caring less who it might trip up, and the other tucked under the chair – made him look cocky. With a stab to her gut, she wondered what David would say about his appearance.

'I was,' she confirmed, hoping that this might put an end to their conversation.

'I've just done the old whizz test.' He angled his head towards a room off the courtyard.

'The what?'

'Urine test. They make you whizz in a beaker. Have you just arrived?' He twisted to look at her.

'How often do they do that?' She was aware of the quake in her voice.

'Every day.'

She felt her eyelids flutter. *Shit!*

'Morning, Mrs Wells. Please come through.' Dr Nagel stood at the open door and beckoned for her to enter. He was wearing a white coat over his black trousers and white shirt and must have been about her age. 'Please take a seat.' He gestured to a chair in front of his desk.

'So, all a bit strange for you, I expect?' he asked kindly.

She nodded and picked at her thumbnail.

'The first thing I need to ask is that you sign this form.' He brandished a clipboard in her direction and handed her a pen. 'It grants us permission to treat you and it also includes a confidentiality clause stating that there will be no sharing of pictures or events on social media and that details of all treatments, classes, interactions with and identities of other residents will remain confidential.'

She looked up at him. 'Why would anyone want to put on social media that they're here or talk about anyone they met here?' She pushed her glasses up, out of habit rather than necessity.

'You'd be surprised!' He laughed. 'Have you had a drink today?' His tone had changed.

'Yes.' She nodded, figuring it was better to be straight.

'Okay. Well, starting from tomorrow we will conduct a daily urine test and if we find the presence of alcohol or any non-prescription drugs, that will be the end of your time here. We run a popular programme and quite frankly we need everyone to be on board with the treatment. Otherwise it's just a waste of your time and ours. We can help you, Romilly, but you need to want to help yourself.'

She scrawled her name on the dotted line and stared at him, wondering if every unit and every treatment started with the same phrase.

The first thing she saw when she returned to her room was an envelope stuck to the door with sticky tape. Peeling it off, she read and reread the short note that had been folded inside. It informed her that her room had been inspected during her absence and that a package had been removed from inside the toilet cistern and destroyed. As a result she was being given a warning; one more violation would mean that she would be asked to leave the programme.

Romilly sank down on her bed and cried again, pointless

tears of longing and regret, wishing that, like Dorothy, she could click her heels and be home. Not that she could be certain of a similarly warm welcome. She looked at the scrunched-up note in her palm. Now she properly knew what it felt like to be waiting outside the headmaster's office. Tilting over, she laid her head on the thin pillow. Thoughts of her family evaporated. She hoped for sleep, prayed for oblivion, but it was as if the booze spectre had placed its dark hood over her head. It was all she could think about, all she wanted.

The routine at Rechtsmittel was very similar to that at The Pineapple, only here she was being medicated. And it helped. During the supervised lakeside hikes and at mealtimes she mixed a little and made two new friends. Leather trouser guy, it turned out, was called Lenny and though originally from the UK now lived in Miami, where he clung to the coattails of those who clung to the coattails of the rich and famous. Romilly asked him if he was a rock star, wondering if that was what had prompted Dr Nagel's speech on anonymity and privacy. Lenny laughed loudly. 'Yes, I am a rock star every single night between 10 p.m. and when I pass out, and I don't even need an audience!' That told her pretty much all she needed to know.

Her other new friend was Sam, a lady from the Home Counties who she estimated to be in her fifties and who was on her sixth stint in rehab. During one group session, as they all sat on the floor in a circle, Sam openly confessed that she had drunk away her house, her looks, her job and her self-respect, gaining quite a reputation in her home town in the process. Most devastatingly, she'd also lost contact with her only son. It wasn't until she came up for air, eight years later, that she properly realised the true state of her life and by then it was too late. As she herself put it, 'Life had moved on; everyone, everything had changed, apart from me. And now what does my future look like? I can't see one a lot of the time. I mean, I've missed his birthdays, his eighteenth, his exams. Maybe he's driving? Maybe I'm a gran?' She gave a small laugh to hide her anguish. 'I'm forty-two and I feel finished.'

Romilly stared at her with her mouth open, shocked to discover her real age. She thought Sam's words were the saddest she had ever heard and was thankful that she wasn't like that.

Dr Nagel seemed to be watching her more than the garrulous Sam and when the session drew to a close, he beckoned her over. Taking up the chair next to him, she sat politely, a little uneasy at having been singled out.

'How are you doing, Romilly?' His smile was fleeting.

'I'm doing okay. Looking forward to getting home eventually, obviously. I miss my daughter very much, but I think it's beautiful here and... I like the walks around the lake.' Nerves were making her babble.

Dr Nagel tapped his fountain pen on the hard-backed A4 book that sat on his legs. He stared at her, his expression questioning. 'This is your second time in therapy?'

She nodded.

'Can I ask you a question?' He crossed his legs, as if settling in for a chat.

'Of course.' She gave a tentative smile but received none in return.

'How did you find it today? What do you think of the people you have seen here in the group session?' He folded his arms, with one hand coming to rest on his chin. With his arms and legs twisted together, he looked like a little human puzzle, which was ironic, she thought, as it was his job to try and figure everyone out, crack the code.

She looked at the window and recalled a few of the faces. 'They all seem very nice,' she said evasively.

'Yes, they are. Do you think you are like them? Or rather, do you think that they are like you?'

Almost instantly she shook her head. 'No, not really,' she whispered conspiratorially.

'You don't see anything in common with them?' He leant forward.

She hesitated, trying to think what it was he wanted to hear.

He didn't wait for her response. 'Let's phrase it a different way. Why are you not like these people? What makes them different to you?'

She decided to come clean, having the distinct feeling that he would keep her there until she told him the truth. 'I don't think I am like these people, no.' She shook her head. There, she'd said it. 'They are addicts, alcoholics, and it's very sad, obviously. I can't stand listening to stories like Sam's or the man who spoke—'

'Wilhelm,' he prompted.

'Yes, Wilhelm. It's horrible to see them distressed and to see them struggle like that, but I'm not like them. I'm not. I'm a scientist; I know how the brain and the body work and I've just hit a bump in the road. I'm grateful to be here, but I'm confident that I'll be back on track soon.' She adjusted her glasses and returned his stare, trying to keep the tremor from her voice.

Dr Nagel uncrossed his arms. It was a second or two before he spoke. 'Wilhelm is a leading academic surgeon in Stuttgart. Do you think he understands the brain and the body? Or what about Markus? He was a test pilot – intelligent and with super-fast reactions. Sam was an interior designer. Lotte, a concert pianist. I could go on. The point I'm making is no one is immune from this disease. Alcoholism. That's what these people are: alcoholics. It's a disease and in my opinion one you are also suffering from.'

Whether consciously or not, she shook her head slightly. 'I'm not that bad,' she whispered.

Dr Nagel stiffened. 'Do you ever feel guilty about your drinking?'

There was a slight pause, not long enough for her to form a response, but long enough for a devastating image of David to appear, hurling their china on to the kitchen floor.

'Are you ever dishonest about how much you drink? Does your drinking cause others to be concerned? Have you ever drunk yourself into oblivion and had no memory of the episode? Can you take a sip, put the lid back on and leave the bottle?'

She stared at him, her muscles tense, her top lip dotted with sweat.

'How bad do you think it has to be, Romilly, before you qualify?'

She shrugged, feeling like a child that had been caught out, disliking the man and his manner.

'I see people like you all the time and the difference between those that get better and those who just go through the motions is the extent to which those individuals are willing to own their problem, see that they need help and accept the help they're given.'

I know I need help. I've hit some lows, but I can do this! I'm strong and I have a hell of a lot to get stronger for. This is just a bump in the road.

The Romilly that returned from Austria was determined. She had stood in front of the mirror at the clinic with fists clenched, jaw set and a steely look of determination in her eyes. She would not drink alcohol. She would not. It got her into all sorts of trouble and she knew that their lives would be better if she didn't go near it. She made promises. She promised to make it up to David. Her drunken infidelity, the details of which he had teased out of her, sat in her throat like a bitter lump, as if visible to all and tainting everything she tasted. She hated, truly detested what had happened and wished that she could rewind that night, politely decline Sara's invitation and stay at home with her family. Her whole body shuddered if she let herself remember waking on that morning... How different things were going to be from now on. Even the idea of this new beginning sent a leap of happiness around her stomach. She couldn't wait to get home and start afresh. With distance, she could see that Sara was not the kind of friend she should spend time with or have around her daughter. She would be polite if they did bump into each other, but otherwise she'd keep contact to a minimum.

Romilly was as good as her word, arriving home with a clear head and a fiercely determined attitude. It was like shaking off a foggy veil and it felt great! She watched the taxi trundle away down the cul-de-sac, then she turned to the front door. David opened it before she had a chance to knock and his face broke into a wide smile, as if for a second he had forgotten and was as delighted as ever to see his Bug Girl. As quickly as he had smiled, his expression changed, became stony. Reality had flooded in. 'Come in.' He stood back, as if inviting in an unwelcome guest, and that was exactly how she felt.

The best way she could describe relations with David was that they were thawing. She didn't blame him; she often wondered what it would feel like if it had been her having breakfast that morning when the key finally found the lock and their whole world was thrown upside down. He had started to look her in the eye and now ate his meals with her and Celeste at the kitchen table, not hidden away in his study any more. She knew he was trying hard for the sake of his family to rid his mind of the memory of her bitten neck, her unkempt hair and that distinctive smell. She'd caught him once or twice, staring out of the kitchen window, mid task – the tap might be running to rinse a cup, or the dishwasher hanging open awaiting powder, but he was distracted, quietly gazing out into the garden in deep thought. About what she could only guess, but judging from the slope of his shoulders, the look on his face and his air of sadness, it was something that filled him with regret.

What she didn't know was how far back that regret extended. To a time before that terrible morning, certainly. But was he also wishing away their early married life, the times he'd laughed off her antics with their friends? Did he even regret dropping to his knee on the suspension bridge, heedless of the tourists trying to squeeze past them on the narrow path? Even the possibility of this sent her into a spiral of self-doubt and anxiety and it took every ounce of her strength not to jump in the car or run four doors up in search of her medicine.

The mums at the school gate seemed pleased to see her back on the school run, no doubt fully briefed on events by Amelia's mum. Frankly, what the parents at Merrydown Middle School thought of her was the least of her worries, and anyway, those in glass houses should never throw stones. Romilly was sure there had to be other mothers out there who came close to losing it after their nightly bottle of Chardonnay in front of the telly.

Celeste no longer gave her so many wide-eyed stares and for this Romilly was grateful, confident that she had very little inkling about the state of affairs. Her daughter was too preoccupied with playing games under her bed or giggling with her friends to fully understand, but that said, there was a certain distance between them now. Romilly tried hard to come across as responsible and reassuring, but she knew she'd let Celeste down and it was inevitable that her daughter would be a bit wary of her.

One morning, a few months after her return from Austria, Romilly was making her second cup of tea of the day when the phone in the kitchen rang. She wondered if it might be Mike Gregson. She was looking forward to his call. They had spoken a couple of days earlier and he'd said they would catch up soon. She knew he had done all he could to smooth things over with the powers that be, but she also knew that, like a leaky dam, there was only so much he could do to hold things off and time was against her. The bosses weren't overly happy about her long periods of unplanned absence. Mike had hinted that they had a replacement lined up and were simply toeing the legal line to make sure they handled her case properly, wary of any repercussions should she feel she had been improperly ousted. Even though she wasn't on full pay, it was more about them being a pair of hands short in the lab than anything else. She decided she would tell Mike she'd come back to work after the weekend. She knew the routine would be good for her and it would send David the right message that things were slowly getting back to normal.

'Romilly, it's me.'

'Hey, Mum.' She tried to keep the sigh of irritation from her voice, not willing to be subtly dressed down by her mum's hints and inferences again. The way she disguised her notes of caution, suggestions for recovery and handy parallels that demonstrated just how lucky she was left Romilly feeling quite depressed. Even her mum's downbeat tone had the ability to filter the joy from an otherwise regular conversation.

'I was thinking that lunch on Sunday would be nice. Shall we come to you, or is that a bit too much? Are you up to it? Would it be better if you came here? The girls thought it might be best, as long as you don't drive, because that would worry your dad to death after everything...'

Romilly counted the seconds of silence, not sure whether her mum had finished wittering or whether there was more to come. She appeared to be done.

'Can I let you know, Mum? Lunch would be lovely. I know Celeste would love to see you all, but I just want to check with David.' *I want to see if he can stand being in a car with me for that journey, if he can stand being with me for a whole afternoon without respite, trapped in your cosy house.*

'Ah, and we'd love to see her, the poor little thing...'

I get it, Mum, a poor little thing because she landed me as a mother and not Ponytail Mum. She swallowed her tears, feeling a rush of love for her little girl, counting the hours till it was time to collect her. She was keen to wrap her in a hug, as though the regular squeezing and streaming of words of affection could make up for the feeling in her gut that she had let Celeste down.

Pat was still talking. 'And yes of course check with David, but tell him I'm making hotpot, you know he loves my hotpot, and if he's good, bread-and-butter pudding for afters.'

'I will.' She nodded.

'And how are you doing, miss? You sound a bit glum.'

I wasn't until you rang. 'No, not glum. I'm fine. You know...'

'Yes, well...' She paused.

Romilly could hear her considering what pearl of wisdom to let drop from her mouth.

'Oh sorry, Mum, that's the front door. I have to go. I'll speak to you in a bit.' And she hung up, just like that, not prepared to hear more of her mum's words, not today.

Romilly fell onto the sofa and had a cry. Her mum was right, Celeste deserved better. She closed her eyes and tried to recapture the feeling of positivity that she'd felt when she'd looked in the mirror at the clinic; she remembered the breathing technique that seemed to slow everything down, including her cravings, and she recalled the way she'd walked tall around the lake, breathing evenly and picturing a healthy future when she was drink-free and happy.

The phone in the kitchen rang again. Romilly wiped her face and took a deep breath before she lifted the receiver, hoping it wasn't her mum again and praying it was Mike. She needed to get out of this rut, she needed to pull herself together and get on with her life.

'Hello?' She kept her tone formal, businesslike.

'Red! Hello, gorgeous. It's Jasper and guess what? I'm outside your house!' He laughed.

Celeste

One of the worst days was the day she didn't collect me from school. I'd made a cake and it was a bit of a disaster – burnt on one side, collapsed on the other and with ugly blobs of caramel-coloured icing slapped on to cover the damage. But I thought Mum would like it anyway and I had it all ready to take home on a tray.

We had a system where parents and guardians had to come into the classroom at the end of the school day and sign you out. That day I waved off all my friends one by one until the classroom was empty except for my teacher, Miss Clements, and me. I wasn't so worried about the fact that Mum was late, it was more the way Miss Clements kept sighing and looking at her watch and then her phone, as though she wanted to be somewhere else and I was annoying her. It made me feel awkward and embarrassed and it wasn't like her. I saw another side to her that day and that made me feel worse, as though Miss Clements had lost some of her sparkle.

We waited about an hour and it felt like an eternity. She took me to the school office, which was both thrilling and petrifying; you usually only went there if you were dropping off the register or if someone was sick. I sat on a padded chair that swivelled round, while she tried calling the house and both of my parents' mobiles. Eventually Miss Clements put me in her car and drove me home. I sat in the back seat with my enormous cake on my lap, wishing I could disappear so she wouldn't keep tapping her thumb on the steering wheel and saying 'Come on, come on...' every time we stopped at a red light.

When we got to the end of our driveway she pulled a funny face and took a good long look at our big, comfortable house. She went ahead and rang the doorbell. A man I had never seen before answered it; he had blonde floppy hair and was quite young. He was smiling and grateful and apologetic all at once and I could tell Miss Clements was flattered by the exuberant thanks and the way the man crushed her to him in a hug. He was well dressed and well spoken and Miss Clements seemed to have got some of her sparkle back as she ushered me up the driveway with her hand on the narrow back of my little red cardigan. I carried my cake in my outstretched arms.

I walked past the man, who ruffled my hair, like he knew me. He stood and waved to Miss Clements.

'Sless... Sless...' That's what I heard coming from the sofa in the TV room. I walked in and Mum was lying on the cushions in her pyjamas. She couldn't say my name properly and her eyes were closed and her head kept tipping backwards until she would jolt forwards as if trying to keep awake.

'Kissittoyourmummynow...' she slurred, puckering up as if she wanted a kiss.

I didn't want to kiss her. She stank. It was a grown-up smell of booze and bad breath and sweat. I shook my head and stood on the spot staring at her.

'Whathefucks wrongwithyou?' She sat up, toppled from

238

the sofa and crawled towards me on the floor, like she used to when we were playing horses. I could see down the front of her pyjama top and she wasn't wearing a bra.

'Youdontfuckinwantokissmehey?' she slurred. Her eyebrows flew up as though she was trying to open her eyes, as though she was looking at me. I wondered if it was because she didn't have her glasses on, maybe that was why she was struggling. I searched all over the floor, which was strewn with cushions and plates and cans, thinking that if I could find her glasses and help her put them on, then she'd be able to see me, but I couldn't find them.

The man came in from the kitchen with an open bottle of wine. He swigged from the top and handed the bottle to Mum, who sat back on her haunches and did likewise. 'What's that?' He pointed at my cake.

I held up the tray so they could both see it.

Mum opened one eye and let out a loud cackle. 'What?' she screeched. 'Whatisit?'

The man sank down onto the sofa and he and Mum laughed and laughed. The two of them were bent double laughing at my cake, clutching at their stomachs and then pawing at each other for stability. I felt my cheeks go red and hot tears slid down my face. I wasn't crying because of what they said about my baking, I already knew it was rubbish. I cried because I thought Mum would pretend it was great and tuck into it, but she didn't. She was laughing at me. It was mean. I've never forgotten that.

'Is it a shit?' He laughed. 'It is, isn't it! It's a big fat lump of shit! You have actually brought us some shit!'

This sent my mum into overdrive, laughing so hard she placed her fingers between her legs and screamed, 'StopstopstopJasper!

239

Ivewetmyself! Jasperivepissedmyself!' She batted his arm as she roared. Sure enough, a dark, wet stain spread across her grey cotton pyjama bottoms and down her legs.

I didn't like it one bit. I was scared and that felt wrong, because I was in my house but I was scared. 'I want my dad.' I remember saying that over and over before finding the courage to leave the room. 'I want my dad. I want my dad.'

I lay in the gap under my bed until it became hot and uncomfortable and so I sat on the bed and waited. Dad did come home eventually. I heard him shouting, so angry. He tore round the TV room like a tornado. He was furious and he was swearing. I'd never heard Dad swear in anger before then, not properly, but that day he used every conceivable word, and it wasn't only what he said but his tone. He sounded like a stranger. I didn't hear Mum make a sound.

He was out of breath when he came upstairs, as though he'd been rushing. He told me he'd come hurtling down the motorway to Bristol the moment he'd got Miss Clements' message. I was still in my uniform, sitting in the corner in the dark. He clicked on my bedside lamp and sat down. I saw his fake smile, a smile for my benefit, and even though I knew he was putting it on, I was glad that he was trying. He stroked my hair as he cuddled me.

'Do you want some supper?' he whispered.

I shook my head. I didn't want anything apart from to rewrite the day and make it happen differently.

He rocked me gently and told me that everything was okay. It didn't feel okay, not at all, it felt about as far from okay as it could get. He pointed to the tray on the floor and asked me what it was and so I told him. 'It's a big fat lump of shit.'

He pulled away and held me by the arms and he shouted at me that I was never to use words like that, *never*! He left me alone and I lay on my bed feeling the loneliest I ever had. It was like everything was messed up and I was scared. First Miss Clements and then my mum and then my dad. It was like they had all been turned inside out and I could see their ugly insides.

I kicked off my school shoes but stayed in my white socks and grey pinafore with my red cardigan buttoned up. I was too scared to go to sleep.

That was a horrible day. I saw worse, heard worse, but that one day sticks in my memory for so many reasons.

Sixteen

'Cup of tea?' Sara croaked from the landing.

'Thanks,' Romilly answered from beneath the duvet.

'I've got a banging headache.' Sara giggled as though this were a badge of honour, proof that a good night had been had by all. Romilly remembered announcing the same thing with the same undeniable note of triumph. She had been sixteen.

Sara hummed as she skipped down the stairs. Romilly knew her friend was over the moon to have her staying with her, guessing correctly that not only did Sara find Romilly's tangled life a good diversion from her own worries, but she was also very glad of the company. For her, however, the situation was as embarrassing as it was distressing. She resented her friend's cheery optimism, as though this was some kind of student gap-year adventure and not a tempo-rary safety net while her whole world fell apart. Romilly could only really cope when she was drunk and didn't have to think about the fact that there was only the space of a football pitch between her and her family; her family in her home, the home which she'd been thrown out of. She was torn between hating her dependency on the woman who she knew was a bad influence and feeling eternally grateful that she at least had somewhere to go. She closed her eyes and wished Sara would stop humming.

Smacking her lips, she could tell she had slept with her mouth open and had probably been snoring as the back of her throat was horribly dry and her tongue thick. Her spit had a rancid bitterness to it. She tried again not to think of her daughter, breakfasting with her dad only four doors away, with her hair in bunches and her bag packed ready for school. She ached for her. Instead, she buried her face in the pillow on the spare bed in her friend's house and let herself cry.

David had been quite clear. She couldn't precisely recall how she and Jasper had ended up on the driveway, him with a bloodied face and her in her pyjamas with her trainers by her side on the grass. And she couldn't remember the finer detail, but she did remember the sense of panic, the shouting, the feeling of utter desolation, as she walked up the cul-de-sac, barefoot with her trainers in her hand. Mr and Mrs Rashid had watched her, and she might have shouted at them. This piece of information was new, actually. She winced as a few more snippets from that evening began to reveal themselves, as they often did days later, bursting through the fog of confusion like a magician's assistant from a box, only instead of a round of applause these came with a dollop of shame and regret.

What had she said to the lovely Rashids? She wasn't sure, but what she could remember clearly was knocking on her own front door the following day. David had opened it a few inches and had spoken through the gap, like she was selling something of which he had no need or was talking about a faith in which he had no interest.

'I don't want Celeste to get upset,' he'd growled, 'so just go.' He hadn't even waited for her to ask if she could come in.

'David... David, please, I'm—' *I love you! I love you so much, proper love!*

'You're what?' he spat. 'Sorry? Is that what you are, Rom? Are you sorry? Again?'

'I just—' *I want to come home! I need you!*

'You just what?'

'I'm—' *I'm sorry! I am!*

'Here's the thing. I'm sorry too. Sorry I ever thought you might be able to change, because I was wrong, you can't. And all I want to do now is protect my daughter.'

Our daughter... 'I love her.' She couldn't stop the sob that was building in her chest.

'She was so frightened. Can you imagine what it must be like for a little girl to have to come home with her teacher and to find a strange man and her mother so drunk that she couldn't stand and then pissed all over the room?' He shook his head. 'The carpet, everything stinks!' He spoke through gritted teeth. 'She is nine years old and I'm damned if that's how she's going to be brought up. You forgot to pick her up from school! You were so drunk, you...' He wiped his brow, exasperated. 'There is no point, Romilly. No point whatso-ever. What exactly is it you want?'

'I want to see Celeste.' She sobbed.

'Not going to happen. Anything else?' His tone was firm, resolute.

'I don't have any clothes or anything,' she managed through her tears.

'I'll send a bag up when I can. I saw you stagger up to your mate's, is that where you're staying?' He looked up the cul-de sac.

She nodded.

He gave a wry laugh. 'Figures.'

And then he shut the door, leaving her standing on the driveway staring at the front door. She laid her hand on it, remembering entering their home that very first time. *'Come on. Together!'* Her fingers flexed as she recalled the feel of her hand inside his and the way they'd both smiled as she'd placed the new key in the unfamiliar lock and turned. She thought about her little girl on the other side, probably in her pyjamas and ready for bed, teeth cleaned and fresh from her bath. Romilly wrapped her arms around her trunk and turned, ready to trundle up the road to Sara's. The sooner she could get wasted, the better. Then, for tonight at least, she might be able to forget.

About to walk away, she paused and gazed again at the front door with the brass furniture that she had chosen and polished. She wondered how long it would be before she was welcome on the other side again, if ever.

That encounter had been two days ago and still no bag had been delivered. Romilly slopped around Sara's house in her pyjamas and when they were in the wash she borrowed a pair from her friend. It mattered little to her; in fact, wearing pyjamas helped her feel like she was poorly, fluey, suffering, and at some level this helped absolve her of responsibility for her drinking.

It was late morning when, from the sofa, Romilly heard a knock on the door. It woke her up; she'd been snoozing there since the night before, too sloshed to make it up the stairs. Her head ached and her vision was fuzzy. She popped her glasses on. At the sound of David's voice, she sat upright.

'Can you give her this?' His tone was no less cold than it had been the other night.

She jumped from the sofa and hurled herself into the hallway. 'David! I need to speak to you. I... I just need a minute, just to speak to you!'

He let his eyes rove over her pyjama top, which gaped with misfastened buttons. Then he ground his teeth and turned to walk back down Sara's driveway.

'Don't ignore her, you prick! She has a right to half, you know. Fucking half! I should know! Been there, done that!' Sara laughed as she leant on the wall.

'Sara!' Romilly mouthed her disgust at the way her friend was speaking to her husband.

In a flash, David turned on his heel and raced back up the path. He stood with his face mere inches from Sara's as he snarled his words, his shoulders back, one foot forward, his index finger pointing in her face.

'You are a nasty piece of work. You know exactly what you're about, you know what you're doing and you know the damage you have caused. What had we done to deserve someone like you? What had Celeste? You are bitter, jealous and fucked up. It must have killed you to see what we had, how happy we were.'

'I want us to be happy, David...' Romilly seized on his words, talking with her hand outstretched as if reaching for him.

He turned his head briefly in her direction. 'We were,

Romilly. But that's finished.' He looked back at Sara, who was holding her stance without a flicker of remorse or fear at his words. 'You have been instrumental in helping my wife fuck up her life. We have a daughter, a little girl...' He stopped. 'And now I am only thinking about her, doing what's best for her and trying to keep her safe. Do not speak to me or my child again. Not one word. Do not look at us or I swear to God, I will be back and you have no idea what I am capable of. None at all.' His voice shook as he strode back down the pathway.

'David?' Romilly called after him. He carried on walking, without looking back. Romilly sank to the floor as she realised that for the first time since she was nineteen she did not have the beautiful David Arthur Wells to lean on.

Sara slammed the front door. 'I don't like being spoken to like that in my own home!' she snapped, arms folded. 'Who does he think he is?'

'He's just upset. It's... It's not his fault...' She instantly tried to justify the actions of her husband. 'You shouldn't have said that stuff about me getting half, I don't want it to come to that and if it did, I wouldn't want anything. I just want to go home.'

Sara stared at her and twisted her lower jaw. Her words, when delivered, were cool. 'I think, Rom... I think it's best if you don't stay here any more. I've been a good friend to you and you didn't defend me once, not once. Even now, you're like, "It's not his fault!"' She imitated Romilly's voice. 'I'd like you to go. I mean, not immediately. You should get changed and have a coffee first.' She flicked her blonde hair extensions over her shoulder and went in search of caffeine.

'I... I don't know where to go,' Romilly whispered as she was gripped by a new, all-consuming fear.

After packing her small bag and slipping her feet into her trainers, she closed the front door of Sara's house and skirted the shiny Mercedes in the driveway. Cautiously, she crept across to her own home and hovered at the end of the path, texting her husband, unsure if he would even read it. Then she hoisted her bag up onto her shoulder and walked up Stoke Hill towards the Downs, making sure to keep her head high and her step light, as if she was like any other woman out for a stroll and not foundering hopelessly, wondering where she might spend the night.

An hour later, clutching her bag to her chest, she tucked her hair behind her ears and stared anxiously at the café. Her face was glowing with the red-hot sweat of need; she'd had a vodka for breakfast and had stuffed the rest of the bottle into her handbag, ready to drink once this meeting was over. The tea room on the Downs was somewhere they had often stopped at for a cup of coffee or to get Celeste an ice cream mid walk, regardless of the weather. She had hoped that choosing a place that was familiar might help her nerves. It didn't, not even a bit. She approached the apron where the little metal chairs and tables were dotted around outside and fought the desire to vomit, she was so nervous. David looked up and saw her. He opened his mouth as if to speak but clearly couldn't think of the words and so instead he slowly pulled out the chair next to him, as if helping a relative who was elderly or infirm.

'Thank you for meeting me,' she whispered, trying to keep her eyes averted, staring at the concrete water tower across the grass and not letting him look directly at her, trying to hide. 'I... I'm sorry about the way Sara spoke to you.'

'You look terrible.' His voice was low, ignoring the reference to earlier, but there was no anger in it now, just pity, which was even harder to deal with. 'Can I get you something to eat?' he asked, coaxingly, like he'd used to do with Celeste.

'No. Thank you.' The thought of food sent bile rushing up into her throat. She swallowed.

'A cup of coffee then?'

'Yes, please.' She nodded. 'Black.' Even the idea of milk made her retch.

He returned to the table minutes later and placed the mug in front of her, along with three long sachets of sugar and a teaspoon. She looked up at him, wondering why he'd brought sugar when he knew she didn't take it. It made her feel like a stranger and it erased a little of their history. Not a little, in fact; a lot. One of the first things he'd done for her was make a cup of tea, and in times of sorrow or celebration they would always flick on the kettle. She couldn't guess the number of hot drinks he'd made her, but it had to be thousands.

'Thought you might like some sugar. I know you don't take it, but, you know, if you don't... don't want anything to eat...'

She smiled briefly, with relief and understanding. A small group of students, boys and girls in skinny jeans, trainers and hoodies, with messenger bags slung over their shoulders, jostled each other and roared their laughter as they ambled along the pavement towards the halls.

'Their whole lives ahead of them…' He watched them and narrowed his eyes.

'How is Celeste?' she whispered. She was still unable to meet his gaze; she was too distressed and embarrassed.

'As you'd expect, really.' His clipped tone gave little away.

'I will try, David. I promise. I will try and… sort myself out.'

'How will you?'

She opened her mouth to speak but realised she didn't have the answer. 'I…'

He tapped the tabletop. 'The thing is, Rom, you've been to two of the finest facilities, both of which promised great results, using quite different methods, but the one thing that was common to them both was that they felt you weren't ready to get better, that you didn't or couldn't see that you were ill. And that's the stumbling block, right there.' He shrugged. 'As far as I can see, you could spend months, years in those places, but until you know here…' He placed his hand on his head. 'And here…' He touched his heart. 'That you need help, then it's a waste of everyone's time and money.'

She nodded.

'And I can see you nodding, going through the motions, but I just don't feel it. Until you accept that you need proper help, I'm shit-scared I'll be coming home again to find my daughter a nervous wreck and my TV room covered in piss.'

She shook her head at the thought, wishing he would stop mentioning it.

He swivelled his head to stare at her, studying her features and letting his eyes travel over her hair. She felt her cheeks colour under his scrutiny and pushed her glasses up onto her nose.

Suddenly he reached into his bag beneath his chair and pulled out a bottle of vodka. He placed it on the table and twisted the label to face her. Her eyes flicked from his face to the bottle, thinking how good it would be to have that in her possession for that afternoon and night. It always gave her a small sense of calm to know that she had bottles waiting for her, and the lack of alcohol at her fingertips had the exact opposite effect, sending her into a state close to panic. It was a curious gift but one that she greatly appreciated, showing her he understood what she needed.

'Okay, Rom.' He turned to face her. 'I'm going to give you a choice. You have me and Celeste sitting here in front of you.' He pointed at his chest. 'And you have this bottle of vodka.' He touched his fingertips to the lid.

She looked from him to the bottle and back again.

'You can only have one today, but not both. Us.' Again he touched his chest. 'Or this.' He rested his hand on the neck of the bottle and she felt a flicker of panic that he might remove it. 'Which will you choose?'

She stared at the man she loved and knew that she owed him the truth. A truthful response to this simple question, but a choice that had repercussions she could only begin to imagine. She felt her face flush with sweat and her head shake with the tremor of longing. She spread her palm on the table and swallowed, letting her fingers creep towards her husband, picturing the two of them wrapped in a white sheet in the afterglow of love, on their bed, in their home, while their daughter slept soundly down the corridor... And then, as if guided by something stronger than her, she reached out and gripped the bottle, sliding it into her lap, from where she placed it in her handbag and laid it snugly next to its twin.

Romilly averted her gaze to the water tower again and wrapped her arms around her form, trying to muster some warmth and stop the shaking. When she looked back, David had his head in his hands and he was crying.

Celeste

When Mum disappeared, I was strangely relieved. I pestered Dad with questions, repeatedly asking if he knew when she would be back, and he was really patient with me. He must have thought it was because I couldn't wait to see her again, but the truth was I was afraid of her by then and I was afraid of being left alone with her. The last time I'd seen her, that horrendous day with the cake, she'd called me a fucking nightmare and looked at me in that awful, hard way she did when she was sloshed, like she only half recognised me. Like she hated me.

Every night when Dad kissed me goodnight and switched my light off, I'd say, 'If she comes back in the night, can you come in and wake me up?' He'd just nod. He looked so sad and so tired. I was terrified that I'd be having breakfast one day and look up and there she would be, a bit scruffy perhaps, like on that morning when she came home and Dad told me she'd been in the hospital looking after Sara.

Then, one Saturday, Dad was making scrambled eggs while I was messing about on the kitchen floor tiles. I had my earphones in and I was twirling, trying to turn in a complete circle and land facing where I'd started from. I didn't manage it, but I kept trying, thumping down on the floor and getting back up again.

After I'd done my last twirl before sitting down for breakfast I asked him again if Mum would be coming back today. I didn't want our nice morning to be ruined. But Dad had left the bread too long in the toaster and a thin swirl of black smoke curled up to the ceiling and set the smoke alarm off. It was a linked alarm system, so once one went off, they all did, all over the house. Suddenly there was horrible shrill beeping in every room.

Dad turned to me and lifted the spatula in his hand, using it like a baton to emphasise his point. He ignored the smoke, the burning toast, the eggs that had caught the bottom of the pan, the screeching alarm and the rhythmic thump of my landings, and he said, out of the blue, 'She's not coming home today and she won't be home tomorrow. She might not be home for months, maybe years. But if she is coming home, I promise I will tell you.' His hand shook and his eyes looked teary. 'But please, please, Celeste, stop asking me.'

So I learnt not to ask and when I stopped asking, she faded a little. Not completely, but enough that it all became a lot easier to bear. I was still anxious, though, and I used to wake in the middle of the night with my heart thumping fit to jump out of my chest. One of those sleepless nights, I even wished that she would die, and that my Dad would come and sit me down, and gently tell me that she was never coming home, not ever again. I still feel really bad about that. All these years later, it's still a memory that plays over and over in my mind.

Seventeen

Romilly had always had a job and she and David had worked out a system when they were fresh out of university whereby a portion of each salary went into a joint account to cover the mortgage, bills and household expenses and the rest was theirs to do what they liked with. Not that there was any financial secrecy. Their private accounts were transparent and holidays and other joint purchases would be paid for by whoever had their bankcard to hand. It was their way.

Romilly had fourteen hundred pounds in her bank account when she left the refuge of Sara's house. With the lack of any other immediate options and not sure what to do for the best, she checked into a modern high-rise hotel in Broadmead, central Bristol. This was to be her home for a few weeks while she made a plan. Everything in the place smelt of plastic, as though the bed, curtains, walls and all the other contents of the room were disposable, temporary. And in a sense they were.

She stayed in her room for the first thirty-six hours, doubling over and fighting for breath every time she pictured David crying or the way Sara had shouted at him. It felt easier not to think about it, so instead she tried to take stock of her dire situation, with the bottle of vodka as her companion. She lay staring at the ceiling, replaying the many times she had driven round the roundabout outside the window, never properly looking up, never considering for a single second that this was where she might one day lay her head, alone.

She called her mum and gave her an edited version of what had happened. Pat sighed a lot, tutted and eventually offered, 'Well, you can of course come here. Just give me a day or so to get your old room straight. I've been using it as a sewing and storage room and it's a bit cluttered.'

Her mum's tone was resigned and angry and Romilly decided that back under her parents' roof was the last place on earth she wanted to be. The details of her situation had obviously been passed on to Carrie and Holly, who both texted her almost immediately. Carrie offered to swoop by with Dr Miguel and pick her up, and Holly suggested that coming to Ibiza might be just the ticket. Romilly had smiled, touched by their sweet concern, and wished beyond wish that she could be fixed and normality restored by a quick trip to the Balearics or one of Dr Miguel's legendary paellas. She was particularly pleased that Holly had seemingly forgiven her; the realisation brought a lump to her throat.

After politely declining both offers, she considered what might make her feel better, what it was she needed most. Then she called the one person she felt might just understand what she was going through. She held her phone to her ear, hoping to hear a friendly voice.

'Red? Jesus Christ, don't tell me you and your old man have tracked me down and he's coming to throw me a left hook to match the right?'

She bowed her head, letting her hair fall in a curtain over her face as she recalled that terrible moment when she'd realised she was lying on the grass and Jasper was by her side with blood on his face.

'I'm in a hotel in the town centre. He's kind of kicked me out,' she managed.

'Hey, well, we're in Stokes Croft, just up the road. Come join us! I'll text you the address.' His posh drawl was as friendly as ever. He clearly harboured no grudges, despite having been punched by David.

She didn't ask who the 'us' was but instead rummaged through the pile of clothes on the floor for her trainers and jeans. Forgoing a shower, she pulled her hair into a ponytail and, using the map on her phone, set off with only three things on her mind: to carrying on drinking, to get drunk and to remain so...

Romilly achieved her goal. She neglected to go back to the hotel for three weeks and so the hotel, having debited the money for her extended stay from her credit card, disposed of her meagre possessions – her clothes, underwear and toiletries and a book on the evolution of the mayfly. Not that she noticed. She didn't notice much.

She had stepped into an underworld that a rational Romilly would have run a mile from. In this dark underbelly of the city, drugs and booze were the only currency of interest and the aim was to block out as many of the daylight hours as possible. She had unsatisfactory, fumbled sex with young Jasper; she had sex with young Jasper's friends and their friends too. It was as much about comfort and wanting to be wanted as it was about being unable to say no when inebriated – not exactly incapable of saying no, but certainly incapable of asking the question, do I want to say yes? Each encounter took her deeper into a dark, dark place of self-loathing, which only made the escape more vital.

Her home was a sofa in a very large top-floor flat occupied by several seemingly unconnected people who came and went. A new face took up residence on every stained mattress, sagging chair and half-sprung sofa as soon as it became vacant. The vast space had no carpets, no electricity other than what the temperamental generator sporadically pumped out and no hot water. A man named Frog, who seemed to have authority over the disparate group, oversaw the place.

Frog was extremely kind, a generous white Rasta who believed that possessions should be shared. He preached about the totalitarian utopia that he saw rising from the ashes of capitalism once the lifestyles of the bankers and the rich had finally imploded. It amused Romilly to see the uber-posh Jasper, beneficiary of a thirty-thousand-a-year education, nodding sagely through a haze of hash at Frog's ramblings. She decided not to mention that she had until recently been residing with her partner accountant husband in the rather smart suburb of Stoke Bishop, where their beautiful home sat in a well-tended quarter acre and screamed middle-class aspiration from its very appealing kerb. Not that she could bear to dwell on that anyway.

Frog was as good as his word when it came to sharing; he shared his opinions, his loud music and his time. Romilly shared her phone, her liquor and the remaining balance in her bank account. That was until the cashpoint flashed up an unsatisfactory message about insufficient funds and advised her to contact her branch at her earliest convenience. She had, in a rather confused state, hurled the useless piece of plastic down a drain and then spent the next sober hour searching for it in the street. Later that evening, without sobriety to fuel restraint, she'd called the house in Stoke Bishop. Unsure who had answered, she rambled incoherently. 'Forthemoney! It was Frog... droppeditdownthedrain... speshllyformenow, s'money! Areyoufuckinglissssning?'

The numerous visitors that hung around the flat were an eclectic bunch. Transient drifters with matted hair and stories of hard luck, free-thinking eco warriors with a passion for anything other than conformity, migrants with limited English who were just passing through, and a whole host of Jasper sound-alikes, lost rich boys enjoying a petty act of rebellion before they returned to privilege.

Romilly came to feel quite safe in her space on the sofa, welcoming the oblivion that she fell into each and every day. She would lie there untroubled as debate raged over her head on any number of topics, from global warming to who'd eaten the last tub of hummus, with the fug of sweet-smelling hash filling her nostrils and furring the back of her throat. She wasn't even that bothered about feeling itchy, whether from lack of personal hygiene or from sharing the couch with Frog's flea-infested mongrel. Catching sight of herself in a shop window one day, she noted distractedly how pale and gaunt she'd become and saw that her hair had dulled to a reddish brown, the burnished auburn now hidden under grease and grime. She often simply forgot to eat; her appetite was non-existent and her calories came mostly from alcohol.

Romilly submitted to this existence. She closed down, folded in on herself and just functioned. She couldn't let herself think about Celeste, couldn't think about David, her home, any of it, because if she did, she knew she might quite literally go insane. Her mind teetered on the edge of the darkest place imaginable, a place from which there would be no return. In her brief sober interludes, she would sob, a wretched, open-mouthed wail that invited hugs and strokes from whoever was in close proximity. She welcomed the physical interaction; it reminded her that she was human and helped her forget things for a little while.

Frog got into a fight; not a fisticuffs-in-the-street scuffle but a feud. It transpired that he was a small-time drug dealer, selling tiny wraps of ganja and the odd pill around the neighbourhood. This hadn't gone down well with the family who considered the streets to be their domain. Romilly woke in the early hours of a damp autumn night to a loud bang and lots of shouting. She was petrified. Her heart leapt in her chest and her breath came in short bursts as though she couldn't fill her lungs. As always, there was a second or two when she didn't know where she was or what was going on. A friend of Jasper's whose name escaped her ran into the room where she was sleeping on the sofa.

'Red! Get your stuff together. We've got to get out. Now!'

Unsure whether she was fleeing from fire or gunshots, Romilly grabbed her bag, which contained nothing of any great use, threw her jacket over her sweatshirt and luckily was already in her jeans. With her trainers in her hand, she followed him blindly down the stairs, not stopping to question the instruction but trusting him to lead her to safety.

As she turned onto the landing, she looked into the dilapidated kitchen, where mould grew halfway up the walls and a gas pipe stuck uselessly out of the wall. Two burly men were holding Frog with his arms pinned behind his back. His head hung down near the floor and a third man was punching him hard in the stomach. She winced, wondered how she might be able to help, decided she couldn't and ran down the stairs and out into Moon Street.

The ill-fitting front door was now completely off its hinges. But apart from the late-night stragglers vacating the Lakota nightclub and bouncing arm in arm on and off the kerb, the place was quiet.

'You okay?'

She looked up at the boy she had forgotten was standing by her side. She nodded.

'There's some serious shit going on back there.' He jerked his thumb in the direction of the flat.

Romilly started to cry. Her mind did this sometimes, opened up a little crack and let her look at herself in the past. In that particular second she saw herself in the middle of the night, tiptoeing downstairs to the kitchen to get a glass of water and stopping at the sitting-room door, surveying the large room and feeling so very lucky. She had a job she loved, a house beyond her dreams and a man she adored; and their beautiful girl was the icing on the cake! She remembered the feeling of pure joy as she padded back up the stairs to climb in next to David. And now here she was, running from a squat in the middle of the night, with all she owned slung over her shoulder in a grubby bag.

'You okay?' he asked again, wide eyed and edgy.

'Yes.' She looked at the garage door they were standing in front of and noted a large new daubing of paint. It was an unfinished work, a female face, half formed. She was devoid of a mouth and her hair and eyes had run in long drips along the metal. It made it look as though she was crying.

'Come on!' He took her by the hand as they loped along Fremantle Road and then Redland Grove, walking with no particular destination in mind. She found out that his name was Levi and he was on his gap year.

Romilly stared at him. 'Of all the things you could have done, all the places you could have gone, why are you at Frog's?' She shook her head.

'He's cool and it's buzzing!' He laughed, pulling from his inside pocket a half bottle of vodka and, just like that, she didn't care who he was or why he was hanging out with Frog; she just wanted to share his bottle.

The two meandered on and eventually found themselves at Westbury Park. Romilly stared up at the grand houses with their distinctive facades of limestone blocks and sandstone quoins, their blinds and curtains keeping the messy world of the street at bay. 'It's not fucking fair!' she shouted, a little more loudly than Levi was comfortable with.

'Keep it down, Red!' He raised his palm and looked across the road.

'WhyshouldI?' She stumbled, managing to right herself before she fell over.

He pointed at a vast house on a corner plot, which, unlike most of the others on the road, had not been divided into flats. 'This is where my parents live.' He pressed the rest of the bottle into her palm and sloped off into the breaking dawn.

'You'reafuckingjoke gapyearboy!' she shouted after him.

He turned and flicked the Vs at her before disappearing inside the gate and out of sight.

Romilly looked around her. She knew she was at the top of the Downs, and what she wanted more than anything was to sleep. Plodding on as the indigo dawn began to burst through the darkness, she made her way across the road and before long was treading on the springy wet grass of Durdham Down.

Spying a bin set in concrete and with a shrub to its side, she decided that this was as good a place as any to catch some sleep. She fell inelegantly to the ground, threw her bag down and placed her head on it. Closing her eyes, she lay in a foetal position, too drunk to fully register what she was doing.

It was an hour later, her eyes still tightly shut and her limbs shaking, that she felt a body curl up against her back, spooning her in the early-morning gloom. Her stomach shrank and her bowels spasmed. Finding herself pinned between the bin, the large shrub and the heavy body behind her, she tried to think straight, tried to decide whether it was best to lie still or make a run for it, uncertain whether her legs would hold her upright.

A familiar, welcome sound caused her to open her eyes. A dirty woollen glove with a filthy long fingernail poking out of it was shaking the remnants of a bottle of whisky over her shoulder. The lid was already missing and the fumes danced up into her nose; this aroma was almost as good as the first taste and every fibre of her being sang with anticipation.

With her hip pressed into the wet grass, her head not five inches from a knotted black plastic bag that bulged with dog shit, she raised her mouth towards the cold neck of the bottle, wanting to feel the glass against her soft lip.

As the liquid touched her tongue, bringing the relief she craved, she heard the body behind her unzip his fly. He pushed up against her. Her jeans had ridden down, exposing part of her flank, now peppered with goosebumps, and his skin made contact. She tipped the bottle higher, hoping for oblivion while he grunted and sighed behind her. She leant forward, bracing herself against the edge of the bin, and as she did so, a tiny spider came into focus. She stared at the little creature, working diligently to repair a gap in its gossamer web. It was beautiful. Romilly stared, concentrating on the pale brown stripe across its back and its stripy legs. *Araneus diadematus*. Beautiful little thing.

She must have passed out because when she came to, the sun was up and there was noise on the road. Cars were ferrying people to work and school, and bus engines were letting out great mechanical wheezes in the heavy traffic. Romilly sat up and gripped her head. Instantly remembering, she reached down to restore her jeans, wiping at the patch of skin where a dirty stranger had taken his pleasure in exchange for whisky. She felt otherworldly, wondering how life could go on all around her while she lay there, in the middle of it but invisible.

She knew she was awake, but surely she was dreaming, as she could hear the sweet, unmistakeable sound of Celeste's voice. *Celeste – the name I gave her because to hold her was heaven and I wanted her to dance among the stars, shining...* It couldn't be real! It must be her mind playing a trick. But the voice sounded so like her daughter's that, trick or not, her gut twisted with longing. Peering through the sparse lower branches of the shrub, Romilly placed her hand over her mouth and let out a silent cry. A thick stream of tears coursed down her face, clogging her eyes and fogging her view, because it wasn't a dream. There, just a matter of feet away from her, was Celeste, walking along the path with a girl of similar age, wearing the same school uniform. A woman, probably the girl's mother, trotted behind them, her ponytail swinging as her right hand tugged at the leash of an inquisitive spaniel.

The pain in Romilly's heart was so real, she thought her heart might stop, and she half wanted it to. Celeste looked so beautiful, and she'd got taller! Her hair had been cut and sat on her shoulder in a handsome thick blunt line. Her school cardigan was buttoned up and she was wearing her red kilt with her school coat over the top. Over her shoulder was her leather satchel, more battered than it had been and now adorned with graffiti and a couple of stickers. Romilly squinted at her name on the label, just visible through its little plastic window. *I wrote that! That's my writing, Celeste! I wrote your name for you. My little girl!* She concentrated on listening to the girls and could just make out a few words as her daughter burbled to her friend '... and we all went outside... so embarrassing, I like him, but I don't love him… nine pounds fifty… Amelia said… not pizza, but if…'

Romilly stared, one hand on her chest and the other reaching out into the shrub, trying to feel the air that her little girl had breathed. *Celeste, I'm here, my baby girl! I'm here and I love you so much! I love you, Celeste. I'm sorry. I'm so sorry!*

Her daughter sounded and looked so much older. A large gulp of distress came from her throat as she realised that she was older! Celeste was now ten and she had missed her birthday. She'd missed it. An image from one of Celeste's past birthdays came into her head; it might have been her sixth. She saw herself icing the cake in the kitchen – in the shape of a butterfly, was it? – while her daughter skipped on the spot behind her, flexing the little plastic rope that made a 'clack' sound every time it hit the tiles and singing, 'Teddy bear, teddy bear, turn around, Teddy bear, teddy bear, touch the ground…' *Where did that time go, Celeste? What happened? Where did I go?*

Romilly watched as the trio rounded the corner and disappeared out of view before sitting back on the damp grass and sobbing. Several hours later, just as Celeste was taking her pink plastic lunch box out of her satchel, Romilly picked herself up off the ground, steeled herself and began making her way down the hill. She had just made the toughest decision of her life.

Late that afternoon, Romilly stood with a clear view of the tearooms on The Downs, dithering on the grass, unsure if she could find the courage to go through with it. She breathed in through her nose and out through her mouth, just as she had been taught. She was shaking so much, her teeth chattered.

And then she saw him and he looked... beautiful.

The tears flowed unbidden. It had been over ten months and she had forgotten how it made her feel to see him. She remembered the time all those years ago on the steps of the Wills Memorial Building, recalled his shy smile, his face young and mesmerising: *'So, is that a silent "Yes, I'd love to come for a light supper on the docks," or a silent "Sod off"?'* The memory filled her with such longing that she closed her eyes and had to fight hard to resist the urge to banish it with drink.

She ran her hand over her stained sweatshirt and rubbed at her face. She knew she smelt and wished she could clean her teeth. David, on the other hand, looked sparkling and neat. She felt a jab of anguish when she noticed that he was wearing the shirt her parents had bought him one Christmas. His wedding ring glinted on his finger, where she had placed it more than a decade earlier, *till death do us part...* She had meant every word. He glanced down at his watch, the one she'd bought him when he became a father, a matching pair with the one he'd bought her, and she felt a stab of disgust as she recalled coming home from that stranger's house and noting that her watch was missing.

David looked up and their eyes locked. Romilly knew him better than anyone, knew every nuance of every gesture and expression. She had watched as he'd set eyes on his daughter for the very first time, had seen his joyous disbelief at the fact that this beautiful little miracle was theirs. She had watched his face as he'd read the letter confirming his first grown-up job, seen the smile of self-congratulation and its undercurrent of panic. She'd seen him cry, and laugh, and laugh until he cried; she'd seen him drunk, and angry. And one sunny holiday afternoon, as he'd found himself struggling in a rip tide off the Mexican coast, she'd seen his look of serene resignation at the prospect of meeting his maker. There was not a single look she could not read, and at the precise moment his eyes fell across her face, she knew exactly what he was thinking. His expression was one of shock, sadness, revulsion and regret.

And it broke her heart.

He gave a small nod and a slight smile. She wiped her eyes and made her way to the table.

There was a strange formality about the way they sat and snatched glimpses of each other; no one could have guessed that they'd been a couple since their teens.

'How's Celeste?' She stared at him, forgetting to look away, eager to capture every clue as to her daughter's wellbeing.

'She's pretty good. She is busy, clever, noisy!' He coughed.

Romilly had promised herself that she wouldn't cry, but it was a promise she couldn't keep. Hearing her beloved girl described in such a way helped her picture her at home so clearly that her heart split with longing. David's tone, as if he was talking to someone that had never met Celeste, made it even worse.

'She misses you of course,' he said, his voice faltering.

She wondered if this was an afterthought, to make her feel better.

'But you know how she is, she gets on with it, and she's

in a routine. Mum stays a lot, helps out and that's working out quite well, because it's familiar.'

'I miss her.'

David nodded and handed her a paper napkin, which was a little stiff and didn't so much soak up the tears as push them around her face. She sniffed. 'I hope it was okay to call you at work. I remembered the number.'

'You said you needed to see me, Rom,' he prompted, kindly but a touch impatient.

Don't call me Rom! It reminds me of the old me. 'I've... I've decided to go away, to London.' She hung her head, distracted by the thought of where she might get her next drink.

'I see.' He cleared his throat.

'I think I need to go to a different city.' She spoke slowly. 'One where I'm not going to bump into Celeste, because that's not fair on her and I know I couldn't take it.' She shook her head at the memory of what had happened that morning: glimpsing her little girl through a shrub as she lay next to a bin, her head inches from a bag of dog shit.

'Do you need money? I can help you out until you get back on your feet.' He tapped the table, awkward at having to raise the topic, yet again showing her how far they had slipped.

'No. I still get family allowance,' she whispered, conscious she had no right to it. 'But thank you.' She meant it. Financially he would be finding it harder now that there was only one salary coming in. 'Just look after Celeste,' she stuttered.

'Of course I will.' He sounded a little cool at the idea that he might need reminding to look after his daughter.

'I miss her so much. Can... can you tell her that I love her?' she rasped.

He nodded awkwardly. She knew he would be true to his word, no matter how difficult he might find it, and all the questions that might follow.

'Your mum said your phone was out of action.' He sipped his coffee.

'I lost it.' *A man called Frog took it. I saw him get beaten up, but I can't think about that, so I shall block it out, shut it away with all the other images...*

'Make sure you give your parents a ring, they're worried about you.'

'*Here we go, a bowl of tommyatoes for my girl!*'

'Can you tell them I'm fine?' she asked, reaching for the napkin again and blotting her eyes.

He gave another nod. 'What are you going to do in London?'

'I'm going to... to try and... to try and get some help.'

He looked up at her with a flicker of recognition in his eyes, a flash that made her think he saw something that reminded him of the girl she used to be, the girl he fell in love with.

'That's good.' He sighed. 'I wish you nothing but good things. Good health.' He smiled. 'Goodbye, Romilly.'

She saw his hands twitch, as if debating whether to touch her arm, her hand. He knitted his fingers, clearly thinking better of it. He stood and hesitated for a second before leaving her alone at the table. She watched him walk away, without looking back.

...for an adult butterfly; a broken wing spells danger. It is

fully formed and therefore cannot grow and doesn't really heal. The insect is probably never going to fly again. The butterfly can, however, live, the question I suppose is, does it want to?

Celeste

My life was pretty settled. Granny Sylvia was living with us by then and she was a stickler for routine, which gave my life a certain rhythm that I hadn't really noticed had been missing, and that was comforting. She had some mad ideas; I loved how energetic she was and how she encouraged me to spread my wings. I was allowed to walk to school with my friend and her mum, and I could go straight out after school as long as she knew where I was and I came home before dark. I liked the freedom she gave me. She was an accomplished cook, my favourites were lamb, and a vegetarian bake that she served at least four times a week once I'd expressed a preference for it. My poor old dad would smile gratefully, pushing bits of broccoli around the plate and winking at me.

It was a strange thing that happened with Mum. We kind of stopped mentioning her as much, carried on as though it was the way things had always been. It was a bit like when you cut yourself and there's this gaping split in your skin and then weeks pass and it disappears to nothing and after that you don't think about it or remember it. The hurt I felt when she first went was a bit like that; it just healed. I was too young and too busy to fully appreciate what was going on but old enough to know I shouldn't be talking about it, as if we were all playing the same game of not mention Romilly. But then after a while that game became real, we didn't mention her so we didn't think about her as much and then we didn't need to mention her. When I did think about her I felt guilty for not thinking about her more and sad all over again that she was gone.

The only exception was if Nanny Pat came to stay. She always wanted to talk about Mum a lot, and Dad would scowl at her across the table during supper, as though she was breaking some kind of agreement. If she gave me any snippets about Mum or reminded me of things that had happened in the past, like talking about the day I was born or when Mum was at school, Dad would always make a point of coming up to my room while I did my homework and telling me that it was okay to talk about Mum, even though it clearly wasn't. He would really go overboard, reassuring me that he wasn't going anywhere and that he would never leave me. This had the strange effect of making me think that he might be leaving me, and so I'd try to get to sleep with this worry in my tummy that Dad might leave too, and then what would I do?

It was my biggest fear, that something might happen to Dad and I'd be really stuck. People told me not to worry, that nothing was going to happen to my dad and that dads didn't just disappear. But I knew different. I knew that parents did just disappear. I knew my dad's dad had vanished and so had my mum, but I didn't say this.

Eighteen

Pat shouted into the receiver, 'For the love of God, Romilly! Where on earth have you been?'

Romilly heard the clatter as her mum placed her palm partially over the mouthpiece of the phone in the hallway that sat on a little table next to the front door. It had been a cast-off of Aunty Margaret's and had graced her parents' hall for as long as she could remember. She could picture her mum, probably with tea towel in hand, panicking as she took the call she had been waiting for.

'Lionel! Lionel! It's her, she's on the phone!' she hollered in the direction of the shed.

'Wh… where are you? We've been worried sick! I got the message that you'd lost your phone, and then David said he saw you and you looked ghastly, and I said to your sisters, she might have lost her phone, but she knows our number, it's the one we've always had and I learnt it to her… I learnt it to her in case she ever got lost…' Her mum's voice broke away in sobs. 'I've been so worried.' She took a deep breath. 'I can't sleep worrying about you. Dr Morrison said he'd give me something, but I don't want to go down that route and end up like Marjorie up the road. Are you okay?' she asked, finally.

'I'm okay, Mum.' It was the best she could offer. 'And I'm working at getting myself together. I just wanted to say don't worry. Don't worry about me.'

'Don't worry about you? How can you say that? I'm your mother! Don't worry about you? Of course I'm going to worry about you. And the girls keep asking for updates and I have nothing to tell them, because I don't know myself. I don't know what's going on, I've hardly heard from Celeste.'

Romilly felt her chest cave, as if she'd been stabbed. The image that she'd suppressed of her beautiful girl was there in an instant. Her mum carried on.

'I said to your dad, I feel like everything is broken and I don't know how to put it all back together again! My family is spread all over the bloody place. I've got Holly in Ibiza getting up to God knows what, Carrie in Bath with Dr Whatsisname and now you, just gone!'

'I'm not "just gone", Mum, I'm in London and I'm trying to find my feet.' She was still getting used to speaking without two of her teeth, the canine to the right of her mouth and the molar next to it, which had flown out of her mouth and rolled away like marbles when she'd fallen face first down some steps. Her tongue had acquired the habit of falling through the gap mid speech, making her sound drunk or stupid. At this thought she gave a small, ironic smile.

'Oh, wait a minute, hang on! Your dad's here, he's coming. Hurry up, Lionel! I don't know how long she's got!' There was a thud and then fumbling and crackling down the line and then the wonderful sound of her dad's voice, his kind and soothing voice, unflustered. *My same old dad.* It was almost more than she could cope with.

'Hello, Romilly,' he began in his slow, singsong tone, as though they'd been catching up as they always used to, with her sitting in the kitchen of the house in Stoke Bishop, chatting over a cuppa while she planned what to make for supper and kept an eye on the clock, or during her lunch break at work, nattering to him in the lab while she ate a plastic-wrapped sandwich and he pottered in the greenhouse. He used to read her snippets of a scientific nature that he'd gleaned from magazines, as though she had an interest in all aspects of science, from space exploration to brain surgery, as though science was science, and she loved him for it.

'Dad…' She was overcome with emotion, which made her feel weak, and that made her feel scared.

'I'm right here. You know you can always come home and you know that I will come to wherever you are, whenever you need me, to *bring* you home. You know that, don't you?' She could tell he was smiling, from the gaps in his breathing and the way he was sounding out his words. 'You just need to say the word and I'll be there, quicker than you can say Jack Flash. I love you, Romilly.'

This was a rare and heartfelt admission from a man who was better at saying it with the gift of tomatoes.

'I love you too, Dad.'

Father Brian had been quite clear when she'd told him that she didn't even know if she believed in God. She'd thought it best to be honest. 'In fact I'm pretty sure there is no God. I'd say I'm ninety-nine per cent certain, with one per cent of scepticism in reserve, in case I've got it horribly wrong and when the time comes I have some explaining to do.'

He had thrown his head back and laughed loudly, slapping the thighs of his grey slacks. 'Romilly, dear...' He stroked his dense grey beard. 'That's the great thing about doing his work: he doesn't specify who we help. And maybe your one per cent of scepticism is a gateway that will lead you somewhere really interesting. I mean, you're not saying that the door is closed completely.'

She smiled at the kindly priest, licking her dry lips. Sobriety was the one condition of staying here and she was finding it challenging. Even the medication prescribed to take the edge off her cravings was only helping a little.

'I think if it's not closed completely, then there's a massive boulder blocking the way,' she levelled.

Father Brian leant forward. 'Ah, Romilly, if that's all it is, then we're laughing. Might I suggest you read Luke 24:3; we do a good line in boulder removal.' He winked. He liked her and this gave her hope that he might be able to help.

The hostel, Chandler House, was a pale brick Victorian building housing a rabbit warren of rooms that were reached via narrow corridors with concrete floors and bare light bulbs. On each corridor hung a large cork pinboard with the rules of the establishment printed out in big fat bullet points, and various leaflets for charities offering Fresh Start training, counselling or therapies for people with addictions. Each room had two bunk beds with a narrow strip of floor visible between them, and each room smelt of human misery. The ones that housed the frail and the incontinent were the worst.

The smell of the place was part of the problem. If she left her room and went out into the fresh air of the pretty little garden at the back or walked the streets and saw the sun, there was a painful period of readjustment when she came back inside. By staying put, she spared herself this. There were showers and loos on each floor and for this small comfort she was extremely grateful.

The hostel was situated a couple of streets back from the designer shops and neon signs of Covent Garden's Long Acre. In her previous life, she too had once sauntered round these shops, brandishing heavy paper bags with fancy ribbon handles. She'd come with her sisters a couple of years back. They enjoyed a posh afternoon tea, went to see the musical *Mamma Mia*, ate noodles late night in Chinatown, bought high-heeled shoes and giggled like teens. It had been the best couple of days. Now, though, Romilly didn't venture too far from the hostel, and she rarely went anywhere after dark. Instead, she lay in her top bunk with the window open and listened to the cabs beeping their horns, the buses with their squeaky brakes ferrying people to their homes, and the loud, drunken voices in the streets that made her own cravings pulse.

One of her roommates was Scottish Gladys, who talked incessantly to herself but avoided talking to anyone else. She occasionally called out into the darkness with some snippet of information – 'I had them all christened, I did!' – usually random, but enough to make Romilly wonder about the life that had gone before. The other roommate called herself T and, unlike Scottish Gladys, liked to speak a lot. Her favourite topic was Leighton, her ex-boyfriend, who was in prison, not that it was his fault. 'No, he was fitted up by his wanker mates, and when he gets out, they'd better run, cos he's had eighteen months to think about how he's going to shit them up...' Romilly refrained from jumping in with the punchline night after night.

She tried to avoid thinking about her own loved ones. It was too painful. But sometimes the least little thing triggered a memory and the tears came. Like the evening she found herself unwrapping a small packet of two fruit shortcake biscuits that someone had given her, the kind you might get on a tray in a budget hotel. As she nibbled the soft edge, dropping sugary crumbs down her nightdress, a conversation floated into her head. *'In fact I sometimes think if I didn't have to shop and cook for you two, I'd still live off biscuits and crisps and the odd bit of toast. I'd go back to being like a little nibbling mouse.'* She saw herself standing in her beautiful kitchen on that glorious sunny morning with the people she loved. The stream of tears made her nose run and her sobs made it almost impossible to swallow the flavourless grains.

She looked for ways to distract herself. After lights-out, she'd pull the thick grey blanket up over her shoulder, lie on her side and stare at a stain on the shiny pale green wall. She decided it was a map of the world and she spent hours looking at each country, thinking about its food and vegetation, its sea, land and mountains, its animals and insect life. She thought of all the places she had visited and those she wanted to visit, using her mind to escape from the room in which she found herself and the desperate, all-consuming desire for a drink that threatened to drive her insane.

Romilly had completed the first phase of the Clean Life, Clean Start programme and had managed to remain alcohol-free for two weeks. This earned her another month in the programme and today she was going to attend her first meeting, the beginning of phase two.

Father Brian smiled and nodded his encouragement as she walked into the room. He had the wonderful knack of making her feel special, and judging by other people's reactions to him, she was not alone. There were filing cabinets and bookshelves lining the walls and she rightly figured that this dusty old place that smelt like a library was used as an office during the day. But now, with all the desks pushed to one side and the chairs placed in a circle in the middle, it was serving as a meeting room.

Romilly was quiet. She pulled her hair into a ponytail and fastened it at her neck as she took deep breaths to try and calm her flustered pulse. She was nervous, scared about so many aspects of this, not least about starting, properly starting something that she didn't want to fail at. She couldn't afford to fail.

Pulling out one of the chairs in the circle, she took a seat and glanced at the other ten or so people gathered around her. It was the usual cross-section – male, female, old, young, black, white. She now understood that this affliction was indiscriminate; it could get its hooks into anyone: a clever, clever girl like her or even an academic surgeon from Stuttgart.

A young woman opposite checked her phone and stretched her legs out into the circle, crossing them at the ankle as she sighed. Father Brian clapped twice, his voice calm but commanding.

'Good evening, everyone, and thank you so much for your punctuality and your willingness to be here. I would encourage all of you to keep your hearts, eyes and minds open.

We're here to see if we can learn from the experiences of others and, more importantly, to help support each other through this difficult time. I'd like to remind you though that the hardest thing is coming here in the first place and you have all achieved that and so be proud of taking that very difficult first step and know that you are not alone. You are not alone.'

He paused and smiled at each of them and Romilly felt warmth spread through her. *I don't want to be alone any more. I miss my little girl. I miss my David. I miss me...* She shook off the emotion that threatened, knowing she had to keep it together.

Father Brian invited a man to speak. He shuffled to the edge of his chair and told of his journey, conquering his nerves to explain how he had been a maths teacher for many years at a boys' school in Kent but had then lost his wife and had been unable to cope. Romilly looked at the girl with the phone, sitting opposite her. She saw how her eyes rolled with impatience and how she stole glances at the large clock on the wall. She then sighed and shoved her hands into the pockets of her bomber jacket and Romilly could read her mind. '*I'm not like these people, these poor bastards. These people have serious issues, but me? I'm different; I've just hit a bump in the road.*'

She didn't realise she was crying until Father Brian spoke to her. 'Romilly? Would you like to say something?'

He smiled and stood to hand her a large box of tissues. She grabbed a few and held them to her running nose. Then she nodded and took a deep breath. She'd sat in on sessions like this so many times before, at The Pineapple and in

Austria, and they'd never felt relevant or real, but this one was different.

'I... I've lost my husband, my home, my job and I don't see my little girl, my beautiful girl.' She pictured Celeste. 'I can't see a future for me if I don't stop drinking. I had it all, and that's the hardest part for me, I really had it all... But I need some help. I do.' She gulped her tears. 'I need some help because... because I'm ill. I am ill. I'm... I'm an alcoholic.' She let her head fall to her chest as she remembered waking with her head next to a bag of dog shit. Her tongue probed the hole in her gum where her tooth once lived.

'I'm an alcoholic.' She sobbed. 'I know it here...' She touched her trembling fingers to her head. 'And I know it here...' She laid her fingers on her heart. Sitting up straight, she looked at Father Brian, who smiled at her. 'I'm an alcoholic.'

Celeste

I guess you could say I grew less curious about my mum as I got older. I knew that she was living in London. Aunty Holly and Aunty Carrie saw her once and tried to fill me in, but it was hard for them to soft-soap what they'd seen, make it appropriate for my young teenage ears, and just as hard for me to hear it. They spoke about her with an affection that I found hard to match. It was as if they were talking about a total stranger. I didn't have the decades of memories and closeness they did or the advantage of adult perspective that could visualise things restored. I tried to picture her with this other life and it made it seem very final. I knew then that she definitely wasn't coming home any time soon, if ever.

Annie, who at that stage was Dad's new friend, made it easier for me to talk about her. She was a wonderful conduit between Dad and me; still is. My life is definitely richer for having her in it.

Ironically, I still used to imagine, sometimes, that Mum had died. I concluded that it wouldn't feel that different if she had: I never saw her, never heard from her, and I was used to it being just Dad and me, with Granny Sylvia coming to stay every so often.

It was around this time that I went to my first grown-up party, the first party where there was snogging and smoking and not party games and cake. It was hosted by a boy called Ben, a friend of a friend who had been shoved into an expensive boarding school and whose parents were living abroad; he'd managed to get the keys for their house, which was bursting at the seams with teenagers. To be there was exciting and scary all at the same time. My friends were desperate to get drunk, swigging at anything that was passed to them. Amelia pressed a glass bottle of beer into my hand. It was open, and half-drunk, and I went to swig from it just like everybody else. But as I brought it near my mouth, the smell hit me. It was just the same as that sour smell that used to be on my mum's breath when she tucked me in at night, that her minty chewing gum could never quite mask. I had a sudden flash of memory of my mum passed out with her pants around her ankles and covered in sick, with my dad standing over her with his sad smile, the one where he was trying to be kind and patient even though every drop of booze that touched her lips just drove him further and further away from her. My friends teased me and said I was being a baby, but I didn't drink a mouthful that night, and I still don't drink. I told my friends I just didn't like the taste, and that's the story I've stuck with ever since.

Nineteen

Romilly was a star pupil and the further she progressed through the Clean Life, Clean Start programme, the more clearly she could see her horizon. After eighteen months, her model behaviour and commitment had earned her a tiny single room in one of the independent flats owned by the trust, a short stroll from Waterloo Station. The Tube trains rattled her windows as they rumbled along beneath her block on their way to Kennington, sending a judder through the entire building that unnerved newcomers, but she'd got used to it. She found the hum of all those people travelling underground like little moles quite comforting.

Her room was sparse, just the way she liked it. Anything more homely might have made it feel permanent and that would have been wrong. This was always going to be a stepping-stone. Tempted one weekend to put up a poster that T had given her, to cheer up the white wall above her single divan bed, she hesitated and thought about the house in Stoke Bishop, the cool, tiled floors, comfy sofas, soft bathroom lighting and fluffy white towels nestling on a rack. She quickly folded the poster and put it in the cupboard. Let someone else prettify the walls, not her. This was a rare slip. She deliberately avoided thinking about the house, because if she did, she inevitably started thinking about the people in it, and to even picture their faces was more than she could cope with.

The ache she felt to be with her family did not fade with time. In fact, the closer she came to feeling 'cured', the more she ached, as if her mind allowed those feelings to stir now that it was all within reach, almost. She had started to look at her recovery in terms of probability, understanding that the longer she abstained from drinking, the clearer her mind became, the more her physical cravings weakened and the less she felt like she needed a drink. And so it went. She was learning that it was important to stay locked in an upward spiral of success, celebrating every day of sobriety and taking great care not to spoil or undo all the work she'd done so far.

Her regular attendance at the group meetings helped. For the first time, Romilly listened, really listened and was able to identify with many of the tales told within that circle of chairs. The routes there were many and varied and they were bound not by where they had started but by their having ended up in that room, rock bottom for many. Among her own group of mumblers, shufflers, nail biters, angry men and crying women was a managing director, a florist, a grandparent, a teacher and a policeman. Ordinary people like her, former functioning members of society who had fallen into the dark crevice, lured by the scent of a cork or the feel of a glass bottle against their mouth.

Romilly walked to Chandler House every day, in all weathers. Pulling her jumper over her hands and buttoning up her coat, she marched over Waterloo Bridge, never tiring of the majestic view of Big Ben to her left and the City rising high into the sky to her right. The Shard stood like a razor, sharp and gleaming in the morning sun. She walked in a throng, everyone but her tapping or talking into phones, gripping cases and bags whose laptops and tablets linked them to the rest of the planet. She, however, felt removed from the world, unconnected, without a phone, computer or purse. She had no real identity, at least not there, and that was the way it needed to be for her.

She knew that, though she was doing well – it was twenty-two months, three weeks and two days since she'd had a drink – she was still teetering at the edge of the crevice, balanced on tiptoes. One harsh word of criticism from her mother, one flippant remark from Holly or indifferent sigh from David and she couldn't guarantee that she wouldn't jump. Only when she could confidently remain flat-footed and steady on the surface, with the crevice behind her and her purposeful stride taking her in the other direction, only then would it be time to pick up the phone or hop on a train. Only then would she make contact with Celeste, when she was certain that she was not going to let her down or harm her ever again.

Romilly stopped every morning to pick up a pint of milk at a corner shop on the edge of Theatreland. It was an incongruous little space among the bars, restaurants, coffee shops and designer offerings of this London postcode. Here, the shelves bulged with cheap white bread in plastic bags, no-brand biscuits, bottles of fizz, a huge variety of crisps, tiny jars of coffee, tinned peaches in syrup, cans of deodorant and a whole range of birthday cards aimed at young girls who loved glitter and cats. Romilly liked it because, for a minute or two while she surveyed the shelves, she could be anywhere, in any little shop in any street in any city, and it made her happy. There were a multitude of memories for her among these shelves, from nipping to the store for her mum, with coins nestling in her palm, to stopping at the shop on the way back to halls after a night out, eager to pick up junk food.

'What are you doing?' the middle-aged man behind the counter asked as she stood with her hands in the fridge, moving stuff around.

'Oh, sorry! I was just sorting your milk. You had the bottles with the older dates at the back, so I was just bringing them forward, otherwise you'll be left with a lot of out-of-date milk tomorrow morning.' She looked at the floor.

'I see. And what else would you like to change about my business?' He folded his arms across his fat belly, which was encased in a zip-up cardigan that had dark stains down the front.

She looked around. 'Well, you've put household bits and bobs like floor polish and scourers next to the cakes – that's no good, they should be separate. People don't want to think about bleach and cake.'

He sighed. 'Anything else?'

She held his gaze. 'You have too many of the same type of greetings card. You should have "Sorry You're Leaving" cards and "Congratulations On Your New Job". There are lots of offices around here and I bet people would pick them up.'

The man scratched at his grey stubble. 'You want a job?'

'Do I...?' She thought she might have misheard.

'What am I, a parrot, having to repeat everything? Do you want a job? The money's crap and I am the worst boss in the world. I will forget to open up and leave you outside in the rain and I am one miserable bastard.' His stony expression indicated he wasn't lying.

'I... I'm in a programme at Chandler House. I drink. Well, I did. I haven't for a long time and I don't intend to again. I'm from Bristol, but I'm here away from my family.' She felt her lip tremble.

'For God's sake, do I look like I want your life story? I don't!' He shook his head. 'So is that a yes?'

'*So, come on! Tell me! Is it yes or no? Don't leave a guy hanging!*'

Romilly smiled at him and nodded her head. 'It's a yes.'

'What's your name?' he asked, lifting his chin.

'Romilly.'

'What kind of name is that!'

'What's yours?'

'Doruk.'

'For some people that might be as odd as Romilly,' she shot back.

He ignored her. 'Three days a week, ten till three. Start tomorrow.' He threw a tabard at her, bottle-green with red piping.

She caught it between her hands and stared at it and then him. Feeling the polyester squeak between her fingers, she smiled at him. This was so much more than a job, this was a chance and it was a gesture of trust that she had no right to expect.

'Oh and Ronnylee, or whatever that was, don't be late!' And he winked at her, flashing a wide, brief smile.

The round of applause was loud and heartfelt; it had been a great meeting. Father Brian stood and started to collapse the chairs, turning the space back into an office.

'Father Brian?'

'Yes?' He continued to work as she hovered in the middle of the room.

'Guess what? She beamed.

'I don't know!' He removed his glasses and returned her smile.

'I got a job! Someone gave me a job! Can you believe it?'

'Yes, I can! And congratulations. At this rate, Romilly, you'll be out of our hair before we know it. I'm so pleased for you.'

'It feels like a big step.'

'It is, that's why.'

Romilly held the doorframe and looked at the man who had helped turn her life around. 'You know, I used to have a great job that I loved, and a lot of responsibility.' She pictured Tim, her lovely colleague, and the kind, kind Dr Gregson. 'But I can't imagine doing that now. I'm different, things are different.'

'Yes. Now they are, but who knows about the future?'

She shrugged. 'I guess. I wouldn't have done any of this without you, Father Brian.'

'Oh yes, you would. You've done it all. I've just provided

the tools, but you've had to work hard with them and you have and you still are. You are a strong woman. Stronger than you know.'

She nodded. 'Thank you. I have never believed in God, not really. I've always let the science part squash that kind of faith for me, but I do think that this place and you...' She didn't know how to phrase it. 'It's special.'

'Goodness me, Romilly Wells, we're not shifting that boulder, are we?' He laughed.

'No.' She shook her head. 'I don't think so. But it may have moved a fraction of an inch to let a thin ray of light into an otherwise dark place.'

Father Brian smiled at her knowingly. 'I couldn't have put it better myself.'

Romilly liked her job very much. Doruk was grumpy but kind, critical but generous and she was slowly learning how to react to him. He made constant jokes about how his wife should be in the kitchen and how business was a game for men. It was only when she met his formidable wife Ayla, saw how he adored and feared her in equal measure, that she realised his talk was all part of his sport. Ayla ran their two businesses and looked after their three kids. 'This is the only place he's safe, Romilly, at least in here I know where he is and he can't cause too much damage! Keep an eye on him for me, will you?' She placed a hand on Romilly's arm as she left.

Doruk watched his wife leave and turned to Romilly with his hands on his hips. 'She's just showing off in front of you. Don't listen to Ayla. It's me that runs things around here!'

'Oh hi, Ayla!' Romilly waved over his shoulder. The speed with which he whipped around, with a look of abject fear on his face, was a picture. She laughed with her hand over her mouth to hide the gap where she'd lost two teeth.

'Ah! Very funny!' he spat and went outside for a cigarette.

It was an ordinary night at Chandler House. There were the usual familiar faces gathered in the circle, as well as a new girl, in her late teens, who'd been sleeping rough. Romilly was struck by how young the girl seemed and her thoughts immediately flew to Celeste. She wondered what her daughter was doing at that moment in time. She hadn't spoken to her family in months and months; it was easier that way. Any snippets of information could keep her awake into the early hours, cluttering her head with grief and longing, making it hard to stay clear and focused, putting her recovery in danger.

Romilly listened as the girl spoke of her journey. She described in such detail the yearning for a drink that coursed through her veins that Romilly felt a flicker in her gut that she hadn't experienced for quite a while. She sat on her hands to stem the shake and swallowed the bitter spit that filled her mouth. She would not give in to it, not now that she had her job and was doing so well.

Father Brian noticed her discomfort. 'Are you all right?' he asked.

'I'm fine. Just feel a bit blown off course tonight. A good night's sleep and I'll be right as rain tomorrow.' She smiled.

'If you're sure. You know where I am if you want to talk.'

'I do. And thank you.' She reached over and gave him a small peck on his papery cheek, unsure if that was the correct thing to do, but not giving a fig.

'Actually, Romilly before you go, I have something for you. It arrived today.'

He made his way to the desk and opened a drawer, removing a slim cream envelope on the front of which was the unmistakeable script of David Arthur Wells.

Romilly was rooted to the spot as she took the envelope into her trembling hands. She sank back onto the worn sofa that lived in the corner of the room and stared at the letter, addressed to her, the first she had received in a very, very long time.

'Are you okay?'

She looked up quickly, having almost forgotten that Father Brian was in the room. She nodded. 'Can I open it here?' she whispered.

'Of course! I'll give you some privacy.' He patted her shoulder and left her alone.

Romilly flipped it over and ran her finger up under the glue that held the flap fast, wondering if he had licked this very edge, if he'd written it at the table in the kitchen, just like he used to. She slowly peeled the cream sheet from its envelope, her heart beating loudly in her ears. Her thoughts leapt ahead, trying to guess the contents. *I would love to see you, Rom...* Her heart lurched at the prospect.

The first thing she noticed was the brevity of the communication: a single paragraph. Swallowing her disappointment, she studied the words. Knowing David, this would probably have been the third or fourth attempt, to make sure he'd got the tone and content exactly right. She adjusted her wonky specs and read his words.

Dear Romilly,
I got your address from your parents. This is not an easy letter to write, but I think probably easier than meeting or even trying to do this over the phone. I am sure your life has moved on, as mine has. To this end, I think it would be a good idea to start the procedure to end our marriage. I have met someone else, but that is incidental. I feel this would allow us to move forward with our lives, which are now so separate. Please advise best address for my solicitor's correspondence.
Very best wishes,
David

She was stunned. She read and reread the lines over and over.

There was no mention of their daughter, the one thing she wanted to read about. His words cut her, not least the assumption that she, like he, had moved on, when every day she was totally preoccupied with surviving. And the very idea that him meeting someone else was incidental – how could it ever be incidental? He was her husband! She was too numb to cry.

The man slapped the table and sent a spray of sticky beer up over her front. She screamed her laughter. 'That's not fair! Not fair!' She wagged her finger. 'I am verysad, veryverysad today.' She leant towards him and breathed her vodka fumes in his direction. 'My goodDavid hasleftme. He didn't... didn't wantowaitf'me!' She sat back, a little confused.

The man laughed loudly, undoing the top button of his shirt as he twisted in his chair. 'I'm sorry about that.' He raised the glass in his hand in a wobbly gesture of solidarity.

Romilly slumped forward and placed her head on the tabletop, where beer and the sticky goo of food remnants and dust stuck to her cheek in a thin paste. 'BugGirl. That'sit, that's my name. He made me laugh and I hadtogetinthecupboard. He was funny. He married me...'

She closed her eyes. A little nap would be really good about now.

She felt a hand shoving her shoulder.

'Come on, Sleeping Beauty, we're closed.' The woman sounded irritated. She wanted to close up and go home, and babysitting the passed-out Romilly clearly wasn't on the agenda.

Romilly roused herself and lifted her head. Her skin peeled away from the table with a sticky, sucker-like noise. She rubbed her face and looked around with one eye closed, trying to recall where she was. The booze had settled in her veins and her brain, cushioning her thoughts and dulling her pain. She liked this slow, neutral state of mind; she'd forgotten what an exquisite pleasure it was to escape like this.

'Seriously, get a move on, will you!' The woman was yelling now, dragging on a cigarette as she collected glasses with her free hand.

'Can I buy a little bottle from you?' Romilly asked as she reached under the table for her jacket and bag.

'No.' The woman opened the door and gestured to the cold outside world.

Romilly felt her face crumple into tears; all she wanted was a little bottle.

'Oh, for fuck's sake!' The woman strode over to the bar, the soles of her trainers sticking to the linoleum floor as she went. Grabbing a bottle of Newcastle Brown Ale, she popped the top and marched back with her arm outstretched, shoving it into Romilly's hand. 'Now piss off!' she shouted.

'Thank you.' Romilly nodded at the closed door. She placed the glass neck to her mouth and gulped.

Looking up into the night sky, she wasn't entirely sure she knew where she was. It certainly wasn't a street she recognised. She wandered along the kerb, uncertain on her feet and finding it easier to keep the raised pavement against her heel to guide her. She was aware of being in among crowds of people, but their faces were indistinct. One or two men catcalled in her direction as she stood still, teetered and carried on her way. 'Fuck off!' she shouted in their general direction, which earned her claps and more catcalls.

Eventually she looked up and found herself by the Freemasons' Hall in Great Queen Street. Recognising the impressive white pillars that towered above her, for some reason she thought it appropriate to salute. In doing so, she fell sideways, landing on the steps with an almighty thud. Her glasses flew from her pocket.

'Oh my God! She's cut her face!' came a woman's voice, kindly and soft. The woman bent over her. 'Are you okay?'

'Leave her alone, she's just pissed,' her male companion said, pulling her away into the night.

'Fuck you!' Romilly yelled as she leant against the step and watched their shapes disappear along the pavement towards Drury Lane. 'I'm a scientist. I am. I am not jus-pissed, I'm a pissedscentist!' This made her laugh. Then her giggles dissipated, replaced by tears as she pictured the note David had stuck on her lampshade. 'Proper love,' she whispered, gathering her specs, newly cracked in the right lens, and hauling herself upright against a pillar with the taste of iron seeping into her mouth.

Father Brian was woken by the noise. He came downstairs with his dressing gown over his pyjamas. Romilly was beating the glass top of the door with her flattened palm. 'Father Brian! It's me, come on! Father Brian, open the door!' she yelled.

Several Chandler House residents screamed down through cracks in the rattly windows, telling her to 'Shut the fuck up!' Someone on an upper floor opened a sash window and threw a half-empty bottle of water in her direction; it missed her by an inch and landed at her feet. She found this hilarious, laughed loudly.

Father Brian slid the bolts and released the chain. He stared at the sorry state of his prize pupil. 'Be quiet now!' he hissed. 'You'll wake the whole neighbourhood. Come in, come on!' His voice was stern.

'You are so fucking righteous, you have no idea whatmy-lifeislike! But you are my only friend, FatherBrian, my only friend... You don'tcare about my boulders, you have helpedme... youhelpme.' She fell over the step and plunged forward, head first, missing the wall by an inch.

Father Brian took her by the arm and led her into his

private study, easing her onto the sofa. He lifted her feet and put them on the arm, before going to fetch a blanket that he laid over her shoulders and tucked around her body. 'Oh, Romilly,' he said with a sigh as he shut the door on her and left her to sleep until the morning.

As the door creaked wide, she opened her eyes and was shocked to find she wasn't in her bed. A split second later, she felt the pain behind her eyeballs and the mother of all headaches. *Oh no... What have I done?*

'I've made you some coffee and here's a glass of water.' Father Brian set the tray down on the floor by the sofa and sat in the chair at his desk.

She closed her eyes again, wanting to disappear, wanting to be anywhere else but there, humiliated in front of the man who had given her a chance at recovery, a shot at the title. Her tears of self-pity sprang.

'You'll need to be rousing yourself, Romilly. I've got staff arriving soon and it will do nobody any good for you to be lying here in that state.'

Slowly she lifted her body and let her legs fall to the floor until she was sitting up. Laying her palm on her throbbing cheek, she felt the congealed line of blood, newly formed over a cut. She reached down for the hot cup of coffee and felt her entire insides shift as she struggled not to vomit. 'I'm sorry,' she croaked, between sobs. 'I don't remember coming here. I don't know what happened.'

Father Brian knitted his knuckles across his ample tummy. 'Do you know what triggered it? Was it your letter?'

She thought about David's words: *I have met someone*

else, but that is incidental. Romilly swallowed. Her spit tasted sour and her breath wasn't much better. She could smell the booze on her skin and her whole body itched as if coated with something.

'I think it was partly that, but it's been a tricky week. I found the new girl's descriptions very unsettling – that hadn't happened to me before, but I don't know, it... it just got me thinking. And then to read that my David, my husband, who I love very much...' She exhaled. 'I know it sounds daft, Father Brian, but I hadn't considered it, hadn't thought that he would meet someone else.'

She sipped her coffee and tried to rid her mind of the image of a woman who looked like Sara walking up the driveway and into her home. 'It floored me. And all I can think of is the promises he made to me and the promises I made to him and I broke my promises and so what did I expect?'

'It's still difficult for you, of course.' Father Brian's tone had softened.

'I'd forgotten, you know... I'd forgotten what it felt like to have a drink. The happiness I felt, it was like nectar. It was magic. And even though I knew it was undoing all my hard work, I didn't care. I didn't.' She shook her head at the admission. 'All that mattered was that second when the booze sat on my tongue and knowing it was going to go into my veins and make me feel better. It's like medicine and poison rolled into one. And I've fought against it for all these months, but yesterday it was stronger than me.' She wished she could stop the irritating trickle of tears that was rolling over her nose and mouth.

'Oh, Romilly, I know exactly how it feels. For me it's been over thirty-seven years, but some days that desire in my gut is just as strong as on day one.'

'Father Brian, I didn't realise that you...'

'Oh yes. I nearly lost everything, my life included, but I'm still here and at least now I'm turning those years into something good.' He cocked his head and looked her full in the face. 'How are you feeling?'

'Shit. Horrible. Sick.'

He nodded his understanding, as if this feeling too was still raw. 'You know the rules, Romilly. This indiscretion means you go back to square one, back to the hostel and back to basics.'

Tears streamed from her bloodshot eyes. 'It's like playing snakes and ladders.' She sobbed. 'But instead of a game, this is my life! This is my crappy life!' She thumped her chest.

'My husband is the beautiful David Arthur Wells and he married me in front of everyone we knew and told me I was his one and only proper love and I so wanted to be, I really did!' She sniffed and wiped her tears with her grubby sleeve. 'He is the father of my child, my girl, who is the most perfect thing I have ever seen and I can't believe I am her mum. I picture them in our house and I always thought that there would be a space left, a place for me, for when I'm better, but they're not waiting for me, are they?' She sobbed again. 'I know they're not. My David has a woman that he loves, I can feel it, and it isn't me! It isn't me!'

Father Brian stared at her. 'Go back to the flat. Get yourself cleaned up, drink plenty of water, rest and I shall see you back here for group meeting.'

She looked up at him. 'But... but you said I had to go back to square one!' she stammered. 'You said that was the rules!'

'I think you have gone back to square one, Romilly.' He sat forward and smiled at her. 'And I think sometimes it's okay to break the rules a bit, don't you?'

Celeste

I don't remember Annie being officially introduced. There certainly wasn't the awkward afternoon tea or a briefing on what I should say and wear, nothing like that. Dad didn't start behaving differently, she just kind of appeared. Looking back, they were already very comfortable with each other by the time I met her, so I guess things must have been going on for quite a while. It was their ease with each other that made it all feel very natural. Uncomplicated.

Annie just slotted into our lives and started picking me up and cooking my supper and buying me clothes or shampoo if I ran out, just normal stuff. She never tried to be my mum, we never discussed it, didn't have to. As I said, it was all very easy. The first time she came to the house, she and Dad cooked and I remember her asking where the pots and pans were, things like that and then the next time she came over and cooked, she didn't have to ask and that's kind of how it was with everything. She stayed over occasionally and then more regularly and then she stopped going home and the bathroom cabinet filled up with her things and just like that we were a little unit. Dad and Annie and me and it was great.

A major turning point for me was when Annie started to

chat to my friends' mums and cook for my mates and organise sleepovers for me and drive me around; that kind of thing. Of course it made me think about my mum, but by then it had been such a long time and she hadn't contacted me and I hadn't seen her and she had faded for me, in every sense. I know that might sound harsh, but this wasn't some movie, this was my real life and that was the truth.

Annie would smile every time she saw me – still does – and that was a lovely contrast to that sick feeling, wondering whether Mum was going to be all over me and doing something fun or whether she was going to go batshit crazy and scare me half to death. I think the best word to sum it up is 'relaxed'. I started to relax and was able to think about school work and boys, normal stuff.

Annie always fought my corner. Amelia wanted a group of us to go to Newquay for a long weekend and stay in a caravan and my dad point blank refused. I went nuts, stormed from the dining table and told him I hated him, which I did for about three seconds. I looked at Annie and she shrugged and said, 'your dad's probably right.' I glared at her, expecting more support. I slumped on the stairs and I heard her say to him, 'that girl is an angel. When I was her age, I'd have snuck off to Newquay and you'd have had no idea where I was, but not her, she tells you everything. You know her friends, her routine... you don't want her to be left out do you? To miss out, not fit in when they're all talking about the rainy weekend they spent in a bloody caravan?'

I crept up to my room and my heart was bursting with love for her. She brought my pudding up about half an hour later and sat on the side of the bed. 'Thank you Annie. I heard what you said to dad.'

'Us girls have to stick together.' She winked.

I took a deep breath and told her, 'It's not true you know.'

'What isn't?' she smiled.

'I don't tell him everything. I don't tell anyone everything.' It was a rare admission from me.

Annie was silent for a moment. I could tell she knew that I was talking about my mum. She spoke softly and kindly when she asked, 'Are there things you would like to tell someone, someone impartial, who won't judge you and has heard it all a million times before?'

I nodded, thinking that might help me get things straight in my head. She brushed my fringe from my face and she said, 'I'll make you an appointment to go and see my friend Erica. You'll like her a lot.'

I never called Annie 'Mum', although she fulfilled the role; and she never asked me to. I guess that was out of respect for Mum's memory and to keep things as straightforward as possible.

Twenty

Romilly was quiet. She was thinking about how she had nearly ruined everything and about how grateful she was to Father Brian, who had been far kinder than she deserved. Her fall from the wagon had shaken her. It had happened so easily, so quickly; it was a timely lesson in the need to be vigilant at all times. She understood Father Brian's admission that even after thirty-seven years clear, his struggle was almost as hard as it had been on day one. This was a battle in which she couldn't afford to lower her shield, ever. It was a daunting prospect and she wasn't sure she still had the strength for it.

'Hey! I was talking to you! Deaf post!' Doruk shouted.

'Sorry, I was miles away.' She gave a small smile.

'Okay, so do you want the good news or the bad news?' he asked casually as he chewed on gum and flicked through the newspaper.

Romilly looked up from where she was kneeling on the floor. She was in the middle of clicking the price gun over a dozen cans of beans, ripping open the cardboard box as she went, to get better access.

'I suppose the good news.' She grimaced at him.

'You are the best worker we've ever had here.'

She stood up. 'Really?' His words had touched her. 'That's a nice thing to say. Thank you.'

'Actually it was a lie. You are just as good as anyone else, in fact slower than Altan, and that's saying something. But I couldn't think of any more good news and so I said that.' He shrugged his shoulders.

'Jesus, Doruk!' She stared at him. 'Okay, well, let's have the bad news.' She folded her arms, bracing herself.

'We are closing the shop. You will be unemployed in three weeks.' He clapped his hands loudly, as if to emphasise the finality of it.

'What? No! Oh!' Her red bobbed hair hung around her jawline as she looked at the floor, trying not to show too much emotion, trying not to panic at this new, unexpected blow. 'Why? Why are you closing the shop?' It had been her lifeline for over two years and never more so than now; a distraction, something to give structure to her day.

'Ayla says we don't make enough money here, so she's buying a fish and chip shop instead.' He tilted his head to one side in a half nod, as though this had been his idea.

Romilly did her best to keep things light. 'I shall miss working here, but I won't miss you. I hate you! You are the worst boss in the whole wide world. But I shall miss working here.'

Doruk closed the paper and hopped off his stool. Coming from around the back of the counter, he enveloped her in a wide bear hug and lifted her off the ground. She squealed and pummelled his large shoulders to make him put her down. 'I hate you too, Romilly.'

He dropped her to the floor and the two smiled at each other, warm, genuine smiles of love and friendship.

'You gave me a chance when I needed it the most and I won't ever, ever forget that.' She felt her eyes mist over.

'Oh for God's sake, shut up! No one wants to hear that shit! And hurry up with those beans!' he shouted, as he took his place back on his stool and reached in his pocket for his handkerchief.

Romilly waved to her miserable boss and pulled her scarf around her neck as she made her way out into the crisp, cold London night. What had shocked her the most in the wake of her relapse was that Father Brian had been right, she had indeed gone back to square one. She had thought that maybe the many months of sobriety preceding this, might have helped in some way, catapulted her further and quicker along the road of recovery, but it didn't work like that. It was a stark reminder that she would always be one drink away from square one and that single fact was petrifying. Her life, she realised, would always be akin to walking a tightrope and even the thought of living that way, was exhausting.

As she set foot on Waterloo Bridge, Big Ben chimed. She played her little game of seeing how far she could get across before it finished its count of the hour. Taking steps and counting as she did so, she gasped as someone walking in the opposite direction grabbed the top of her arm, swinging her round and almost knocking her off course. She looked up into the face of a young man she vaguely recognised but couldn't quite place.

'Red? Oh my God! I thought it was you! I don't believe it! How the devil are you?' He grinned.

It was Jasper's friend... Levi! That was it, Levi. The last time she'd seen him was the night Frog got beaten up. They'd escaped together, and then she'd ended up on the Downs, crashed out by that bin...

'Levi.' She smiled weakly, pleased to have recalled his name, awkward at seeing him there. The anonymity that London gave her was crucial to her ability to function, and seeing him there, on her route home, compromised that anonymity. Her hand flew to her mouth as she self-consciously tried to hide her toothless gums. She pulled off her glasses, not wanting him to see the fine crack across the lens.

'What are you doing up here?' he asked.

She wasn't sure how to answer, how much to tell, and she certainly didn't want it getting back to anyone that might know her in Bristol. 'I'm staying up here for a bit and working.' This was true.

'Me too! My dad's got me a job with some of his mates in the City.' He tugged the sleeve of his long, navy wool overcoat, like a child showing off their uniform on the first day of term. 'Not really my cup of tea, but what can you do? Can't put off taking the plunge forever. Do you fancy a drink?' He beamed.

Do I fancy a drink? That's funny. I do. More than anything, I fancy a drink. I want one now, and I know I always will, but I can't have one. I can't and I won't because every drink, every mouthful will push me off balance and I will fall, each sip is a step backwards in my journey to get home to my little girl and I don't want to lose her to another woman, another mum who might take my place and there's nothing incidental about that... but I am tired, so tired of living like this.

She shivered. 'I can't, Levi. Sorry.'

'Ah, no worries. Next time.' He smiled with a mixture of disappointment and relief.

'Do you still see Jasper?' She wanted to change the subject, knowing there would not be a next time. Romilly saw him hesitate and was prepared to bet they'd had a falling-out of some kind. Their relationship was built on the precarious rocks of hedonism and selfishness, no model for longevity. She thought of Sara.

'Oh, Red.' He placed his hand on her shoulder and held her gaze. 'I thought you knew.'

'Thought I knew what?' She shrugged loose from his touch and squinted to focus.

Levi lowered his voice and took a step towards her. 'He died.'

'What?' She thought she must have misheard him. Surely not the smiling, gorgeous Jasper, that beautiful boy.

Levi nodded. 'Jasper died. He shot himself. His father found him at their country house. We were all devastated. We *are* all devastated. He was such a great guy. I really miss him.'

Romilly felt her knees sway a little. She pictured sitting next to him at The Pineapple. *'They lock their booze in their gun cabinet...'* She wondered if he had simply gone looking for drink and had seized the opportunity, or whether it was planned and had felt like the best solution.

Walking over to the side of the pavement, she placed her hand on the white-painted railings that ran the length of the bridge and gazed at the dark, whispering water below. 'He was... He was...'

An exchange from one of their chats at The Pineapple came back to her. *'Do you find everything funny?'* she'd asked. *'No, but I'm very good at hiding behind my funnies.'*

She glanced at Levi. 'He was just lovely.'

She bent over and stared again at the water and cried, for pretty, young, funny Jasper and for the bloody waste of it all. She thought about his parents, who had now laid both their boys to rest, and she wept fresh tears for them.

Levi placed his hand on her back. 'Are you going to be okay?'

'Yes.' She nodded. 'I just want to be on my own.'

'Okay. Well, I'll see you around, Red.'

She barely acknowledged him leaving.

Romilly stared at the water for some time, watching the currents swirling, endlessly chasing each other. She liked the look of the murky depths, thinking at that moment that if she couldn't lose herself in the oblivion of drink, then maybe there was another way to end her pain, to find the peace that she craved.

She pictured herself lifting Celeste and dancing with her in the cereal aisle, remembering the way they had laughed. *'I am the walrussusses!'* She smiled. Shedding her coat, she let it fall onto the pavement behind her and tossed her bag on top of it.

Gingerly, she climbed onto the wide edge of the bridge railing and balanced there with her arms outstretched and the wind whipping her Titian locks around her face. She pictured herself on her wedding day, standing among a cascade of pale petals; she could almost smell their honey-like perfume. David was staring at her and she him, and she knew that she would never stop loving him. A man further along the bridge was shouting, 'Hey! Hey, you! Hang on! Don't jump, just stay right where you are. I'm coming!' She was only vaguely aware of his voice. Instead, she looked down and there was Jasper, beckoning her in, smiling. It was really good to see him again. She closed her eyes and tipped forwards.

Her hair fanned around her like a golden, fiery halo and the cold stopped the breath in her throat. She heard David calling to her. 'Bug Girl! Hey, Bug Girl!' And he tipped his head back laughing, waiting for her with arms open. Celeste was standing on a step singing 'You Are My Sunshine', loudly and slightly off key. Both the grandmas clapped enthusiastically at her efforts, while her dad plucked fat, ripe tommyatoes and popped them in a basket. And then Father Brian appeared, in front of a brilliant white orb of light. She stared at it, wanting to reach it, desperate to know where it led. The closer she got, the warmer she felt, and all doubt and all hurt fled from her, leaving her spirit soaring and her bones like new. 'We have moved that boulder, Romilly,' he whispered. 'Concentrate, stay with it and focus on the light. Look at it, you're nearly there...'

Celeste

I was eighteen when I received the letter. I hadn't heard from my mum in a few years and I didn't know how to react. Part of me was so happy that she had written to me, because it meant that I hadn't faded from her mind, like she had from mine. Another part of me was frightened, because her letter sounded like she was saying goodbye. I called Annie to come up to my room. I handed it to her without saying a word and she read it out loud, making it real for us both. When Annie got to the bit about me singing 'You Are My Sunshine' to Mum when I was four, her eyes welled up. She said addiction was a cruel illness and the saddest part was how much my mum wanted to go back and do things differently.

It was the first time I had truly thought of Mum's drinking as an illness rather than something she chose. There's one part of the letter that is still indelibly etched on my mind:

> I wish I could have one last chance to do things differently. But deep down I know that I could be given an infinite numbers of chances and I would not change a thing. I would still end up here alone with this pen in my hand, shaking, with my heart fit to burst and my nose and throat thick with tears.
>
> I would not change a thing because I can't.

That made me so sad, and the intensity of it scared me, too. I thanked my stars for the hundredth time that I had always managed to say 'no' to alcohol. It made my life so much simpler. I think that's one of the reasons I loved having Annie in my life, and definitely one of the reasons that Alistair's family mean so much to me. They aren't complicated and difficult; I love the straightforwardness of his life, his heritage; there's no topic off limits, no person who can't be mentioned. Reading that letter, I wished I'd known my mum more, before her life went off the rails, and I wished she could have known Alistair. But after the life I've led and the heartache I've watched Dad go through, there is one thing I'm certain of and that is that wishes don't come true. Well, not all of them.

Twenty-One

Saying goodbye to Father Brian had been a huge wrench, harder than she had imagined; he'd picked her up after so many falls. She gulped back the tears as she pictured him sitting patiently by her side all those months ago, waiting for her to come round. But she'd made it to Pewsey, just as she'd told him she would, from her hospital bed. Remembering that day always brought a lump to her throat. She'd woken up with a start, frightened by the beeps and the harsh strip light in the unfamiliar room, but reassured to see him there. 'Where... where am I?' she'd asked.

'You're in St Thomas' Hospital. You were fished out of the Thames in the nick of time. Luckily a man saw you jump, or you might have been a gonner.' He smiled at her. 'You were hypothermic, delirious, and rambling more than usual, but you're safe now, girl.' He patted her arm.

'I saw you.'

'You saw me where?' he asked softly.

'Under the water. I saw you. You told me to look at the light.'

Father Brian looked at her and gave one of his kind, gentle smiles. 'I did say that,' he confirmed, 'but you weren't underwater Romilly. It was when the doctor was trying to check your pupils, he shone a great big torch in your face.' He laughed. 'Besides, I can't swim.'

'I want to go home,' she whispered.

'All in good time, dear.'

'I don't mean now.' She swallowed, weakened by the effort of talking. 'I mean when I can. I want to go back to Bristol, to be nearer my parents and nearer my daughter...' She let this hang. How would she manage, without Chandler House, without him?

Many months later and that time had come. As she'd sat in Father Brian's room for the very last time, he'd taken her pale hand inside both of his. 'This is another big bend in the road, Romilly, and you must do what you feel is right. But remember, it's been a long time for everyone who loves you. You've been absent and things will have changed for them, just as they have changed for you.'

She nodded. 'I know. I'm not expecting much.' This was half true.

'And the danger is that when things change or disappoint you, there might be a temptation to—'

'I know.' She cut him short. 'But, Father Brian, that temptation is there no matter what. At least now I feel able to make the right decision. You've given me the tools, remember?'

'I do.' He smiled. 'And how are we doing with that boulder?'

She thought about it. 'I'd say it's been reduced to a large rock.'

'Well, that's a step.' He chuckled.

'I don't think there are enough words to say thank you, Father Brian, so can I just give you a kiss?' She wrinkled her nose at him.

'Romilly, sweet child, if you think it's okay to tell me that I am "fucking righteous", then a kiss should be fine too!'

'Oh God, I didn't, did I?' She placed her hand over her eyes, remembering the night she'd relapsed. 'I'm sorry.'

'I'll be here, you know. Always.' His voice was solemn. 'But find a group that suits you in Bristol and attend.'

'I promise I will.' She meant it, knowing she would need the support, possibly forever.

'Because you won't really know how you'll cope until you're tested.' He spoke from experience. 'I shall miss you, Romilly Wells.'

'And I you.' She raised his hand to her mouth, kissed his fingers and cried, remembering how she had climbed up onto the railings...

'Ah, come on, this is no time for tears; this is a good thing, a happy thing! You are going home.' He beamed.

She nodded, unsure of what home looked like, or even where it was.

'She's here! She's here! Lionel! Lionel! Girls!'

Romilly heard her mum shout up the stairs and along the hallway as the taxi from the station dropped her outside the house. She had refused the offer of a lift, wanting to use the time to compose herself as she arrived back in Wiltshire.

She felt a jolt of love for her family home after so many years away. She eyed the narrow concrete path, which had been set with so much care by her dad one hot summer. He'd done his best to keep the three girls off the wet sludge; they'd wanted to leave their handprints and write their names in it, and Holly had wanted to bury her Barbie there. The boxy hedging was now wider than the path it was meant to edge, reducing the front garden by a good margin. She wondered if they'd noticed or if it was like many things that you lived with every day: you stopped really looking. Wasn't that a lesson she'd learnt in spades, she thought bitterly. And over a hell of a lot more than a straggly hedge.

Romilly shook her head; this was no time to be thinking too deeply or too far ahead. She adjusted her short hair around her ears, practised her tight-lipped smile and took her first step on the path.

'You cut your hair off!' Holly shouted, as she rushed up to hold her sister in a tight hug.

'Yep.'

'What happened to your long hair?' Carrie yelled, as she found a gap and wiggled in to join the huddle.

'She cut it off.' Holly answered for her.

'Oh, will you look at that, Lionel! All my little girls together. All together again.' Their mum unfurled the tissue that had been scrunched inside her palm and blotted her tears.

Lionel stood at his wife's shoulder. Romilly caught his eye and smiled. Her dad looked much, much older and a little stooped, but his expression was the same as it always had been; he was glad his girl was home.

Romilly settled back on the familiar sofa while her sisters sat on the floor and her mum and dad took the two chairs opposite. All four stared at her. After a second or two, she coughed. 'I know I look very different. I suppose I am very different.' Her tongue darted to the gaps in her mouth.

'You look grand, Romilly.' Her dad winked.

'Yes, but you do look different,' Holly started. 'Though not in a bad way. I mean, you need to put on some weight, but not as much as Carrie, obviously.'

Carrie punched her twin on the arm.

'You look better, calmer. Not totally bonkers crazy like you used to.'

'For God's sake, Holly!' Pat tutted.

'No, it's fine, Mum. It's good to be open about everything. I've learnt that.'

'Are you staying? You can stay as long as you want, you know that,' Pat said quickly, as if to counter the implication that the family had been less than frank with Romilly.

'Thanks, Mum. I will for a bit, while I get things sorted in Bristol.'

She noted the snatched breaths and the wave of unease that rippled around the room at her mention of Bristol.

'Oh, don't worry. I don't mean Stoke Bishop; not home.' It felt odd calling Stoke Bishop 'home'. 'Just Bristol, where I'll try and get a job and somewhere to stay and things.' *To be nearer my girl, my beautiful girl. To build a bridge that might help her find her way back to me...*

Pat clapped. 'I think this calls for a little celebration!' she said. Then her face dropped. 'Oh God! I didn't mean... you know... I just meant a cup of tea and a slice of Victoria sponge.' She looked close to tears, mortified.

'It's okay, Mum,' Romilly reassured her. 'You can say the word "alcohol", and you guys can have a drink if you want to. I just won't. I can't and I never will be able to. It'll kill me and I've come too far to let that be an option.' She didn't want to burden her parents with the details of her liver damage and the other health problems caused by her drinking, but it was good to be upfront, set the rules.

'Do you still want a drink, or have you been cured of that?' Holly asked.

'No, Holl, I can't be cured, sadly. I'm an alcoholic.' She let the word linger. 'But I've learnt to live cleanly, without being dependent on booze. I guess I've broken the habit and I really want to keep it that way. The longer I don't drink, the more I feel positive that I never will.'

'So can you just have a drink at Christmas or your birthday or whatever?'

'No. Not ever. It's toxic to me.' She looked at her sister, saw her horrified expression. 'Like a poison, an allergy, and that's just the way it is.'

'Like one of those people who's allergic to peanuts and puffs up like a balloon if they get within three feet of a Snickers?'

'A bit like that.' She smiled.

The following week, Romilly was pushing the trolley up the aisle in Pewsey's supermarket, trying to find the Fig Rolls that her dad liked with his afternoon cuppa; her mum's goodies cupboard was running low. Her new phone beeped in her hand. It was a number she didn't recognise. Opening the text message, she read the words and gripped the handle of the trolley. *Would be good idea to meet up. Are you in Bristol any time? David.*

She read and reread the message, scouring the fourteen rather formal words for subtext. The fact that he hadn't used

her name was strangely hurtful; there was no *Hey Rom!* or
R. The temptation to call him back immediately, to hear his
voice and bombard him with questions about Celeste was
strong. Her pulse raced.

She inhaled deeply and focused on her breathing and
keeping her head clear. The technique came quite easily to her
now. Closing her eyes briefly, she managed to slow her pulse
as she pictured herself floating above the clouds, soaring high
and looking down on the world. She saw the verdant patchwork of fields below, the hedgerows and flowers, and a large
rectangular pond with the sun glinting off its surface, where a
woman and her child dipped sticks into the murky green water
and laughed and laughed. This helicopter view helped her
make decisions, helped her see consequences and look further
down the line, rather than reach for the instant gratification
that lurked three aisles away and came in stoppered bottles.

She clutched the phone and slowly composed her reply.

Romilly sat at the little metal table by the path, enjoying
the view of the water tower and the Downs beyond. There
was something wonderful about being in a place that was
so familiar to her, but there was a lot of sadness too. She
pictured herself walking out of the café a dozen years ago,
with Celeste gripping her hand, stealing a few licks of the
ice cream before passing it to her daughter. She let her gaze
wander down the road that led to Stoke Bishop, just a couple
of miles away; to the house whose front-door key she'd
owned and whose wallpaper she'd chosen.

A cough from behind interrupted her thoughts. Romilly
closed her eyes for a second and tried to compose herself.

Suddenly, there he was, by her side. The years since she'd last seen him fell away and the flip to her stomach was the same as it had been on the steps of the Wills Memorial Building a couple of decades before.

He had aged, of course, but was still her handsome man. His eyes still crinkled in the same kindly way, his jaw was still chiselled, despite the beginnings of a small pouch under the centre of his chin. The smattering of grey hair that peppered his temples only made him look distinguished. She didn't recognise the suit he was wearing and that made her heart skip a beat. It was something obvious yet unconsidered by her, that the clothes she always pictured him in, his smart slacks, washed jeans and favourite jersey, would have been replaced by new items, chosen by a person who had supplanted her, clothes that had not felt the touch of her hand.

Smiling a little awkwardly, David bent and grazed her cheek with a formal, fleeting kiss that was more heartbreaking to her than if he hadn't kissed her at all. As if she were a grandma, a whiskery aunt or an elderly neighbour.

'Well, this feels a bit strange, doesn't it?' he began. She had forgotten the soothing velvety tone to his voice.

He sat in the chair opposite and took in her short hair, weathered face and no doubt the missing teeth. She cupped her right hand over her mouth, inadvertently drawing attention to them.

'It is strange. You look well, David.'

'It's good to see you, Rom. You look a lot better than the last time we sat here.'

All she could really remember about that day, the day

she'd decided to leave Bristol for good, was the pull of the bottle in her bag, and the look of revulsion on his face.

'I am. Thank you.'

The formality was hard to stomach. Who would have believed the two of them had once rolled naked under the sheets, had bathed together in their grotty student bath, and had held hands, crying in unison, as they were delivered of a daughter.

'How's Celeste?' She swallowed, keeping her tears at bay by sounding a little colder than she intended. This was a technique she'd learnt and it was far better than collapsing in front of onlookers, and David.

'She's... you know, so grown-up! I expect your mum's told you about her love of learning. It always makes me think of you, to see her with her face buried in a book, studying some obscure data about a rock or something.' He smiled. 'She's hoping to study geography at Southampton University, if she gets the grades. Fingers crossed. She should be fine – you know, the harder you work, the luckier you get!'

She smiled at him, recalling his mantra from the early days of their marriage. 'University! God, it doesn't seem possible.' They looked at each other, both of them thinking about their own uni days, a mere hop from where they now sat, a heartbeat ago.

I miss her so much, it makes my heart hurt...

'Can I see her? Do you think she'd want to see me?' Her tone had softened a little and with it her composure slipped a fraction. She sat up straight.

He gave a slow nod and drummed his fingers on the table-top. 'She knows I'm seeing you today and she did as she always does, took it all in and will think about it, talk it through and then come up with questions. She's quite analytical and very level-headed. Mature, really.'

'She must take after you. Did she get my letter?'

'Yes.' He shifted in his seat, coughed and flattened his lapel, 'yes she did.'

'I wanted to tell her how I felt and what it's been like for me.'

He nodded, 'it did that. She was a little frightened, thought it sounded a bit like a final note...'

She held his eye and smiled, shyly; he had no idea how this was nearly true. 'So do you think she might want to see me?'

He sat back in his seat. 'I think the answer is, all in good time, Rom. You know? Let's not rush her. When she's ready, she'll come to you and she knows she won't meet any resistance from me.'

'Thank you for that.' Her voice cracked a little. She was grateful. A different man might have advised their daughter differently.

'That said, I don't want her to get hurt.' He looked at the sky, as if searching for the words. 'She's in the middle of her A levels and I don't want anything to throw her off course.'

Romilly nodded. 'I do understand. I'm not drinking, David. Haven't for a few years.'

'Yes,' he said, already in receipt of this knowledge. 'But...'

She took a deep breath. 'You're right, it is a "but". It's a daily battle, but one that I'm winning and I want to keep on winning.'

'Well, for what it's worth, I'm really proud of you.' He held her eye.

Don't say you're proud of me; don't be too nice to me. I don't want to cry in front of you, not today.

'I expect you're wondering why I wanted us to meet up?' He coughed again, as he did when he was nervous or tired. 'The thing is, Rom, as you know, I met someone a while ago...'

No! No! No! Please, David, not this.

'She's called Annie and she's great. You'd like her.' He looked up, as though he'd just remembered who he was talking to. 'And the thing is, we're looking at our future. None of us are getting any younger, are we?' He gave a small smile. 'And, well, I do want a divorce, Rom. I mean, we were done a long time ago and I want to move on. I regret sending that letter when you weren't ready to receive it. I'm sorry. But I think now it's time we properly moved forward. It's what I want and I'm sure you do too...'

She knew he was speaking, but the words were muddled in her mind. *I used to think that one day I'd be back at that sink, washing out the cups, making us tea, ironing your shirts. I guess I thought I would slip back in, seamlessly and fully repaired, back into my old life, and you and I would laugh at how far we'd come and all the things we'd been through. Your Bug Girl, back in your arms. I can see how odd that must sound, but that's what I thought. I have thought about your note on so many nights and I concluded in my own muddled way that you must have meant that this woman was 'incidental' of no great importance. It got me through many a dark night, lying against a magnolia-painted wall, thinking it was only temporary, just until I was better and I could come home...*

'So what do you think?' He sighed, clearly relieved to have delivered the words that he had no doubt been practising for some days.

'I think you're right, David. I just want you to be happy.' She tried her best to smile. *I guess I knew it was never going to last. I always knew that someone better than me would come along and steal you away.*

He nodded.

Her voice, when she found it, had an unmistakeable quiver. 'I… I would like to see Celeste, but I do understand. I don't want to push her or scare her or unsettle her in any way. But I really, really would like to see her.' And then her tears broke their banks, her control was lost and she wept.

David's request swirled through her head as she walked the length of Blackboy Hill and along Whiteladies Road. It was hard for her to imagine him writing messages to another woman, declaring 'proper love'. She felt diminished. Even during their years of separation, she'd still been his wife, the wife of the beautiful David Arthur Wells. He had picked her! And that had given her some sort of status. But now that was coming to an end. He and his Annie would be a proper couple and Celeste would be part of that and where did that leave her?

Romilly came to a standstill on the pavement and realised that this had already happened. They *were* a unit, and any piece of paper would be a mere formality. She looked across the street to where the sign for The Vittoria pub creaked in the wind; it seemed to be calling her.

She loitered at the bar, looking from the dark-wood furniture and low-hanging lights to the door through which she'd just walked, wondering whether to leave or stay.

'Yes, love?' The young man with the goatee beard leant towards her with his eyebrows raised.

'A double vodka, please.' She nodded. *Yes, a double vodka.*

'Anything with it?' He was in a hurry.

'Orange.' She averted her eyes guiltily as she searched for her purse.

With the drink in her hand, she made her way to a table in the corner and placed the glass in front of her. Tiny beads of moisture ran down its smooth sides and onto the beer mat. Placing both hands on the cold glass, she tensed her fingers and her jaw, imagining what it might feel like in the next few seconds to place the hard rim against her lip and let the booze flow into her veins. Her stomach hopped and her brain fired shots of ecstasy in anticipation. Her mouth was dry and her hand shook. Raising the glass, she inhaled the scent of the sweet orange and the subtle tang of vodka.

She held it there and closed her eyes. Father Brian's image came into her head and he was smiling at her. *'I've just provided the tools, but you've had to work hard with them and you have and you still are. You are a strong woman.'* She pictured waking with her head next to the bin, the feel of the man's breath on the nape of her neck. And she thought about her daughter, who was the prize, her reward for staying clean.

Romilly placed the drink back on the table, left the pub and ran. She ran all the way to the Royal West of England Academy, past the Triangle and on to the Wills Memorial building. She panted her way up the steps and stood looking down Park Street. She was smiling and then laughing.

'I'm winning!' she shouted at the top of her lungs. Her head was thrown back and her tears fell. 'I'm winning!'

'Good for you, love!' the man in the van hollered back from the line of traffic, just before he pulled away.

I'm going to be okay. I am. I'm going to be okay. She turned her head and for a second she saw the image of a young woman and a young man, students, standing a little way behind her; they were young and happy and her beautiful long red hair cascaded down her back.

Celeste

It wasn't long after receiving her letter that I first saw her again. If I'm being honest, it was a shock. I won't say I wouldn't have recognised her, that's not strictly true, but I was surprised by how much she'd changed. Her skin was yellowy, quite different from the creamy, English-rose complexion with the lovely blush to her cheeks that I remembered. Her eyes were more sunken, her lips were thinner. She looked... She looked like she'd had a really hard time, which of course she had. Her hair was short – again, quite the opposite of how it was in my imagination. Some of her teeth were missing, and the teeth she did have were dark. I felt sad for this woman who, according to my dad and her sisters, had once shone so brightly. I was sad for her and sad for me.

It was an awkward encounter. She wanted to hug me, I could tell. I did give her a small hug, but it felt a bit forced. She sat too close to me and I kept taking little shift to the right to move further away. She touched my hair and it creeped me out a little. I understood her desire to do that, but it didn't feel comfortable for me. The conversation was just horrible. How do you catch up? How do you exchange information on so many missing years? There's too much to cover and it felt like too much of an effort, almost like it was easier not to.

And… this makes me sound like a horrible person, and I don't mean it to, but Dad and Annie and I were so happy that I almost wished Mum hadn't come back into my life. It was like it was too late, like she was just rocking a very steady, happy boat.

I couldn't wait to get home and talk to Annie. She was amazing about all that. I started opening up to her about Mum and how I felt, and Annie was her usual lovely self. She encouraged me to try and see things from Mum's perspective, to be more sympathetic. She was almost like a go-between for a bit. The biggest thing, though, was that she made me realise I didn't have to choose between them, that it wasn't a question of having either her or Mum in my life. It was possible to have them both.

Twenty-Two

Romilly trod the path and put the last of her bags into the back of Carrie's car, slamming the door on the rather bulky load.

'Promise to call me when you get there. And when you're settled, your dad and I will be over as soon you give us the nod.' Her mum fussed in the doorway.

'I will, Mum.' She smiled.

'Flippin' 'eck, she's only moving to Bristol, not the other side of the world!' Carrie tutted.

'I know. But I've got used to having her here.' Pat was a little tearful. She turned and hollered up the hallway. 'Lionel, she's off!'

Lionel came rushing through the house in his slippers. Making his way up the front path, he presented her with an empty ice-cream carton full of ripe red fruit. 'Some tommyatoes for your new flat.' He winked.

'Aww, thanks, Dad!' She reached up to kiss him.

Quite unexpectedly, he held her close. 'I am so very, very proud of you, my clever girl.'

'Well, it's only an admin job at the museum, but it's a start.' She smiled, ever thankful to Dr Mike Gregson for having pulled some strings for her.

'I wasn't talking about the job, but it's the start you deserve, love.' And he kissed her again.

It was now four months since she'd taken the job and she felt happy to be in a routine that she loved. Her little rented flat in the Montpellier district was all she needed. The tiny bedroom, kitchenette, shower room and sitting room had been skilfully constructed above a double garage and was a perfect six hundred and twenty-five square feet. Far from finding it cramped, Romilly considered it cosy. With the addition of a couple of large aspidistras, her stacks of books on entomology, which had nothing to do with Egypt, and the multi-coloured Indian beaded silk throw that hung on the largest wall, the place was bright and interesting.

Switching the light on when she arrived home at the end of her working day filled her with happiness. She would forever be grateful to her lovely mum and dad, who had helped her with her deposit and the first month's rent to get her started. The flat felt like a safe anchor; after years of rootlessness, this alone gave her a sense of strength and wellbeing. Life was good.

Her boss had been impressed at how much she knew about some of the insect exhibits in the museum and had suggested she might like to give talks to visiting groups. Romilly had beamed; it had been a long time since anyone had given her that kind of responsibility and it felt wonderful. The more talks she gave, the better she got at it, learning what to repeat, what to leave out, until she had it down to a fine art. It was after one such talk, as Romilly was gathering up her prompt cards and stacking chairs, that she noticed a woman loitering at the back of the room, stealing glances at her.

'Can I help you with anything?' Romilly smiled at the lean, middle-aged woman with the long dark hair twisted into a loose bun, wondering if she was lost or had a question. The woman walked over and Romilly took note of the jeans, T-shirt, walking boots and tight black zip-up fleece. The two of them studied each other's faces. Romilly knew what she was going to say before she said it.

'I'm Annie.' The woman put out her hand and smiled.

'Right.' Romilly studied her angular face and unselfconscious manner. She was make-up free and had made no attempt to hide the few grey hairs that wisped around her forehead, nor to pluck her rather unruly brows.

'Can I talk to you?' Annie's tone was calm and confident. She hitched her rucksack over her shoulder.

The two made their way to the front of the museum and took up seats at either end of the wooden bench by the main entrance.

'I've got half an hour for lunch,' Romilly pointed out, curling her hair behind her ear and then folding her hands into her lap to stop herself from fidgeting with them.

'I hope you don't mind me coming to see you.'

'It's fine.' She didn't know how to react. The image she'd carried of this woman was very different to the reality. She wasn't the sexy vamp that she'd pictured but was instead quite homey. A sexy vamp would have been easier to bear, actually; the opposite of her.

'Celeste said you met up?' Annie smiled again.

Romilly nodded.

'It must have been wonderful to see her after all this time.'

'It was. I was nervous,' she admitted. She clenched her

jaw, annoyed at herself for sharing this with the woman who'd snuck in and taken her place.

'I can only imagine. I bet you both were.' Annie smiled again and ran her palm over her face; she seemed to grow prettier the more Romilly looked at her. 'I think it took a lot of guts. But at the end of the day, you're her mum.'

Yes. Yes, I am.

'So…' Annie slapped her thighs. 'You must be wondering why I've popped up out of nowhere, interrupting your day?'

'Yes.'

'Well, here's the thing. I have had the privilege of playing a small part in your daughter's life over the last few years and I have a bit of inside information that I know David would be crap at handing over.' She shook her head as if exasperated.

She'd done it. She'd mentioned the man that they both loved, the man that was their common ground and the source of their embarrassment. Romilly stared at her, finding it hard to feel hatred or even the spike of dislike that she might have expected. Instead, it was comfortable, like hearing from a close relative or at least someone who was on your side.

'So I thought I could fill in your gaps! You can ask me anything and I will try and help you build a picture and it will help you get to know her all over again. What do you think?'

Romilly swallowed the lump in her throat and looked sideways at Annie, still not quite sure what to make of her. 'Okay', she whispered.

Annie dipped into her rucksack and pulled out a punnet of strawberries. 'I thought we could share these.' She sidled closer to Romilly on the bench and handed her a disposable plastic fork. Peeling back the flimsy plastic lid, she skewered a strawberry and popped it into her mouth.

Romilly cautiously took one too. 'Can I ask you something?'

'Of course. Fire away, that's the idea!' Annie spoke with her mouth full.

'Why would you want to help me, why would you even want to meet me?'

Annie lowered her fork and considered her response. 'I've wanted to contact you for a while, almost as soon as I started hanging out with David, but I didn't know how. I wanted to let you know that I'd do my best to be a friend to Celeste and that you weren't to worry, and that I didn't want to be any more than her friend.'

She paused and smiled at Romilly. The unspoken words shone brighter than the spoken. *I'm not trying to be her mum; that's your job. I'm not trying to take your place.* 'I lost my own mum when I was fourteen and I would have given anything to be able to tell her all the things she missed. I know I would have felt more complete had she known all about me.' She reached over for another strawberry. 'And in the relatively short time I've known your daughter, I can see that she is pretty special and I can't bear the idea of you missing a scrap of that, just because you were ill.'

Romilly had hated this woman from the moment she'd first heard about her. She'd twisted every snippet of information that had filtered back to her. But now she felt a wave of gratitude towards her, for having thrown her this magical, generous lifeline. She was stumped, genuinely overcome. 'I don't know what to say.'

'Well, that's okay. You don't have to ask me everything today – that might take longer than your half an hour.' She laughed. 'But we can do this any time, just meet up and have a natter, if you want.'

Romilly nodded. 'I do want.'

Annie shoved a vast strawberry into her mouth and spoke around it. 'You're not what I expected.'

'In what way?'

'I dunno... I guess I thought you might be a bit...' Annie paused. 'I don't know how to phrase it without it sounding harsh.'

'Oh God, don't worry about that.' Romilly shrugged.

Annie took a deep breath. 'I suppose I thought you might be a bit like the winos you see hanging around the city centre. You know, a bit... grubby, a bit down on their luck. I know that sounds awful, but that's what I imagined. But you look lovely and you seem very peaceful.'

Romilly couldn't help but smile at the compliment. 'I was exactly like those winos for a long time, that's the scary thing. But I am at peace and it feels good. And for the record, you're not what I expected either.'

'No?' Annie cocked her head.

'No. I thought you'd be a bit more...'

'Come on!' Annie prompted. 'If I can speak my mind, so can you!'

'I always imagined you to be the opposite of me – you know, one of those women who wears heels and lipstick, a bit racy.'

'Racy!' Annie laughed and choked a little on her strawberry. 'That's the funniest thing ever! I am so not racy!'

The two laughed, giving Romilly time to think of her first question.

'Does… does she have a boyfriend?'

Annie straightened her back. 'No. Friends who are boys, but not one special boy. I think she held a bit of a candle for a boy named Josh who was at a different school, but I don't think anything came of it. And a boy called Ollie took her to Prom. He was lovely; polite and sweet, and nervous, looked like he'd borrowed his dad's suit, but again, just friends, I think.'

'What colour was her dress?' Romilly had turned to face Annie on the bench now, fixated by the keeper of secrets she was desperate to learn.

'Oh, let me think. It was pale blue and she had her hair twisted up in a loose chignon with a large diamante clip; she looked very *Downton*. I think I have a photo on my phone.'

Annie reached into her bag and slid through the shots on her screen, and there she was. This was quite different from the photos Romilly had seen on the mantelpiece at her parents' house. It took her breath away. She stared at the snapshot of the gorgeous young woman, who looked relaxed and happy as she smiled into the camera. Nothing like the tense, awkward girl of their recent encounter.

'Beautiful.' She handed the phone back. 'Does she have a drink when she goes out?' she asked.

'No.' Annie shook her head.

'I expect I put her off.' She bit her lip.

'Yes, that's what she said. I think she's tried it, but she doesn't drink now. I think she's a bit scared of it.'

'I think I scared her. In fact I know I did, sometimes.' She thought about the days when her little girl had shrunk away

336

from her grasp or had hidden upstairs while she ranted or passed out.

'Yes, she said that too.'

Romilly liked her honesty, no matter how hard it was to hear. 'Does she... does she ever talk about me?' She looked ahead at the road.

'Sometimes. More so now you're back in Bristol. It's like she's allowing herself to think you might be around. I think she was nervous to talk about you too much, allow herself to miss you, you know? Like she closed down just to get through it.' Annie looked at her.

Romilly nodded. 'I know how that feels.' She paused. 'I wish I could turn back the clock and do things differently.'

'That's the thing; even if we could turn back the clock, we'd probably do the same things, make the same mistakes.' Annie held out the punnet and raised it for her to take one. 'It's only the future we can fix.'

Romilly found herself warming to Annie. She spoke a lot of sense, and she was kind.

'If you don't mind me saying...' Annie spoke with her mouth full again, then swallowed her strawberry. 'There's no point looking back at what your life was. Just concentrate on what's ahead, build again from the ground up.'

'Yes, and things are getting easier for me. You know how it is, the harder I work, the luckier I get...' Romilly gave a rueful smile as she reiterated David's tag line.

'Oh God! Yes, that!' Annie chuckled at the reference. 'Well, I must be due some luck, cos I'm bloody knackered!'

And the two women laughed. Like they had known each other for an age. Like they shared a history. Like friends.

Celeste

When I met Alistair, I didn't know what to tell him about Mum. I was nervous about explaining our family situation and how Annie fitted in and how I had only been in touch with my mum for a relatively short while and there was this big chunk of time missing in our relationship. I was embarrassed in case he thought her disease was hereditary. I worried he might judge me, think I was damaged and change his mind. But of course he didn't.

I'm ashamed now, for having felt that way. Mum was sick. No one would choose to have her illness. It took me quite a while to realise that. Even after we'd met up a few times, I still didn't really get it. Then I started writing down my memories in this notebook and that's really helped. I feel a lot more settled about things. A lot more settled about everything.

The thing that made the most difference was rereading the letter Mum sent me when I was eighteen, especially the bit about her being two different people. It makes so much more sense now. And it's so sad.

It's as if there are two of me. The shy me, the nice me. Smiling and enjoying the good fortune of others, wanting to do good, wanting to love and be loved, wanting nothing more than to laugh and laugh some more; the woman who puts her family at the centre of everything. That woman is smart, interested and interesting. She wakes with a spring in her step and a lift to her heart, happy to have a place in the world, a woman who looks forward to the future.

And then there is the other me, the one who has another love, a love that can't be broken. A destructive, all-consuming love that casts a long, dark shadow over all that is good. This other love is so strong that she will do anything, anything if it means they can slope off together and snatch some illicit moments of pure, pure joy.

My mother's other love is alcohol. It's been the most influential relationship of her life and it has clouded everything.

Things are a lot more normal between me and Mum now. We've had some good chats and I've told her all about Alistair. I'm going to introduce them to each other soon.

I had a real urge to see her yesterday. I phoned her and she was out on the Downs, going for a walk, so I drove over and met up with her. She was by the water tower. As soon as she saw my red car pull into the layby, she budged up on the bench. I plopped down next to her and tipped my head back, letting the sun kiss my skin.

I decided to plunge right in. 'My therapist advised me to make notes,' I told her. 'To look back at the past and write down how I felt about things. I've been doing that for a long time now.'

'That sounds like good advice,' Mum said. 'Has it helped?'

I was quite nervous by then. 'Yes. And I just wanted to say something...'

Mum looked nervous too.

'I think I blocked you out a lot, Mum, when we weren't in contact. Almost as if I couldn't let myself love you, not properly. It saved me from worrying about you and stopped me getting hurt, like a little snail hiding in its shell. But now I'm older, I realise that I've got these two amazing women in my life. Annie, who's wonderful, steady, like a good mate. And then there's you.'

Mum turned towards me, but it was as if she couldn't quite bring herself to catch my eye. She stared at a ladybird on the bench instead.

'And I just wanted to say that I will forever be thankful that you grew me, fed me and set me on my way.'

She looked like she was close to tears, and I was getting very gulpy myself, so I blurted out the rest of it a bit faster than I'd intended.

'And the thing is, I love you. I love you very much, Mum. We are joined forever, aren't we? You know, proper, forever love, because you're my mum.'

And then Mum broke into the biggest smile. She looked me full in the face and gripped my hands and said, 'Yes, my darling. Proper, forever love.'

Epilogue

Sylvia rocked baby Freya from side to side, cooing to her as she slept.

'She's such a doll! Is she a good baby?' she asked Dr Miguel, who couldn't take his eyes from his daughter's face.

'Oh yes, an absolute angel. And Carrie is a natural.' He beamed across at his wife, who was trying to catch the peanuts being lobbed at her by her twin sister from across the kitchen. When she succeeded in catching one, Holly ran and jumped into Carrie's arms and they did a victory lap around the table.

'For goodness' sake, you two!' Pat tutted and adjusted her fascinator, which kept slipping forward onto her forehead.

Lionel strolled around the garden, happy to observe how his planting had taken hold over the years, liking the thought that this riot of colour was largely down to him.

Annie flitted from guest to guest, pouring refills of Buck's Fizz and offering tea. It was testament to the Shepherd/Wells clan that they could all happily spend the morning crammed into the house in Stoke Bishop together. The atmosphere crackled with anticipation and celebration.

Upstairs, Celeste stared at her reflection in the full-length gilt mirror, smoothing imaginary creases from her bodice.

Her dress was a simple sheath of raw grey silk and she looked gorgeous, like the princess she'd always imagined. All she was missing was something blue.

Romilly stood just behind her and could barely contain her emotion. 'You look absolutely stunning, Celeste. So beautiful!'

'Thanks, Mum.' She smiled at the reflection. 'You don't look so bad yourself.'

Romilly beamed, pleased that the double crown that now filled the gap in her mouth had given her the confidence to smile properly once again. Her russet hair hung in shoulder-length layers that framed her face beautifully.

The bedroom door eased open and David cupped his hand over his mouth and chin. 'Oh, love! Goodness me, you look so beautiful.'

'Don't! You'll start me off!' Celeste giggled as her dad pulled out a handkerchief and dabbed at his eyes.

'I've got something for you and then you'll be complete. Close your eyes.' David nodded at Romilly, who smiled back.

Celeste did as she was instructed and held out her hand as her dad placed something in her palm. She closed her fingers over it.

The body of the mayfly was made up of tiny sapphires; the turquoise wings were fashioned from translucent slivers of shell set in filigree silver. It was delicate, beautiful.

'What do you think, Rom? Reckon it matches her frock?'

Romilly smiled, too choked to comment on the perfect gesture.

'Oh Dad! Mum!' Celeste paused. 'I love it! Thank you. I love you both, very much.'

'And we you.' David nodded emphatically. 'Been a bit of a bumpy old ride, eh, Rom?'

She raised her eyebrows a little in acknowledgment. That it had. She touched her hand to her daughter's veil.

'I gave this to your mum on our wedding day.' David said, as he pinned the brooch to the bodice of Celeste's gown.

Celeste fingered the family heirloom, which perfectly complemented her wedding gown. The sunlight caught it, sending a beautiful iridescent sheen across the jewels.

'There, now you are perfect.' Romilly smiled.

'Did you enjoy your wedding day?' Celeste directed the question at both of them.

'Enjoy it?' David laughed. 'It was one of the best days of my life. I had snared the wonderful Romilly Jane Shepherd and, just like Alistair, I felt like the luckiest man on the planet.'

Romilly beamed. 'And I couldn't believe that the beautiful David Arthur Wells wanted to marry someone like me.'

'Oh, I did, Rom. I was happy.'

'I was happy too.'

Celeste watched as he took her mum's hand and squeezed it gently.

Annie poked her head into the bedroom. 'Oh, my word! Celeste, you look incredible!' Romilly handed her a tissue and she blew her nose. 'I just came to say, cars will be here in ten minutes! Better start making our way downstairs.'

A fluttering movement near the open window drew their attention. All four looked up. They watched as a tiny mayfly spiralled up into the bright blue sky. Romilly pictured it floating high above the clouds, looking down on the world. She imagined the verdant patchwork of fields below, the hedgerows and flowers, and a large rectangular pond with the sun glinting off its surface, where a woman and her child dipped sticks into the murky green water and laughed and laughed. The mayfly hovered, beating its wings, seemingly enjoying the glory.

Celeste stared at her mum, who was transfixed.

Romilly's face lit up at the sight. It didn't matter that she had seen this little creature a thousand times before; every time was like the first for her. A slow tear trickled down her cheek. She cried because she found it so beautiful and because she knew what fate awaited it but was powerless to intervene.

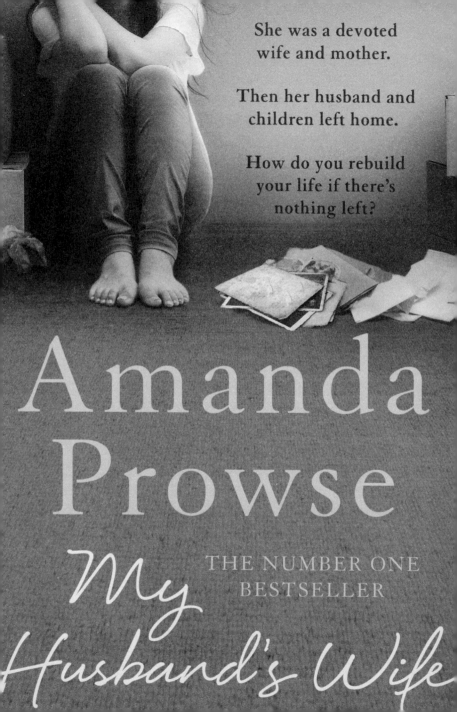

She was a devoted
wife and mother.

Then her husband and
children left home.

How do you rebuild
your life if there's
nothing left?

Amanda
Prowse

THE NUMBER ONE
BESTSELLER

My
Husband's Wife

Prologue

Rosie always laid three places at the dinner table.

Mum, Dad and herself.

Three knives, three forks and three wipe-clean placemats with scenes of Venice printed on them.

Every evening after school, she ate her tea with pictures of the Grand Canal, St Mark's Square and the Bridge of Sighs lurking beneath her plate. She had a hankering to visit these places despite having no idea where they were. They looked mighty impressive, even with an escaped baked bean sitting astride a gondola or a blob of ketchup in the middle of the grand basilica.

Her dad never mentioned their eating arrangements. He simply smiled, handed her her plate and gave the same monotone instruction that she sounded in her head with precision as he spoke it. 'Mind out, the plate's hot.'

She would wait until he went back into the kitchen to fetch the gravy or the glasses of weak orange squash that accompanied their evening meal and then she'd touch her finger to the edge of the china. It felt daring and illegal and was about the closest she got to misbehaving. The temperature was only ever warm at best.

The first time her friend Kev came home for tea he hadn't been invited as such, he just happened to be sitting in front of their TV when her dad popped the macaroni cheese under the grill to bubble. It felt rude not to invite him to stay. Rosie set the table with four places to accommodate their guest.

Kev smiled as he took his seat and looked up at her. 'You've set four places,' he pointed out, as if she had done so in error.

Rosie felt panic flutter in her throat, unwilling to admit that she always laid a place for the mum she had never known, let alone eaten with. She liked Kev, but she didn't know if she could trust him to keep this secret. Recounted out loud, it might make her seem weird, and at school weird was poison; it isolated and alienated you. Like all her class-mates, Rosie feared weird.

She was trying to think what to say, how to explain, when her dad walked in carrying two plates heaped with golden-crusted macaroni cheese and slices of ham.

'Four places set, Rosie?' He looked at Kev and tutted. 'She never was very good with numbers. Mind out, the plate's hot.'

Her dad gave her an almost imperceptible wink and Rosie felt a rush of love for him that was new and overwhelming.

It made her forgive him a little, for having driven her mum away in the first place.

One

Having lived in the small seaside town of Woolacombe her whole life, it was hard for Rosie Tipcott to see it the way visitors saw it. Where tourists might rave about the surfing, linger for hours in the famous sand dunes or spend every afternoon on the crazy-golf course, Rosie was often preoccupied with what to make for tea, how many shifts she'd get that week or whether she'd remembered to switch off the iron.

There was of course the odd day when she would take a moment from her chores to sit on her favourite bench up on the Esplanade and look out at the big, big sea foaming against the deserted beach at Barricane. Or when her eyes were drawn to the dazzling red sunset, as beautiful as any on earth. Either could stop her in her tracks and quite take her breath away. But what she really loved about the North Devon town was that it was home, the place where she lived in a quiet backstreet with her beloved husband and daughters.

Today was not a day for taking time out to appreciate Woolacombe's charms. In the cramped cloakroom under the stairs of their stone-built terrace in Arlington Road, Rosie peered at the peach-coloured hand towel that she had just lobbed over the little wooden shelf so as to hide it from view. She took her time, washing her hands and then drying them by flicking the droplets into the sink and finishing them off on her jeans so she didn't have to move the towel. Her stomach leapt in anticipation and she closed her eyes to quell the excitement. She then applied a squirt of hand cream that she massaged into the gaps between her fingers, sniffing the intoxicating scent of jasmine as she did so. This was one of her small joys, a little luxury, courtesy of Auntie Mags last Christmas.

'Mum?'

'What, love?' Rosie let her head hang on her chest. All she wanted was five minutes! She'd even laid the foundations so she could disappear for that small window of time, asking if either of the girls needed a drink or the loo. They had both shaken their heads and she had mistakenly thought she was safe.

'Leona's got my rubber!' Her daughter's Devonian accent turned the last syllable into the longest.

Rosie sighed; having to referee between her daughters was a constant. When her day was going well, it was amusing, the things they found to squabble about. But when she was tired, it was draining.

'I'll be out in a minute, but tell her to give it you back.'

'She can't!'

'For goodness' sake, Naomi, I'll be out in a sec! Can you just give me one minute please!'

'It's my favourite one. You know, the one that came in that set from Nan that looks like a little poo with a face on it.'

Sweet Jesus! 'Just ask your sister nicely to give it back to you, please, love. Just give me one second! I'll be out in a mo.'

Her daughter started knocking on the door in a slow rhythmic beat, as if her blathering through it wasn't irritating enough.

'I can't! She put it up her nose and now she can't get it out.'

Rosie closed her eyes as her eldest kicked the door, making the bottom flex.

'Don't kick the door!' As so often with the kids, she found herself shouting.

'But she's got my little poo rubber stuck up her nose and I need it!' Naomi shouted back.

Rosie grabbed the fringed hand towel that had been hiding her pregnancy test and stared at the little clear windowpane. Only one blue line. Negative. Bugger it. There was no time to properly consider her disappointment, the quake of regret in her gut. That would have to wait until the great rubber-up-the-nose debacle had been resolved.

Wrapping the white plastic spatula in a wad of loo roll, she shoved it into her bra and pulled her sweatshirt down sharply to hide it. She'd throw it in the bin later when the girls weren't around. But even wrapped in loo roll, hidden inside an old cereal box and with gravy scraped on it, there was still no guarantee that they wouldn't go foraging.

She pictured the early morning the previous year when she'd woken to the sound of her girls' laughter. Happy that they were playing nicely she'd taken her time, coming to leisurely, finding her slippers and checking for chin hairs in the magnifying mirror she kept in her make-up bag by the side of the bed. She also checked before she went to sleep but knew that, unlike regular hairs, they could sprout overnight and take hold. It was only when she crept out onto the landing that she saw the kids peeling condoms from their fine foil wrappers, stretching them to their full length and flinging them down the stairs with a pencil.

'Aaaaagh!' she screeched, her hands outstretched, carefully trying to find the right words that would neither alarm nor interest the kids too much.

'Where... where did you find those?' she asked tentatively.

'They were just in the bathroom.'

'Just in the bathroom?' She couldn't believe her husband, Phil, could be that careless.

'Yes,' Naomi confirmed. 'In the bathroom. In the cabinet. In Dad's washbag. In the side pocket. Wrapped in a flannel...'

Rosie smiled at the memory of how she'd gingerly scooped up the slippery, rubbery nest from the bottom of the stairs and begun offering breakfast options, as if her hands weren't full of discarded prophylactics. 'Who wants what? We've got waffles, cereal, toast...'

Opening the cloakroom door, she came face to face with Naomi, who was still in her school uniform of grey skirt, red sweatshirt, white polo shirt and black tights but had, for some reason which Rosie knew there was no point in trying to fathom, put a pair of her dad's Y-fronts on and stuffed her skirt into them, making it look like she was wearing padded sumo pants. One of her bunches had worked loose, her face was covered with purple glitter paint and she resembled...

Actually, Rosie was stumped as to what her seven-year-old resembled, but the words 'nut house' and 'hedge backwards' sprang to mind.

'Right, you have my full attention. What's going on that couldn't wait for five minutes?'

'Leona asked if she could borrow my rubber and I said no and she said she was going to have it anyway and she took my pencil case and I hit her with my yoghurt spoon and then she tipped all my stuff out and I called her a shitstar and then she took my little poo rubber and shoved it up her nose.'

'Can you take a breath, please?' Rosie kept her tone low-key, having learnt that if she raised the volume or level of hysteria, the girls would follow suit. The earlier exchange of shouts concerning door-kicking being a prime example.

'I don't really know where to start with that, Naomi.' She replayed her daughter's words. 'Actually, I do. Don't hit your sister, even if it's only with a yoghurt spoon. In fact, don't hit anyone, ever, with anything. And don't say shitstar, ever, to anyone.'

Naomi twisted her mouth and considered this. 'What if it's someone's name and I have to ask them a question?' Her daughter stared at her, unsmiling.

Rosie shook her head. 'How do you mean?'

'Supposing I was a teacher and I had a girl in my class and her name was, say, Naomi Shitstar, and I had to do the register and I had to call her name out, could I say it then, like, "Naomi Shitstar? Has anyone seen Naomi Shitstar?"' She added a grown-up voice for full effect.

Rosie felt her laughter wanting to erupt. She turned her lips inwards and bit down hard.

'Are you crying, Mum?'

Rosie shook her head and let out a little squeak. She took deep breaths and leant against the bannister, trying to compose herself. 'So...' She coughed and decided to change the subject. 'Leona has a little rubber that looks like a poo up her nostril?'

'What's her notstril?'

'Her nostril, her nose hole?' Rosie pointed to her own face, remembering to keep her patience.

'Up one of her nose holes, yes.' Naomi gave an elaborate nod.

'I know I'm going to regret this, but what does she have up her other nose hole?'

'Erm, it's a piece of my compass.' Naomi picked at a loose thread on the men's underpants she was wearing.

'Please God, not the pointy piece?' Rosie's tone was becoming more urgent.

'No, Mum, it's like a little silver bolt thingy that holds the end on.'

Rosie ran her fingers through her thick, dark, wavy hair, gathering it into a knot at the base of her neck, as was her habit. 'And why does she have this piece of compass up her nose hole?'

'Because it wouldn't fit up the other hole because she already had my poo rubber up it!' Naomi widened her eyes at having to state the obvious.

'Of course she did. Where is your sister now?'

'Under the kitchen table.' She pointed along the hallway.

'Of course she is.'

'It wasn't my fault, it wasn't anything to do with me, not

really.' Naomi avoided her mum's gaze, telling Rosie all she needed to know.

The two hurried to the little kitchen. Rosie dropped to her knees and smiled at her five-year-old, who sat huddled forward between the chair legs with her arms and legs folded and a pirate patch over one eye.

'Hey, Leona.'

'Hi, Mum.'

'Naomi says you might have some things up your nose that you can't get down, is that right?'

She nodded. 'Yes.' It sounded more like 'Djes.'

'Can you come out from under the table so I can have a look?' Rosie coaxed gently.

Leona shook her head vigorously and closed her one uncovered eye. She still believed that if she couldn't see anyone, then no one could see her. She had been doing this since she was a baby, when Phil used to call her Little Ostrich.

'All right! All right!' Rosie lifted her palm. She was worried about what vigorous head-shaking might do to the small compass part and tiny eraser that were currently lodged inside her youngest daughter's head. 'I do need to have a closer look, love. I'll try and come to you.'

Rosie moved one of the four chairs from the kitchen table and poked her head into the cramped gap. Her knees hurt from contact with the cold, tiled floor and a tiny round pebble, probably delivered from the sole of a shoe, bit into her skin. It was on Phil's list of jobs to lay some lino and remove the tiles that she found quite hard to keep clean. 'Shitstar!' she muttered at the sharp pain. This was all she needed. 'Nearly there!' She kept the tone light and jovial rather than give in to the panic at the images that had started to creep into her mind. She wondered how close to your brain 'up your nose' actually was.

Wedged between two chairs, she smoothed the long fringe from her youngest daughter's face. Leona's beautiful, curly, caramel-coloured hair sat on her shoulders in waves. It was Rosie's pride and joy and caring for it one of her great pleasures. It was one of the things she had dreamt about when she was a little girl – having a mum who would wash and style her hair, brush it and fix in it a bun for parties.

It was cramped under the table and Rosie wished she was a more comfortable size twelve so that she didn't have to heft her size-sixteen bottom into the small space.

'Right, let's have a look at you.' She gently held her daughter's chin and tilted her face to the right, swallowing her horror at the unmistakeable bump that sat almost at the top of Leona's nose. A quick investigation revealed a similar shape on the other side.

'Okay, well that's all good,' she lied. 'I need you to come out, Leona, so I can have a better look in the light.' Rosie began reversing out, only to find Naomi blocking her exit from under the table.

'Did you get them out, Mum? Can I have my rubber back?' she asked.

'Not yet, darling, but we will. It's all going to be fine.' She looked back at Naomi and smiled. It was this particular combination of words and actions that had proved to be the best weapons she had as a mother, a combination that could make monsters disappear from under beds, quash nervous tums before special events and even soothe pain when they were poorly.

'Shall I call Dad and tell him he needs to take us to the hospital again?' Naomi was now bouncing on the spot, delighted by the drama and the possibility of more to follow.

'No! Of course not! Don't be daft!' She squeezed Leona's hand. 'I'll have a little wiggle in the light and they will pop out, I'm sure. If you could just move out of the way, Naomi, so I can get out.'

'I know what you need, Mum, one of those beeping warnings that lorries and forklift trucks and diggers have, so you don't run anyone over!'

'Yes, thank you, love. I probably do.'

'Beeeeep! Beeeeep! Beeeeep!' Her daughter's sound-effects accompanied the rather ungainly manoeuvre.

It was an hour later, as the trio sat in the A&E department of North Devon District Hospital, that Phil arrived, harried and covered in plastering dust but grinning at his girls.

'How you feeling, Leo?'

'Okay.' The little girl shrugged and then yawned. It was getting late.

'The nurse said it shouldn't be too much longer and it'll be a quick solution.' Rosie turned towards her husband, twisted her index finger into a hook and mimed putting it up her nose and pulling down.

'Are they going to stick something up her nose?' Naomi leant forward in her chair, quick to comment, as her sister's eyes widened at the prospect.

'No! Well, maybe, and if they do, she won't feel a thing,' Rosie said soothingly.

'What do you look like?' Phil stared at his eldest, taking in her school skirt, which was crumpled into a creased mess, and her matted hair. 'You look like you've been living in a barn!'

'Leona May Tipcott?' The doctor stood in the brightly lit, rectangular room and called her name, louder than was strictly necessary, Rosie thought, considering that the only other patients waiting were an elderly man who had cut his head and a young male footballer with a dodgy looking ankle, neither of whom were likely to go by that name.

Naomi answered her dad just as loudly. 'I haven't been living in a barn, Dad. I'm all screwed up because I was wearing your pants, but Mum said I couldn't go out in public like that.'

Rosie smiled at the young medic and wondered what their little family must look like to a stranger: she in her jeans, blue Converse and sweatshirt, stressed and with the fish pie she had made for supper splattered over her front; Phil covered in plastering dust; Naomi with her sparkly purple face, wild hair and screwed-up skirt; and Leona with a pirate patch on her forehead and a bump up each nose.

'Yep, that's us!' She stood up.

Taking Leona by the hand, she smiled at her husband. 'This is nearly as embarrassing as the time we went to look at that show house and she took a dump in the bidet!'

'I remember.' He laughed.

As Rosie bent to pick up her little girl, a wad of loo roll fell out of her bra and landed on the floor, in the middle of which sat her pregnancy test.

'What's that?' Naomi yelled and jumped on it, pulling the

plastic from the paper and removing the lid, before placing the soggy tip in her palm. 'Urgh!' she shouted, then held up her hand for her dad's inspection.

Rosie held her husband's eye, gave a gentle shake of her head and swallowed the desire to cry. I wanted this baby, Phil. I wanted it so very much...

Hello lovely reader,

Thank you for reading my novel – I hope you enjoyed it.

It's both nerve-racking and exciting for me when a new book is published. There's very little you can do, other than watch it drift out towards the horizon and wait to see how it is received. So, if you have time, please take a minute to **write a review of this book** or share it on social media **@MrsAmandaProwse**. Hearing your thoughts would make me very, very happy!

I write stories for women about women. Women like you and me, women we would like to take for a coffee and get to know. Some of these women have terrible secrets, some of them have to face great adversity, some pull through, some don't, but each and every one of them is confronting challenges that women like us face every day.

I invite you to join my online community and **sign up to my magazine at www.amandaprowse.org**. Here you can put your feet up, grab a cuppa and enjoy exclusive stories, special offers, events, competitions and much more.

With love and thanks,
Amanda x